THE SWEETNESS OF LIBERTY JAMES

THE SWEETNESS OF LIBERTY JAMES

Janey Lewis

Book Guild Publishing
Sussex, England

First published in Great Britain in 2014 by
The Book Guild Ltd
The Werks
45 Church Road
Hove, BN3 2BE

Typesetting in Sabon by
Ellipsis Digital Ltd, Glasgow

Printed and bound in Great Britain by
CPI Group (UK) Ltd, Croydon, CR0 4YY

A catalogue record for this book is available from
The British Library.

ISBN 978 1 84624 991 4

1

'Bundt tins? Where the hell are my Bundt tins?'

Deirdre James was flinging open cupboards and scanning shelves, flinging vast numbers of cake tins all over the kitchen floor, making a complete mess.

Liberty looked up from her hot chocolate with as bemused an expression as a six-year-old girl can muster. Her normally serene mother was covered in flour, with chocolate from the recently grated Valrhona chocolate for Liberty's drink spread down her apron, while her hair, most unusually for such a well-coiffed lady, stood on end, again with a light dusting of flour. Her almond-shaped grey eyes flashed with emotion and her mouth quivered.

For any other mother who had been baking twenty Genoese sponges for a large wedding the following day, and getting her daughter a snack after school, this may have been normal, but Deirdre James was a baker extraordinaire. She had a great number of satisfied clients who lauded her cakes to everyone they knew; she and Delia Smith had both appeared on television screens around the same time. Deirdre had taken the mystery out of baking for many housewives striving to be perfect mothers, wives and career women, and her calm elegance, more usually associated with stars like Catherine Deneuve, appealed to the husbands who watched avidly alongside.

Liberty loved coming home from school to be greeted by heavenly scents created by her mother in the beautiful yet supremely practical kitchen that took up a good portion of the ground floor of their stunning double-fronted village house in

East Sussex called The Nuttery. The magic smell of baking goods drifting from the house kept the villagers continuously hungry, as walking into a supermarket towards the freshly baked bread counter might do. Deirdre had added cinnamon, vanilla and cardamom to her sponges, and the perfume of the spices was wafting out of the kitchen window at that very moment, to mingle happily with the honeysuckle and wisteria that covered the front of the house.

'What on earth is the matter, Mummy?' asked Liberty. 'You know your Bundt tins are kept in the chest below the window.'

Liberty was already an excellent helper in the kitchen. Both her parents had encouraged her, and with Deirdre as her mother, and her father being Alain James, triple Michelin star holder and chef patron of The Dark Horse, a restaurant with rooms outside Tunbridge Wells, she had fabulous experience of all types of food, and was very interested in learning how to cook. She hopped off her chair, one of a dozen mismatched wooden ones scattered round the huge scrubbed kitchen table, which had been fashioned from a great slice of oak. Gnarled and cracked along the edges, the table had been Alain's wedding present to Deirdre twenty years ago when they moved into the house, and it was decided that Deirdre would work from home and Alain would open a restaurant. He would be home only on Mondays and Tuesdays, better able to do the hours demanded of a top chef by living on site. They thought their stressful lifestyles had prevented them from having children – that, and barely seeing each other while Alain worked every moment God sent. In those days, they were not aware that it is common for male chefs to have infertility problems, owing to their nether regions spending so much time very close to hot ovens.

But six years ago Liberty's birth coincided with Alain's award of a third Michelin star. He called her his lucky star, and she was named Liberty, because at the time Alain thought that freedom from pressure came with the award and time would be spent with his beautiful newborn child. Sure enough, he doted on Liberty, as any father would on such an angelic baby. But to keep his three stars he had to work as hard as ever, if not harder. Pride was at stake; handsome, swarthy and half-French, Alain James had a lot of pride. He also had the arrogance of any successful artist.

When Liberty was born, Deirdre gave up her television work and concentrated on her baking and private catering, selling to upmarket delicatessens and department stores all over the county, who were aware that with her name attached they could sell any and all of the patisserie and cakes she could provide.

This happy if unconventional arrangement had worked for the past six years. Occasionally, Alain was content and willing for Liberty to be in his restaurant kitchen, crawling between the sous-chefs' feet. Sometimes Deirdre and Liberty would stay in Alain's apartment above the restaurant during the weekend, but most of the time Liberty was the only child to be excited about Mondays, knowing that when she got home from school Daddy would be there for two blissful, spoilt nights. Despite his arrogance and complete dedication to his work, Alain was incredibly loyal and a wonderful father. He insisted on quiet and calm in his kitchen, and at home, too, and he and Deirdre had a good partnership and were very popular. Their dedication and love, combined with a healthy sense of humour, helped them get through some tough times. The recognition that came from their success attracted the fabulous and the famous, many of whom became their friends in the 1970s, when it grew more acceptable for social classes to mix. Invitations to glamorous parties plopped through their letter boxes every day, though they were usually not honoured, as either work or Liberty kept them at home. When they did venture out, the paparazzi – a small version of the clamour of today – loved them; their beauty and happiness shone through and sold countless magazines. They were celebrities, albeit discreet ones.

As Liberty hopped off her chair and approached her mother, she said, 'Shall I get the cakes out?' She looked at the Aga, in front of which lay three cats, two pugs and an ancient Labrador, who raised his head, hopeful of a treat. 'I think I can smell burning,' she said. This was quite unusual at The Nuttery, and things must be extremely bad if burning could be smelled through a heavy Aga door.

She gazed at her normally calm mother and was astonished to see tears plopping down her beautiful face. 'Mummy, what is it? Can I make you a hot chocolate?' This was, she knew, the only thing that could possibly help in such a situation.

'My darling girl, I think we had better go outside. I do believe we need some air,' said Deirdre, as she retrieved the burning remnants of what should have been Liberty's rabbit casserole from the Aga. Thankfully, the cakes had been prepared and cooked earlier. She propped open the windows and called to the animals to escape through the French doors into the walled kitchen garden, planted with espaliered fruit trees, herbs and vegetables. An ancient walnut tree stood at one corner. This was used by Liberty to clamber over and escape to meet her friend Savannah, whose garden, or rather park, abutted their property.

Together Deirdre and Liberty sat down on an old swing bench that hung below the veranda at the back of the house. Laburnum tickled their hair as the fronds wafted in the breeze, and apple blossom sent its fragrance to calm the situation. Late flowering narcissi and pheasant's eyes were still winking over the scene. Deirdre had collected herself slightly. She opened her mouth to talk and then stopped. She licked her lips and tried to begin again. Then Liberty wriggled off the seat and shouted, 'Mummy, I want to play with Savannah, her daddy has a new foal by one of his horses and she said I could go and take a look.'

'Darling, I need to tell you some news, so please sit down again, and try to be brave for me.'

Liberty gazed up at her mother, green eyes glistening, at last understanding that this was something important.

'Daddy will not be coming home this evening.' There was silence. *Oh well,* thought Liberty, *that's not so bad.*

'More inspections?' she asked.

'No, my dear, Daddy has decided he wants to live at The Dark Horse, with . . .' At this point Deirdre started to cry again. ' . . . with a new lady.'

'What do you mean, with a new lady? What's wrong with us ladies?'

'Nothing, nothing at all, my darling girl, but sometimes things change, and Daddy is going to have a new family, so . . . so . . . well, you will have someone to play with.'

Deirdre was doing her best to be brave and positive. Having only been told the news by Alain in person that morning, she was still trying to digest it herself, but she knew it was important not to criticise him to Liberty, as he was, after all, still her father.

The news that Alain was about to have a baby with Genevieve a Bois, a recently retired ballerina, and by all tabloid reports a huge diva, had come as a bolt from the blue. She had already thought there could have been an affair. But making a home with the woman? Now Genevieve (surely not her real name, didn't she come from Surrey?) was expecting a baby and Alain said it was certainly his. He told her he had decided to do the right thing and create a home with Genevieve. As Alain spoke, Deirdre had for the first time in twenty years of unflinching support lost her temper and started flinging crockery, chairs and anything else she could reach. Dogs ran in all directions as she screamed 'How can that be the right thing? Be like any other unfaithful bastard, pay for her upkeep, buy her a bloody house, give her maintenance, but the RIGHT THING would surely be to stay here, at home with your family, your wife, your daughter! How can you do this to Liberty?' At this point Alain burst into tears, but he simply shrugged, said, 'What can I do?' and drove off.

Liberty was by this time not sure herself whether to cry, comfort her mother, or ask one of the numerous questions going round her head.

'Did I do something? Was it because I wasn't here last Monday when he came home? When I was riding with Savvy?'

'No, no, my angel,' Deirdre said as she hugged her daughter close. 'No, sometimes we oldies just need to do something different, which is surprising for the rest of us.'

'What do you mean? Someone to play with?' The penny had just dropped. 'Daddy is going to have a baby with this lady. So he won't want me any more.' Her lip quivered and she fainted dead away.

Half a minute later she came to; her mother was leaning over her anxiously, shaking her shoulders rather hard out of fear.

'Oh, there you are my darling. Golly, you gave me a fright. Come on, let's be brave together. He still loves you just as much as ever, and you will still see him just as much as ever. You can go and stay with him – it will be fun!' She enveloped her daughter in a hug, but Liberty shook her off.

In her moment of unconsciousness, Liberty had grown up somewhat. 'No, I don't think it will be fun, but it will be OK. Especially if you stop burning things. Can I have my supper now? I am really hungry.'

Deirdre looked quizzically at her daughter, hurt at being shrugged away, worried that her daughter seemed to be on autopilot. 'Yes,' she said, 'maybe we could have an apple tart as a treat. I think we need one.' *And,* she thought to herself, *a bloody great stiff drink once Liberty is in bed.*

The horrid smell of burning had diminished from the kitchen. As they walked slowly back inside Liberty said, 'But where has the smell gone?'

'Well, the windows and doors have been open and the breeze blew it away,' explained her mother. 'That's good, isn't it?'

Her daughter was concentrating, looking round the room with her brow furrowed. 'No, I mean I can't smell anything at all.'

'Try this.' Deirdre pushed across the now cold mug of chocolate, infused with cinnamon and vanilla. 'This should still smell lovely, especially if you stir it around a bit.' She took a teaspoon from the cutlery drawer and placed it beside the mug.

'No, I can't smell anything at all.'

Deirdre was now slightly more concerned; she crushed a clove of garlic and held it under Liberty's nose. Her daughter sniffed it, then bit into it.

'I can't smell anything, and I can't taste anything either.'

Deirdre, Alain and subsequently doctors diagnosed a reaction to the shock and said no doubt it would wear off. However, as the weeks and months and eventually years went by, Liberty's sense of smell – and therefore taste – refused to come back.

Liberty's parents did not have much contact during their divorce or afterwards. Deirdre continued living at The Nuttery together with her daughter. She gave up her baking business, allowing it to wind down by refusing new orders, instead building up a well-received cookery school which kept her busy while Liberty was away at boarding school, and she could choose not to take classes personally during the school holidays. It also gave the village of Littlehurst new life.

Meanwhile, Alain became renowned as something of a Lothario. This proved to be very good for business; the out-of-town lunch market had always been difficult to fill. No such problem existed now. Tables were booked by a stream of elegant ladies who lunched, waiting in line to take the post of the next Mrs James. Many of these had an opportunity to become familiar with his more primitive side, but none got further than a few months of his attention before his kitchen and cooking lured him back into focusing on food.

2

Liberty blossomed into an elegant, tall, green-eyed beauty. She had a symmetrical strong nose and cheek bones and a jaw worthy of Audrey Hepburn. She was one of those girls who even other girls couldn't stop looking at, just for pleasure. Everything simply seemed to be in the right place. Taken on their own you might have thought her nose too large, her mouth too pouty and her eyebrows too strong, but put together she somehow looked wonderful. It was as though God the designer had downed His tools and claimed this face as His best creation that couldn't be improved, putting Him out of work.

Her long legs were usually encased in a skirt as beastly trousers were mostly too short. Being too tall and too slim was not something she felt able to complain about, given that some of her friends struggled to find anything large enough to fit them. Her elegant figure was maintained through a lack of interest in eating or drinking wine for enjoyment. Some of Deirdre's friends were sure Liberty was destined for the catwalk, but her intelligent and slightly aloof nature kept her studying, and she emerged from school with great exam results, heaps of friends and a wonderfully strong relationship with both her parents. Sadly, there was no hope of a friendship with her stepsister, a spoilt child who had moved to the United States with her mother one year after she was born, when the relationship between Genevieve and Alain fell apart.

Amazingly, Liberty had not a stick of arrogance about her. Neither of her parents had allowed her to rest on her natural assets, and insisted and instilled in her that unless she used her brain, her looks would fade and she would become ugly, as no beauty is complete without knowledge. Experiencing a divorce when you are a young child is pretty grounding, too, so Liberty had never taken adoration for granted. It also made her vulnerable to anyone who showed her affection.

Despite losing her sense of taste and smell at such a young age, Liberty was fascinated by her parents' work. In her school holidays she earned pocket money by washing dishes or waitressing. Alain knew he was extremely lucky to have kept a good relationship with his daughter. He put that down to her ability to love and to forgive unconditionally, something that terrified him when she started having boyfriends.

Savannah, Liberty's friend, came from Denhelm Park, the estate which encompassed the land around The Nuttery and a good deal more. She was blonde, petite and pretty. Her father was Jonathan de Weatherby, and he owned the estate, most of the village of Littlehurst itself and a great deal of other property in the county. They were sent to different schools, but they always stayed in touch, and during the holidays it became a tradition to race each other on horseback from the capacious stables at the park to visit their secret friends the gypsies who lived in the forest. There they would pretend to fall off their ponies, and run shrieking into each other's arms, each speaking over the other so fast it was like watching two squirrels arguing over whose nut was whose, and just as noisy.

Liberty went on to university, after excelling in music, art and sport at school, as well as being head girl. However, she had gained her lowest mark in home economics, much to the amusement of her parents, who knew she could make a pistachio soufflé with hazelnut chocolate sauce by the time she was thirteen – in fact, a better one than her father – despite not being able to taste or smell, just from instinct.

'It bugs me,' she explained. 'They make rock cakes, for heaven's sake. Who eats rock cakes? And the teacher sticks her false teeth into the sugar and the cocoa jar before putting them back in and sucking!'

'Yuck,' said her mother. 'But you must try, in all your subjects.' And she turned away, so as not to show she was smiling.

Liberty decided not to take a year out before university, as many of her school friends did, as she couldn't see the point of that. She didn't particularly enjoy studying, but wanted to get out in the world and start living, and she thought it best to get on with it.

She went to Trinity College, Cambridge, simply because they accepted her. Having celebrities as parents had caused a few problems over the years. Sometimes, friends persuaded Liberty to ask her father to secure a table in his restaurant for their parents' birthday parties. But Alain stuck to the 'first come, first served' basis, which kept the rich and famous clamouring and gave the general public an equal chance. It also made Friday and Saturday nights near impossible prospects. Liberty would say she would try, but her father bent the rules for nobody, not even for her, and she felt such guilt at causing disappointment. If the supposed friend was told by her parents to drop Liberty – silly, stuck-up family, who do they think they are, just a bunch of bloody cooks – Liberty, with her soft heart and willing nature, took it very hard and believed she had hurt people's feelings and cried down the phone to her parents. It took a lot to persuade her that people who only want to be your friend to gain something are unworthy of your friendship.

Liberty had always wondered if any friendship was based on equality, but kept her opinion to herself. Everyone else, not after a freebie, liked her and wanted to be her friend, but because she was self-conscious and uncertain as to who was a true friend, she gave the impression of being rather cold and distant. Because they recognised this, her parents advised her to apply for universities that took students from all walks of life.

An argument that had been a thread throughout her childhood was Deirdre saying she should have been sent to a bigger school further away, one that took girls from similar backgrounds to their own, whilst Alain remained adamant that his little girl was going to school within easy driving distance of home and his restaurant. He couldn't bear the idea of boarding school and, having a French mother, had practically been home-schooled until he was ten, and then had gone to a local lycée. The dispute was only solved when they discovered a nearby boarding school that would give Liberty the freedom from her parents and ability to grow in herself that Deirdre wished for, but was also an easy enough drive from home to satisfy Alain.

Liberty studied history of art and English literature. She justified this by saying it would give her a broad spectrum to choose her career from. University was a series of parties and social events, as any good first degree course should be. She had two major assets: good looks and the ability to whip together a feast for sixty from what appeared to be a few tins of beans, some good sausages and a 'few pinches'. (Her mother had sent her off with an unusual emergency pack. Most mothers would have given first-aid kits, condoms or advice on hangovers, but Deirdre, desperate for her daughter to regain her lost senses, and mindful that in a different environment this may actually happen, made up her special spice mix, saying every six weeks she would refresh it. 'Just add a pinch to any dish you cook, or add a sprinkle to some unappetising meal you have from the canteen–' her mouth contorted as she was forced to use the word '–and it will magically transform it into something delicious.')

Deirdre dreamed of the day Liberty would phone and tell her she had regained her sense of smell, no matter if it was because she had fallen in dog poo or sustained a bang on her head. Deirdre just couldn't imagine life without the smell of cooking. She had written her first cookery book while travelling through Italy on her gap year. She had never admitted that all she did was write notes on what she ate, something to take home with her as a sort of food diary. On one of her last days she was enjoying the sights and smells of Palermo, supping a chicken broth flavoured delicately with herbs and lemon and given substance with tiny fluffy tortellini. She scribbled in her notebook 'must grow herbs and improve British weather, everything tastes ten times better when eaten al fresco'. A man at the next table, who had become very aware of her silver eyes and bewitching expression, asked her, by way of introduction, what she was writing.

Vaguely recognising a voice of authority and a very smart suit, Deirdre tried to impress by saying, 'A cookery book to educate my friends,' at which point the man's eyes lit up and he introduced himself as William Pointon-Chase, partner at P-Chase and Bloom Publishing.

'Oh!' Deirdre had the grace to blush, but he ordered a bottle of Prosecco, having first invited himself to join her at her table. He claimed it must have been fate for them to meet like this. She wondered if his dining companion, who was now paying their bill and walking slowly out of the restaurant, occasionally throwing poisonous looks in his direction, thought the same.

'Oh, don't worry about Chris, he works for me and hates the fact that I'm ancient, married and still get the girls!' As he said this, he guffawed. Unable to tell if he was serious or not, Deirdre took no offence, and she spent a thoroughly enjoyable, if a little surprising, afternoon in his rented villa.

Coming downstairs, now aware that what actually went on in the bedroom was very different to the romantic novels she devoured, and thank goodness for that, she was horrified to find him sitting sipping whisky and reading the scribblings and sketches in her notebook.

'Oh no! I may have embellished somewhat on the quality of my writing.' She blushed, and tried to draw his attention away from the notebook by sitting on his knee.

'My dear!' he exclaimed. 'As beautiful and sexy as you are, and though my heart may have fallen at one glimpse for your sparkling eyes and long legs, my head is entirely that of a businessman, and I would like to offer you an advance for this book. Sketches have to be included. Your words and pictures bring the food of Italy alive. I feel I could sample the dishes if I licked the page!'

Deirdre had underestimated her scribblings, as she had called them. An avid diary writer from a young age, she had put her life down in words and pictures. When she arrived in Italy it made sense to write about the food, as that was what the people seemed to spend most of their time talking about, shopping for or devouring. Coffee, wine, olive oil, which bread to choose, and how much. I mean, where else can you go to a bakery and they cut you a wedge, as an entire loaf would be a waste for one person? A few touches to polish the writing by a newly assigned editor, and Deirdre's life as a cookery writer began.

William Pointon-Chase returned to London, to his wife and his job, where once again they were amazed at his skill in picking new talent. Deirdre went on to become one of their biggest money-spinners over the coming years. And most importantly, William Pointon-Chase paid his assistant a large enough salary for him to be discreet about how the new cookery author, and many before her, had been found.

It was during her first semester that Liberty attended a party given by an art dealer. Her new great friend J-T, which stood for Julian and some unmentionable middle name, had told her about it. He was tall, immaculately groomed, blond, giggly by nature, but with an excellent eye for beautiful things. Her other friend, Bob, was also there. Olive-skinned, dark-haired and beady-eyed, he was short and stocky but very beguiling, and seemed to say little but always commanded the room when he decided to talk. Already displaying considerable knowledge of the art world, Bob kept buttering up gallery owners in and around Cambridge to invite him to previews in the hope that he could establish relationships with artists and their agents alike, as he was trying to wriggle into the tangled and competitive life of an art dealer. The friends he invariably invited along would consume vast amounts of the free booze on offer. At one of these events Liberty was standing drinking Evian water, looking up at an enormous canvas of a fat pink pig surrounded by little stick men. The title of the picture was *Pigs' Reverence*, but it gave her no greater insight into the meaning of the piece, so she started to wonder if people were given free drinks at these jollies to make the art look better. She happened to relay her thoughts out loud to no one in particular, but a tall, well-built, smartly dressed man responded.

'Art is all in the eye of the beholder. Beauty is worth much more.'

As Liberty looked up she saw that at least the stranger was smiling rather than looking lecherous.

'Is that your best chat-up line?' she asked, realising that despite his tweed jacket he was similar to her in age.

'Golly, I hope not,' he replied in a clipped, very English way. 'Percy,' he continued, and stuck his hand out. Liberty's hand was engulfed in a warm, dry, pleasantly firm one, and she was instantly attracted to his blue eyes that twinkled in a naughty, un-English way, and the smooth, well-shaven, chiselled face with a strong jaw and a strangely predatory, hawk-like nose. At that moment Bob scuttled towards them and put his arms around both their waists as he wasn't tall enough to embrace their shoulders.

'Have you ever seen such crap?' he asked, glancing at the price of the piece they were gazing at in horror. 'I should take up making plasticine pigs. Shall we get out of here?'

In throwing them together Bob was being just a tiny bit wicked. He had overheard Percy talking to a successful dealer, saying his appreciation had led him to hope he could invest in art for his future to make the glum, dull days of working in a bank more manageable, and he would love to enjoy the excitement of the auctions. Bob privately wondered why, if this Percy loved paintings so much, he planned to work in a bank, unless what he was really interested in was money, in which case Bob would be his 'uncle'.

Percy had managed not to flinch when this obvious poof put an arm round his waist, but he had overheard the gallery owner talking about Bob Forest, a new chap to look out for, as he knew what he was talking about, despite his youth and silliness. Once Bob had a gallery of his own, he would soon be snatching up all the promising young artists as he was in their peer group, and other gallery owners would be missing out if they were not careful. Anyway, this beautiful, leggy, doe-eyed girl was obviously Bob's friend, and he definitely wanted to get to know her. So J-T, Bob, Liberty and Percy joined a group at a local wine bar, frequented by students and artists, or those who could afford to drink wine and those who were sufficiently attractive to encourage others to buy it for them.

Percy obviously could afford to buy. He started the table off with two bottles of Bollinger.

'Well done, Liberty,' whispered J-T, nudging her in the ribs. 'And not bad looking either, despite wearing his grandfather's clothes!'

'He seems charming,' replied Liberty loyally. After all, he had just spent an entire student allowance on their drinks.

'Are you not joining us?' Percy asked Liberty, noticing she had only a glass of water.

'Oh, you don't know her guilty secret, then?' joked J-T.

Percy stepped a few paces back, worried he had just tried to press champagne on an alcoholic.

'Oh, don't pay any attention,' laughed Liberty. 'I just don't have any sense of taste or smell, so I don't bother to drink. It would be wasted on me.'

'I know, I know,' said J-T, giggling and shaking his head. 'We just drink to get bladdered and this little poppet doesn't see the point. I blame the French influence on her, they are all far too serious when it comes to wine!'

Percy smiled and in doing so looked far more relaxed and handsome. He sat down beside her. 'So tell me,' he said in a stage whisper, 'I'm dying to know all about you. Beautiful,

French and able to put up with this lot. I find you intriguingly different already!'

Liberty was flattered by such attention. She was used to being passed over by straight men, considered too aloof, too beautiful, and therefore out of their reach. They didn't bother chatting her up, thinking she was above them, and she was often lonely as a result. She had rarely been asked for a date. Once a lovely chap had asked her to dance at a school ball, but she had been horrified to learn, after kissing him behind a rack of chairs, that it had all been a bet. The gaggle of giggling, pointing boys standing nearby gave it all away. The lad who had kissed her had only recently started at her school and was from South Africa. All the boys in his group had bet him a fiver that with his funny sense of fashion, cowboy boots and blazer, there was no way he could get to kiss a girl.

Liberty had fled back to her mates in horror, thinking she would never trust a boy again, until her father, hearing of her decision, said she was very smart.

'My dear, all boys are as bad as each other. They, and I speak from experience, as I was once one of them, just want to get into your knickers. I would wait until you come of age and meet a gentleman.'

Alain had spent most of his fatherhood years preparing to shoot any boy or man who set eyes on his beloved little girl, so was thrilled to discourage his daughter from joining in the dating game.

Liberty turned to Percy. 'I'm not French, although my grandmother was. J-T simply assumes anyone with a food background must be French, but thank you,' she said sheepishly, 'for calling me beautiful.'

Percy was charming. He listened attentively and asked questions, was well-mannered and kept jumping up to order more drinks. He told her his family owned a bank. It had been founded by his great-grandfather, who had bought a stately pile in the Sussex Weald when he became successful, and this had been passed on through the generations.

'How extraordinary!' exclaimed Liberty. 'My family home is in East Sussex. It's such a beautiful part of the country, and relatively unknown.'

'Oh my goodness, you aren't Alain James's daughter, are you?' asked Percy, the penny dropping. 'My family spend all birthdays and celebrations at The Dark Horse!'

Bob and J-T looked on, J-T pleased for his friend, Bob jealously trying to get in on the conversation as Percy had just admitted to Liberty that his aim in life was to own at least one genuine Impressionist masterpiece; his parents' home, he announced somewhat flippantly, was full of stuffy old masters! Bob could barely contain himself.

J-T was aware of Bob's attempts at becoming an entrepreneur, and also recognised his sexual inclination. 'Don't worry, darling,' he whispered. 'When he and Liberty start dating she can persuade him to buy his pictures through you. Much more subtle that way.'

'Oh!' shrieked Bob. 'You sneaky little so-and-so. By the way, are you seeing anyone?'

'Well, I was, until tonight.' And with that they started snogging at the table with the enthusiasm of puppies finding a lost sock to share. This caused loud whoops of joy to come from their friends, and Percy to take a large swig of his champagne.

Liberty looked at this handsome, eloquent man, shocked and pleasantly surprised to find someone undaunted by her parents' fame and success. Percy's family were not at all put off by the celebrity of her father's restaurant. Unbelievably, some of the more snooty, snobbish people in the area around Fickledown had refused to dine there, claiming that a chef's reputation should be on the plate and not in the papers. And this was despite the excellent food, the best in the south-east.

Alain had always claimed that if ignorant people were the only ones who paid to eat, La Colombe d'Or in St Paul de Vence would have shut down long ago, so he didn't care if people with closed minds chose to stay away. He still raved about the Colombe's ratatouille, never making it himself again since trying theirs. 'No point, theirs is the best.'

Percy insisted on dropping Liberty back at her hall of residence, and with the promise of a phone call the next day and a peck on the cheek, off he went.

3

The first call the following day came not from Percy, but from J-T. 'Is Percy still there? Am I calling too early?' he asked.

Liberty yawned and said no, but why was he up so early? He must have the biggest hangover ever.

'Only from too much sex,' giggled J-T excitedly, and then Liberty knew he had not really phoned to find out about Percy, but to regale her with his own night of passion.

She heaved herself out of bed and made a cup of instant coffee with the tiny kettle in her room. She settled back against the pillows, the only place to sit comfortably, so she could listen to J-T chattering away about the most amazing, wonderful man he had ever met, how both earth and bed had moved more than once, and how he was madly in love.

'Oh? Oh yeah?' laughed Liberty. 'Heard that one before. How long do I give it this time? A week, tops?'

'No, no, this is very different, I'm sure,' insisted J-T. 'How about a double date?'

When Percy did call later that day – *very well-mannered,* thought Liberty – he was quite clear that a double date was out of the question. Liberty could almost feel him recoiling from the phone like a dog thinking he had found the best stick, only to discover it was an adder.

'I think I would rather court you in private.' *Pompous or romantic?* wondered Liberty. Was he homophobic, or was it just an aversion to double dates, which she happened to share. She agreed to meet him the next Saturday at REDS, a bistro run by a Russian who shouted at the customers and thrust vodka shots down their throats, but who cooked the most sublime veal in white wine and sage, and who was known as one of the best chefs in Cambridge. Percy had taken note of Liberty's parentage but not that she could neither taste nor smell what she was eating. However, she was flattered that he wanted to take her to such a grown-up establishment, and she could appreciate attractive food as well as the next person.

Percy appeared to be the essence of charm and a fine example of a perfect gentleman. He ordered two glasses of Sauternes to accompany the sautéed foie gras. The plates were accompanied by twists of toasted caraway-seeded black bread. Liberty politely sipped the wine, enjoying its honey texture, and she could see the liver was cooked to perfection: slightly crisp on the outside, soft and yielding within. But her principles about well-raised and fairly treated livestock, not only important for the animals but also for the taste of the meat, according to her father, who refused to use crated or caged animals, led her stomach to tighten and she only took a few bites.

However, manners prevailed and she didn't complain to Percy. For their main course he had ordered a whole turbot, albeit a small one, between them. It came accompanied by tiny pieces of roast beetroot and a sour cream chive sauce.

Over dessert of blackcurrant kissel, Liberty realised she had thoroughly enjoyed his company. He was interesting, his knowledge of art and books was extensive and he was well-travelled. His parents had seemingly been very indulgent, taking him to France, Italy and the States, and also to various countries in the Middle East. This was mostly to follow his father, who travelled professionally. She wept openly when he told her his sister had tragically drowned at only nine years of age, in the pond on the family estate. A horrific accident, caused by unknown underlying health issues, and which no one could have foreseen but his mother blamed herself, had the pond filled in and covered with rose bushes because the girl's name was Elizabeth Rose. But nowadays she was barely mentioned.

'I'm impressed that your father works at his bank. I thought most privately owned banks were run by the City lot nowadays,' said Liberty, genuinely interested.

'Oh, he always insisted that we are new money and must work to show the difference between us and the lazy upper classes,' laughed Percy. 'I'll be expected to spend my days there after my time here.'

'Don't you want to do something connected with art?'

'Yes, in an ideal world, but as it's a family bank, I really have no option. Being their only child I do feel a certain responsibility.' Percy shrugged, seemingly with a typical English lack of ego. He appeared to be close to both of his parents, and to love them deeply and visit them often. They had a home in London so he could overnight there when partying in town.

'Maybe over the Christmas break I could bring them to your father's restaurant and they could meet?'

'Gosh, that sounds serious! Do you think we will last that long?' laughed Liberty. It was only October.

'I think so, don't you?' asked Percy, raising a quizzical eyebrow in a disarmingly attractive and naughty way.

During the meal Percy had noted how Liberty took little wine, and ate only small amounts. *She definitely fancies me,* he thought smugly, but wasn't surprised. He was a good catch, after all. He appreciated her shiny conker brown hair and her gleaming green eyes, her smooth ivory skin. Her shapely but slim figure that he had admired at the art gallery was shown off to its best effect tonight in a clinging Hervé Léger jersey dress that looked as though the designer had taken hold of some beautiful bandages in silver grey and wrapped them round her like a mummy, only stopping to make sure her breasts were pushed up becomingly like snow moguls. He appreciated beauty whether it was on canvas or a human being, and he realised he had found a rarity. Not only was she well-educated and widely read, she was kind, compassionate and uncommonly thoughtful.

He admired the way she subtly pointed to her shoes to

indicate to some poor unfortunate woman she had loo roll stuck under hers when she came out of the ladies'. Most girls he knew were only too pleased to see another attractive female embarrass herself. She spoke warmly of her family but didn't push their fame, didn't seem interested in fame herself and looked altogether very down to earth. A little lost in life, perhaps; she had no idea what she wanted to do after university apart from helping others, but as he told her, what good comes of giving too much of one's self before one knows who oneself is? That was no obstacle in a wife, though, for wasn't he looking for someone he could guide and shape to his needs?

And Liberty, if he was honest, was who he was looking for. He was too young, he knew, to marry now, but he was ambitious and wise enough to know already that behind every great man is an enabling wife. What luck to have found such a perfect girl, what a relief. Now he could stop hunting and start enjoying life. And gosh, she was someone he could grow to enjoy!

Percy did not see himself as callous, merely realistic. Being an only child, son and heir, he had a heavy weight of duty on his shoulders; not only a family bank that would some day be run by him, but also a vast family home and land, reminding him of his family's presence. If he could make Liberty happy, they could marry when they were ready and produce future heirs. Though even the thought of babies repulsed him now, he knew it was expected.

Liberty was entranced. Percy set about courting her in earnest. Over the next few months a weekly display of scented flowers arrived at her door. (J-T told her this. He knew that Liberty couldn't smell them, and scented roses cost a lot more than average.) He took her punting, followed by a prearranged picnic. They were both popular students and between them were invited to a great many parties. Liberty was on the student board, arranging several of the balls for the following summer, and was so ablaze with love and lust she booked them a table at one to include some of their mutual best friends, despite the ball being a good six months away.

Percy did rowing and was on the debating team. Liberty helped with routing charitable donations to a local premature baby unit in a well-known hospital, and their first term swept by.

Deirdre, having heard lots about Percy during her weekly chats with her daughter, was eager to meet him and encouraged Liberty to invite him for a weekend if they could find a free one over the Christmas vacation.

Their first kiss was planned to perfection. Percy took her to a bar which they could walk home from, and he wrapped his jacket around her to protect her from the chilly December air. He pulled her to him, and they kissed. Liberty didn't feel butterflies in her tummy, but she assumed that must only happen in romantic novels, and she was swept away by his physical strength and assuredness.

A few days later, Liberty phoned her mother. 'Percy would love for his family to come to The Dark Horse, or lunch at yours, to meet both you and Daddy.'

'Um, well,' said Deirdre, imagining Alain storming out into the restaurant from his kitchen, knife in hand, demanding to know who dared entice him from his lair and scaring the bejesus out of Percy. 'I think it would be fine to introduce him to Alain, but perhaps it would be best to invite him here.'

'Don't you think it's time you saw Daddy again? It's been years.'

'Maybe not the occasion to do it though, darling,' said Deirdre, thinking how stressful it could be, as she and Alain might have a row in front of the prospective in-laws. 'I just can't imagine the Cholmondly-Radleys would like to sit down between the human equivalents of Israel and Palestine building bread walls and throwing Exocet sausages at each other.'

No, maybe not, thought Liberty. So she arranged to go to The Dark Horse for lunch with Percy and his parents, then on to afternoon tea at her mother's home.

'I'm not sure it's the best place for you to meet my father,' she worried out loud to Percy, wringing her hands together as he drove her down the A21 towards Fickledown, the pretty village where her father's restaurant nestled into a cosy meadow set in a Wealden valley.

'Why not? We know how good his food is, and I'm sure he will be thrilled to meet my parents, as they will become even more regular visitors.'

Alain surprised them all by coming over to meet them.

'Daddy! How lovely!' No carving knife to be seen, no chef whites.

'I thought it would be better to get to know your young man if I sat and ate with you,' said Alain with a twinkle in his eye. He took Liberty through the portico to a charming reception resembling a domestic hall, with a round mahogany table in the centre atop an intricate Turkish carpet. There were bowls of fresh flowers set on side tables, and a large sofa in front of the fire which was crackling in a comfortable, cosy way. There was also a ceiling-high Christmas tree, its branches bent low with baubles.

A small door to one side of the fireplace was slightly ajar. It appeared to lead into an under-stair cupboard, and indeed it was exactly that, but it held a small desk with a computer on it, and out popped Gary the manager, who held together The Dark Horse and was the ballast between the stormy chef patron and his clients.

'Good afternoon, and a warm welcome to you, sir,' he said to Percy, and he gave Liberty a bear hug. He had known her since she was a young child. At that moment the Cholmondly-Radleys entered the reception, and Alain greeted them by name. Charmed to be remembered, the rather stern, beautifully made-up face of Mrs Cholmondly-Radley broke into a delighted smile. 'And there's my darling boy,' she exclaimed, reaching out with both hands for Percy, who, understanding the invitation, went over to his mother, guiding Liberty by the arm while whispering in her ear, 'This is going rather well already.' Then out loud he added, 'Mother, Father, this is Liberty.'

Percy's family, the Cholmondly-Radleys (pronounced 'Chumly-Radleys'), had owned a huge pile in East Sussex for the last ninety years. It had been purchased by Percy's great-grandfather, eager to try the lifestyle he thought should go with owning your own bank, trying his hand at hunting, shooting and fishing, and giving up quickly when he realised that the reason the upper classes had the time to enjoy all these pursuits was simple: they didn't need to work and they didn't feel the cold. Percy and his parents spent most of their time at their home in London, as Anstley Hall was freezing in winter and terrifically gloomy in summer. They were a sociable family, preferring the art gallery openings, restaurants and parties of the capital city to the hunting and shooting of their ancestral castle.

'Delighted to meet you, my dear,' said Mr CR, his highly coloured cheeks turning even pinker. He looked rather like a deer hound, with bushy brindle eyebrows and long legs encased in tweed. Liberty imagined he was wagging his tail, as he seemed very jolly. 'Call me Cecil,' he beamed.

Isabelle, his wife, was slightly more guarded. A bit like a terrier, not sure whether to bite or delight, she simply shook Liberty's hand and announced she was thrilled to meet both Liberty and Alain.

Before any awkward silence could prevail, Gary suggested they took drinks in the drawing room whilst perusing the menu.

Alain had arranged for champagne to be served, and he left them to have a drink while he checked the kitchen hadn't collapsed without him.

Liberty settled herself in a comfortable sofa next to Cecil. He was entertaining and charming, making everyone laugh and putting Liberty at ease. Despite her rather bland appearance, Isabelle was extremely interesting, well-educated and doing her best to be pleasant, which Liberty realised she considered was her job as mother of their only son and heir. She was obviously a delightful woman, and she and her husband made a warm and happy couple.

As many a child of divorced parents, Liberty loved the feeling of security and solidity that happily married parents seemed to ooze. She realised she was enjoying herself and felt that Percy had given her a fabulous Christmas present; an extended family. She felt more in love with him than ever, and loved glancing over to where he sat in a large checked armchair looking relaxed, elbows resting on the arms, head back, with a big smile on his face.

This was what Alain saw as he re-entered the drawing room, having established that the kitchen was managing somehow without him. Smug was the word that flashed through his brain. *He looks like a smug, handsome toad that has been kissed by the princess. My princess.* He supposed the romance would be short-lived, so tried to be as pleasant as possible.

Liberty, however, knew her father very well, and picked up quickly through small gestures and comments he made that he was less than charmed, unlike everyone else including the waitress, who blushed sweetly when Percy touched her forearm while asking if she would kindly top up his mother's glass.

Liberty merely assumed Alain was being protective. She was convinced that when he knew Percy better he would be as bowled over as she was.

Of course, the lunch was excellent. They enjoyed a light tasting menu; small portions of delicately cooked fish, meat and vegetables set off by fragrant sauces, followed by a selection of local cheeses, and at the end a trio of pears for dessert: one, a poached pear set on a see-through thin slice of crisp sweet puff pastry with the pear's syrup reduced to a sticky sauce; two, a tiny pear almond sponge, as light as air, on a puddle of crème anglaise; the third a pear and nutmeg sorbet.

'Amazing,' pronounced Isabelle. 'Normally after a tasting menu I can barely breathe, but I feel I could even manage the petit fours that I know come with coffee.'

Alain puffed out his chest visibly at the compliment and took Isabelle's arm as they went into the conservatory for coffee and Armagnac. Isabelle was delighted to have been recognised by friends who had been looking over admiringly at their table, and who then trapped her in the ladies' and asked how she had managed to get the notoriously reticent Alain James to dine with them. 'Isn't he just gorgeous?' they gushed. She was feeling rather frivolous after more than two glasses of wine. She found Liberty charmingly innocent and utterly beautiful, and had surprised herself by liking the girl, who chatted eloquently and entertainingly. She was thrilled her son had found such a suitable mate, and admitted to Alain she had been worried Percy would fall for some new-age hippy at university, who would persuade him to become vegetarian and smoke dope rather than knuckle down and study for a good degree.

'Oh,' responded Alain, 'I think he knows exactly what he wants.'

The afternoon tea at Deirdre's home was somewhat less successful. Although she knew they would have eaten well at The Dark Horse, Deirdre couldn't help herself and had prepared a full high tea, with tiny sandwiches and quiches, scones, clotted cream, angels on horseback, black pudding brioche, sausage rolls and a blackberry sponge cake.

As they all stood around in Deirdre's sitting room chatting amiably, she thought she must have left a CD playing because they all looked as if they were swaying to music. She suddenly twigged that they were shuffling about, attempting to make room for the huge spread laid out on the nearby coffee table, precariously balanced on the vast array of books and magazines that she hadn't bothered to clear. Deirdre was considering how killing her prospective son-in-law by over-feeding him on their first meeting would go down when her exuberant Labrador, Dijon, took matters into his own paws. When Isabelle opened the wrong door to the hall the dog, delighted to be invited in, albeit accidentally, with one smooth tail movement swept all the sandwiches and quiches off the tiered cake stands and on to the floor, where he happily wolfed down the lot. Nobody attempted to stop him, and the relief was evident.

Deirdre was very taken by the jolly Mr CR, who had enjoyed a nap on the drive over, and the handsome, chiselled face of Percy, who in his tailored suit looked nothing like the snotty student she had envisaged. Isabelle was looking at Dijon as though he were a yellow Hermès Birkin. She announced to Cecil it was high time they replaced old Mouse, who had died the previous year.

'Every home needs a dog,' she said firmly. Deirdre decided at once they were her sort of people, and told Liberty so the next day on the phone. Liberty, knowing that dogs were everything to her mother, resisted telling her that Percy hated pets of any sort, but was thrilled that she approved, when Alain had so obviously not.

More surprising, then, when after years without contact, a letter arrived for Deirdre from Alain saying that if things became serious between their daughter and Percy then he would like to step in, as he thought there was something amiss with the relationship. But as Deirdre now had so little respect for his views on love and relationships she didn't respond.

After their final year at university, Percy proposed to Liberty, offering her his grandmother's emerald engagement ring. Her mother's only comment was, 'Emeralds? Aren't they supposed to be unlucky, darling?' But by now Liberty was used to her mother's scepticism where marriage was concerned. He proposed after a long day's drinking and watching his pals playing cricket. ('Sorry, sorry, can't let the boys down, but I had put today aside to ask you to marry me, so stop making a fuss, just say yes.') And that was that.

Deirdre hosted a large engagement party and after their white wedding in the local church their reception was held in her garden in 1998, where they were surrounded by 250 family and friends.

Tatler's Bystander pronounced it the wedding attended by everyone who was anyone, and the most elegant of the year. Thankfully, the bride was so utterly beautiful in her Neil Cunningham gown that she managed to outshine all the lords, ladies, dukes, duchesses and the odd rock and film star in attendance.

4

Liberty and Percy were both beautiful people, willing academics and admired by their peers, and they were happy to be together from their first meeting. Undoubtedly, there was an intense sexual attraction, but they could both relax knowing their parents' fame and money were not the only reasons they had come together. After Percy came down from Trinity he went straight into the family bank. No thought had ever been given to his doing anything else. He settled into his office nicely and charmed the staff, something that came very easily to him. Within his first month they stopped muttering behind his back about the 'unfairness of it all, sliding into a post he hadn't worked for, posh toff'. Instead, he became one of the boys, able to drink his colleagues under the table (and pay the bill) and get to work on time the following day. He also ran the Boys' Club, a private drinking club that anyone could join, as long as they were useful socially or had enough money to keep up.

The path had never been as clear for Liberty. She had moved in with Percy and his parents in their London home at his invitation. They had their own floor at the top of the house, so Liberty didn't put up too much of a fight, although her parents were appalled. She got on extremely well with Mr and Mrs Cholmondly-Radley. Although she had never thought of going into banking herself, she applied for, and got, a job in the Radley Bank, when Mr Cholmondly-Radley suggested she might find it interesting to learn about the family business. She was almost surprised to be there every morning when she arrived at the smart old Georgian building, together with a crowd of East

End boys who spent their days running along corridors and carrying messages across big airless rooms full of telephones and computer screens.

Gradually, she drifted along in her own direction. Liberty was excellent at dealing with people, and with her practical mind she was very good at problem-solving. She was offered a position in PR and felt much happier than when she had been an equities trader. Because of this, she excelled at what she did, smoothing the road for the directors and making the bank appear to be a modern, forward-moving, people-friendly establishment, whereas in reality it was stuck in the past and simply lucky with the quality and loyalty of the men and women it employed.

As a wedding present, the Cholmondly-Radleys gave them the amazing gift of a sweet little mews house in Belgravia. Percy had found the deeds when going through a trunk years earlier. The Cholmondly-Radleys had been unaware they owned it, and Percy thought the rent the tenants had been paying for the last forty years was an abomination. Against his parents' wishes, Percy announced, 'We have tipped the tenants out, it's ours now.' His parents had simply hoped he would keep it as an investment and were truly sad to say goodbye to their delightful daughter-in-law and their only son.

Liberty wanted to start a family and sell the house to set up her own company. There would be money left over to buy a small place in the country. Percy, though, was reticent. He knew at some point an heir apparent would have to be produced, but he couldn't bring himself to imagine the horror of a baby messing up his day. He didn't say so, just encouraged Liberty to remain in her job for a little while. 'We have the rest of our lives to settle, let's have some time together first.' So she used one of her many practical talents to decorate their mews house. This was a tricky job as the place had very little natural light and small rooms. Liberty managed to make it look fabulous with the help of her friend J-T.

Bob and J-T had also (unbelievably, after J-T's own admission of a somewhat debauched past) been an item since the night Liberty first met Percy, the only two of Liberty and Percy's friends who had remained together for the full three years of uni and emerged at the other side still an item. Fabulous, camp and ineradicably stylish, J-T had known that after reading English (because that was what one did, darling, after Eton) he would set up an interior design consultancy, and be brilliant, expensive and very, very famous. Within three years of opening his showroom J-T had succeeded in all three ambitions, and now spent most of his time phoning Liberty to ask her when she was going to let him into Anstley Hall. He was prepared to create something really sumptuous for her in-laws, and when could they begin? Liberty simply giggled, knowing that Anstley Hall would remain the showcase for years of family life, not plumped cushions and perfect colour schemes, but she embraced J-T's enthusiasm and passion.

J-T was forever clothed in Dolce & Gabbana, and it was rumoured that even his pyjamas bore their logo. He was always immaculately turned out, with his slicked back blond hair and one eighth of an inch of stubble perfectly clipped every day by his valet, José. Bob, dark and plump as a Botticelli cherub, was usually dressed in pink cashmere. He had opened his own gallery, showing an interesting mix of new artists and established painters. The couple were adored by their French bulldogs, Feran and Bulli, who never told them off for coming home at 5 a.m. after too many Martinis quaffed at the most recently opened club. After all, it was their job to meet all the latest TV and football stars, and somehow to let them know, in a most subtle way, that nobody except the two of them had any idea at all about what good taste was. What was more, Bob and J-T were there to create wonderful interiors and provide art for all these nouveau stars and give them an indisputable air of 'having arrived'.

This was their primary skill. The introductions were vital. After that, they would introduce their style. Most interior designers have a specific style. A potential client will look at their 'book', like what they see and invite the designer to come and give their home a makeover, or 'do their space', interior design speak for redecorating a home. This makes most homes which have been designed by a specific company look almost identical, and as most designers watch out for the latest trends and use the latest patterns, most of these homes look very similar.

J-T was different. He listened with great care to the clients. He then followed them around for a month or so to see what type of personality they had. If a footballer hesitated over a gold dolphin tap sticking out of a wall in a hotel, he would find an antique one to match, or have one antiqued to look as good. The client usually thought he, or more usually she, had chosen it personally.

J-T would recreate your house interior so it appeared as though you had personally collected every item yourself, but somehow things fitted together and looked miraculous, and of course incredibly stylish (and oh-so-expensive, darling). He was 'quietly clever', as Liberty put it, but like Botox, you only told your nearest and dearest friends that you had employed him, because you wanted all your acquaintances to know just how intelligent and designer-savvy you were, and of course, he always bought the art through Bob, which in turn meant that Bob's gallery received unheard of success very quickly.

J-T knew Liberty well enough to tell her that she had no need of his services, and he could do no better. He had spent most of the long uni holidays at The Nuttery, and having seen the beautiful house, he knew that Liberty would want more of the shabby but lived-in look, and that she was perfectly capable of achieving this herself. And, selfishly, it meant he wouldn't have to deal with Percy, whom he found an insufferable prig, bullish and homophobic, although of course he would never dream of explaining this to his dear friend for fear of losing her.

After three years of married life, Liberty was still floating through her days. Nothing seemed very real to her. The parties were fun, she stayed at Le Manoir or Gidleigh for appropriate birthdays and anniversaries and she found her working days so easy they barely registered in her brain.

Because she was so beautiful, she had advantages, but she had so many friends simply because she was a genuinely good, kind person. She would always be the first to help or listen to any of her colleagues, and once she had accepted someone as a friend she was loyal, generous and loving in a rare way. But this seemingly perfect girl had two fatal weaknesses. She was far too innocent, and she was loyal to the end.

From the moment her parents had separated, Liberty had disappeared emotionally into a tortoiseshell of protection. She had never regained her sense of taste or smell, so had kept a fine figure; although she retained considerable interest in her parents' professions, she believed she could never emulate them as she couldn't taste the outcome. Instead, she pursued perfection for its own sake, whether it was working hard ensuring her employer's bank became better thought of, being a good friend or running marathons for charity.

5

After three years of being badgered by Liberty, who was very keen to try for a baby, Percy decided they should produce an heir. However, twelve months later, nothing had happened. Despite checking dates in her diary with her usual care and ensuring she was ovulating (Liberty did not have a regular cycle, but everything appeared to function well) there was no pregnancy. After another six months, Liberty and Percy went together to the doctor and asked him to recommend a specialist. As Percy reminded Liberty, 'Obviously, it's not me.' This was not intended as any form of criticism, but simply a fact in his mind. He was a fit man from a good family who had never had problems in that department.

Liberty was referred to the Snow Fast Fertility Clinic. Mr Probert was a remarkable man, specialising in IVF. He had only recently opened his own surgery in Tunbridge Wells, designed with an operating theatre. Like many specialists, he kept on learning about his subject, as he was keen to keep up to date with every new treatment and procedure, and he travelled frequently to listen to speakers on infertility and curiosities concerning the human body in the modern age. He was interested in the dichotomy of the Western world, which had good medicine and diet yet a high infertility rate, while poor countries produced more babies per woman despite their poor health. He also asked the question: why were so many couples in industrialised countries either putting off trying to start a family until they were too old to create a baby, or not managing to when they tried early on in their adult lives?

On the day of her appointment Liberty drove herself down from London to Tunbridge Wells. Percy was representing his bank at a conference in Paris, but Liberty, as ever impatient to get on with things, agreed to the first slot offered to her by the clinic. She arrived at the large Victorian building, parked her Range Rover with difficulty in a space meant for something smaller, and looked around her. The house looked smart; the windows were freshly painted and it seemed somehow both welcoming and efficient and nothing like a hospital. *So far, so good,* she breathed to herself.

As she unwound her grey scarf from her neck she was greeted by the friendly nurses in reception and asked to sit in the large airy waiting room, obviously once the drawing room. She glanced furtively at the other people sitting around, reading or pretending to read the latest country magazines. Most of them were about her own age, some girls on their own, others with partners, but there was one man who was about seventy-eight at a polite guess while, shockingly, the girl he was with was a young slip of a thing, probably not even out of her teens. *I hope that's her grandfather,* Liberty thought to herself.

The women in the room were trying hard to look relaxed, either reading magazines or chatting quietly to others, but they all had a set look about them, one that Liberty recognised from her own reflection in the mirror. It was a sort of terrified desperation, all of them hating their bodies for making them be there, wondering why it was that so many women could pop out five babies without a thought before they hit thirty while living on benefits, McDonald's and alcopops, whilst they, with their macrobiotic diets, yoga workouts and alcohol-free lifestyles, were keen to try anything to get pregnant, but couldn't. There must be some sort of evolutionary unfairness. But maybe that should be the advice: live on cheap food, smoke and never get any fresh air. Look as pasty as possible and never get out of a tracksuit, and then drop twins nine months later. She smiled at the thought.

It didn't help that the latest *Hello!* on offer included a ten-page spread of a supermodel who had just delivered another baby from her billionaire boyfriend, got her figure back in a mere six weeks and was now cavorting round their swimming pool in her minuscule bikini, while her baby was God knew where. 'Oh, I barely knew I was pregnant,' the quote stated, 'it was just so easy. Everyone should have a baby. It was such fun. Anyway, I am off to New York on an assignment next week, leaving darling Tia with Nanny. No, I don't think small babies should travel round the world, do you?'

OK, so that's it. The anorexic models are fertile and the poor breed like rabbits. Was everyone but Liberty having babies? *Obviously not,* she thought, looking around the room, feeling guilty and selfish. *All these people need help too.*

Thankfully, stopping her mind from spiralling into insanity, Liberty heard a text arrive on her phone from her godmother Paloma, a glamorous and successful restaurateur in the south of France and a Sophia Loren lookalike. Paloma was born in London, but moved to France after falling in love with a man ten years younger then herself. His parents owned a tiny restaurant, set in the hills above St Tropez. The parents died, the man disappeared to 'find himself', and Paloma was left with the restaurant to run. Somehow along the way she became pregnant, so also had a baby boy to feed.

Liberty's parents had met Paloma when Alain helped her out after she was left with a large restaurant and little knowledge. Deirdre soon learned that Paloma was pregnant. Best of all for Liberty, Paloma was asked to be her godmother. She was a true fairy godmother, whisking her down to France to stay for the summer holidays, where she got to know little Claude, Paloma's son, and they spent many a happy summer playing on the beaches and in the dusty hills. As the years went by, wonderfully, Deirdre, Alain and Liberty stayed in touch separately with Paloma, sometimes going down to the resort for some relaxation, sunshine and excellent French cooking.

'Well done, darling,' read the text, 'try for one of those test tube babies for me, is it like those ships in bottles? How will you get it out? Remember to come and stay for some R&R when preggie, it will happen my angel.'

Liberty giggled and relaxed and felt much better. Her mother also texted and as Liberty looked at her phone again she laughed aloud. 'Should I start knitting? Maybe will stick to baking. Tried making you a baby cardie but it ended up being full of holes. Good luck, darling, Martini waiting in Littlehurst when you need it.'

How lucky she was to have such a positive family. She had joined her father earlier in the week for lunch. He had been laughing about his latest squeeze, whom he had dumped unceremoniously when she told him she was 'off carbs' and their affair had appeared in the red tops. 'I don't bloody understand, it's not as though I've sold myself out to *Hello!* or the other ghastlies, so why the hell should they be interested in my personal life?'

'Well, maybe, Daddy, it's because Angel has sold herself out! She has told the world how you tried out your latest sauce by pouring it all over her breasts and licking it off in the middle of your restaurant! I think the tabloids may like that sort of thing . . .'

Alain roared with happy laughter, and then looked sheepishly at Liberty.

'Well, darling, it is all about passion, something I am blessed with.'

'And what happened to wife number three? I didn't even meet her!'

'Well . . . she is now singing in a pop group all paid for by muggins here, and sleeping with some aged punk. She is still a spoilt brat, too.'

'I see.' From her expression, Liberty obviously didn't.

'Oh, darling, I am so proud of you,' said Alain. 'Forget about my silly vacuous life, I hope this IVF business will bring you happiness. I don't think it's a walk in the park, you know.' And then, with amazing insight for someone with such a bad reputation, he said, 'I don't think it is the easiest process if the relationship isn't strong. I just wish you could live your dream.'

'Whatever do you mean?' she asked. 'Our relationship is great!' But he just looked at her with his head on one side and changed the subject.

'Mrs Cholmondly-Radley?' Liberty suddenly realised the nurse had been calling her name and was now standing in reception looking round the room. The nurse smiled at her in a 'seen it all' kind of way, and said Mr Probert was ready for her now. Liberty followed her up the stairs, which were covered with a rather unpleasant carpet. She laughed to herself, realising that her surroundings really didn't matter.

The nurse knocked on the mahogany door, then stood back sharply. This was a wise move because the door was flung open and round it popped a cheery, slim, impish face. Mr Probert looked more like a long-distance runner than a doctor, but his manner was kind and Liberty felt immediately at ease with him. He gestured to a chair, then sat beside her in the bay window space. His head wobbled as he spoke, making him look like a nodding dog, and as happens in such singularly stressful situations, her mind became transfixed on the oddest of things (she couldn't help focusing on his Adam's apple, a very prominent one, that seemed to have a life of its own, bobbing up, down, up, down . . . oops, where is it now?).

'Mrs Cholmondly-Radley? Mrs CR?' Liberty suddenly realised he was talking. *Well, of course he is, you silly woman!* She liked being called Mrs CR.

'Well, what seems to be the problem, Mrs CR?' *Strange question, considering where I am.*

'No conception after a year and six months of trying for a baby. Well, I can be honest because my husband is not here with me. It's been two years of trying, as I gave up taking the pill that long ago, but I didn't tell him.'

'Any previous illnesses?'

'Nothing specific. I had mumps, measles, that sort of thing. My periods have not been regular, but according to those sticks you can buy I do ovulate, and my temperature goes up and down at the right times of the month. We have sex, I hold up my legs for twenty minutes every time afterwards, and – oh, I am talking too much. I am a bit nervous.'

'No need to be nervous with me,' he said, putting on the seen-all-this-before voice and smiling cheerily. 'What we need to do first of all is to eliminate all the obvious reasons why things are not happening as they should, and then we will work out what we need to do.' He reeled off lists of blood tests, hormone level checks, said that he would examine her internally then give her a sonic scan, to see whether there was anything he could pick up on.

Forty-five minutes later Liberty found herself up on the bed, legs in stirrups, while Dick Probert – and really, was that his name? – chatted away, waving what looked like a mean dildo at her. Liberty couldn't listen to a word he was saying (is that really going in there?) in-between praying to whoever was up there that she would love a baby no matter what sex it was, *but a boy for Percy would be easier, oh but I don't want to be greedy, but please, please* . . . 'Ow!'

'That, my dear, is your left ovary, looking nice and healthy.' *Oh, for goodness' sake,* she thought, as the no doubt very capable but not so gentle man decided he needed to look 'a bit further this way, my dear', and with that he guided the internal scanner smartly round and up to what felt like her lower rib cage, while leaning on her right leg as though it were a sturdy tree trunk, with no sensitivity at all.

'So that's where we go from here!' he announced as he whipped off his thin surgical gloves with aplomb and flung them balled up into the bin. He reeled off more tests, including one only Percy could perform, and explained the whole bionic process of stimulating her ovaries to produce unnatural amounts of eggs that they would 'harvest', then select the best, put it with Percy's sperm, all being well in that department, and then grow to blastocyst stage. All being well – golly, that phrase could get tiring – when the cells stopped dividing by two and really got going to show they were a healthy little embryo, they would be implanted back into Liberty's hormone-happy uterus, and all the time Liberty would be injecting herself with hormones and putting horse-sized pills where the sun don't shine.

Thank goodness Percy isn't here, thought Liberty, *he would run a mile at the thought of injecting me; then again, I might do the same if he came towards me with a needle.* And she smiled listlessly.

'Well, thank you, I think,' she said, as she heaved her squeezed, thoroughly prodded body off the examination table.

'No problem,' said Mr Probert. 'I know it's easy to say, but do try not to worry, we have a very high success rate here. You are a good age, and we haven't found anything that would indicate any problems.'

With a smile, a nod and handing her a large amount of reading material, Mr Probert helped her out of the door. As it closed behind her, Liberty felt a strange sensation of being on a conveyor belt come over her, but on her way out of the clinic she felt a definite spring in her step. At last! Mr Probert had said there was nothing wrong, they were on their way to having a baby! Contradicting herself, she thought if only Percy were there, he would be over the moon! She tried his mobile, but he was obviously still in his conference. She would have a baby! She felt a smile the width of the Thames crossing her face.

About five minutes later she was in the mental condition that anyone who has started the month of IVF knows only too well. Her thoughts ran along the lines of – well, if there is nothing wrong why haven't we had babies yet? What is so wrong with me that I'm the one who can't have babies? It seemed to be making her doubt herself more than ever. She fiddled with the idea of going home to see her mother as Littlehurst was so close, but she knew she should go back to London to be there when Percy arrived late. He would need a long bath and supper. The drive into London allowed her to sort her thoughts out and feel positive, if a little nervous about the process ahead of them, and she did worry that if the problem was Percy, or rather Percy's sperm, how he would react. When she reached their mews home she was surprised to see his car, and thrilled that he had taken an early flight home to check if she was all right. She walked into the kitchen to pour a much-needed glass of white wine, then put the kettle on instead, thinking that from now on alcohol was a real no-no! And a cup of tea would also be most welcome, after all. Percy's voice could be heard boring down the hall. 'Hong Kong would be nice, but Shanghai is the place to be now!' He came through the door and looked surprised to see her.

'Oh, my darling, thank you so much for being here,' she said tearfully. She threw her arms around his neck as he put his phone in his pocket.

'Well, you know me.'

'What happened, darling, was your meeting cancelled?' She looked up at him.

'No, it just finished early.'

'Anyway, let me pour you a whisky and I can tell you all about my meeting with Mr Probert.'

'Sorry, love, who's this Probert? New client? Well done, you can tell me over supper. I only popped in on the way from the airport to pick up my other phone. I have to get back to the office. Toodles.'

And off he went, just like that.

Liberty had to let her brain tell her that as little as she wanted to admit it, Percy had obviously forgotten all about her appointment. His conference had been very important. Liberty was never a person to think badly of others, until confronted by strong evidence. *There is no point in winding oneself up over what is often the mind playing games,* she comforted herself. So she did the only sensible thing: said 'Bugger it, I'm not on treatment yet', and poured that much needed glass of wine. Then she went through all the forms and paperwork that Mr Probert had given her. And after that she had a long, very hot bath to make herself feel human again, scrubbing the feeling of being a baby factory from her body, and called Scalini, their favourite Italian restaurant in Walton Street. Maybe over a bottle of Chianti Percy would be responsive to the news that he would need to have a sperm check and answer some fairly personal questions about his sexual history. Funny, how women have to put themselves through the most humiliating of examinations as a matter of course every few years, yet ask a man for a few vials of blood and a sperm sample and they will run a mile (or try to) rather than agree.

Meanwhile, Percy, on his way back to the office, was thinking hard. He had forgotten all about her appointment, but the ridiculous name Probert had brought it back. *I still don't really want a baby. Does every man go through this?* he wondered. *It's going to change everything, and knowing Liberty, she's not the sort to put up with a nanny, she's going to want to do it all herself, have no time for me and look a state, with no thought for entertaining my clients. Life will be dull, dull, dull.*

That night, over a plate of pasta and a bottle of wine, Percy said, 'Well, darling girl, I'm sure they will find whatever is wrong with you and then they will sort something out, but if you insist, I will agree to whatever tests you and this Mr Probert think I need.'

'This IS the last resort,' said Liberty firmly. 'We are infertile together, and we have to try either IVF or embryo implantation if we want to have a family. You would have to come to the next appointment with me. I can't believe you forgot about today.'

'I did not,' spluttered Percy, who as usual had consumed most of the wine, while Liberty sipped sparkling water, her need for alcohol satisfied by her calming drink earlier. 'If it's so bloody important to you, I will come, I've said I would. Now can we drop it?'

'Drop it?' squeaked Liberty. 'You are the one who needs heirs or graces for your bloody pile.' And then she did something that horrified both her and Percy. She burst into tears.

'Come on, old girl,' reassured Percy in his best way, patting her on the shoulder, whilst looking around the restaurant, hoping that no one had noticed his blubbering wife, which of course they had, but they were doing their utmost to pretend not to be listening. 'Let's get out of here, and talk on the way home.' With that he threw a wad of notes on the table and guided her out before they had finished their meal. It seemed to be raining, which they both knew meant taxis would be full, so they started to walk, Percy hesitant to take Liberty to a bar where she may start to blub again.

'I thought you wanted babies as much as I do,' said Liberty. 'We were doing this together.'

'Come on, calm down,' said Percy, feeling a bit of a wretch. 'You know that women always feel this more keenly than men, and it must have been an emotional day for you.'

Feeling somewhat comforted, and in need of his umbrella, Liberty held tightly to his arm all the way home.

Percy reluctantly gave in to the tests, and allowed Liberty to go ahead with the IVF. He reassured himself that if it worked, he could still have fun, despite having a squawking brat in the house.

Mr Probert was lovely, as were his nurses. Tunbridge Wells was lovely. The building was lovely. The weather was lovely. But IVF was GHASTLY. When they tell you about the procedure and give you all the information, there is scant mention of the fact that it will be like PMT times one million. You put up with horrible bloating, terrible flatulence, spots, daily injections, the general self-conscious horror of having various implements stuck up holes only your lover should investigate, being prodded and poked like an experiment, being told that nothing physical is wrong with either of you. But it doesn't help.'So why can't we have a baby, then?' sobbed Liberty after the first attempt, when her tiny embryos had given up the fight for life after only five days of being implanted.

She had wondered how she could wait through the ten long days before doing a pregnancy test, after the procedure to place the two embryos chosen from a dish of seven grade A ones (according to the technician who developed and looked after the dishes of growing cells like a shepherdess, only in scrubs in a laboratory, surrounded by Petri dishes and vats of nitrogen instead of sheep). Those embryos not used were kept for another time or given to a couple unfortunate enough to be unable to make their own.

'We don't really understand everything about infertility,' explained Mr Probert patiently. He still seemed like a mad scientist to Liberty. He attended all the conferences on the subject, kept up to date with all the latest procedures. But the conferences forgot to stress the human touch. His pre-op room was about as comforting to a patient about to go through an emotional procedure as a gaol cell. It had a specially designed chair to keep her body in the correct position, but it was windowless, and about as big as a tube of Smarties. It gave a horrible feeling of claustrophobia, so no one could relax after being told they had to be as calm and peaceful as possible if the procedure was to work. Liberty could see the set-up was ideal for the medical side of things, but for the patients, not so good.

Percy could barely bring himself to speak to Mr Probert, apart from reluctantly realising he had to go and have his sperm checked. 'What did I tell you? I am a well functioning male. All the males in my family have produced heirs, otherwise I wouldn't bloody be here, would I?' He gave his sample, which would be separated and injected individually into each egg harvested from Liberty, produced as a result of all the hormones injected into her body.

Percy avoided the clinic. He refused to be there when they implanted the embryos. 'I won't come to see your gynaecologist. Why would I want to see you so degraded? Legs in stirrups while a little man with a long syringe plays around with your fanny.'

Because I feel lonely, and yes, I do feel hugely degraded, was what Liberty was thinking, but she understood in a way. Most of her girlfriends' husbands refused to be there when they gave birth, or at least, refused to sit at 'that end'.

Despite the horror, the fluctuating moods, and the emotional trauma when it didn't work, Liberty persuaded Percy to try for the third time in as many years. Ten long days to wait. She was sure it was going to work this time. Mr Probert had told her she would definitely have a baby this time. She made sure she went to see Zita West, an acclaimed ex-midwife who advised on nutrition and lifestyle, and gave her acupuncture, which had been shown in some studies to help with conception. It also gave Liberty something to do. She was feeling so helpless.

Percy insisted on their continuing to socialise, but Liberty felt so ill and out of sorts, she couldn't bring herself to dress up and be her usual charming self. It was the one time in her life she would kill for a glass of wine, or a stiff whisky, just for the sake of the alcohol numbing some of the feelings of worthlessness and uselessness which seemed increased by the hormonal upheaval. But she steadfastly refused any type of alcoholic drink. Percy worked and played hard as he always had. Liberty worked, went home and had long baths, breathing in herbs and aromatics prescribed by her naturopath to help her to stay calm and conceive. She wanted her husband to cuddle her, to enfold her in his arms. But he couldn't understand why.

'Third time lucky,' said Mr Probert, as he waved her goodbye. 'Phone us in ten days, when you have taken your test. I know you can do it.' He gave her an impish smile, and went back inside to help another couple make life.

6

Liberty had a pregnancy test ready and waiting; not that she needed it. She knew her body. And it was different. She had previously put on weight when doing IVF, but this time, instead of feeling like killing someone – anyone who looked at her, spoke to her or touched her – she felt calm and serene the whole time. A funny 'Ready brek' glow seemed to envelop her and she had the feeling that nothing could touch or damage her. She was like a walking, talking, padded cell, and she was protecting her baby!

Liberty even stopped on her way back to the mews to stare through the window of Rococo chocolates, imagining the warm smell of the ground cocoa beans, the vanilla and cinnamon her mother used to add to her hot drink. She couldn't wait to be making breakfast for her child. Maybe the pregnancy would bring back her sense of taste and smell. The doctors had always insisted it was psychological and that another shock or major change in her life could well help it to return. For the first time in memory, Liberty found she missed her long-lost senses, and wished she could feel the joy she remembered from a freshly baked cake. Home and comfort were her associations with baking, or the wonder when a new taste crossed her tongue; she had to be able to experience these things again, didn't she?

As she let herself into the house, she was surprised to find Percy standing in the kitchen.

'Darling! You didn't say you would make it home before you left on your trip.'

'Well, you know you have the perfect husband. I have been

telling you a white lie; I don't have a business trip this week. Come on, my love, I am not a completely insensitive loutish idiot. I am taking you away. Go and pack your bag for a few days. We need to be smart. Oh, and here is a little something extra.'

He paused, leaned towards her over the kitchen island, and then put his hand in his jacket pocket and took out a box.

'Oh my God!' she breathed. Percy had only ever given her jewellery when they became engaged, and that was inherited from his maternal grandmother, or in fact taken from his grandmother's finger by his mother and given to Percy in front of Liberty, as Mrs Cholmondly-Radley was horrified Liberty didn't have a ring to wear on her finger for their engagement party.

'Go on, open it, you'll love it,' said Percy, a smile on his face.

Liberty pulled off the ribbon and opened the box and the case inside.

'Wow!' That was all she could say. In the box was a very over-the-top diamond and citrine necklace. It had a great deal of filigree detail dripping from it. It was not to her classic taste at all, but what did men know? And anyway, it was so very thoughtful, and was for the baby, really. She knew she had to thank him.

'Oh, sweetheart, I didn't know you were so romantic, and after all these years! I am so happy I shall burst!' She threw her arms round his neck, kissing him all over his face. 'After eight years you still surprise me, and there was me beginning to worry that you were somewhat dissatisfied with your lot in life. I haven't managed to produce your heir, and I was worried you were tiring of me, and what must your parents think of me!'

Terrified she was going to start crying (these hormones were making life with the normally steady, capable Liberty a little chaotic) Percy removed her arms and told her to run and pack her bag.

'And when do we leave for wherever it is? How will I know what to pack?'

'Smart, but it should be warm, and in twenty minutes we will have to find a cab,' said Percy as he poured himself a coffee. 'So go on!' He had noticed she was still rooted to the spot.

Liberty raced up the stairs as quickly as she could, found a dress bag and, using her over-practical huge Hermès Birkin as a holdall-cum-handbag, flung in some DVF wraps as they would fit round her tummy, grabbed her bikini and a couple of cocktail dresses that always made her feel dressed up and smart, no matter what her mood. How forgiving a bit of black crepe can be when Karl Lagerfeld is behind the design! She then topped off the bag with passport and toiletries and at the last minute remembered her pregnancy test (or eight).

'Come on darling, ready? Are you all right?'

Liberty noticed that Percy was wearing his thoroughly pissed-off face.

'I'm not late?'

'No, no, but come on, let's get going.'

'Is everything OK, darling?' Liberty asked. 'We don't have to do this if you need to be at the office; just the wonderful thought is enough.'

Percy half smiled. 'No, nothing wrong there, no, come on, I have to set the alarm.'

A few years ago Percy rewarded himself for his own hard work by finally achieving his dream and acquiring a Pissarro, which now hung behind a false painting that was on a slide to hide the exquisite masterpiece and which was only revealed when they were entertaining or using the sitting room themselves. Bob, Liberty's friend from uni, had always been a bit funny about the arrival of the painting, which seemed to come with an odd selection of small Warhols and Hockneys. All the paintings, said Percy, had come from private collectors, which was why they were unknown, but he refused to enlarge on where they came from, just saying someone needed the cash quickly and therefore was practically giving them away. Bob said to Liberty when they were alone that the paintings collectively would be worth well over a million.

How Percy had raised the cash Liberty didn't know, but she understood the importance of setting the alarm, after one hormone-induced stupid moment when she had run out of the house, slamming the door but leaving a window open. She had been late for an important meeting following an appointment with Mr Probert. When Percy got back to the house and found the window open, he had taken her watch, a twenty-first birthday present from her father, and her charm bracelet, which her mother gave her, followed by a charm each birthday, the two possessions she cherished most, and sold them to a jeweller. It took all her own savings to get them back, despite pleading with the wily businessman behind the counter, and she never, ever left the house without setting the alarm again.

So, alarm set, they jumped into a taxi, Liberty relaxed and excited, holding Percy's hand and begging him to tell her where they were going. Florence!

'Florence! I haven't been there since I was sixteen. Daddy used to take me there, how I love it and how I love you!' exclaimed Liberty as she kissed Percy.

'That's enough, you don't have to keep doing that,' said Percy, conscious of the grinning taxi driver looking in his rear-view mirror.

'That's all right, sir,' said the driver. 'So nice to see a couple in love. Usually get the arguments at the end of the night – you two carry on with my blessing.'

Liberty grinned like a schoolgirl. How could she have doubted Percy? This was going to be amazing.

As she settled into her business class seat on the plane and strapped herself in, a smile crept across her face. Everything felt right and good in the world for the first time she could remember in years. *At last, I don't have that nagging sensation that I am living in an unreal world, with things going on around me that are outside my control. This is my life; my husband is in love with me. This is happiness. And I didn't even realise that I wasn't living.*

She had always wanted to do work to help other people, but felt that by working for the family bank she would please her husband and his family. Now she felt very secure. Her husband did love her, and she would produce a baby to carry on the generations of CRs. *Everything is falling into place, and when I get home I can quit my silly job and concentrate on doing something important. I shall research doing charity work. Whatever have I been doing these past six years?*

She hadn't appreciated until now how much she had felt ill at ease, and how much she disliked her job. She was good at it because she put all her effort and skill into anything she applied herself to. But she wanted to do something that truly fed her creative spirit, and having a baby was just the thing!

'Glass of champagne, or juice?' The steward was leaning towards her with a tray.

'Water, please.'

'Oh, for God's sake,' said Percy. 'I've paid good money for these tickets.' He took two glasses of bubbling champagne from the tray. 'And you can bring the bottle back when we have taken off,' he reminded the steward.

Liberty glanced at him.

'Well, what is it?' he asked. 'You seem so pleased with yourself, quite different, really.'

'Well, you know, it's best to be positive,' she responded meekly, feeling surprised that Percy wasn't as excited as she was about the impending pregnancy test, and worried he had been working too hard as he kept snapping. Trying to please him, but feeling no need for alcohol, she took a tiny sip of champagne.

She only knew it was champagne because of the bubbles running over her tongue, and felt an immediate furring in her mouth. 'Yuck.' When the steward passed by she said to him, 'Can I have some water, please, when you have a moment?' He brought her a large bottle and smiled sweetly at her before letting his face fall and handing Percy a bag of nuts. Liberty wondered if he had spat in them, remembering J-T's steward friends telling her in peals of laughter what they did to rude passengers' food and drink. Then she shut her eyes until they took off, to clear her mind of all negative thoughts.

Through her dream Liberty heard the roar of the engines and opened her eyes, which were feeling rather heavy, although she had only had a very quick nap.

'Welcome to Florence,' said Percy, smirking. *Oh God,* thought Liberty. *Whoops! I must have slept the whole way.* 'You seem to have been tired,' said Percy, his smile odd and cold. Liberty wondered how much champagne he had drunk. 'Are you going to sleep the whole weekend? I'm spending a fortune on this and if your hormones are going to make you sleep the entire time, I shall have to buy a book.'

'Sorry, sorry,' said Liberty, feeling embarrassed. The passengers around them, now standing to retrieve bags, were listening with interest whilst turning on their mobiles and stretching stiffly.

Percy raced to passport control, then to the baggage carousel, as though they were late for something. He rushed off to find the hotel car and was chatting animatedly to the driver as she pushed through the crowds, trying to keep up. Not exactly relaxing so far. Liberty felt more like a spare part than his wife. He had given her this special treat and now she just seemed to be doing everything wrong and was acting like a failure. She must make more of an effort. Maybe she had been too self-absorbed recently.

She didn't speak Italian as fluently as he, but she understood 'names wrong, stupid man' and 'phone ahead' being snippets from their conversation. *Oh dear, I hope the hotel hasn't made a mess of our booking,* she thought.

'Come on, get in the car. I just wanted to check the rooms were ready before we arrived. You know what a fuss these hotels make, even if I did book the rooms bloody six months ago.' How did he know six months ago they would be coming here for this particular weekend? An alarm bell started ringing, but she decided to ignore it. This was going to be the most wonderful, romantic weekend of her life.

They drove through the cobbled streets of the old town in silence, Liberty struck dumb by the beauty and symmetry of the buildings. The sun was dazzling and made the contrast between grey London and roseate Florence even more noticeable.

As they drove up the steep winding road to Fiesole, Liberty realised they were staying at the Villa San Michele, where she had been as a teenager with her father. It had been converted from an ancient monastery into a five-star luxury hotel, cleverly done in a relaxed but grand way, as though it was a private house full of lovely things rather than a designed 'space'. The staff were always waiting to attend to the guests' every wish or command, but they carried out these wishes in a discreet, subtle way, and therefore were never intrusive. Staying at the hotel was like being a guest of very good friends in their grand family home, with the best food in Tuscany served on the loggia overlooking the city of Florence. There were huge white hydrangeas blossoming in large terracotta pots on a terrace just below them, interspersed with lemon trees, also in pots, hanging with fragrant fruit.

As Liberty glanced around, savouring the clarity of the light and the cypress trees reaching up in columns to the sky, a man came dancing down the steps to the car.

'Mr Cholmondly-Radley, welcome; Luca di Campo, manager of the most wonderful hotel in Italy, if not the world,' he said by way of introduction as he stuck out his hand. Percy took it, and said, 'That's quite a claim. I hope you can back it up,' and then sotto voce to Liberty, 'Bloody Italians, arrogant little Eyetie. They should stick to pinching bottoms and making handbags.'

'Come on, darling,' replied Liberty. 'He seems charming, and this hotel is very beautiful.' She gazed up at the facade of the building.

'Attributed to Michelangelo,' announced the manager

proudly. 'Please come with me, we will get you settled on the terrace with a refreshing drink while we take your luggage to your suite.'

'I would rather check in first,' stated Percy.

'No need, we don't do things like that here,' explained the manager kindly. 'We have your booking, no need for any more formality, you are here to rest! Come to the terrace and relax.'

Percy professed himself disappointed to find there was no real bar, just a table set on the loggia, laid with a linen cloth holding a few bottles and glasses and a fridge for the peach juice and Prosecco in case anyone wished for a Bellini.

'Giovanni will look after you from here,' said Luca. 'Welcome again and enjoy your stay. Anything you need, let me know. Our little bus will take you into town, it leaves every half hour, or we can arrange a taxi.'

'Thank you,' said Liberty, gazing out at the heavenly view towards Florence in the distance, and entranced by the hilltop setting of the hotel.

The maître d' appeared as if from nowhere. 'The best table has been reserved for you for dinner, sir.' He indicated a table at the far end of the terrace, slightly apart from the others, and furthest away from the piano.

'Come and sit in the garden,' said Giovanni, somehow manoeuvring them into two comfortable chairs overlooking the distant city. 'Now, my dear lady, a fresh peach juice for you, I think? And what would sir enjoy?' Percy looked aghast at the term of endearment directed towards his wife, and Liberty could almost hear him thinking 'Bloody Eyetie!'.

'Whisky, single malt,' said Percy, 'and make it a decent size!' he shouted at Giovanni's back. The maître d' acknowledged this with a nod of his head and a smile. He was used to hassled visitors who were unable to unwind from their hectic lives. A few days here and things would change.

While they waited for their drinks Liberty sat back on her comfortable cushion-filled chair, and took in the incredible beauty of her surroundings. The gardens were terraced, flanked by one wall of the hotel. Swathed by an ancient wisteria, small garden rooms could just be seen tucked under the lower terrace where the gentle splash of water in the swimming pool soothed their ears. Near them was the lemon garden, with beautiful metal chairs covered in thick white cushions carefully arranged in groups so as to provide instant comfort wherever wanted. Some had small tables shaded by white fringed parasols, just slightly moving in the light breeze, and the whisper of the wind gave the right amount of relief from the otherwise pressurising heat of the late afternoon. Liberty felt so fortunate that she could experience this intense beauty, so far removed from the real world, and she marvelled that once in a while man could get it right, and create a paradise on earth. She made a mental note that she must tell J-T and Bob to visit; they would adore it. Percy broke into her reverie.

'Damn the Eyeties, they are just too bloody familiar. The Ritz could teach them a thing or two. Next they will be telling us what to wear for dinner and what to eat.'

Liberty knew full well they would do exactly that, or at least strongly recommend their special dishes. All Italians try to help visitors to realise in which direction they should be going, whether culinary, sartorially or any other which way, rather than sticking to their own known world. The manager would understand that as an Englishman, Percy could well order pasta for a main course, and would try to sway him tactfully towards it as a first course, to be followed by a little meat or fish, so she simply smiled and said, 'But Percy, just look at this place – have you ever been anywhere quite so stunning? And when have you ever stayed at the Ritz?'

Percy ignored the question and said, 'Well, August the twelfth is pretty damned bearable if you are in the Highlands, when you have a gun in your hands.'

'I am sure the management could arrange some shooting

here, and they probably have game on the menu. Let's just enjoy our drinks, shall we?'

She sipped her white peach juice, and settled herself back in the cushions as she realised just how delicious her drink was. This was not only because she knew it should be so, but because she felt that this drink was truly tasty. She sat bolt upright. Then she recognised it had been subtly enhanced with lemon juice.

'What's wrong?' asked Percy, glancing up from his smartphone.

'Nothing, nothing,' said Liberty, not daring to hope that pregnancy may indeed have been bringing back her taste buds. But she kept that fact to herself. She was so excited that her sense of taste could be returning in such a magical place, but would hate to make a thing of it, just in case it was simply the miraculous setting that had made her imagination run riot. 'Cheers, darling, and thank you again. I feel so lucky to have you, although I do wish you didn't work so hard, you are meant to be relaxing!'

Percy looked up at his exquisite wife, in the unique setting, and wished he could be anywhere else in the world. He knew the subject of her pregnancy would pop out the moment they got to their room. Trapped. Trapped by baby, trapped by job. Why was life turning into such a chore? Didn't he deserve some fun? This weekend was meant to be oh-so different. But he managed to put his phone down, and with some effort raised his glass and said 'To life!', before downing the amber liquid in one.

7

They chatted idly as they finished their drinks, and before they felt in any way impatient a member of staff was at their side saying their bags were in their room, and would they like to go up now?

He took them up the narrow mahogany staircase, along an arched hallway and stopped at Room Eight. He opened the double doors and they walked into a beautiful vaulted room that took up the entire width of the hotel. An enormous bed with a half-tester stood proudly in the centre against one ancient stone wall, draped heavily in red velvet; comfortable chairs sat cosily around a table; whilst all mod cons had been hidden in wooden chests and cabinets. To see the view from the shuttered windows they had to step up slightly to a ledge wide enough for both of them to stand on together. One of these windows afforded them a full vista of the bowl that held the city of Florence, like a teacup containing an exquisite hibiscus flower.

Liberty immediately moved up to the ledge, pushed open the shutters just enough to glimpse the golden dome of the Basilica di Santa Maria del Fiore in the valley below and gasped at the wonder of the sight before her. She knew Florence was a noisy, bustling city, but from their vantage point they only saw the glamour, the beauty, the well-known skyline, without the noise or polluted air. All was serene, bar the sound of knives and forks and happy chatter wafting up from the terrace, as late diners were still enjoying their luncheon, although by now it was nearly five o'clock.

There was the sound of a bottle popping behind her. 'Look

what I ordered – Krug '99,' said Percy. 'Come on, here is a glass for you. Funny they didn't offer you alcohol downstairs.'

Liberty opened her handbag and said that she wanted to get unpacked first. She couldn't help but think only of the pregnancy test she wanted to do. Percy wanted to get drunk.

'Come on, just one glass to celebrate, and then I need to check my emails and make some calls before we go down to dinner.'

Liberty accepted the glass from Percy and took a sip, again not experiencing anything but bubbles. But she was convinced she had been right about her taste coming back before, so surely it would again? They sat with the sun peeping through the shutters, until Liberty glanced at him and blurted out, 'So, aren't you desperate to know?'

Percy looked startled for a moment. 'Know what, my darling? Oh yes,' he corrected himself sharply. 'Well, go on then, but you are so sure already that little Charles is on his way, aren't you? I'm already celebrating, as you can see, but I hope that at least you won't eat for two and get all podgy like Conrad's wife did. The poor man couldn't look at her for two years until she went to that fat farm, and now everything still sags, he says.'

Oh great, thought Liberty. *Well, I suppose that is what men want. A wife, a baby, the immaculately presentable family that seems perfect but without any change in bodily substance. Must remember to do my best to remain svelte for as long as possible, but if I AM pregnant, nothing else matters.*

She wandered through a huge arched doorway that led to the stunning bathroom, wide bath set below a window, vast shower for at least two, and an enormous vanity table inset with two basins, all enrobed in Carrara marble. In fact, it was hard to find anything that didn't seem to be carved out of the gleaming grey and white stone that flattered every skin tone, whilst adding a sense of serene calm and good taste. The ceilings were as high as those in the bedroom, with frescos along one wall that looked as though they could date from the fifteenth century, but had probably been added later. *J-T would have a field day here*, thought Liberty as she emptied her cosmetics out of her seemingly bottomless Birkin. 'I know I put in at least ten of the damn things, and now I can't find one,' she muttered. 'Aha!' she exclaimed as she found a pregnancy test, feeling triumphant, like Mary Poppins when she discovered her hat stand.

For a brief moment she wondered whether being pregnant might not be the dream she had hoped for. Percy had seemed so distant the moment she said she was sure it had worked. Then she checked herself. Did she not love Percy, didn't she respect him at all? What was she doing with such a superficial man, anyway? Why hadn't she noticed his behaviour before now? She supposed it was because she had always made such an effort to be exactly the woman that Percy wanted, the perfect wife and partner, whereas now she just didn't care any longer, all she wanted was to be a mummy and have a family, with Percy. She was sure he would be a good father. He was probably just nervous. After taking a few deep breaths leaning over one of the sinks, she reassured herself that he was a good man; not too good at showing love or emotion, perhaps, but kind nonetheless. She tried to remember the man she had met all those years ago, filled with passion and drive. He would be a fine father, she reasoned, it would just take a little getting used to for him. She regained her excited feeling and threw doubt to the wind.

She tried to open one of the plastic wrappers to get into the pregnancy test and observed they were made for organised people who carried scissors wherever they went, so she hurried back into the bedroom to find a sewing kit or something similar. There was no sewing kit in the room that she could find. She looked around and saw a bottle opener on the table. Percy must have left the room to make his calls. There was a letter next to the bowl of fruit on the table that she had not noticed before. It must have just been delivered. It was addressed to Mr and Mrs Percy Smith. Out of curiosity, she opened it.

'Welcome to the Villa San Michele. We hope to make your

honeymoon a very special and memorable one.' It was signed Luca di Campo, Manager, San Michele.

Oh no! she thought. *We have been given their champagne and now their fruit, and it's all a mistake.* She called down to reception to correct the error.

'I think you have mixed us up with some other guests,' she said.

'Oh no, Madame, we have had you booked in here since you came in May,' said the lady at the end of the line. 'I specifically remembered your husband when I saw him coming out of the elevator, so I do know that you are our special honeymoon guests, and I welcome you back to Villa San Michele. I look forward to greeting you again in person at dinner. We have your favourite Martini on ice already.'

The receptionist was pleased with herself – she would get high praise for her attention to detail. When she had arrived for the evening shift, she found that Luca, usually such a stickler, had left the note he would normally deliver himself while checking a guest's room was prepared to his satisfaction behind the desk. She had hurried upstairs, really not in her job description, and placed it in the room. It was then she saw Mr Smith walk down the corridor, talking on his phone.

Liberty's legs started shaking and she felt instantly sick. She replaced the phone in its cradle without replying. She sat down on the sofa and gazed around her. She saw Percy's briefcase by the armchair, and walked over to it. Hesitating only for an instant she placed it on the sofa and opened it, not caring about snooping, something she would abhor in any other situation. She rummaged about until she found his diary. He was sufficiently old-fashioned still to use a paper one, and also had a secretary who entered his appointments in it. Although he also put things in his smartphone, he didn't yet know exactly how to retrieve them, so this was his backup.

Sure enough: 'September 1st–4th, Florence – send money for undies.' All through June, July and August until the shooting season started a little tick appeared on certain days, and then on 12th August, when he had been in Derbyshire, 'make sure G invited'.

Liberty's entire body now began to convulse. Percy had made some excuse to her, telling her that it would not be a good idea for her to go to Derbyshire this year, saying the men were shooting without their wives this time, and 'anyway, darling, you wont feel like it after taking all those medical hormone things'.

She almost smiled when she thought of old fusty Mary, Percy's personal assistant, trotting out to Agent Provocateur to pick out underwear. God, Percy had never bought underwear in his entire life, whether for himself or anyone else.

As she sat there, twisting her hands together, everything began slowly to slot into place. Percy was trying to make himself unattractive to her, because he wanted her to become fed up with him. That bloody necklace, the horrid thing, must be G's taste. She felt very sick, and then howled as a terrible pain tore through her gut. She ran into the bathroom, feeling the familiar hot sensation as the tiny life left her body and blood trickled down her leg. She crawled along the floor, grabbed her pashmina that was hanging over the towel rail and wrapped it around herself, suddenly freezing cold. She could hear gut-wrenching sobs escaping her body. It was a known sensation; she had experienced it twice before. She had been so sure, almost felt she knew the little soul that was now leaving her body. She sent a prayer up, raising her face towards the God she hoped was doing this for a greater purpose, allowing the tears streaming from her eyes to escape down her temples and trickle down and cool her neck. She tucked herself under the vanity table, trying to curl up and hide. She hoped God would listen and take care of the tiny entity. *Why am I so useless? I can't hold a man or a baby.*

She lay there on the marble floor for a while, unable to think of what to do next. What was there in life? No baby, no husband, no nothing. She sobbed. She had allowed her life to float by, not caring about anything; she had nothing of her own of any significance. She had achieved nothing meaningful, she had let others tell her what she should do. Had she no thought of her own? What was the point of life, anyway? She felt pain and horror and grief washing over her in waves like an ocean trying to wash her away. She wanted to be carried away, to disappear out of the world.

Someone was hammering at the bedroom door, and she crawled over to let the bastard in.

'Signora?' said Luca, gazing down at her with consternation written all over his face. She looked up at him in a daze and he seemed to disappear, at which point she realised she was not really there herself . . . a few moments later an elderly lady stood before her, and managed somehow to persuade Liberty to her feet and into bed. Gently, gently she was undressed, while the strange but oh-so-kind lady chatted away all the while in Italian, not one word of which Liberty understood in her semi-comatose condition, but she gathered comfort from the attention given to her by this remarkable woman. It all seemed like a hazy dream, or nightmare, and somewhere far away she could hear Percy's voice, some shouting, some rather soft Italian voice, but she couldn't bring herself to care what was going on, she couldn't think what was happening, she was just full of sadness. She must have fallen asleep, as the next thing she knew it was dark outside, the shutters had been opened to let in the cool night air and several lamps had been lit in the room. She sat up, and her first thought was, *Oh God, the blood!* She threw back the exquisite sheet, horrified at the thought that Luca had put her to bed and seen all the mess. It might be a five-star hotel, but there are limits!

She suddenly felt amazingly calm. Sad and forlorn, yes, but it was as though her face wouldn't move or show any emotion ever again. She was set in this calm mode for ever. She worried she was just a shell with nothing left inside.

She was amazed to find herself in her negligee with a towel

beneath her. She went into the bathroom, and noticed that all evidence of the pregnancy tests had been removed along with her IVF notes and folder, and the horrid mess. After splashing her face with cold water, she also saw that although her toiletries and make-up had been neatly placed on the table beside one of the basins, she was positive she hadn't done that. There was nothing, nothing at all of Percy's. No shaving gear, no toothbrush, no toiletries. She returned to the bedroom. No bag, no briefcase, no half empty bottle of champagne, just something else. What was it? An aroma. A heavenly aroma of rosemary, a little garlic, and the heady scent of decent chicken being cooked with a touch of nutmeg. The memory of smell must be strong. For the first time in twenty years Liberty salivated. She was starving. She looked around her, but there was nothing to eat in the room; the fruit must have been cleared away. She didn't want to leave the room for the time being and have to face anyone, but she could certainly eat a horse, and of course if she asked for one that would probably be brought to her, as she was in Italy, she thought ruefully.

She sat on the edge of the bed. What to do? At that moment there was a gentle tap at the door, followed by the appearance of the woman who had so wonderfully cared for her earlier. Liberty blushed at the memory. The woman was in her late sixties and had a large knot of grey hair elegantly pulled back from her kind, wizened face to the nape of her neck. She wore a black, simply fashioned dress and black shoes, and was essentially a typical wealthy Italian matron. But what really caught Liberty's attention was the tray she was carrying.

On the tray was a basket overflowing with different freshly baked rolls, some crusty, pointy and white, some knobbly with walnuts and sultanas. There was a bowl of tiny olives like shiny black pearls, a dish of walnuts so fresh they gleamed, and another filled with a puree of red peppers and anchovies. Yet another was filled with the new season's olive oil, green and succulent, with tiny specks of chilli and chopped herbs. And then, pièce de résistance, a tureen of chicken broth.

As the woman removed the lid and ladled some into a shallow dish, Liberty couldn't help but lean over, almost drooling with anticipation. Fresh vegetables, gleaming like coloured jewels, swam happily among handmade tortellini filled, she was to discover, with the lightest chicken liver mousse, gently seasoned with nutmeg and parsley, which had been poached in the broth.

'Come, my child, sit.' Liberty allowed herself to be led by the hand to a chair, have a napkin tied around her neck like a child might and, even more amazingly, let herself be fed, slowly; a spoonful of soup, bread with some puree, a torn shred of bread dipped in oil with one or two walnuts perched on the top. The flavours exploded in her mouth. The rosemary in the oil was healing her body, she could feel it infusing her very soul; very subtle, not overpowering. The oil was so fresh and green; it was rehydrating her. The calming, restorative flavours seemed to flood her whole body and pulse through her veins, the very opposite of the anaesthetic that forced its way through her when the tiny embryos had been implanted only ten days ago. All that horror seemed light years ago now. The chicken broth, so sweet from the carrots and pea pods, but savoury with parmesan and fresh chervil; the pasta, so light, and the mousse it contained danced lightly on her tongue, before slipping down like the best medicine. With each mouthful, she could feel herself growing stronger.

Both women were surprised when they realised she had consumed everything on the tray, except for the glass of Chianti, which she now raised to her lips. Only then did she feel able to speak.

'Molte grazie, signora,' Liberty sighed, *'molte grazie.'*

'My child,' replied the woman, 'you are safe here. Luca is my son. He has, er, removed Signore Radley. You need rest and to heal, yes? I regret to say, Luca had no idea, when you arrived, of the matter. He would not have interfered, but mamas understand these things.'

'Where is Percy?' asked Liberty.

'Gone, Signora. You must stay as long as you need to. Don't think about anything but rest at the moment. You are safe here,' she stressed. 'Sleep now, my child.'

Liberty did indeed feel overwhelmingly tired.

'Do you need to see a doctor? I have arranged for someone to visit you in the morning, but if you need someone now, he will of course come. You know your body, of course, better than anyone else.'

'No, thank you, I think I had just best return home.'

'Not yet. Wait a few days. You need Tuscany to restore you. *Alora*, we can speak about it in the morning. Now sleep.'

Liberty allowed herself to be put back into the bed, and tucked in. 'Thank you. *Grazie*,' she managed to whisper again, unable to put into words the utter gratitude and relief she felt, before the restorative haven of sleep enveloped her.

Liberty awoke feeling alive again. Not alive in the sense of 'OK I am breathing, and can see and hear' but alive in the sense of being full of energy, vitality and excitement. *What can I achieve today, tomorrow and for the rest of my life?* she thought. *I have been reborn,* she decided. *Now. Today. The rest of my life begins at this moment.* She felt physically drained, exhausted, despite her long sleep, which, unknown to her, had lasted almost thirty-six hours. Signora di Campo had checked on her and slept outside the door in a chair, placed there by her bewildered son.

'How could he do anything to hurt that exquisite creature?' he asked his mama.

'Life is one long trail of confusion, hate, love and experience,' she responded. 'We must not judge, but she needs care, and you men have no clue at times like these.' She enjoyed the feeling of being needed again, after spending eighteen years as a widow and watching her son in the arms of his wife. Her heart had gone out to the girl, who had allowed herself to be mothered. The screams that had filled the air while she slept had torn at the heart of the elderly woman, who thought she had seen it all, but she was pleased her son had called; he didn't always have the answer, capable as he was, and he still needed his mama!

Liberty stretched, got out of bed and staggered to the shutters. As she flung them open, she realised she felt nothing of the grief that had enveloped her two days earlier. Percy and the horror of the miscarriage seemed to have been swept away in her dreams. She had no memory of being held tightly by Signora di Campo as shouts and screams ripped from her body and filled the room while she slept.

I am going to live, to really live, to feel alive, to experience new things, she decided. She felt able to make things right somehow; her skin seemed to zing with newly found nerves, as though the sensation of air was massaging her soul, sending thousands of messages to her wretched body, to stop wasting life, stop dwelling on what had gone by and start thinking of the future. *My life can start now; I can make people happy, myself happy!* She knew it sounded strange, even to herself, but she felt it was remarkable that out of such horror, such positive change could come.

She leapt about like a child, gathering clothes, running to the bathroom to splash her face, to look in the mirror, expecting a different reflection to the one she had seen in recent years to peer back at her. *No, still me.* But to the outsider, a new determination and gleam would be seen, filling the green eyes, behind which a new beginning was slowly unfolding.

This baby's tiny life would not be wasted. Liberty would not sit and mourn, for what would that achieve? *Starting from now, everyone will be seen through new eyes. Life is so short and I will not just coast through it any longer.*

She had a long, hot shower, followed by a cold blast, dressed quickly, combed her hair and made up her face. She looked herself straight in the eyes in the mirror. She saw a woman in a navy wrap dress, cheeks glowing, and smiled. This was her life. *Let's go, girl*, she said to her image.

Once out of her room, she felt a little more uncertain and alone. *Oh, come on girly!* She mentally kicked herself, and reminded herself of her quest. She wandered downstairs. Luca was at the reception desk. He came forward with a genuine smile, not unbearably sympathetic, and led her through to the vaulted dining room which had been laid for breakfast, although most of the guests had chosen to dine on the terrace.

Along one wall of the room were two tables covered with heavy cloths, groaning with plates of cold meats, smoked cheese, fresh ricotta, smoked salmon, Prosecco for a breakfast mimosa. Luca was describing the selection of breakfast dishes as though none of the horrible events had happened.

'Signora, I have set a table for you in the garden. Shall I prepare a plate of food for you?' Fabulous.

'*Grazie*, and do please make sure there is plenty of that wonderful bread,' she replied, pointing to baskets of walnut and sultana sourdough and rye. 'Ooh, and some of that, too,' she added as she spied a huge leg of Parma ham being sliced by a waiter.

'And a Bellini or a mimosa?'

'Bellini, I think, and a strong coffee. And thank you,' she said as she looked at him earnestly. 'Your mother has taken great care of me, and I am both humbled and incredibly grateful. How can I thank you?'

Luca looked serious. His facade as manager slipped for a second as he said, 'The happiness and well-being of my guests is of utmost importance to me, but sometimes I need a little help. The only person who knows better than me is my mama, so it was to her I turned.'

Understanding he would be uncomfortable to talk any more, Liberty allowed him to lead her past the other guests, who were restricted to the loggia, and sat alone in the garden, blissful in isolation, away from the stares she felt might be forthcoming, although, of course, no one else had any idea what had happened.

As she sat in the morning sun and dunked yet another piece

of butter lemon cake into her coffee, Liberty emailed her godmother and invited herself to stay. Much as she loved the hotel, she felt in need of a home, but was unable to return to her own. Unwilling to force herself on either of her parents, she would escape for a while, maybe take a course in baking, and help in Paloma's restaurant. A change of scenery was just what she needed most. There followed a brief email exchange:

P: Of course, darling, how long for? Is Percy coming too?
L: No, will explain later, will come tomorrow if I can get a flight. Can I stay for a while?
P: Let me know your arrival time and I will send Claude to the airport for you. Love you.

Liberty leaned back in her seat and breathed in the scent of the pine trees, the aromas from the kitchens where lunch was already being prepared, the lemon bushes in their tubs. She even thought she could smell the grass growing. What had she been missing all this time? Her tongue was alive with taste, and she almost felt it was asking her 'What next?'.

Like a child with its first mash of solid food, her taste buds were tingling with excitement, her skin was twitching with pleasure and she understood the importance of good food and its setting for the first time. All those silly magazines were there to help one to diet and to reject food. But food was there to help one to live. Respect food, respect your body, respect life. It was like a new mantra for her.

The energy that her breakfast gave her was now coursing through her body. She got up from the table, happily replete, and walked through to the hall that served as the reception area. A black-haired woman glanced at her and immediately looked sheepish.

'Good morning, signora. What may I do for you?'

Liberty recognised the voice as belonging to the receptionist on the phone from the day she arrived, welcoming her back and insisting she had been there before. She smiled warmly at her to show there were no hard feelings, because, after all, it was hardly the woman's fault that Liberty's husband was a shit and a liar. *Golly, odd to even think of him!* She found herself pushing his memory to a nook in the back of her mind, something she would deal with later.

'I need to book a flight to Nice for tomorrow, please, to arrive mid afternoon, if possible.'

'Business class? Yes, I will arrange, and a car to transport you to the airport? Meanwhile, shall I reserve a table on the terrace for you for dinner this evening, or will you eat in town?'

'A table at eight thirty would be lovely. I shall go into Florence now. Can you recommend somewhere for lunch?'

'I will reserve a table at Buca Lapi, here is the card. They will expect you. I can get the driver to take you, or will you find your own way?'

'I will walk from where the minibus drops me, thank you.'

She stepped into the sunshine and climbed into the little bus that took guests from the hotel into town whenever they needed it. She was joined by a young American couple who were discussing the meal they had eaten the evening before.

'We come from San Francisco, and we thought we had great pasta there! Now we are not sure we can eat outside of Italy.' Their faces beamed with pleasure at her, and she felt a joy for them and their ability to appreciate, and not simply want an imitation of what they had at home.

As the bus drove them down the hillside and through the outskirts of Florence, Liberty looked out at the shops. Fresh linen in neat heaps, little market stalls hanging with leather bags, cafés bustling with people standing drinking their cappuccino or espresso before rushing off to work. Dust, drains and roasted coffee filled her nose and she loved it. Even the driver's strong cologne did not disturb her, although Percy would have complained loudly. Every hint of an aroma excited and amused her. This was living!

The minibus dropped them in the main square, right by the Duomo. Liberty left the young Americans examining their street map. She could see them as she turned; they were already surrounded by touts and men offering horse and trap rides, while she strode away not caring in which direction she went. She wanted to explore and enjoy absorbing the atmosphere of beautiful buildings, people and history. She smiled as she walked past a café, the owner of which was yelling at the top of his voice to a delivery driver who had apparently forgotten his quota of peaches. The driver simply shrugged, and the owner smiled in typical Italian style, everything quickly forgotten as he saw Liberty, a prospective customer.

'Cappuccino? Espresso? Signora?'

My mouth almost hurts from smiling, she thought as she declined, anxious to see the city. Spying a beautiful shop adorned with linens and plates, she thought she had better phone J-T. He had told her to call the moment she knew the results of her test. In fact, her mother, father and boss had better be told where she was. She could picture her mother at the Aga, eyes glancing towards the phone, wondering why she hadn't heard, whilst wrestling with a new recipe or a kitchen full of students. Unwilling and unable to speak to a kind voice yet, Liberty thought maybe a cappuccino would be a good idea. *But I want to find a local café, in the Italian style, no chairs, somewhere I can stand in a very disorderly queue and wait to shout loudly enough to order my coffee over a bar, and then watch the world go by as I drink it.* She filled her mind with as many ideas as she could, to remove any negative thoughts.

She wandered through some narrow alleyways where washing hung from one side to the other way above her head, and then came out again into a large square with a church at one end. She found a café of the sort she wanted at last, and waited for attention. She was baffled and amused at the same time by how the barman could work out who was next in line, as it seemed utter chaos to her, but she watched for a while, learnt quickly, and then just shouted over everyone else, her height and looks helping.

'Milano, espresso?' asked the waiter.

'Milano,' she replied, the beans being smoother and sweeter. He handed her the cup. By now, 11.30, it was already too late for a cappuccino; she would be considered a tourist by any café owner if she insisted on ordering one, and despite being just that, she had no intention of advertising the fact, as her coffee would probably be taken by someone she had just queue barged. She took her cup on to the street, and looked along the narrow passageway, lined by ancient wobbly buildings, each as beautiful as the next, finished in intoxicating Tuscan colours: terracotta, dusky pink, burnt umber. Flowers spilled from well-tended baskets and urns, smart new wooden shutters protected the long windows. She imagined that behind the beautiful old exteriors were stunningly expensive and exquisite apartments, judging by the buzzers attached to the huge wooden doors.

It was tempting to begin a fresh life and live somewhere new. She had always loved both Italy and France; the joy that both the Italians and the French seemed to take from life had long fascinated her. They always took time to enjoy each day and never allowed it to pass them by, whereas the English always expected and demanded so much from the world around them. She thought, *We need to learn to stop, look and love, to breathe, to do what we want and not as we should.* Liberty knew that she was English through and through, and although the idea of moving abroad was a tempting one, she also knew she had to get on with living, and that did not begin with running away.

She strolled off down the street, and back into Via Borghese. She decided, first things first: new woman, new clothes!

8

Two hours later, loaded down by huge bags from many of the great fashion houses, Liberty headed for Buca Lapi, a well-known traditional trattoria, run by the same family for decades and the oldest restaurant in Florence. The owners used fresh produce and wine from their estate in the Tuscan hills. Hungry, and loving the sensation, the moment she started to think about stuffed courgette flowers with fresh ricotta she actually thought she drooled. She wiped her chin worriedly, then laughed out loud.

She found the restaurant tucked down some stairs in a passage just off the Via Borghese.

'Signora! Welcome!' A tall, slim man took Liberty's bags and put them behind his desk, then offered her his arm. Silver hair, handmade suit and shirt; Liberty summed up instantly that he was the owner rather than merely the manager, as he led her past the tiny open kitchen.

'I have a special table for you. You like to be private or to observe?'

'Ooh, definitely observe!'

Carlo, as he introduced himself, raised a finger and immediately a waiter in a shoulder to ankle striped apron appeared and moved the table so that Liberty could slide on to a comfortable bench with her back to the window and look around the room. How typically Italian, she thought. A table for one, and they give you the window, just in case you want to keep an eye on the street. The table was larger than some of those laid for two. She giggled to herself – Italians obviously expected you to sit almost on top of one another if it was to be a romantic dinner for two.

The elderly waiter brought out sourdough bread, crostini with tiny Tuscan olives and a glass of Prosecco.

'May I choose for you, Signora?'

'Oh, yes please,' sighed Liberty, thrilled to empty her mind and let someone else do the thinking. The restaurant was just filling with diners. Those who had already finished their meals were presumably tourists, unused to the hours kept by the Florentines. Water rather than wine on the tables, maps everywhere and pasta being eaten as a main course. This early 'tourist' service allowed the tables to be filled for a second time at a normal lunch hour for Florence, and the restaurateurs loved it. The earlier sitting was at midday (who eats at such a stupid time, they sighed, but it was so easy for the kitchens); probably only a plate of carpaccio as a starter, followed no doubt by a big dish of pasta carbonara, followed by maybe a cappuccino (and who drank milk after a meal anywhere civilised?) then a rude wave of an arm when offered a limoncello on the house.

The locals were arriving for their luncheon. Italians are used to taking a decent lunch break during the working week, although longer than one hour is frowned on in the modern, uncivilised world. But now it was Saturday, time to relax and enjoy life to the full. Elegant ladies and gentlemen, couples and families, grandparents and grandchildren, all exquisitely clothed, all buzzing with the excitement of eating together, of filling each other in on their news, sharing their silly problems or happy developments of the past week. They were simply here to enjoy catching up, gossiping and, of course, the food.

One couple at a table close to Liberty's had obviously had a bit of a set to. They sat side by side, as the restaurant encouraged couples to do, the man holding the girl's hand, whispering in her ear as she looked the other way, her huge doe eyes glistening with hurt tears. He started to stroke her cheek whilst continually whispering sweet nothings in her ear.

Carlo appeared and placed a dish between them. On it sat a solitary ravioli. One sage leaf atop, it was surrounded by butter.

Liberty imagined the butter flavoured with the sage and perhaps a little garlic and pepper and wondered what the pasta envelope held within. Carlo silently placed a fork on each corner of the square dish and two small glasses of what looked like Marsala wine next to each of them.

The man picked up his fork, the girl her glass. For one moment Liberty thought the contents of the glass were about to land in his lap, but no, they were Italian, after all! She took a sip, and he cut the corner off the ravioli, so soft and yielding, but then the fork found just a touch of resistance in the pasta, to show just how perfectly cooked it was. A little puff of steam was expelled from the centre and Liberty could discern sage and maybe butternut or onion squash, and she watched as the creamy filling spilled out on to the dish.

The man placed his fork under the girl's nose, as a parent might a child, and then lowered it to her trembling mouth, still glistening from the wine. Liberty realised she was holding her breath – would she? Wouldn't she? The lips parted; slowly and gently he placed the small portion in her mouth. As her lips closed around the aromatic pasta, the corners of her eyes lifted and she chewed slowly and then swallowed. He smiled. She turned her head and gently kissed him. She then picked up her own fork, and tiny mouthful by tiny mouthful they fed each other. Not a word was spoken throughout the whole transaction. Liberty thought she had never seen anything more erotic in her entire life.

Carlo appeared. Liberty had assumed the ravioli was an amuse-bouche for the whole restaurant. But it seemed they cooked different remedies for different maladies (perhaps this was really an Italian hospital?). On her own plate, miraculously placed before her while she had been examining her neighbours' performance, lay a few wide ribbons of pappardelle. She could see and savour small pieces of rosemary, a few slivers of pancetta and some very green, freshly podded broad beans.

Carlo shaved some pecorino on the pappardelle and drizzled the dish with a little of the vibrant local olive oil.

'Enjoy. It's good for you.' He smiled.

Liberty thought for a moment. Either the hotel had, along with reserving her table, given the restaurateur a full rundown of her disastrous love life, or, being an Italian man, he thought her too thin.

She picked up her fork and scooped up a bit of pasta, a piece of the ham and a bean, gazed at it momentarily, and then tentatively placed it on her tongue. The aromas flew to her nose, whilst the flavours, delicate together yet individually strident, exploded in her mouth. What she hadn't seen on the plate she now tasted. The fresh pasta had been cooked in water with a bay leaf to give it an aromatic flavour, the minute amount of rosemary was just enough to uplift and heal, the salt of the pancetta was enhanced by its partnership of fennel seed and pepper, and the new life in the tiny broad bean gave energy and a touch of sweetness, gently offset by the slight tang of the sheep's pecorino.

There were probably only three medium-sized mouthfuls on the plate. Liberty ate carefully so as to make seven, and then sighed heavily, as she had to relinquish her fork and greedily mop up the last vestiges of oil with a mouthful of bread.

Well, she thought, *were I to die now, I am healed and happy.*

Three courses followed: a single courgette flower stuffed with a light veal mousse and coated in a fresh tomato sauce; a few griddled baby squid flavoured gently with wild garlic and finally a single lamb cutlet, also griddled, and served with a herb and olive oil dressing enhanced by anchovies and capers.

Liberty sat back, pleased that she hadn't devoured the entire bread basket, but in no way did she feel over full. They knew how to balance a meal.

She sipped her small glass of red wine brought with the food – fruity, light Chianti. She smiled and felt genuine happiness for the couple who were now chatting away happily, waving their hands to demonstrate their meaning, and from what she could understand of the conversation, talking about the apartment they were moving into, although it was obviously not the one the girl had picked!

Families were conversing over coffees, children were playing together around the tables and the staff from the open kitchen had to dodge as they played games of chase around their feet.

It was almost four o'clock in the afternoon, and Liberty knew she needed to walk and see more of the city, but she was enjoying herself too much. Carlo approached her table and looked down at her in a paternalistic way.

'I am so happy you enjoy our lovely town properly, signora. It is so calm in here, and so happy, I feel you are seeing more of the true Tuscany in here than out there with the tourists. Well then, an espresso and you can have a walk along the river. It will not be too crowded, as many tourists leave around now to go for a rest before early dinner.'

The espresso arrived with a tiny sliver of hazelnut and chocolate cake, a shot glass of zabaglione and a small ball of coffee granita, sprinkled with toasted hazelnuts and cocoa. 'Try it, you will love it and ask for all my recipes,' said Carlo with a smile.

Indeed she did. 'Sadly, I never divulge recipes,' Carlo joked as he brought the bill.

'Then why say that I should ask for it?' she responded.

'I didn't say that you should, I said that you would. I gave my heart and the recipe for the cake to someone in Rome once, and she made it, only without love and without the essential ingredient . . . It only tastes as good with the butter from my cows, who live outside Florence, so unless you want to come and milk my cows every night, when the milk is richer, there is no point in my giving you the recipe.'

Liberty smiled up at him with a glint in her eye. What was happening to her? When did she last flirt, for heaven's sake? And what did happen to the lady who made the cake?

'Well, as I said, she made the cake without love; I could tell, all beating and no care. I couldn't love a woman who baked like that, so I returned to my family, found a lady who knew how to caress both human flesh and butter and cream, and from that moment on, no one gets the recipe apart from her! I am a married man, but you have made my day, signora, and you may return and eat at my humble *ristorante* any time you wish. You should come up to the estate and have lunch *con la famiglia*!' offered the smiling owner (or should she call him doctor?).

Liberty knew well enough that this was the restaurateur speaking, but she appreciated the offer. 'Thank you so much, signor, I hope to return soon.' With that, she paid her appropriately large bill, feeling she had indeed been in a hospital, and asked for her bags.

'They have been taken to your hotel, signora, to free you for your walk,' responded the lady at the desk. *Wow!* thought Liberty, *now that's service*, and she climbed back to street level and headed towards the river. The tourists had indeed thinned a little, but in normal terms the city was still crowded. Liberty decided she had had enough, and suddenly needed to get away, back to the peace and sanctuary of the hotel, so she hailed a taxi.

As the Fiat wound its way up the hillside towards Fiesole, Liberty realised she was shaking with apprehension. She had lost herself for a few hours; she had left her true situation and taken a fantasy day out. Now she was terrified in case Percy had returned, not because of what he might do to her, but simply because she knew she never wanted to see him again. She wanted truly to rid herself of him and everything she had ever shared with him. She felt different, cleansed almost, and was ashamed to find herself realising that she was almost happy, able to be herself for the first time in years. She also felt deeply sad, but only because she had been wasting her life for so many years.

Percy was not at the hotel. Two envelopes were waiting for her. One was to inform her that an 11.30 flight had been arranged to take her to Nice the following day, and a hotel car would collect her at 9.30. The other contained an email that had been sent care of the hotel concierge.

'Liberty, expect you to have calmed down. No hard feelings. Will see you Monday when I get back from work.'

Liberty sat on the terrace with a cup of English tea and thought about herself, her life and her position in it. As she looked around the garden, reality flooded into her sore head. She did not want to, but it was necessary to acknowledge Percy's message. She thought for a moment. She knew she would not go back to live with him. She had few possessions to call her own, and she didn't want them. Or did she? Her diary and other personal papers were all at work. Her passport was with her. She certainly didn't want to walk into the room she had been secretly transforming – in her mind – into a nursery. She had bought several rolls of Quentin Blake wallpaper, tiny baby gowns, cashmere blankets, several teddy bears. They were no longer needed. They were not part of her life any more. She realised she had no need whatsoever to return to the mews.

The message she tapped out on her BlackBerry was concise.

'Am staying with Paloma in St Tropez for a while. Will not be back.'

As she pressed 'send', Liberty knew it was the right thing to do, but felt sick to her stomach and had to race back to her room to weep in private, grieving for her beloved parents-in-law and her lost security, and wondering what the hell she would do next.

Finding herself weeping on her bed, Liberty thought, *This is getting silly*. Doing something better with her life did not include soaking Frette sheets with salty water and being a complete drip. She needed to do something constructive; despite a wave of tear-drained exhaustion enveloping her, she wondered if she had packed a swimsuit. Rummaging around, she found her bikini tangled amongst her lingerie and slipped into it, covered it with a discreet San Michele robe, and ran down to the pool. This too was built into the hillside and was surrounded by a lemon grove. The last rays of the afternoon sun still warmed the flagstones along the side. A few couples were lying on the loungers on the grass area surrounding the pool, but the water itself was temptingly turquoise, empty and calling to her.

Wow! she thought after diving in. The cool water enveloped her, enlivening her instantly, and she swam with energy and enjoyment, clearing her mind and loving the sense of burning off bad emotions in a healthy way. After twenty minutes she clambered out, for once feeling no need to be her normally elegant self, but more like a child. She gulped huge breaths of air as she realised how hard she had worked her body. She had needed to. The still-warm sun caressed her legs and she knew her cheeks were red with exertion. She felt alive, happy and excited about her trip to see the gorgeous Paloma.

The next morning, after a deep and prolonged sleep, preceded by an excellent but light supper on the terrace, Liberty woke early and packed her suitcase with her new clothes, shoes and toiletries. She had even bought some scent for the first time, Aqua Di Parma, as it was a classic, and for the time being she didn't know which would become her favourite anyway. The name sounded like ham, and that had to be alluring! Did they make a freshly baked bread scent?

She went downstairs for an early stroll, to pay the bill and enjoy a final breakfast in Italy. Luca was ready for her.

'There is no charge, signora. We hope to see you soon again under better circumstances. My mother wishes you a happy return home.'

Liberty was stunned. 'But you can't not charge me. I know how much the rooms cost here, and . . .' she felt embarrassed and stopped mid-flow, not sure how to continue.

'Direct orders from my mother,' said the smiling Luca, 'and she is far more terrifying than any CEO. We hope you will return for longer and in happier days.'

'Thank you, a million thank yous, and this is for your mother. Please see that she gets it, with my gratitude.'

Liberty handed over the exquisite hand-printed silk scarf she had found the previous day, knowing that a scarf would be the only splash of colour an Italian widow would consider wearing.

9

The stewardess opened the aeroplane door, and Liberty stepped out into the white glare of Nice. The chaos and throng of August had ended with its last hours, and travelling on the first of September, Liberty found herself through immigration in no time. Claude was waiting for her. He was Paloma's son, and although it had been assumed his father was the light-foot who had run away when Paloma's beauty and vivacious personality had taken over 'his' restaurant, she had never acknowledged this directly. Deirdre, Liberty's mother, had always said the father must have been someone else, and that was the true reason Paloma's husband left, but Paloma wasn't telling. Claude had always been the apple of his mother's eye, a delightful, charming boy with a ready smile, who turned into a whippet-slim, dark-haired Gallic jaw-dropper. As a young boy, he had frequently sat at Liberty's feet in the St Tropez garden, gazing up at her beauty while Paloma and Deirdre gossiped about food and lovers. Deirdre had moved through several, some rather infamous, lovers as 'therapy' to get over Alain's departure, thus making her somewhat too well-known for the wrong reasons, but she sold a few more books as her infamy brought her to the attention of a new generation of would-be cooks. It also won the respect of Liberty's friends, much to her embarrassment.

'Liberty!' breathed Claude in her ear as he bent to kiss her on each cheek; very erotic, very French, but she thought to herself that he was wearing too much cologne, something she had not been aware of until now. They instantly returned to the happy-go-lucky brother/sister relationship they had enjoyed for so long, quickly getting rid of any sexual tension that may have existed back when Claude was twelve and his hormones encouraged him to think he was in love with her, even though she was two years older than him. He used to run after her on the beach, bringing seashells and other treasures for her to admire, thrilled when she ruffled his hair in an older sister kind of way and rewarded him with an ice cream. But his attentions had turned to French girls since those days.

'Come along, let's get to the car, and we can enjoy the drive along the coast to St Tropez. Paloma is desperate to hear your news, but she is busy with the restaurant. We still have to work all hours for the four-month season here where the room bookings are concerned.'

'But the restaurant now has such a good reputation. You must be booked all the year round, surely?'

'Well, yes, but the people who come during the summer spend money on wine, whereas the rest of the year tends to be booked by real foodies who appreciate what we serve, but who spend less.'

They had arrived at the car, an ancient white E-type Jag. 'Lucky I travel fairly light,' giggled Liberty, as he struggled to get her newly filled bags into the back.

'It's OK, we will have the roof down,' said Claude, shrugging in a typically French way as he helped her into the front seat.

'And such manners. Your mother has done a fine job!' noted Liberty.

'She always told me manners got the girls, so I had no problem concentrating on those lessons,' Claude divulged with a wink. As he swung on to the highway west, they took up the restaurant theme once more.

'Isn't it more interesting cooking for foodies?' asked Liberty.

'Of course it is, but although they appreciate and really savour the food, they tend to drink only a little, which, sadly, these days, means little return for a great deal of effort. Paloma can tell you all about it.'

'How long have you called your mother Paloma?'

'It just seemed more natural, really, especially when I had to speak to her in front of the punters.'

He drove fast but easily, glancing around only occasionally at the view of the outskirts of Nice.

'Now, you tell me, how come you look so wonderful? I thought there would be a tragic heap to meet at the airport. Have you dumped that moron at last?' And he leaned over and put his hand on her leg, just for a moment.

'Watch it!' screamed Liberty, as Claude swerved out of the path of a wayward lorry, and she grasped his arm. 'I forgot how badly people drive down here.'

Claude laughed and drove in silence for a few minutes. Then he continued, 'Didn't you always know how I hated Percy?'

'You don't know anything about it. I didn't say a thing in my message,' she huffed at him.

'Yes, but Maman can see through these things. She put two and two together and made sixty-five, as usual; she knew you were finding out if you were pregnant, and when you asked to stay she figured it was for a reason. Come on, she knows you well, little fairy godsister.' Claude smiled at her in a sympathetic way that Liberty hoped wouldn't last.

'I am not over it yet, so be careful what you say.'

'Yes, I know you too, and Maman can read you like a book, and she told me Percy has always been too much the upper-class Englishman, but without the good manners or redeeming qualities.'

'Just don't let him hear you saying that.' But Liberty found herself smiling; she supposed it was true. Despite his good breeding and lovely parents, Percy seemed to lack the natural charm and manners of most of his upper-class English men friends, once he had got what he wanted. He was lovely while he was wooing her; she remembered how charming he was when they first met. But she quickly swept all thoughts of him out of her mind, determined to enjoy herself.

'I just need to get away for a while, and I think I want to learn how to cook.'

Claude swerved the car and had to fight to correct it. 'You! Learn to cook? But you are not the slightest bit interested in food – in fact, you hate it.'

'No, that's wrong, I just haven't been able to appreciate it without being able to taste or smell. There is a difference! You try enjoying fine dining with a leather tongue!'

'You mean you have grown taste buds all of a sudden? What has happened? Paloma is going to be so excited.'

Throughout Liberty's youth, it had always been accepted by those close to her that she was the only member of her family who couldn't embrace every aspect of the kitchen, food selection, preparation and cooking. It was going to be a huge change for them all.

They wound their way through slow-moving traffic into St Tropez. Claude asked whether she would like him to take her through the port for old times' sake, and when she said it would be wonderful, he swung the car through the hustle and bustle. There were few boats at this time of year, but the tourists still promenaded and the cafés seemed to be doing good business. With the roof down they could hear all the chatter and noise of the crowds.

There were appreciative gasps from people-watchers seated in the cafés along the seafront as the glamorous couple in the E-type drove slowly past. Paloma had become quite stuck in the 1970s vibe of St Tropez, and she refused to buy a more modern car. Liberty breathed in the smell of the diesel from the boats, the sweaty workmen walking past from their lunch, the sewers from the streets, and said, 'Right, Claude, thanks so much for coming to fetch me. Now, before the full interrogation begins, I need a drink. This new sense of smell can have its dark side!'

The car drew up in front of the restaurant, where the last of the lunchtime diners were enjoying their coffees and cognacs.

'Liberty, daaarling, come here at once!' Paloma, a vision in a flowing DVF tunic and four-inch wedges, came gracefully past the bougainvillea lining the steps up to the peach-coloured Provençal villa that served as a restaurant with rooms, with her own apartment in the back wing.

Liberty was enveloped in a warm, scented embrace that seemed to go on forever. Then Paloma pulled back, held Liberty's face between her hands and studied it, squinting as a result of refusing to wear the spectacles she now needed.

'You look awful.'

'Ha ha!' laughed Liberty, turning to Claude, who was struggling to reach for her bags over the seat of the car. 'You see, honesty at last!'

'Come in, come in. Let's go round to the back. I have asked Vevetine to arrange refreshments on the terrace.'

The building was L-shaped, perched on a hill above the old town of St Tropez. Even though it was run by the 'crazy English woman', it had survived for many years, despite people either having to drive or stay overnight as it was just too far to walk from town – a testament to its excellent food.

The tall shuttered windows overlooked the vine-covered hillside towards the coast, and a veranda covered in bougainvillea, wisteria and vines shaded diners who wished to eat outside. Huge banks of lavender edged the terrace, and a Moorish fountain splashed water merrily in the courtyard to make everyone feel cool even when the temperature reached forty degrees.

They settled in easy chairs, positioned to take advantage of the views, normally occupied by people smoking or taking digestifs after luncheon or dinner. It had been reserved for them by Vevetine, the restaurant manager, who now placed before them a bottle of rosé wine ensconced in an ice bucket, two chilled tumblers and a bowl of lavender and rose petals.

Alongside these arrived a plate of the lightest cheese crisps made from local sheep's cheese melted and mixed with wild thyme and black pepper, as Paloma explained while she offered the plate to Liberty. Expecting her to refuse, she almost moved the plate away before her goddaughter had the chance to help herself. Paloma's eyes widened as she noticed the delight with which Liberty took up a crisp, savoured it beneath her nose, and then appreciatively chewed it slowly.

'You are eating, child, what has happened to you? Are you starving or what?'

At that moment Claude rejoined them. He poured the wine, sprinkled some lavender flowers and rose petals on to the top of their glasses and announced he had to go to pick up supplies. 'Don't tell Paloma anything without me, I will look forward to dinner, be back at eight.' And with that he was off, leaving a drift of cologne in the air.

'He must have a girlfriend,' said Liberty. 'Goodness, how he has grown up.'

'Actually, I think the perfume was for your benefit. And don't change the subject. The last thing I know from you, I was waiting to hear about the results of the IVF. Now you turn up on my doorstep, not only eating but sniffing your wine and noticing Claude's cologne. I am not even going to give you the chance to freshen up. Tell me all. Should I get your mother on the speaker phone?'

Liberty sighed, and told her story. As she related the past few days (was it only days? It felt like months) she found herself looking at Paloma and admiring what she saw. She had always known how glamorous she was: a mixture of Sophia Loren, Diane von Fürstenberg and Claudia Cardinale. Amazing bone structure, olive skin, gleaming chestnut hair in soft waves to her shoulders, no doubt helped along by the hairdresser, but all the better for that. Not a wrinkle in sight, although nobody had any wrinkles these days! But there was something extra, an indefinable something which gave her true beauty: she was kind. She had experienced life, and been seriously hurt by it, and this instilled in her the ability to give advice when needed and be aware of when to keep her own counsel. She had probably had many lovers, many famous ones, according to the red tops, but always unnamed, including the elusive Papa Claude, as Deirdre called him. Since following her heart down to the Côte d'Azur in the mid 1970s she had found happiness. At first she was front of house staff, while her partner cooked for the restaurant he leased. She was so glamorous that the rich boat owners flocked to see who was being talked about at all the cocktail parties. As she was also very friendly and welcoming they eventually wanted to be seen with her, which in turn brought journalists and photographers. Her reputation at the restaurant had truly taken off in the early 1980s, when St Tropez became rather trashy and nouveau riche, and many of the more discerning visitors decamped to St Paul de Vence and further along the coast to get away from the yuppies. Would-be guests had to book several months in advance for a simple luncheon, which made Paloma laugh, and then cry, when her partner François left in a huge Gallic huff at the beginning of the summer because she was receiving all the attention.

Thankfully, by then, and with a great amount of support from the lovely local girls who helped in the restaurant, Paloma had picked up sufficient knowledge to struggle through her first season. She then heard of an up-and-coming chef in England, Alain James, and she entreated him to come and teach her the fundamentals of cooking over the winter months, when both their respective restaurants were closed, his for renovations, hers as the season had come to an end. His advice, when he saw how excellent she was at front of house and that she struggled to cook a meal for one, let alone fifty hungry diners, was, 'If you must stay, find a good chef, and fast. Pay him an excellent salary to keep him, and between you and a huge miracle it may just work.'

She had decided to stay on in France; the weather and the people suited her, and she quickly picked up the language, although her accent was described as *'exécrable'* by the locals.

Deirdre joined them after some weeks, and the two became

friends very quickly. 'I have to stay here,' Paloma had said to her new friend after a couple of months. 'I am pregnant.' But she would not divulge who the father was, not even to Deirdre. Of course, the paparazzi had a field day, but her reputation was enhanced by her dignity and beauty during her pregnancy, and eventually she managed, by employing a nanny for Little Claude, to make a huge success from what had previously been a rather quiet little eatery. Now she was chef patron of one of the most successful restaurants in the south of France, so successful it could remain open throughout the year.

She had redecorated and modernised over the years, putting in decent bathrooms to appeal to the increasing numbers of Americans brave enough to travel, and furnishing it in her own style. Plates and old wooden garden rakes hung on the walls, plants in vast terracotta pots served to create privacy for tables and make it feel like an exotic garden room. The soft scent of lavender wafted through the shutters in high summer. She decided to grow as much of her own produce as possible, and with the help of a green-fingered god, her gardener Antoine, had created her own herb garden and a new walled potager to serve the kitchen, complete with working bees. The walled garden was a sixtieth birthday present from Claude, who had built it with his own hands, importing old bricks from a reclamation yard in England. For years he had listened to Alain and Deirdre talking about theirs, with its knot pattern of planting, and he knew how his mother wished she could have one. Eventually, he obtained permission to buy a plot of land behind their restaurant and had it cleared and the soil improved. Deirdre and Alain had both helped with the design. Over a period of two years, Claude had built a one hectare walled garden with a pleached avenue of lime trees running down the centre, lines of a variety of fruit trees trained up the walls, and a sundial with the inscription 'With Love From Your Beloved'. For several months there was a vast tent over much of the garden, and Paloma had thought her son was building a home for himself. But in her typical way she had not thought to ask, as she did not want to interfere. It had been unveiled during her sixtieth birthday party.

For the first time in years Liberty had seen her parents, both of course invited to the huge party, getting on as friends. Nobody could have been miserable on such a midsummer night in St Tropez, surrounded by soft jazz and simple but fine food. The A-list from the surrounding countryside and the boats were all there, seemingly having invited themselves. Lavender and blackcurrant filled the air. Deirdre had told Liberty how it brought a warm scent to the proceedings as guests' bodies accidentally brushed the bushes as they passed and released the perfumes. She explained how the perfume made the local wine taste as good as a Burgundy, but she never made the mistake of filling up the boot of the car with Provençal wine to return to England. The damp and cold air removed all perfume and taste. Liberty had thought little of it at the time, not appreciating just what a difference wonderful scents could make to an evening, but now it was obvious as she sipped her glass of rosé and the warm honeyed air filled her nostrils.

Liberty finished telling Paloma her story, starting with the miscarriage, as she needed to say that quickly, as though it hadn't really happened at all, through to telling Percy she wouldn't be returning to him. She appreciated Paloma's lack of curiosity or nosiness. Unlike so many people, Paloma never dwelled on or enjoyed the misfortunes of others. She listened with total concentration and a sympathetic expression. In Liberty's experience many of her so-called friends would encourage their women companions to say more and more, showing a sad face while preparing to recount this further to other women, adding, 'Well, at least it's not me it's happening to, she has always been so lucky, she deserves everything she gets.'

Instead, Paloma listened to Liberty with mind and body, and at the end asked Liberty if she wanted any comments and thoughts from her, or whether she should just let it be.

Liberty said, 'I think the reason I wanted to come here was to hear what you think. And then I want you to teach me how to cook, please!'

Paloma's eyebrows lifted as far as her perfectly Botoxed face allowed – not too much and not too little. She stood up, came behind her goddaughter and hugged her tightly. She said, 'It's all your bloody parents' fault, my dear. As much as I love them, they got wrapped up in their own lives. Your father didn't even think how it would affect you when he moved out, he only concentrated on what he thought was the right thing to do. So many people get divorced these days, it's as though they don't believe it affects the children any more. From the moment your mother told you she and Alain were going to separate, you have lived in a small part of your brain that nobody, absolutely nobody, could reach. You have always done whatever you thought you should do; trying to keep the peace, and probably keep both of your parents happy, maybe even in a childlike way trying to bring them back together. You went to the right university, studied hard and forgot about your love of food entirely, even though you had made the best hollandaise and béarnaise at the age of six. The Michelin inspectors were accidentally given it on a frantic Saturday evening, and still gave your father his third star.' She smiled at the recollection of Deirdre's excited phone call. 'Liberty clinched it for him!'

'You married someone you thought was "the right sort", and SAFE, and sadly he turned into just the opposite. And being very impertinent, if I may, I will also say that your inability to have a baby had a lot to do with suppressed emotions. But perhaps that is the hippy in me. I can't tell you how extremely alive you look now; it's as though you had been dormant for the past twenty years, and now you have been born again.'

Liberty decided she did not need to tell Paloma that was exactly how she felt. Instead, she asked in a small, rather frightened voice, 'But what now?'

'Right now, another glass of rosé, then a bath and a good meal. I must attend to guests. Your parents are both very concerned about you, naughty girl not telling them. You knew they were waiting to hear the results of your test, but now I understand at least, and I can call them. You need sleep and lots of rest in order to recover your health. Even though you look fabulous, your body must be reeling from these shocks it is experiencing, not to mention the physical damage. Do you still have to take any hormones or anything?'

Liberty bit her lip, feeling more than a little guilty for not phoning her parents. They didn't even know she was out of London. 'I haven't called the clinic, but having been down this road before, it's just a case of spending the next few months getting rid of all the leftover drugs in my system, and trying to pretend that nothing is wrong, feeling ghastly and overweight for no reason, and my mood swings should go after a while.'

Paloma looked at the girl's forlorn face, as well known to her as her own son's, and just as dear. She felt wretched to be unable to do anything for her, and told Liberty so. 'At one point in my life I could be of help, but my hippy self has nothing to offer apart from a safe place to rest and recuperate.'

'But that's exactly why I came, and that's what I knew you could do,' said Liberty, 'along with something else far more important!'

Paloma looked up from the glass she was draining, ready to go and greet dinner guests. 'And what, may I ask, is that?'

'I know what I want to do already!' exclaimed Liberty excitedly. 'It came to me on the journey here, and sort of in a dream! I want to feed the world, I want to introduce people to tastes and flavours. If I can "wake up" after twenty years of having no sense of smell or taste, and feel so fabulous, then everyone in Britain needs to recover from fast food and cheap, tasteless, chemically filled rubbish and feel as good as I do. I am going to open a bistro, maybe just a small café, in England, and enlighten people!'

Paloma gazed open-mouthed at her goddaughter, marvelling both at her forcefulness and her determination, both of which had been dormant for many years, and felt the excitement streaming from Liberty, excitement that was infecting Paloma as ideas poured into her head.

'Well,' she began, 'you need to start with our herb garden. If you want to feed people with flavour, you need to know how to grow the flavours. And then you must progress to the potager, because you have to understand what good vegetables are, how fresh they must be if they are to taste healthy and succulent.

'Then you should learn about the animal, its meat and its dairy products. You need to eat from the earth up to the sky! Choose your own terroir well. If the soil and the air are healthy, you can convert anyone to eat your food. That is what la France has taught me. And no, you do not need this beautiful climate, it just helps. When the French chefs left their country after the revolution, they found work in the stately homes of England, Germany, Spain and so on. They took with them their need for fine produce, and because of their requirements hothouses were introduced in England for fruit, and walled gardens were developed for vegetable growing, as they kept out that dreadful wind which ruins so many otherwise wonderful crops. And you will need the very best available meat, although I don't suggest you try animal husbandry quite yet; give yourself one task at a time.'

Liberty looked at Paloma, and burst out laughing, 'Golly, I didn't think you would be so encouraging, let alone so verbose!'

At that moment Vevetine came out of the restaurant and approached them.

'Excuse me, Madame, but we are about to open. May we begin serving?'

'Forgive me, Vevetine,' replied Paloma, 'but for the first time since I can remember I am going to miss a night's work. I am sure you will manage perfectly without me, and I am here should you need anything. My darling Liberty and I have battle plans to draw up.'

And so an un-bathed and un-rested Liberty and a devoted

godmother put their heads together while an unmanaged restaurant lit up and filled slowly with guests, and nobody suffered; indeed, everyone was suffused with the atmosphere of happiness generated by Liberty's 'recovery'. Plans were drawn up – literally. Paloma's own files were filled with drawings and notes for gardens, kitchen layouts, customer profiles, lots of advice from various sources, named and unnamed.

'A lot comes in the form of well-educated customers,' explained Paloma. 'I had to learn the ropes as I went along. Any constructive criticism went down in this book.' It included one they giggled over, where an inexperienced Paloma had poured wine over a client's lap when he had asked at the end of a meal for a special favour, something personal. 'It turned out he meant to return here with his wife, whose birthday it was to be, and could we make a cake. It would have been almost tragic, if he hadn't been so calm. It was in the early days, and almost any comment like that meant whoopsie back then. Believe it or not, he still came back with his wife and a huge party. They had meant to celebrate in Paris, but chose to come here instead, which was rather a coup, even if I did have to pay for the dry-cleaning!'

Paloma pointed out that many things she would need to learn could come from her parents.

'Most importantly, you need to get back your natural instincts for food, but first of all we will see how you are with your sense of smell. Starting tomorrow, you will have to name a great many items blindfolded, and identify flavours put before you and in the air. You will have to recognise whatever you are eating and drinking, in detail; and yes, you will have to taste soil! Then you must decide where you want to open this café of yours!'

10

After a very long sleep Liberty rose from her narrow but extremely comfortable bed and opened up the shutters on to a soothingly bright morning.

As she stood gazing out at the distant hills, stretching in front of the window, waiting for her eyes to adjust, an appreciative whistle sounded from the garden below.

Liberty gasped and leapt backwards. She had been stark naked, unaware that she was being observed by Claude and Antoine, the head gardener. Not sure which one had whistled, and bristling slightly because the other had not, Liberty dressed quickly (Capri pants, Tod's loafers and a simple Breton top) and ran downstairs.

'Stop!' screeched Paloma's normally calm voice. 'OK, right now, what can you smell?'

'Um . . . um . . . butter, unsalted, as it smells slightly sour, coffee, um . . . guessing here, Milano beans, but only because I know you like them, stock, beef and fish – or is it fish soup? Saffron, bay, lemon, orange . . .'

She listed the scents that filled the air, sniffing around and looking a little like a Labrador that had lost a bird on a shoot.

'Well, that confirms it. You still have your natural palate. Nothing to worry about at all. Quickly, have your coffee.' Paloma handed the younger woman a small steaming cup of black coffee with one hand and a croissant with the other.

'Yum,' mumbled Liberty, spilling flakes of the lightest pastry. 'Baked here?'

'No, they do them so well at the Café Tropézienne. We pick

them up there together with our order for the Tarte Tropézienne, a very light brioche baked in a round tin filled with lemon-flavoured crème pâtissière that is very famous hereabouts. In fact, before you open your own place, you should come up with your own original, something that people will come from miles around to eat. Anyway, to return to this morning. Into the garden with you. Antoine is waiting.'

Yes, thought Liberty, *I know*.

'And Claude will be around to do the translation. Although I know your French is excellent, plant names may baffle you. And don't forget a notebook,' she added as she thrust pen and paper into a startled Liberty's hands.

Liberty disappeared outside after a gentle push, and Paloma thought to herself that keeping her busy would be just the thing. She had telephoned both Alain and Deirdre to fill them in and assure them all was going well with their daughter. Both of them expressed some anger when Paloma, in her usual forthright manner, blamed them for Liberty's difficulties, then each of them insisted on rushing straight to Nice. Paloma had managed to persuade Deirdre that it was a bad idea and she was dealing with everything perfectly well, but Alain had closed the restaurant for the month of October as he couldn't bear the old crones, as he called them, who travelled round in coaches after the school holidays came to an end on their cheap deals. They insisted on parking their caravans in the car park, then ordered water and one course, complained about the expense, and remarked loudly that 'the Little Chef was just as good and very much cheaper'. They often stopped there on their way to Eastbourne, and as soon as Alain got the measure of them he closed his restaurant for the entire month and flew somewhere warm to sail. This October his yacht would be jaunting around the Mediterranean, and would moor in Marseilles, so it would be silly to refuse his wish to come along and see his daughter.

'OK,' Paloma had agreed, 'but let me have her for at least a couple of weeks first, and no grumbling about your customers, this is about Liberty.' *For once in your life*, she thought, but kept this to herself.

Five weeks later Liberty was suntanned, fit from digging and preparing seed beds and glowing from a fresh fish, vegetable and rosé diet.

Antoine had delighted in having such a hard-working and beautiful assistant, and he was amazed at her ability to pick things up. She had just got on with the work, and he, in turn, learnt quickly it was a mistake to assume that a pretty face hid a very small brain.

He had shown Liberty into his private domain. It was the first time he had ever taken anyone in there. Neither Paloma nor Claude had ever been inside the ramshackle shed at the bottom of the terraced garden, well hidden by trees and shrubs from the restaurant's terrace but with full south-west views of the coast. Liberty gasped. The wiry little man had created beauty in the garden, but seemed to have few, or no, other interests besides his work – even in girls, which was unusual in a forty-five-year-old Frenchman, which no doubt explained the lack of the second wolf whistle!

The rather messy outward appearance of the shed belied what lay within. Old stained glass panels, presumably from a deconsecrated church or chapel, filled one wall. This created an unusual greenhouse effect, the colours of the glass muting the direct heat, which was also tempered by banks of bergamot growing outside the window. The simple tiled roof appeared to be set in large hinged panels to let out hot air, and the smell inside was incredible.

It was like a greenhouse on speed. A powerful aroma rose from the rows of peppers, greens turning to reds. There were chillies, tomatoes in various reds, deepening to dark burgundy, greens, yellows. Fruit, including what looked like an ancient vine, added a sweet perfume to the almost intoxicating tomato elixir. The size of the produce also varied considerably, from huge melons to tiny grapes, and courgettes with their flowers ready to be stuffed or braised in the kitchens. It was the scent of the chillies and tomatoes that almost sent her reeling, a heady, healthy perfume that forced its way into her nostrils and her eyes and seemed to fill her stomach, although she had tasted none of it. And honey! Where was that smell coming from? Antoine pointed casually to a wall, where she assumed there must be the most enormous bees' hive.

On a high trellis reclined the huge arm of a vine. Plump red grapes dripped from branches, a bunch of which Antoine picked using his very ancient, very sharp penknife, without which he felt as lost as a city dweller without his mobile phone.

He laid the bunch reverently on an old tin plate. The bloom was untouched, still perfect, something you would never see in a shop. He then reached for two old scratched tumblers, gave them a cursory wipe with a cloth he probably normally used to wipe vegetables, and placed them on the rickety table. He spent a long time fiddling with keys and a padlocked trapdoor set in the floor, all this time in silence. Liberty began to wonder if this was where he kept his wife, and she became increasingly worried. She had only known this little man for a few weeks, after all, and she was sure nobody would look for her here if she failed to turn up for lunch. Perhaps it was an ancient Provençal ceremony, to drain a female's blood and use it to wash the first grapes of the season? But no, he now reached into the cellar he had revealed, and pulled out a bottle of red wine. The only label on the bottle was a rudimentary sticker with the date 1984. He pulled the cork, poured a little on the floor and then filled each glass with the glistening liquid, made all the more colourful by the refracted light streaming through the stained glass.

He handed a glass to Liberty and at last said, '*Je vous remercie, Mademoiselle. À la votre!*' He raised his glass.

The nectar, for that was what it was, glided down Liberty's throat. It may not have been Château Pétrus, but it held 1984 in its belly. She could tell it had been a wet but hot summer; the blackcurrant was strong but not too prevalent, there was a honey scent, but not overbearing, and lots of iron from the local soil. She could also feel the love and smell the toes, in a good way, that had gone into making it. Antoine nearly ruined the romance and moment by spitting his wine on the floor, but Liberty reminded herself this was meant to be a gift to the gods, and at least the next mouthful stayed in place.

Speaking in French, he said to her, 'Mademoiselle, you have the greatest natural ability and desire of any kitchen gardener I have known, but you must always love what you nourish and then it will prosper and surprise you in ways that you simply cannot imagine. If you can do that, your food will delight and surprise, and make all those who consume your food happy. You will succeed, I feel sure. Good luck.'

11

Struggling through a pastis, Liberty decided it was an acquired taste. She related her morning to Paloma.

'Well, bloody hell!' her godmother responded. 'I've known Antoine for at least twenty years, and I have never seen anyone admitted into his hovel. We all assumed he buried vermin and wove spells down there, but we just let him get on with it as he is such a wizard in the garden.'

Liberty twirled the glass round in her hand, deciding she would leave the cloudy elixir to others. 'I really feel I have a basic knowledge to start my kitchen garden, although I will have to enlist help back home. I've had the details emailed through of tea rooms for sale in the south-east, but they all look very pretentious, and not my idea of what I want at all. I really need to go there to extend my search, but I don't feel ready to visit home soil as yet, and anyway, I need to start learning how to make pastry.' She rubbed her hands together excitedly.

'And it will start, at two o'clock tomorrow morning!' boomed a voice from the French doors.

'Daddy!' 'Alain!' shouted Liberty and Paloma at the same time.

'What on earth are you doing here, Daddy?' said Liberty, throwing a knowing look at Paloma, angry and thrilled at the same time, as only true love can allow. She threw her arms around his neck and looked behind him. 'Where's the latest squeeze, then?'

'Oh, Giselle was definitely a passing phase. I am here on *Liberty Five*, my new boat, to visit a few restaurants, check on the competition and rescue you.'

Liberty turned back to Paloma, who had the decency to blush. 'Well, I did think he might turn up. But your mother is definitely not coming. She said she would be waiting at home with a Martini and some recipes for you to try. She always used you as a taste tester. When you were a young girl, she said you had the purest palate.'

'Don't change the subject! You knew I was trying to escape from everyone.'

Liberty was trying her best to remain cross, but now her father was here she actually felt a great reassurance. Although when her parents split up it had affected her in such a dramatic way, she had maintained a fantastic relationship with both, and as an adult had grown to be quite excited to meet her father's latest glamorous, ever younger model, and to find out how daft she really was before he got bored and moved on to the next one. She had once asked him how, or why, after her mother, who was so dynamic, and with female friends such as Paloma, who was so driven and interesting and well-educated, he could settle for such bimbos. Even his second wife had been a ballerina, someone really worthwhile, if a little dramatic, proud and self-assured. Alain simply told her that it was a search for something to take his mind off the restaurant. 'But the restaurant is my life, so it never works. I have no time to interest myself in anything else, really, although I do enjoy holidaying on the water. But, of course, I do have you to look after and care for,' he joked, winking at Liberty. And that was the end of that discussion. Paloma had years ago mooted that he really regretted leaving Deirdre, and it had been the biggest mistake of his life, but neither she nor Liberty were brave enough to bring that subject to his attention.

Alain was a seriously enigmatic, elegant man. His manners proclaimed him as a true gentleman, and his dress code spoke of his Englishness. He wore impeccably tailored suits, shirts and handmade shoes when he was not clothed in chef's whites. Now, on the Côte d'Azur, he was wearing his white linen shirt, dark blue linen shorts and Tod's loafers. His silver hair was slicked back to the nape of his neck, and his dark green eyes flickered with amusement and excitement as they always did if beautiful food, wine or women were in evidence.

He had always been very ambitious, and his greatest achievement was gaining and maintaining his three Michelin stars. But he was also hugely caring and emotional, unusual in an Englishman, a trait probably encouraged by his French mother, Josephine, who, along with Liberty's other grandparents, had sadly died before she was born. He adored Liberty as only a father can. It was easy to be proud of such a stunning, bright and intelligent girl, and he was thrilled that she had so easily succeeded in her career, but along with Deirdre, Paloma and several of Liberty's friends, he was sad she had not realised what he thought was her great potential, whatever that might have been. After all, she had the need to achieve in her genes.

He recognised now that the person standing in front of him was a changed woman. Yes, the statuesque brunette was still there, but the life force gleaming from behind her eyes he had only seen when she was a little girl. *My, my*, he thought, *here's a woman to be reckoned with*. He ordered a pastis from Vevetine, and sat down. He picked up a tiny pastry from the selection before him. 'You made these?' he said, looking at Liberty as he bit into the finger of buttery puff pastry, topped with a rubbing of tomato and herbes de Provence.

'Yes!' squeaked Liberty in excitement. 'How could you tell?'

'No French pastry chef would undercook puff pastry. And they were not properly chilled before being baked, which is probably why they haven't risen properly.'

Paloma picked one up and stared at it. She could not have told the difference between the canapé she was holding in her fingers and one that Louis, her pastry chef, had produced. As Liberty stormed off on the pretext of needing the loo, Paloma raised an eyebrow and looked sternly at Alain. 'That,' she said, 'was a Michelin inspector's opinion. These are perfect.'

'No, they are not perfect at all. There is a faint softness in the centre, which makes the butter taste slightly rancid. They should have been much colder so the water in the butter really exploded in the hot oven and released all the steam necessary to make the layers puff up. She will be a really excellent pastry chef one day, but I need to push her.'

'Go easy,' said Paloma softly. 'I think she is still in shock. It's bound to hit her at some point. I hear her screaming in the night; she seems fine, but under the surface . . . We must be careful. Don't forget, the last time she had an emotional shock, it left her physically damaged. It must be her body's way of coping, some sort of self-protection, so that when something goes wrong in her life she either explores a new subject or loses one of her senses. Let's hope she doesn't lose her marbles as well.'

'She is my daughter, and I see a lot of myself in her. I know what I am doing.'

Liberty came back to the dinner table, looking a bit blotchy in the face but determined to stand up to her fiercest critic.

'OK, Daddy, two o'clock tomorrow morning. I will be in the kitchen.'

'Oh, not here, darling, I was only joking. You will be in the way of the professionals. I know this restaurant, and the kitchens are buzzing all night long with the bread and pastry chefs. Come and stay on *Liberty Five* and I will teach you all I know.'

'Why on earth at two o'clock, then?' asked Liberty.

'Because it gives you the discipline. If you want to run a restaurant, you will be doing this every day, all day.'

'But I don't want to run a restaurant. I want a café or tea room.'

'Don't be silly, darling. I know you. You will eventually want to serve lunches and breakfasts to attract decent punters. Tea rooms are for softies who want a cup of milky tea and an old scone for a euro a pop. It would drive you mad in no time. If you are going to turn a decent profit, you need to attract the people who will appreciate it, and therefore happily pay for it.'

Oh, bugger, he's right, thought both Liberty and Paloma, but neither would admit it, and so they silently sipped their drinks.

Alain's phone suddenly sounded, a loud hunting horn ring tone that he loved. He found it very funny to assign the same ring tone to his new totty; at least then, when he was having problems getting rid of one, if they heard the horn and it was not they who were calling him, they tended to get the message, no matter how stupid they were. However, sitting with Liberty and Paloma it had the reverse effect. They both gazed at him and then at each other and burst into hysterical laughter, which is what the poor girl at the other end of the phone, sitting at the reception desk of Daphne's Restaurant in London, heard.

'Who on earth is that woman laughing with you?' she squawked. 'I thought you went to rescue your daughter. I'm not impressed.'

Alain left the table, making shushing movements with his hands at the two women and went to whisper sweet nothings in her ear. She was a dear girl and he didn't want any of that jealousy nonsense that sometimes soured his relationships.

'Will he ever grow up?' sighed Paloma.

'Doubt it, but he is a catch, I suppose, even at his age. It's unusual to be so relaxed a person considering his profession, let alone so glam and gorgeous. Even I can see that, as his daughter,' said Liberty.

'Well, as we were talking of phones,' said Paloma, 'sort of, have you been in touch with Percy, or any of your friends?'

'J-T has tried to call me several times. I will need his help with the restaurant. Whoops, I am already calling it that, bloody Daddy, I mean the café, and I am desperate to catch up with him. And strangely, I had an email from Savannah, my very old friend from home. I thought she had married the Aga Khan or something, and moved to the Middle East. I haven't heard from her in years. I still don't want to talk about what has happened between me and Percy, really. Apart from with you, of course, and I am sorry to have burdened you with my problems, really I am.'

'My darling girl, I am just so pleased you are relying on someone at last, and I am even more thrilled that it's me you have chosen to confide in. Stay here just as long as you need, although Claude seems to have gone all gooey for you again, and I think his last fling has been flung, so go easy on him, please. You just don't realise how easy it is for men to fall in lust and love with you. Men never expect to find a woman with the combination of stunning beauty and extreme kindness, warmth and generosity. They want to make love to you, and for you to mother them. And now you are becoming a professional cook! It's going to be a lethal combination.'

With that Paloma stood up and walked into the restaurant. She had been keeping a distant eye on the proceedings within, and she had suddenly spied a man who appeared to be dissatisfied with his meal, so she wanted to soothe his brow personally. She left Liberty in a state of amazement. The young woman had never really thought of herself at all, and of course her lack of awareness of her beauty and abilities was very much part of her appeal.

For the first time in thirty years Alain wanted to delay the opening of his restaurant, much to the chagrin of people who had managed to book a table, as the bookings were only taken one month in advance and the phone lines were jammed from nine to six on the first of each month. Eventually, his second-in-command persuaded him that the staff were perfectly capable of opening without him, and not to fuss. Alain was not so sure; he hated to take his hands off the controls. It would merely mean a very expensive phone bill, as he wanted constant updates, to have a say in the menus and to call producers personally if they didn't deliver. But it was for Liberty, and for her nothing was too much.

While he tried not to worry over supper with Liberty, the great and the good of St Tropez, or the rich and the rolickers, depending on your point of view, were drifting into the restaurant. Often the clients who came out of season were the people who owned the fabulous villas dotted around the coast, rented out for the too busy, ghastly 'season' in July and August, and they delighted in returning to their favourite restaurant for the delicate tomato and herbes de Provence tarts, partridge braised in peas and wild fennel, served with caramelised endive tarte Tatin, followed by a chocolate *délice* with sesame seed brittle, pistachio crème anglaise, and copious amounts of local wine.

The evening was warm, with a cool breeze bringing in the first scent of autumn; perfect for most, but Claude wept quietly in the centre of the walled garden and vowed to become a monk until Liberty looked at him as a man instead of a younger brother. He had no idea that the following morning his hangover would take him to a local café, where he would bump into an angel sent from heaven to feed him slurps of black coffee from a spoon interspersed with small mouthfuls of croissant, delicately torn by her magical long fingers, and his heart would be lost again.

12

The following weeks were spent intensively learning the art of bread and pastry in Alain's tiny galley. Patisserie, chocolate, sweet treats – anything that would make a person be grateful just to walk past the establishment that sold the sensuous delights and stare in the window, knowing by then their fate was sealed; they would have to buy one of the gleaming, glazed fruit tarts or a loaf of crusty bread. It was also two weeks of very little sleep. Alain was determined that his girl should do things right. He saw no point whatsoever in making her go through the usual channels of working in a kitchen under a pastry chef, as he knew she would waste time being made to feel completely worthless, both because she was a woman, and because she was an apprentice.

Before they began her training, Alain sat Liberty down in a deep leather armchair in Paloma's home, handed her a glass of rosé, and said, 'Got your notebook? There are a few rules to observe. At your age, my girl,' he said, smiling at her, 'we have to get you up and running quickly. It would take at least five years of working in kitchens to get you to a basic standard, not because you don't have the ability, but because you have to earn your praise in any commercial kitchen worthy of teaching you, by doing the same thing perfectly over and over again. And that would simply waste too much time. You will have to prepare your doughs and pastries very early in the morning, or late at night, for morning baking. Your customers will cotton on very fast if you attempt to sell them day old bread. A French *boulangerie* bakes twice a day. We in Britain have lost the need for this, as so many people are now used to preservatives in their food. And that includes their bread. Thankfully, the majority are now aware that for your body to function well, you have to eat well. A lot of people nowadays feel they have an "allergy" or cannot digest bread comfortably. This is usually because the bread they eat is not left to prove and rise with time, it is all rushed artificially with fillers and additives, and that doesn't allow natural yeasts and the gluten in the flour to process.

'The wonderful artisan bakeries now able to open in the UK are relishing the fact there is a demand for high quality, beautifully made breads, using only the finest ingredients.'

Alain paused, remembering he was tutoring his daughter, not telling her the state of the food industry.

'To even begin to compete with the other artisans, you will want your own "starter" mix for a good sourdough. Most bakers will have been using the same mix, taking the majority for one batch and then "feeding" the starter again. This means they have even more flavour after years of fermentation. We have had the same one on the go for at least fifteen years. It would have been longer had I not gone away and forgotten to remind the oafs in the kitchen to put it somewhere cool. Damn thing exploded! But I digress.'

Liberty had the feeling there would be a lot more digressions, and wondered how long this would take, but, aware of the time her father was generously bestowing on her she sat, took notes and tried hard to be the perfect student.

There were recipes, all rough estimations. 'Depends on your flour, the weather, the kitchen, the starter or yeast you use,' was all Alain could say. 'Practice will make perfect.' And practise they did. He gave lots of advice, all of which she noted down and sorted out into her huge and growing files for later, should anything go wrong.

'You will need your own signature tart or cake, something special only you make, something people maybe take home to serve as pudding, then their guests ask where they bought it, and your reputation spreads. So start thinking about that now. And flavours – experiment. Don't be afraid of them. Specialty breads are always popular, but it's ordinary, basic bread that ordinary, basic people want to buy. Fennel and sultana breads are fabulous, but not everyone will buy them. You are not after the masses, but to get started you don't want a lot of waste, it's too expensive. Garlic, onion, and the basic Provençal flavours are wonderful in summer: tomatoes and herbs. In winter, people eat more blue cheese, so I suggest walnuts, as they go so well together. Find a walnut bread somewhere, or walnut and fig.'

'Fig?' Liberty's nose was wrinkling.

'Fig. Exactly. It's a wonderful fruit if used correctly. Think along the lines of connecting two seemingly random tastes, experiment with them, read everything in the cookery books endorsed by the great chefs of the world, including mine, of course, and you will eventually produce your own signature. You will be very unlikely ever to invent anything new, as chefs have been experimenting for hundreds of years and by now we know exactly what works, more or less, but your own mix and availability of flours and grains, for example, or the use of local honey in spelt bread, will alter the flavours. If you can introduce local ingredients, the bread will taste all the better for it, as somehow, eating something local gives it a certain je ne sais quoi, as you breathe in the same air which goes into the item you are eating.'

'Like eating fish and chips outside!' Liberty giggled. 'Everyone has always told me they taste far better eaten outside. I must go to the coast when I return to England, and see if it's true.'

'Exactly! In a funny way, that is a really good example.' Alain smiled. 'Just remember, everyone says eating in the fresh air is better, and it's quite true. The plants around you, the terroir, even the pollution – it all goes into the food you are eating, so in a sense you are getting a third more flavour. It's just like matching the wine to your food. The natural yeasts are great in the south-east of England. They will make your starter dough taste wonderful, and are a good example. Eat Italian, drink Italian, eat French, drink French is always my choice. Fennel with salami and Chianti from Tuscany, where you have just been – they go well together, because the pigs grew fat on the same land that produced the wine and the fennel plucked for the salami.'

Liberty coughed and showed Alain her empty glass, which he filled for her without comment. She felt exhausted, but in a good way. Her brain was whirring with excitement, both thinking of well-known flavour combinations and imagining new ones that she wanted to try, although Alain kept insisting that in England she would find everything had to be rethought.

'I have often written down an entire month's menus for the reopening in the autumn, only to get back from my vacation and realise that the game tastes different there, the fruits are not as rich, the dairy has had a different summer and is so much creamier than it is in France or Italy, but perhaps not as sharp, and so on.'

'So it's all about adjusting to what produce I have to hand and being flexible, I guess,' mused Liberty.

'Exactly!' said Alain. 'I know you are tired, and it's the last thing you need to hear, but all the work you did with Antoine, as important as it will be, I feel is over the top now. Paloma gets great ideas in her pretty head, but there is no way you will be able to make a garden to supply your restaurant–' as he insisted on calling it '–in the time you want to open, which knowing you will be as soon as possible. We need to be practical, and no dreaming allowed!'

And on it went, father to daughter, teacher to pupil, on into the night, which would end cruelly. Almost before her head touched the pillow, Alain woke her for practical lessons.

13

Liberty's arms ached from hand-kneading kilos of dough a day. 'Of course,' her father had told her, 'you will have a machine in your kitchen, but you have to get to know and to understand dough, how it lives and breathes as we do.'

Thankfully, her father's passion was contagious, and she had definitely caught a dose of it. Normal, balanced mortals would have told him just to shut up and go away, as he could talk about food twenty-four/seven. Alain had also been chatting to Paloma.

'She is still having the most terrible nightmares. The screams from her room are gut-wrenching, and some of the surrounding boats have complained!' He tried to make light of it, but did add, 'It is lucky I don't let her sleep long. God knows what they would say after eight hours.'

Paloma knew, however, how worried he really was, and said she would speak with Deirdre. 'I think she should go home, deal with her private life. But I understand her need for a diversion. Give her some time off. You don't want to make her ill on top of everything else!'

The following day Paloma, Alain and Liberty met up for an aperitif.

'Perhaps that is why you choose such silly girls to bed,' laughed Paloma. 'So you can concentrate on your first love – food! They can listen to you chattering on, while thinking about their next pedicure, so they don't need to comment. Nor are they able to, of course.'

Even Alain had to admit that one girl he spent a week with

in Amalfi had been an excellent sounding board for menus; so good, in fact, at listening that when, at the end of the week (spent mostly making love and writing down new food ideas on his laptop in the boat's cabin), he had asked her to return to London for a party with him the following weekend, she replied, *'Quoi?'* It turned out she actually spoke no English at all, not one word. Nor did she understand the language.

When he related this to his daughter and his friend they both fell about laughing, but had to admit that his passion for food had benefited them hugely, to the exclusion of others who took no interest in it.

'But how can people ignore what fuels them and gives them the energy to get through their day?' asked Liberty.

'You, my girl, have done exactly that for years.' Liberty's father looked at her, feeling grateful. Both he and Paloma were thankful that her sense of what was so important to them both had returned.

Liberty sat back and thought about that statement.

'I suppose I have,' she riposted. 'But my family have always been so immersed in food, either writing about it or cooking it, and I think I have just not appreciated its importance. But now I do, and I am living the dream. So I am going to cook supper for you both. Won't be long!' And with that she swept off into the kitchen to make an omelette.

Paloma and Alain looked at each other. Both were thinking the same thing. This time a year ago Liberty was simply another stunning young woman, who took people's breath away with her captivating eyes and grace, and who could hold a conversation with anyone from the local dry cleaner to the Greek ambassador, as she treated everyone with empathy and intelligence. But now she gleamed, as though her pilot light had been switched on. Like a young horse turning from a riding school hack into a thoroughbred, her eyes sparkled and her skin gleamed. Passion flooded through her, and it was obvious. Her interest in food had only increased her womanly curves rather than adding unsightly pounds to her hips, and the hard work in the kitchens had given her a bit more strength and form.

Liberty soon rejoined them, bringing plates that held *omelettes aux fines herbes*, and a green salad tossed with olive oil and lemon juice in an earthenware bowl. They ate quickly and silently, Paloma because she had to return to her kitchen, the others because Liberty was terrified of the criticism bound to flow from Alain's mouth, and Alain because he was amazed at the perfect seasoning and delicate flavours on his plate.

'You do have a natural ability to taste what you are cooking,' Alain said when he laid down his cutlery and wiped his mouth with a napkin. 'You can add a pinch of something here and a sliver of that there, until the combination of flavours in the mixture is exactly right. Not everyone can do that. Not everyone has the ability or the need or the passion to do it. I have no qualms at all about your cooking. You already have business skills, so I say, go ahead with your venture. You need to find your property and to prepare it for your opening, and I need to get back to work.' And Alain hugged her.

'You also have to find somewhere to live, and to sort things out with Percy,' said Paloma tentatively.

For the first time since she had left her husband, Liberty suddenly felt very frightened. 'I have to go back,' she said in a small voice. 'I know. I have to. It's time.'

'Call your friends and your mother, and go and stay with her,' advised Paloma. 'It is definitely not a good idea for you to live in a hotel on your own for the time being. You should see your in-laws, too. You were always very close to them, and they deserve your explanation, because goodness knows what Percy has told them about your split.'

'They may not want to see me,' replied Liberty.

'No need for negatives. You don't know that until you phone and ask if you can go to visit. You have never been a coward, so don't start now.'

Paloma felt as though she was losing a daughter. She felt the tears pricking the back of her eyes, so instead stood up and suggested having 'a small party' to send her off. 'I haven't had a party since I was sixty and we decorated the restaurant and garden with Chinese lanterns.'

Liberty tried to insist she didn't want any fuss made over her, but Paloma only replied, 'Do let me, darling, for my sake if not for yours. You will be very much missed by all of us. It has been my great pleasure having you to stay for a few weeks.'

14

Alain and Liberty flew home after a very late party, into that grey that only Heathrow can reflect after one has returned from sunnier climates. Each thought 'Why do we love England so much?' as they gazed out of the plane window. But by the time they were ensconced at the Ritz by a roaring fire, eating dainty sandwiches and drinking champagne, they were smiling again.

Liberty felt awful for taking her father away from The Dark Horse, knowing he felt it unfair for people to turn up, expecting him to be behind the stoves. She also felt bad for heaping herself on to Paloma. She relayed her apologies, but he simply said, 'Don't be so silly. We were only too pleased to be the ones you could ask for help. Your mother will be fuming, but I know Paloma has spoken to her and explained that I insisted on turning up.'

However, he had to be up and out at four the next morning, so as to drive back to Fickledown, his village, his true love, his kitchen, to throw a bit of a tantrum to show he was back in charge. He admitted to Liberty he was a little miffed at how well they seemed to cope without him. 'All these years of sweat, tears and never a day off, and they simply coast along as though I'm not needed!' Liberty knew he had an excellent staff of sous-chefs, commis chefs and a whole pastry section, but she understood he needed to feel at the helm, to be in control at all times. She smiled at her dear daddy and said, 'You are a control freak, but I am so proud of what you have achieved. If I can manage to accomplish a fifth of what you have done, I will be pleased.'

Alain took her hand and explained, 'As much as I look forward to my time off, I crave and miss the buzz and excitement of the kitchen, the mad rush of my days, just as much as the day I opened the restaurant all those years ago.'

Now he was picking up messages every five minutes and sending emails and texts on his BlackBerry. He made sure supplies were ready for delivery, checking with his restaurant manager and sommelier, who had reported several thefts over the past weeks. It never failed to amaze him how much people would remove, from whole place settings, to ashtrays, to glasses. Once a painting had disappeared from the hallway. Alain had assumed it had been taken by a member of staff, until after an embarrassing and upsetting police investigation it was proved it must have been a customer. After several waiting staff – and good ones are a little like hens' teeth – had left, an expensive alarm system and CCTV cameras had been installed .

'I can't believe that people are happy to pay £500 for lunch for four people and then steal a loo roll, but it happens,' he had once explained in an interview.

Liberty sipped her champagne and watched her father go red in the face as he heard the news that, due to inclement weather, some of his fresh produce was stuck in a refrigerated lorry somewhere in the Channel, and his garlic from the Isle of Wight hadn't been delivered for the garlic soup to be served as part of the amuse-bouches at tomorrow's lunch. She realised how attention to detail was so important, and how much she would have to maintain control of every single tiny thing if she were to obtain anywhere near the results her father did, year after year. She didn't want a Michelin star, but she wanted to give her little place and her customers the impression that she was capable of one, if that was what she desired!

They walked from the hotel to eat at a local Italian bistro, as both wanted a light meal before an early night. Liberty was going to meet up with her parents-in-law the following day and needed to compose herself. They spent the entire meal drinking a rather mediocre Chianti, but as the food was really terrible – faux Italian, too many ingredients, over-cooked pasta – they didn't eat much, so found themselves wobbling and weaving back to the Ritz in a melancholy mood. As he kissed his daughter goodnight by her room, Alain asked if she would like him to accompany her to see Cecil and Isabelle, and when she sighed and said 'yes, but no, if you know what I mean', he simply told her to call him the moment she had left them.

They hugged goodbye and both went to sleepless nights. Alain rose at two in the morning and left the hotel, excitedly jumping into his old Porsche which the hotel had stored for him in their long-term parking area, and whizzed down the motorway, thrilled to be getting back, trying not to worry on Liberty's behalf.

Liberty eventually got up, feeling grotty and a little apprehensive, had an espresso after checking out but left her bags at the hotel. Her luggage contained the summer wardrobe she had picked up in Florence, and she shivered in the early November air as she was wearing only a light dress and jacket.

'First things first,' she said to herself, striding towards Regent Street. 'Warm clothes, and then somewhere to put them.' She didn't know, but assumed, that her car would still be parked in the mews garage where she had left it. Percy would be at work, so she would pick up her car along with the few photos and personal possessions she wanted to keep. She had decorated the mews house, but the furniture had all been gifts from her in-laws' other homes. It had been a place where she had lived, but not hers. Before that she had lived with Isabelle and Cecil, so had felt no need for her own ornaments or paintings. All the wedding gifts of china and glassware she was happy to leave, and she knew that if she even touched the art works, Percy would call the police. Not that she wanted to – they were all his. She decided she needed backup, so she phoned J-T and asked him to go to the house with her.

'Darling! You're back at last!' was J-T's greeting. 'Where the hell have you been? What's going on? Oh my God, you need to fill me in. Is it true you have left Percy? Gossip is flying here!

I would love to have you to stay, but Bob has got an opening tonight, and everything is complete chaos here.'

Liberty stopped his verbal diarrhoea. 'Don't worry about that, I just want to see Mr and Mrs CR, and then get out of town ASAP. But I need your advice on a few things, and I know how hard it would be to get you to leave the safety of the city, so if you just help me get my car and a few things, I'll buy you lunch. I need a little lubrication before I see them.'

'Meet you at the mews in one hour.' He put the phone down.

Off sped Liberty to Browns, where she could find a complete winter wardrobe under one roof. She accomplished this within the next half-hour, as she knew what she liked and never wavered from the classic styles. She had shopped there for years, and the staff looked after her quickly and efficiently. They suggested bags, boots, scarves to go with each outfit. Satisfied with a grey, camel, black and white group of clothes, Liberty hailed a taxi and returned to the Ritz, collected her suitcases and then, full of trepidation and baggage, told the driver the mews address. And that was how J-T found her, standing on the corner of the street surrounded by huge shopping bags and five large suitcases.

'Is this camouflage, or are you now the smartest bag lady in town?' he asked as he threw his arms around her and enveloped her in a long hug.

'Aaaargh!' he yelled in mock terror. 'Breasts! Get them away from me.' Then, as only a gay best friend can, he stood back and grabbed them gently, as though appraising them. 'Bloody hell, darling, how much did THEY cost? Amazing work. AND you have had Botox and fillers. Is this the new, single you?'

They both snorted with laughter as Liberty told him no, it was just the result of food and happiness.

'Right, well, let's get this over with and then I can ask you all the info you haven't told me.'

Although J-T was incapable of being frightened unless Dolce & Gabbana ran out of white suits, he was nevertheless rather nervous about the thought of breaking and entering.

'But it's not,' Liberty consoled him, as they heaved her bags down the quiet mews to her old house. 'I have keys, darling.' He looked visibly relieved.

As she looked up at the windows, she felt no longing for the home she had shared for so long with Percy. It just resembled another perfect house in a row of perfect houses, with absolutely no individuality.

And that about sums up my life, she thought.

'OK, I'll go in, grab my car keys and get my photos. It will only take ten minutes, tops. You stay here and keep watch.'

J-T stood surrounded by all the paraphernalia of Liberty's shopping trip and summer adventure. He stamped his feet to keep the blood flowing in the chill of the London November morning, and felt as though he looked like an extremely well-dressed burglar scanning the street. A shiver went up his spine. He had loved Liberty from the moment they giggled over a lecturer saying 'bottom' whilst reciting from *A Midsummer Night's Dream*. He would never have allowed her to leave his life as some of her girlfriends had done when Percy became jealous of Liberty's friendships. If she was too friendly with any of her girlfriends, Percy phoned them to say she did not want to see them any longer. She had remained ignorant of this as he was clever about it and so they simply stayed away. She had spent their years always thinking the best of him in every situation, until the last journey they took together, so she had believed her friends did not want to see her.

J-T had seen the tougher side of Percy. Never one to admit it, Percy had nonetheless been rather a homophobe. Combined with his desire to control his beautiful, popular girlfriend and eventually wife, this had led to some uncomfortable moments. Once, at Liberty's twenty-fifth birthday party, held at Le Manoir, Percy had come to the bedroom J-T and Bob were sharing. Using very clear wording, he told them that such was his influence in the City, and his parents' influence in top social circles (although Mr and Mrs Cholmondly-Radley were nothing but delightful), that if J-T and Bob dared to show him up, embarrass him or say anything whatsoever untoward, he would make sure their business was closed within weeks.

The gay couple were known to be somewhat flamboyant in their behaviour, but being told how to behave was the red rag to the bull. They shared a bottle of champagne before getting a taxi into Oxford, where the owner of a famous drag shop awaited their arrival. He kitted them out. J-T looked like a giant Kylie Minogue, while Bob resembled a male Anne Robinson. They turned up to the dinner complete with a karaoke machine which was beating out ABBA songs and sang 'Happy Birthday to Liberty' before presenting her with a magnum of pink champagne and a feather for her hair.

J-T and Bob were in fact impeccably behaved, and had warned the restaurant staff in advance and asked if they would like the drinks to be held outside. Everyone screamed with laughter. Even Mr and Mrs CR got up to have a bop. But the next day, after a really fun evening, Liberty and Percy had come down from their room and they left the hotel very early. At breakfast a concerned waiter had sidled up to J-T and told him that Liberty had literally been hauled out and was nursing a bruised face. J-T was horrified that his actions had caused this to happen, but was aghast that Percy was capable of behaving so badly. He had always been an arrogant, bigoted twit, but a wife beater?

Liberty had never mentioned the incident, but it had lengthened J-T's list of why he hated his best friend's husband.

J-T kicked his well-shod foot gently against Liberty's suitcase. Percy looked like a pompous ass, he thought, and he acted like one, too. He became a really, truly arrogant ass when he was drunk, he always put Liberty down, and he was a bully. He also hated dogs, and in J-T's mind anyone who hated animals, especially dogs, was worthless. This may have had something to do with Percy's attitude towards Feran and Bulli, J-T's French bulldogs, which attended every party, every gallery event. More seriously, he had also punched a mutual friend at university, breaking his rather perfect nose, after the friend had whispered something too flattering in Liberty's ear.

J-T had always thought that Liberty had stayed with Percy because she believed he gave her security. Percy constantly reminded her that nobody else would ever put up with her, and she believed him. Nobody else had been allowed to show any interest in her. Percy had seen to that.

But from the time of the birthday party, J-T had constantly hoped that Liberty would break free. He had always seen her artistic potential, in the way one artist can understand another. The fact was, that despite being without a sense of either taste or smell, her dinner parties were legendary, merely from her natural instinct and ability to make everyone welcome, and people wanted to be with her. When she spoke to someone she really paid attention to what they said, so that the next time she saw them she would enquire about a sick wife or racehorse, or ask how the hedge fund (that Percy's boring friends ran) was faring. It was one of the reasons why she had been so successful in public relations. When Liberty spoke to you, you felt you were the only person in the room. You were made to feel really important. This, combined with her arresting looks, had managed to clinch many a deal for herself, for J-T and for Percy, although Percy would never admit it, and if he saw her speaking in an intimate way with a client of his, a friend of J-T's or anyone he thought she liked, they were simply never invited to dine with the couple again, in case a friendship evolved.

The more Liberty had matured into an empathetic woman, the more he had tried to suppress her. J-T understood why Percy did not want children; it would have meant her primary attention was focused on someone other than him.

J-T jumped when Liberty shouted 'Quick, no time!' as she ran from the house and down to the garage, calling for J-T to follow her. Managing to simultaneously press the button on her key fob to open the electric garage door, which thankfully slid up quickly, and to press the unlock button on her car, she flung open the door and started pushing her newly purchased goodies over the seat into the back. Considering this was only a Golf, the manoeuvre was quite tricky. At last they were whizzing along Sloane Street, J-T resembling one of his dogs, sticking his head out the open window so he could breathe in the narrow seat, squashed on either side and in front by Liberty's shopping bags.

'My suit will go all black!' he squeaked. *Maybe I should hang my tongue out and try to look adorable*, he thought as they stopped at traffic lights and a rather handsome young man gazed wistfully at him. *No, on second thoughts, that only works with dogs*.

'You do realise you are saying that out loud,' said Liberty, laughing as she changed up a gear. 'You have Bob, you silly man. No one could be more adored.'

'Mmm,' he replied. 'Maybe it's time to get out of town.'

As Liberty pulled into a parking space outside the Enterprise they both burst out of the car, Liberty giggling with relief and J-T smoothing down his crumpled suit.

'You shouldn't wear white in winter,' she chided.

'It's my signature, darling,' he responded. 'Anyway, it's bloody cold, and I am in desperate need of a strong cocktail. And it's time for you to tell me all about your adventures.'

They parked their bottoms on bar-side stools alongside the reporters who were pretending to read newspapers whilst listening out for the latest gossip.

'A Grey Goose Martini for me, and a Malvern water for the lady,' said J-T to the barman.

'Wait a mo,' interrupted Liberty. 'I'll have a whisky mac, please, with lots of ice.'

'Blimey, you didn't tell me you were drinking now!'

'Only a little – well, sometimes a lot, but no point when I couldn't taste the stuff.'

'You are a funny one. Most people can't stand the taste, they just drink to get happy, or to forget something.'

'Well, that's all wrong for a start. But that's enough of lectures for the time being. Now, about bloody Percy . . .'

As they enjoyed their drinks and felt warmth flooding into their bodies, they giggled over Liberty's story. Percy had been very wily. He had not changed the locks, but had changed the alarm. Thus, it didn't go off when Liberty pressed the old code, but did something different she couldn't understand. She was gathering up her things when suddenly Percy's voice boomed out of a speaker.

'Liberty, I know that is you inside the house. I am coming home.'

'If he hadn't said he was coming home, I would have thought he was in the room, his voice was so close. I nearly wet my pants. It must have been a recording.'

'I wonder if he wants you back,' said J-T thoughtfully.

'I doubt it. I don't think he really wanted me in the first place.' She then told J-T about discovering Percy's affair.

'You were the perfect wife, and that is what he wanted. But funnily enough, you were probably two quite similar people. I don't think he feels emotion that much. He certainly doesn't like showing it, and you were, for a long time, just happy living the perfect life together. Or that is how it seemed to your friends.'

'I would have stayed with him if we had a baby to love together,' Liberty declared suddenly.

'Yes, but darling girl, he didn't want a baby, really, did he?' said J-T very gently. 'I think he went along with the idea of a baby, as a dream, or someone to inherit his worldly goods eventually, but not as a father.'

Liberty looked at her hands. 'Whoops, widow's fingernails. Better have a manicure very soon.'

'Stop ignoring the facts, Liberty. You needed to escape from him, and as sad as your miscarriage was, especially after all the horrible experience of IVF, the fact is he gave you a bad time. And you were just not prepared to see things as they were until you discovered he was being unfaithful.'

J-T and Bob had briefly flirted with the idea of having a baby with a surrogate mother, and had looked into the process, so both of them understood what IVF involved.

'You will see in years to come. Your miscarriage was perhaps a blessing from your baby. Anyway, let's get something to eat. You need your strength and I want to see what gives you your fabulous new look.'

They ordered a typical London lunch, a bottle of Sauvignon Blanc and a warm salad of frisée, walnuts and goat's cheese with beetroot foam that looked pretty and didn't taste of much. *Too cold*, thought Liberty. Both played with the bread basket; J-T as he avoided carbs alongside alcohol and Liberty as she had acquired a taste for good bread and felt there was little point in eating anything else.

'So that is how Europeans stay so thin!' declared J-T. 'They only eat what tastes good, which cancels out a lot. Anyway, you had better have a double espresso, as you have to drive. They do those well here.'

'No, it's OK, it will be a nice walk to Mr and Mrs CR's.'

'And then what?' asked J-T. 'Where are you staying? I was only kidding, of course, Bob would love you to stay.'

'No, no, so kind of you, but don't worry. As I said, I need to get on with my plan. I am driving down to Mummy's this evening. Anyway, I only had one glass of wine.'

Whoops! thought J-T, realising how much he must have drunk. 'Bob needs me to be on form this evening, but it's a bit late for that! I'll have a double espresso and another Martini,' he announced to the barman. 'So what advice did you want from me?'

'Well, it will only be for the café's decor.'

'Oh, darling girl, you have got your personality back with a zing, and you will know much better this time around what china, wallpaper and so on you will want. I will happily source things and ensure you get discounts, but I think my old pal is back on course, and we must let you blossom! The only advice I will give you is that the word "café" sounds very working class, and not you at all!'

Liberty gathered herself together from this outburst, and told J-T it was time to go before she started to have second thoughts.

J-T downed his Martini and wobbled off to find a taxi, only pausing to bend down and kiss his old friend on the top of her head and tell her to call him when she had found somewhere or when anything interesting happened.

So probably tonight! she thought.

Number 12 Westchester Street was a lovely, beautifully proportioned Regency town house situated in a quiet garden square in Belgravia. Black railings enclosed a small front garden filled with huge terracotta tubs holding neatly pruned bay and box and winter cyclamen, with ivy trailing in an orderly way, all maintained by Gordon's of Belgravia. Steps led up to a glossy front door with a gleaming brass handle and bell, no doubt polished that very morning by Mrs Stickybunns, Mr and Mrs Cholmondly-Radley's plump, loyal and improbably named housekeeper. As she answered the doorbell she gave Liberty a wide open smile which allayed the younger woman's fears immediately. Acting most unlike the very proper housekeeper that she was, and had been for the Cholmondly-Radleys for over thirty years, she enveloped Liberty in a giant bear hug, as only a tiny woman with a remarkable resemblance to Mrs Tiggy-Winkle can manage. More alarmingly, she also burst into tears and said, 'My darling child, come in, come in.'

Liberty almost expected to be taken downstairs to the kitchen and have hot milk and shortbread thrust on her, as she had done in difficult times when she and Percy had lived in the house.

'Mr and Mrs CR are in the yellow drawing room. Go on up and I'll bring tea.'

With some trepidation creeping back, Liberty mounted the staircase. She had always cared deeply for Isabelle and Cecil, her parents-in-law. They were deeply decent, kindly people. Fed up with the draughty rooms of Anstley Hall, they spent most of their time in London, but this was not the only reason. Just before their eldest child Elizabeth, Percy's older sister, celebrated her ninth birthday, she died in a terrible accident on the estate. During a family picnic she had fallen into the pond and drowned quickly before any of the family could do anything about it. Her parents would never forgive themselves. Percy, who was only eighteen months old at the time – a happy mistake – had from that time on been spoilt and indulged by Cecil, and mollycoddled and protected from life's turmoil by Isabelle. They were both painfully aware that perhaps their son's shortcomings resulted from their treatment of him. They also genuinely adored Liberty, and had taken to her as some sort of recompense for the daughter they had lost.

As Liberty entered the pretty, sun-filled room, they both immediately rose and embraced her.

'Welcome home, darling,' said Isabelle as she ushered Liberty into a Nina Campbell two-seater sofa by the fire and sat next to her.

'Whatever has been going on? We haven't seen you for simply ages,' Cecil shot at her in a friendly but demanding way. At a discreetly raised eyebrow from Isabelle he bumbled his apology, and retreated, saying, 'Well . . . well . . . um, maybe I will leave you two gels to it for a while. I will be in my study if you need me. Just let me know when I can safely return!'

Isabelle smiled sweetly at him and mouthed a thank you. As Cecil left the room Mrs Stickybunns came in with tea and cake. 'I'll have a whisky in my study, please, Sticky,' he said to her. 'I need something stronger than tea.'

As 'Sticky' poured the tea, and made a bit of a fuss with the milk jug and teaspoons, Isabelle asked after Liberty's parents, her health and the weather in France. She knew full well that the housekeeper was desperate to find out all the news. Although Sticky, as she was known by everyone, was essentially part of the family, having been with them for so long, and would no doubt find out all the news in her own way, Isabelle didn't want to grill Liberty with an audience. All Percy had told them was that the IVF had been a mistake, and that Liberty needed some time to recover. This had been quite enough of a shock to his parents, as Percy had been unable to discuss their infertility, and therefore his parents hadn't realised they had problems in that department, let alone had been undergoing IVF.

Liberty thought Percy would have kept them informed, but Percy, in his anger and annoyance at his wife's actions, had completely forgotten his parents' ignorance of the matter.

Eventually Sticky, after fussing over plates, napkins and cake forks, moving each cup and saucer about the table and checking for drips from the tea strainer, could find nothing more to do, so she reluctantly retired to 'get on with the evening meal'. Liberty was perfectly aware Sticky could produce a fabulous, if plain, meal with the ease of a chef for up to 150 people, without ruffling a silver hair on her head. Besides supervising the cooking she would ensure the silverware was perfectly polished and all the carpets scrupulously vacuumed, but she always had to fuss and make it known how hard she worked. Liberty knew she was rewarded handsomely, with apartments of her own in both houses and a high salary.

'Right, my dear,' said Isabelle, once Sticky had left the room. 'Poor Percy is in such a state. He has rigged up cameras all over your house and connected them to his computer, so he can see when you return home. It seems like something out of a film. What on earth has happened between you both?'

Well, that explains the booming voice, thought Liberty.

'I am not sure how much to tell you,' she said. 'In any case, whatever I say will not really explain everything. Percy is your son, and I do not want to criticise him in any way to you. Therefore, I can only say it is impossible for me to remain living with him as his wife. I will not ask him–' or you, she implied '–for any monetary settlement, and of course I have brought Cecil's mother's ring back.' She had returned to their marital home specifically to retrieve the original ring box, which she now placed carefully on the mantelpiece. 'I have to ask you to trust me when I say that I simply cannot continue living with him.'

Isabelle, a woman of the world, had been married to Cecil for fifty-five years. She had endured her fair share of affairs, deceptions and tragedies, and felt she could honestly say that marriage was about working these things out, getting past them and finding the relationship was stronger for the experience. 'I know Percy can be selfish – he is a man, after all – and we are terribly sorry about the IVF not working, but don't you need a few cycles for it to be given a chance?'

Liberty decided now was not the time to enlighten her mother-in-law.

Isabelle continued, 'I know you, my dear. You are not a girl who gives up on something so easily. Percy is devastated. He had a month off work, which is unheard of. He said he had to think, which is also unheard of!' She tried to smile, but failed.

'I suppose,' stuttered Liberty, now feeling more than a little guilty and like a naughty schoolgirl, 'it's a lot to do with me. I am not sure I have been myself recently, and the things that Percy and I have just gone through have brought matters to a head. I cannot go back, as I wasn't being the person I feel I am inside. Percy doesn't like the real me, so I spent years being who I thought he wanted, so as to make him happy. I thought I was happy at the time, but now I know I must be true to myself. So for Percy's sake as well as for my own, it would be fruitless to try to return to the marriage. I am very sorry, I know you must be terribly disappointed in me, but for both our sakes we have to live apart.'

'But you have been together for so long, you can't just give up and go away. Heavens, Cecil and I would have separated years ago if I walked out at the whiff of a flirtation, or if he spent too much at the races.'

Liberty was feeling rather nauseous. 'All I can say is that this is slightly different. I am sorry you don't understand. If Percy chooses to tell you more in the future, then he can. But I don't feel able to. I am truly sorry. I had better go.'

'I am so saddened,' sighed Isabelle and, horror of horrors, Liberty could see tears welling up in the normally controlled eyes. 'Please remember, I still consider you as part of our family. Do stay in touch. I beg of you not to give up, and I hope that you come to your senses very soon. I do understand what you are going through – more than you know. Don't forget, I lost a daughter. Your brain does funny things when you are mourning a loss. You have lost a baby, too, and maybe when you have recovered from that you will contact Percy. Please, for our sakes, don't divorce him until at least a year has passed. It took me well over nine months to smile again after Elizabeth died, and it never gets better, or easier, but you learn to live with it. Every day you feel less guilty for smiling or feeling happy, and it gradually comes back.'

Christ, thought Liberty, *now I feel doubly guilty – her loss was far greater than mine.*

Cecil was called, and both the CRs hugged her closely and with genuine warmth. But as she left, the engagement ring in its velvet-lined box was pressed into her hand, and Isabelle repeated, 'Don't give up on Percy. He may be spoiled, but he is your husband, and he wants to remain that. At least think about it for some time. And do stay in touch.'

Liberty now felt claustrophobic, both because of the grey city surrounding her, and for all the emotions pressing down on her. She had not realised that Mrs CR would make her feel so very guilty, and for the first time she really did wonder whether she was doing the right thing. Had she been too hasty?

As she raced to her car, eager to flee the city which had for so long been her home, Liberty tried to list why she had left Percy. *Were the reasons justified?* she asked herself. Had she simply jumped out of the situation, as so many before her, when she should really be putting all the bad things she did not like about her husband into the past, and moving on? Would Percy have her back? At this last thought her body went into such involuntary convulsions that she was afraid she might have to sit down. No, she certainly could not live with him any longer. The last couple of months had allowed her to realise there had been occasions when she had felt wrong, but at the time she had simply pushed all negative thoughts from her mind. The Percy she had originally got to know was a strong, athletic young man with ambition, but in the usual way of the over-indulged he was also selfish and spoiled, and that came to the surface when things didn't go his way, or when he was drunk or high, which had become more regular over the years.

He also had a passion for the darker side of life. Cocaine had been a great friend, as it can be to the rich. It gave him a great deal of false confidence and turned him into an aggressive bore. It also left him depressed and uncommunicative after a binge. His ambition led him to make waves in the City, but he was so driven by the need to better his contemporaries at whatever they did that he lost his friends as quickly as he made them. Anything he attempted that didn't work out was labelled 'someone else's fault' or swept under the carpet, and anyone who succeeded in finalising more deals or bigger contracts would be relegated to the 'oh well, but he is an ugly bastard and only did well because of luck' bin. Liberty was originally happy to live with this, but it filtered down into her and suffused her normally happy nature with cynicism. After she discovered his affair and lack of desire for a family, she finally knew for certain that he was not the man she wanted to be with. She knew she wanted children, and she could not really tell his parents that he didn't. She realised they were desperate for grandchildren; despite their never putting pressure on her, there had always been casual comments such as, 'Well, we can't clear out the attics, dear, we may need the Moses basket again soon!'

As Liberty got into her car, she realised she was emotionally exhausted. Slumped in the driver's seat, her only thought was, *I need my mother. I need to go home!*

15

Adrenalin got her through the journey, enabled her to cope with the usual stop-start of the M25 and down the A21. As she pulled up outside the stunning house situated on one side of a pretty village green, surrounded by a muddle of charming cottages, Victorian houses, a pub and a shop, she felt absolute relief. Her home! She was safe, and about to burst into tears. Liberty didn't even bother to get out her cases; she just grabbed her handbag, slammed the door without locking it, and raced up the path which led through pretty gardens from the lane encircling the village green to the oak front door of the house. As she looked up at the windows she thought, *Is my mother even there?* The house was a typical Queen Anne manor, built for a wealthy sheep merchant, the originally bright orange brick walls now charmingly pale peach and warmed by the fading sun. The large windows gave good light to this aspect of the house, and as a child, Liberty had thought the facade looked like a face, and that the building was keeping an eye on the comings and goings of the village. In summer the entire frontage was smothered by an ancient wisteria, which at the moment was just displaying its silver-grey skeleton, as though it was in some way cuddling the house, holding it against the chill of the autumnal afternoon.

The door was thrown open. Deirdre said nothing, but drew her daughter into her arms, allowing her at last to let go and sob openly. Her mother held her for a few minutes before calmly saying, 'Come on, my darling, let's get you inside, you are home now.' Paloma had phoned three days before and told Deirdre to expect her; therefore, she had slept little, eaten nothing and worried incessantly, as only a mother can, until she heard the car draw up in the lane. Deirdre, like her daughter, was more than used to putting a brave face on things; her relief at having her daughter home was both intense and unsettling. She was good at looking after wounded puppies, so she knew what to do.

'Come in, come in. You are letting the cold air in,' she said. She was covered in a very pretty Cath Kidston apron and a lot of flour. As they walked together along the flagstone floor towards the back of the house, she explained why. 'It's my Kids Bake Day. Come into the kitchen by all means, but I warn you . . .!' Sensing Liberty's reluctance, but unwilling to allow her out of her sight even to freshen up, she led her blotchy-faced daughter forcibly along the hall.

As they approached the kitchen, the sounds of shouting grew louder.

'That's MY cookie cutter! Hands off, you little fucker!'

Liberty glanced at her mother before they entered the room.

'A lot of them come from the workers' cottages by the river,' whispered Deirdre by way of an explanation. 'I am not sure whether this is for the parents to take time out, or for the benefit of the children, but they seem to improve and calm down as the term progresses.'

Bam-poof! Perfect timing; as Liberty opened the door, a flour bomb hit her square on the chest, throwing flour all over her black cashmere jacket and dress. Silence. Absolute stillness. The children seemed to realise they were in the presence of a lady worthy of better behaviour, a lady who looked like a supermodel to them, and definitely not an appropriate target for a flour bomb. As Deirdre sometimes surprised them with a celebrity chef friend, they wondered if they had really goofed this time and would be sent home. Even though they were prone to playing up, they all loved the feeling of success when their cakes and biscuits rose and baked close to perfection. Sometimes this really did happen, and then they were allowed to take their produce home and give it to their families. It gave the children a sense of worth. They were now terrified this privilege could be taken away.

Thankfully, after what seemed like an eternity, Liberty started shaking with laughter. She then took off her jacket, donned an apron she saw hanging behind the kitchen door, and said, 'Right, who can I help, and what are we making today?'

One hour later the two women were stacking and washing dishes, cleaning work surfaces and wiping floors. Liberty's emotional arrival long forgotten, she felt tired, but happy. They were helped by Sarah, a young woman from the village who assisted Deirdre as a cleaner, and kept things as tidy as possible during the classes. Now she was washing the walls.

'Sarah, it's time for you to leave!' stated Deirdre eventually. 'Liberty, you go and bring in your bags and have a bath. Your room is all ready. I'll bring you up a drink.'

As instructed, and in the way that children, no matter what age, follow their parents' instructions when under their roofs, Liberty grabbed her things and took them up the stone staircase to 'her room'. It was actually her mother's main guest room, with an en suite, and whoever happened to be staying at the time had the room named after them. Thankfully, it was no shrine to Liberty's teenage years. She sometimes looked with horror into guest rooms in friends' houses – kept in a sort of 1990s time warp. It was as though the parents thought the children hadn't really left. Posters of pop stars remained Blu-tacked to the walls, candy pink curtains frilled at the hems hung at the windows, teddy bears sat perkily at bedheads. Perhaps it was just an excuse not to spend money on new curtains. It could be somewhat disconcerting for guests, though.

Liberty's room was in a beautiful double-aspect corner and looked out on to the village green. She had a prime view of the shop, pub and tea room, to which Deirdre supplied patisserie. The room itself was a calm sea of pale green toile de Jouy and yellow stripe, which her mother had somehow made work.

Deirdre had an exceptional eye for decoration, and in the early days of Alain's restaurants had enjoyed making them into centres of relaxation, which added to the dining experience. She went by the psychology that you didn't want to notice your furnishings, only that you felt extremely comfortable and serene. She knew that the correct furniture for the setting, especially dining chairs, played a big part in this, and always said one should feel one knew a room the moment one walked into it. She couldn't bear modern decor but she understood the need for it.

When Liberty came downstairs after a hot bath and a hair wash, feeling fully herself once more, she sat down by the open fire to let her hair dry. She was joined by Custard, the fawn pug, beautiful to those who knew her and therefore loved pugs, and glared at by Dijon, the elderly golden Labrador, who always took the prime place by the fireside. Liberty gave in to his wishes, and shuffled along so the sweet dog could curl up and warm his bones after being left in the garden while the children were enjoying their class. As Deirdre said, 'Otherwise, he spends his entire time being fed by them. He can't resist food and they can't resist feeding him, and he would end up like a balloon.'

She entered the sitting room and handed her daughter a drink. Liberty took a gulp and nearly choked.

'My God, this is neat vodka. What are you doing to me?'

'No, my darling. This is an absolutely fabulous dry Martini. I thought you should try one now, as I have heard from Paloma – why I had to hear from her is another thing – that your sense of taste and smell have returned. You know how I have prayed for this moment – I'm not going to go on at you, but really.' Deirdre looked flustered.

'I'm sorry I didn't tell you straight away,' said Liberty, feeling guilty, but Deirdre was not going to dwell on the whys and what-have-yous and waved her hands at Liberty to shut up. 'But you should only sip, not gulp. It is the very best medicine in the world, although for some reason my doctor disagrees with me.'

'Why, are you ill?' asked Liberty, looking worried.

'No, no, darling, it's just that I see quite a lot of Dr Brown around the village.'

Liberty raised an eyebrow inwardly and smirked to herself but made no comment.

They sipped their drinks and Liberty filled her mother in with her news. She left no detail out, and recounted a full report of Alain's help in France. Deirdre took this surprisingly well.

'He would certainly be the best person to teach you about baking, and I quite agree with his theory that if you had to work in restaurants to get the experience you need it would take years. Do you now consider you have really learned enough to open somewhere of your own, or are you going to have to go to college?'

'College?' Liberty laughed. 'All the people I know who went to catering college can manage to do is deep frying and short-order cooking, and that's it. I really want my place to be about baking, pastry and patisserie, either savoury or sweet. And then seasonal salads, cheeses – that sort of thing.'

'Will you be licensed?'

'I don't think I will start with that, as I want to get established quite quickly, but we will see. People can always bring their own.'

Of all the people Liberty had told of her plans, she was most desperate for her mother's approval. Deirdre worked in the real world, and lived in the area of the country where Liberty wanted to open her restaurant, so she would know if there was any need for another eatery. She simply said, once she had listened carefully to her daughter's plans, 'This area is crying out for a decent place to go to for a cup of fine tea or coffee, and good cooking. The problem with touristy villages in Britain is that you just get the crappy stuff, because people put up with it. Foreigners expect British food to be terrible and the English want cheap food, so the foreigners stop at the first place they find, and the English go somewhere they can find a huge piece of cake, or worse, a burger served with frozen chips, because they think their children want that. Children only want it because they are not used to better food. What was your favourite meal when you were a child?'

'Freshly baked bread with unsalted butter and Valrhona chocolate grated on top, or a buckwheat galette with cheese and ham and béchamel,' replied Liberty without hesitation, even though she had not thought of these childhood pleasures for years. 'Oh, and your home-made strawberry jam spread on sour cream cake.'

'Goodness, I haven't made that for years. I remember it as a cheesecake, with no base. It was flavoured with ground almonds, nutmeg and cinnamon, if I am not mistaken?'

'Yes, it was always a bit different – you changed the spices, sometimes cardamom, but always yummy.'

'The children could make that next week,' mused Deirdre. 'They all have a sweet tooth. Just need to make the candied peel to decorate it, but the oranges are coming into season now, and they are delicious. You can help me tomorrow, maybe. We could do some clementines and lemons as well. How about it?'

'Oh, sure! I was planning to visit estate agents, but we can do that in the afternoon.' Liberty's fatigue had disappeared the moment her mother had been so enthused by and encouraging about her plan. 'The agents I have contacted are being typically useless. Why is it they all say they have exactly what I am looking for, and then send me terraced houses in towns fifty miles away from here, with no business licence? They either don't listen, or they just want to sell me what they have left on their books. Maybe I should become an estate agent!'

'God, no!' answered Deirdre. 'Please, not – but you could pay one of those property finders to do it for you. Although, hold your horses. I need to phone Jonathan tomorrow. When I saw him last week he mentioned that the lease of one his estate shops was coming up for renewal soon. Let's find out which one. Location for this type of venture is everything.'

Jonathan de Weatherby was the 'Tzar' of the Denhelm Estate

that encircled Littlehurst. He and his family lived in the vast, freezing yet beautiful Tudor house with later add-ons that sat in the valley at one end of the village. Its driveway led from one side of the green through wrought-iron gateposts, added in Victorian times when it was important for wealthy landowners to advertise their status and intimidate the poor and lowly who worked for them and kept the estate going. At one time his ancestors owned the entire village and most of its occupants. Not much had changed since, as Jonathan's ancestors had managed to move with the times and looked after their tenants and workers well. As a child, Liberty's best friend was Savannah, his youngest daughter, reckless from birth, who enjoyed getting Liberty into trouble by encouraging her to ride off on her father's thoroughbreds and hide them in the local gypsy camp. There they played with the children, who in turn taught them to ride bareback at high speed. Savannah had always dreamt of becoming a gypsy princess, as portrayed in Hollywood, transforming into Ava Gardner and living in a painted fairytale caravan, but of course one with all creature comforts and no pooing behind the bushes!

Liberty and Savannah, together with Leo and Titan (two of the children from the gypsy camp), spent endless summer days swimming in the lakes on the Denhelm Estate, or climbing trees and riding. Jonathan, whose wife Helena had died giving birth to Savannah, had managed to remain friends with Deirdre as she had been close to them both, and there were no complications – all the other women in his life, either single or married, seemed to want to become the next Mrs de Weatherby with all that went with it, but he said his heart would always belong to his beloved wife Helena.

Jonathan's two older children, Edmund and Grahame, had known and therefore missed their mother terribly. Edmund, the elder, was twelve when his mother died. He was always serious and never climbed trees. Liberty had not been close to him when they were children. Grahame, on the other hand, was a beauty like his sister, and he had been Liberty's first love. She and almost all the girls at the local primary school, which the children attended before being sent off to boarding schools, adored him. Their father was intent on their having local friends, as he had been sent away to school at the age of seven, but even he became exasperated with Grahame and Savannah living like gypsies most of the time, and he was relieved when he could hand them over to the firmer hands of housemasters and mistresses, who had none of the guilt a parent feels and were therefore able to instil a little more discipline. Or, that was the theory.

Savannah and Liberty had been sent to different schools. The parents had got together and deliberately decided on that. The children were devastated; Liberty, because her parents were in the process of separating and she felt lonely enough; Savannah, because, deprived of both her family and her best friend, she felt horribly restricted by school, and imprisoned without a huge estate to run about in. School in the centre of town, even one as smart as Cheltenham, was no substitute for freedom and friends. She rebelled and was expelled pretty quickly. Liberty had heard little of her since she was sent to Switzerland after eight English schools had done what they could. She had read in *Tatler* of the forthcoming third marriage of Savannah, who had become a society beauty, to a Middle-Eastern sheik, but had no idea whether this had taken place.

Edmund had gone into the City. His desire to solve the energy problems of the world, along with inner city poverty, took him successfully into venture capitalism. Grahame went into politics, where his good looks and charm made him incredibly successful with both his constituents and fellow MPs. He said what he thought, and didn't care about upsetting the apple cart. A people's politician.

'Come back to the kitchen while I say goodbye to Sarah,' said Deirdre to her daughter. 'Anyway, we have to make something to eat.'

They took their empty glasses through.

'How is Jonathan?' asked Liberty.

'Oh, just the same as ever – out hunting at every opportunity, keeps himself busy with the estate. I'll call him before his morning ride. When I heard him mention the other day that one of his tenants was thinking of leaving, I'm sure it was the tea rooms!'

'That would be too strange a coincidence – almost fate! It couldn't be true that I could start my café right here, could it?' Liberty paused for a moment before saying, 'Why haven't you mentioned Percy yet?'

'Haven't I? We need to eat, but before that, more drinks. Come through to the kitchen. Oh, Sarah, are you still here?'

'I just thought I would wash the floor before I left.'

'Go on, you, get off home. I'll pop in and see you tomorrow.'

As Sarah closed the outer door, Deirdre said, 'Marriage problems,' to Liberty by way of explanation. 'Her husband is sleeping with Dilys, the publican. All the village seems to know about it, and Sarah was the last to find out, so now she hates going home, knowing he is at the pub flirting in front of everyone and making a fool of her while she minds the children.'

'Why doesn't she leave him?'

'Can't afford it. And anyway, they have two little ones,' said Deirdre as she threw two duck breasts, which had been marinating in salt, thyme and juniper, into a cold pan to render the fat slowly. 'Make a salad with the leaves you'll find in the fridge.'

Liberty looked in the fridge and found a bowl of squash roasted with garlic and rosemary, some toasted walnuts and some winter leaves with spinach. *That will do*, she thought. She put everything on the table and mixed a vinaigrette with walnut oil and red wine vinegar. Deirdre, more anxious than she wanted to appear, poured them glasses of claret and lit a cigarette. Then she leaned against the Aga and looked Liberty in the eye.

'While the duck rests you can have my thoughts, but as a

mother it's as simple as this. If you are happier without him, then I am happy for you. If you think you have rushed out of the marriage, then maybe think before you go to a solicitor.'

'That's it?' asked Liberty.

'What else do you want me to say? I love you and only wish you to be happy.'

'I expected you to say you hate him and he never deserved me, like Daddy did.'

'But darling, that would only make you feel stupid. After all, you did marry him, and you were choosing at that time to spend the rest of your life with him, and to have babies with a man too pompous to be true, a big bully with red cheeks and too much aftershave, who was rude to your poor mother the first time he walked through my front door and after a few drinks rude to just about everyone.'

'OK, OK,' said Liberty, laughing, 'that sounds more like you.'

'I'm sorry, I really am. I am desperately trying not to say everything I am thinking, as you may yet get back with him, and then you would hate me for what I said, and we wouldn't be friends any longer.'

They embraced, and after a delicious meal felt as though they understood one another very well.

They enjoyed a light as air apple tart with thick Jersey cream, then sat back in the sitting room sipping coffee, while the dogs snored in front of the fire. Finally, exhausted, Deirdre apologised, saying she had recorded the final episode of *The Apprentice* and was going to watch it in bed.

'Tomorrow we will start the search for your café. Breakfast at eight o'clock prompt.'

16

The following morning Liberty woke at six thirty to the intense smell of orange, cloves and cinnamon. Mmm, happiness was being at home. She dressed quickly and went downstairs. The dogs were lying treacherously in front of the Aga while Deirdre coated orange and lemon peels with hot sugar syrup and hung them on pegs on a string along the heavy stone mantel above the stove.

'Morning, darling, help yourself to coffee. Why are you up so early?'

'I couldn't sleep any longer. Shall I take the dogs for a walk? I need some fresh air.'

She grabbed the leads, although neither dog was ever held by one, and started off down the garden and out through a back gate on to a permissive foot path that led through the Denhelm Estate.

As the dogs rootled along the hedgerows in the first light, setting up pheasants and rabbits, Liberty gazed at the beauty around her. She didn't notice the cold, only the rooks calling to one another, the mist rising and the trees shedding their leaves and showing off their figures in the early morning sunlight. In the distance she could make out three riders on horseback, galloping along the centre of a field. *Must be hard going*, she thought, and then realised a sort of gallop had been pressed like a wide footpath along the middle of the ploughed field. She watched as the able riders made it to a high hedge and sailed over easily, one by one. They were soon out of sight. *I must begin riding again if I am going to live back in the country*, she thought, and then realised she would probably have no time to do anything like that if she ran her own business. *Am I doing the right thing?* she asked herself, and she carried on asking the same thing over and over as she walked for another hour.

'God, the dogs look pissed off,' said Deirdre as she arrived back at the house. 'Dijon hates the cold; it affects his arthritis, poor thing.' And she towelled the dogs off, then laid a blanket on the floor by the warm Aga. 'You couldn't have lost either of them. Custard you can hear miles away, and Dijon never leaves your side these days, as I am sure you noticed. Where on earth did you get to?'

'Sorry, Mother,' said Liberty, feeling chastised. The one thing that upset her mother was people not taking care of the dogs. 'I was just thinking, and enjoying the fresh air. I forgot the time.'

'Poor darlings,' Deirdre said, putting down a bowl of hot milk for Dijon and feeding him Liberty's bacon. 'Far too crisp for her to eat now, anyway,' she told her dog. She lifted her head. 'He's eighteen, you know, and he has been the best companion anyone could ask for.'

Liberty had been so caught up in her own thoughts, she only now realised her mother was actually crying.

'Mummy, I didn't mean to upset you; he seemed to be enjoying the walk.'

Deirdre sniffed noisily and wiped her runny nose on a tea towel. 'Oh, God, I am being so silly, but the vet said his arthritis was so bad and he is so old I should think about having him put to sleep! But he seems happy enough, and I don't think I could bear it, not yet.'

'He IS happy, so change the bloody vet,' replied Liberty, hugging her mother. She knew it was the anniversary of the day her parents' divorce had finally come through, so she understood the over-the-top reaction. 'Sit down while I make some toast.'

Over a pot of extremely strong coffee, some excellent marmalade (home-made, of course) and toasted brioche, Deirdre gradually felt better, and said she would phone Jonathan.

'Have you any particular properties lined up through agents?' she asked.

'Only two, both in Tunbridge Wells, and I know that's the wrong location. There are very good cafés there already, and as I said, the agents have been pretty dreadful. I had planned to see them today and gee them up a bit. I want a country location, really.'

'Well, let's see Jonathan first, and then we can drive around the villages.'

Deirdre set up a meeting for ten o'clock that morning. 'It's the old butcher's shop on the corner of the green,' she told Liberty after she came off the phone. The butcher had shut up shop years ago, and had been replaced by a delicatessen run by an elderly Italian couple who had now decided to retire. 'I could have sworn he was talking about the tea rooms. No point you setting up next door to them,' said Deirdre. 'Sorry, darling.'

'Well, we could look anyway. Would it be big enough?'

'Only one way to find out – and Jonathan would be a fabulous landlord, as he is only interested in what is good for the village. His rent will be very reasonable for the right tenant.'

Jonathan de Weatherby had set up a food hall on his estate. It was somewhere between an upmarket farm shop and a butcher's. It was run by a charming girl. It sold local produce, meat from the animals reared on the estate, game shot there and cheese made on site, and since the Italians had departed it also contained a new deli counter. They also had baked bread, but fortuitously for Liberty they had been forced to sack the baker for stealing, so were looking either for a new supplier, or a new baker. In the meantime, Deirdre told Liberty, she had been supplying them. 'So you will be doing me out of business!'

The food hall had raised the profile of many local producers, who made small amounts of good quality produce, including many farmers and their families who had been forced to diversify after the foot and mouth trauma.

It was why Mr de Weatherby was such a popular landlord

and agent. He had helped many of his tenant farmers financially during the crisis, and had given a few of them loans to set up kitchens and had advised them on health and safety issues, and all the impossible paperwork.

The two women met Jonathan outside the old butcher's shop at ten on the dot. It was a beautiful, if cold, day. Low sunlight bounced off the red-brick building and the cottages surrounding the green, most of them constructed from the same brick, or weather-boarded. The sky-blue window frames of the houses owned by the estate gleamed with fresh paint, and all the front gardens looked as though they were waiting to take part in a competition (which took place in June, judged of course by Jonathan, along with the vicar's wife, who was in her late twenties and rather more interested in who was wearing what and flirting with Jonathan than boring gardens, but did her husband's bidding and tried very hard to be a good church wife).

The green had a small duck pond, which held an eclectic mix of Indian runners crossed with wild mallards. A young family in the village had raised a group of runners in their back garden, but the children had tormented them so much the sweet creatures decided to find friends and safety elsewhere and fled to the pond, and since then had raised many clutches of eggs.

The village shop and post office were next to the old butcher's, and on the other side was a dear little tea room, presently doing a roaring trade in morning tea and coffee, with people sitting in the window munching on delicious pastries baked by Deirdre.

Jonathan greeted them both warmly and for a while they chatted about their respective families and generally caught up with news. Deirdre told him about Sarah's terrible husband, and Liberty merely said she had decided to leave the rat race in London and change her career path. (She was fully aware her mother would have told him the real situation, but both she and Jonathan were sensible and sufficiently English to refrain from mentioning it.)

Liberty was also desperate to know how her old friend and Jonathan's daughter Savannah was, but they agreed it was far too cold to chat any longer outside; further news could wait.

As Jonathan unlocked the door and stepped through the large glass paned door, Liberty felt it was the perfect place for her. She already knew the location was good. The main road ran close enough to catch passing trade and the parking around the green was sufficient. The building was perfect. The main room, which would be the restaurant, was cluttered with a large deli counter, but was a great size for about ten small tables. Two bay windows looked out over the green, and as it faced south-west the room was flooded with natural light – maybe a problem in summer, but nothing shutters couldn't help with.

Liberty could imagine the flagstone floor covered in old heavy rugs (firmly stuck down so people didn't trip), a few leather armchairs and shelves full of teapots, jugs and cups and saucers, alongside displays of home-made jams, preserves and pickles. There was enough space for a bread basket display and a patisserie counter, and the little kitchen was a perfect site for fresh tarts, quiches and salads to be prepared. She was hoping that to start with she could bake most things in her mother's school kitchen, and then, if she found a house close enough, in her own, as most of the baking would have to be done early in the mornings to be cooled and ready for sale by nine o'clock.

'If we moved this partition we could set up the coffee machine with a small counter from which to serve espressos. It would take up too much room in the kitchen,' mused Deirdre.

'I love it,' said Liberty. 'But what about the tea room next door? I can't imagine you would want me to take away their business, as they have been here for ages, and they look busy.'

'Indeed,' responded Jonathan, 'but until your mother started helping them by making their cakes they only sold bad scones and old teacakes with watery tea. They had been losing money for years, but carried on, as they enjoyed the gossip and wanted to be part of the village. Neither Gwen nor Paul had any interest in cooking at all, and were going to have to close until, as I said, your mother helped out. I bet you don't even charge them for your cakes, or for using your name to advertise, do you?' He looked quizzically at Deirdre.

'Well, no, but Gwen is so lovely, and she was a little desperate. She thought they were moving here to enjoy the quiet life, until her beast of a husband told her she was to start a tea room, when she could barely cook fish fingers for her kids. They have been here for a while, and he was blaming her for the slow trade. I couldn't imagine them sitting looking at each other all day in their tiny cottage, until one of them decided to murder the other with an old iron railing, just for something to do after watching two hundred reruns of *Midsomer Murders*.'

'You strange woman,' was Jonathan's only response to this. 'Anyway, I decided Gwen might be the perfect waitress to help with your café. The locals all like her, and she would pull them in before they had time to moan about change and the way things have always been done. And she is really good with customers. She can be trusted, and she works very hard. She is only in her late fifties, and although I disagree with your mother that murder is the only alternative, I'm not sure she could sit at home with that husband of hers either! She definitely wants to carry on working.'

'But what about their tea room?' asked Liberty, her brow furrowing.

'Well, I have thought for a while that the village needs more independent shops and a young chap who used to be in wine, supplying restaurants in town, has shown an interest in opening a fine wine shop. The property would lend itself better to being a shop, whereas this place is much more atmospheric. He will sell online as well – he has already set that part up and it is doing well – but he gets fed up on his own, sitting in an office with just a computer and warehouse. He is in the business park just outside Wadhurst, and would love to be among people again. We think the holiday rental cottage people would use him. They always seem to have oodles of spare cash, and we know some of the villagers have an interest in wine.' And at that he glanced at Deirdre.

'*Moi*? I never drink! Well, not on my own. Well, not more than a glass with supper – and maybe one after work, well . . .' And she went quiet, blushing an attractive burgundy.

'Anyway, let's look around the rest of the place,' said Liberty to save her mother's embarrassment.

There was a good-sized cloakroom ('Loos are always so important,' said Liberty) and a good-sized storeroom at the back, ideal for baking ingredients, coffee beans and teas, and two rooms upstairs with a bathroom. There was also a lovely courtyard at the back. With a bit of jiggling, tables could be put outside during the summer. It was walled and had some good planting. *It's not ideal to live over the shop, but I could stay here until I find a cottage*, she thought. *It could be extremely pretty, lots of pots, that sort of thing, and some decent chairs and tables.* An ancient apple tree drooped in one corner and a wisteria clambered over the back of the building. 'It must be lovely in summer,' she said out loud.

As they exited by the front door, Jonathan told Liberty to turn around. She stood in front of her restaurant-to-be and looked. Yes, she loved it. She now noticed that a wisteria also climbed up the front and over the bay windows. It covered an old sign with the original butcher's name painted on it, and she thought of getting the local blacksmith to make a sign that could swing over the door.

'Right, you love it, and you are about to love it even more,' said Jonathan. 'Take a look next door.'

'The shop?'

'No, the other way.'

Along the right-hand side of the building was a narrow alley, and on the other side of that a low wall enclosing the front garden of a stone cottage. In the centre of the wall that ran along the lane a pretty white gate opened on to a box-lined stone path that led up to the front door, painted a lovely gleaming green.

Bay windows on the ground floor flanked the door symmetrically, and upstairs were other windows with what looked like eyebrows, as the cottage had been recently thatched. A sweet array of birds and animals had been added to the thatch. Aran, the thatcher, had been so chuffed with himself – it was his first job after being an apprentice for years – that when he finished the work he decided to add them to all his roofs as his signature. 'He adds them as his calling card, apart from on those where the owners don't pay on time,' Deirdre told Liberty.

'Why are we looking at it?' Liberty asked a beaming Jonathan, who was feeling rather smug.

'This,' he explained, 'is Duck End, so named because it is located in what used to be the wet end of the village, where the ducks would naturally come before humans re-routed and made village greens with ponds for cattle and livestock to graze and drink on. It was where the sheep used to be washed too.' He smiled at the two bemused women. 'It is also for sale!'

The front garden was neatly laid out in four squares, surrounded by lavender, each divided into triangles of roses, which had to be exquisite in summer. Two huge pots sat by the front door. They seemed to contain hydrangeas, but were covered with fleece as frost protection. Over the porch rambled honeysuckle and winter jasmine.

'I've always thought it the prettiest cottage,' said Deirdre. 'Everyone who comes to the school says it's like the dream country house, but what about the delightful'– she made little air quotes at this point for Jonathan's benefit –'Sabrina and Neville? They spent a fortune doing it up as a second home, and I haven't seen them for ages.'

Jonathan was by now looking smugger than ever. 'They have now fallen in love with Marbella, and have decided they prefer the sun to quaint village life, which as you know they never embraced, so they have visited only twice, both times coinciding with our hunt ball, which, as villagers, they get an automatic invitation to, although goodness knows why they would want to attend. They always seemed so uncomfortable.'

Deirdre was giggling despite the cold, remembering the tiny gold-sequined dress that Sabrina had worn to one of Jonathan's balls. 'She was so cold, poor dear, we had to wrap her in a duvet.'

Jonathan was rather sensitive to the temperature of his ancient home and blustered on. 'They rang last week to ask me to recommend an estate agent, and if it would be all right to put up a for sale sign. I told them we probably need not bother with the sign, and since your mother's call, I think I was right, hmm?'

'Oh, yes, oh my God, yes!' Liberty was totally overwhelmed. 'When can I see it?'

'I happen to have the keys in my pocket.'

An hour later the three of them were sitting with steaming cups of coffee and sour cream cake at Deirdre's kitchen table, with Dijon drooling by the Aga, hopeful for a piece, and Custard far more obvious, sitting beside Jonathan's chair gazing wistfully up at his fingers. They chatted about how miraculous it was that so many events had made possible the perfect starting point for Liberty, and all in Littlehurst.

'If I didn't know better, I would think you had planned all this!' Liberty was trembling with excitement. Duck End was a dream come true. Take out all the suits of armour in the hall, the vast flat-screen TVs above the fireplaces and the zebra rugs, and it was simply stunning. Sabrina and Neville Smythe (everyone in the village knew they had changed their surname from Smith to Smythe to make themselves sound smarter, as Miss Scally, the doctor's receptionist and serious gossip, had gleefully told them so), despite having appalling taste and little time for locals, did have heaps of money, with which they wanted to make their home their castle and show it off to all their city friends. Encouraged by Jonathan, who intimidated them slightly as they saw him as Lord of the Manor, they had employed the best local joiner, stonemason and builder, to bring Duck End out of dereliction after being lived in by the same family for 150 years. The workmen had re-coved and pointed cornices, wired and plumbed. The original flagstone floors had been left untouched throughout the ground floor, and there was a huge family kitchen, a dining room, a small office and a sunny sitting room downstairs. Upstairs were five good sized bedrooms and three vast bathrooms. Modern comforts of underfloor heating upstairs and a new Aga helped the house to feel cosy, but the games and cinema room they had put in the cellar could be stripped out and the room turned into a bakery with some decent ventilation. Without the silver wallpaper and bright red lacquered walls which made the dining room look like a bordello, and the pink marble kitchen, it would be a heavenly home. Most of the horrors were in the furnishings, and they would leave with the unfortunate Smythes, who had never fitted into village life.

'I just need to know what the agents will value it at,' said Liberty. 'I know the demand for commuter homes here is high, and that it will create a lot of interest; one look at the pretty facade in a magazine will see to that. I could imagine a bidding war, and I'm not sure I could compete. I have to be sensible and think of the café as well. I shall have to offer them the asking price and hope they really are desperate to leave.'

'Well, I shall get Digby and Rest on to it,' said Jonathan, smiling. 'They are good local agents, and sold it to the Smythes two years ago. They will advise. With the housing market as bad as it is, they would be unwise to turn down your offer. Do you need to release money from the house in London?'

Liberty explained that her previous home had been a gift from her in-laws, and therefore she had no claim. But she had her savings, and there would be no problem.

As Jonathan rose to leave he said, 'It's so lovely to have you here again. Savannah will be thrilled to hear you are back. We may even get her over for Christmas. Although, she is now living in the Middle East, and Khalid, her husband, seems a little reluctant to come. We will just have to persuade her that it's a good idea for the children to experience an English Christmas.'

'Oh, my goodness me!' exclaimed Liberty. 'In all the excitement I forgot to ask after her. I must catch up on all her news, and on Gray, as all Grahame's friends called him and I suppose they still do.'

'Well, then, do come for supper this evening. Mrs Goodman will be delighted to have people to cook for rather than my usual omelette. See you at eight.'

With that he stood, kissed them both and left by the back door to walk back through his park, leaving Custard thoroughly put out and hungry.

'Here, darlings,' said Deirdre as she placed a piece of cake in each of their bowls. 'Isn't he a sweetheart?'

'Yes, he really is. Any romance there? You seem very close.'

'Yes, too close – he is more of a brother than a possible lover. He was so good to me after your father left, making sure I didn't hear any of the local gossip, and trying to stop the more insulting stories. He enabled me to stay in the village without feeling like a leper. So many of my girlfriends whose husbands went off had to move away from their family homes where they had happy memories of bringing up children, and so on, as they seemed a threat. Single women and friends who had often had them for a meal, or parties, abandoned them in case they flirted or took their husbands, and all that after fighting to keep the house they had lovingly looked after for years. Your father was always very gracious, letting me stay here with no question of my having to buy him out.

'Now, we do have more important things to discuss. You may have no need of Percy's money, but you will have to contact him and let him know what is going on. How long has it been since you spoke to him?'

'Three months,' replied Liberty wearily. 'Must we talk about this on such a very happy day?'

'Just phone him, leave a message and see if he gets back to you. Or at the very least, email.'

17

Back in London, Percy was amazed to see Liberty's mobile number light up on his BlackBerry – so amazed that he didn't pick it up. He had to collect his thoughts before speaking to her. He knew he must control himself and not do what he felt like, which was to give the bloody bitch a tongue-lashing. He had been humiliated by her, by the hotel manager in Florence, and humbled by his parents. After Liberty had met with them, he had been summoned to their home, and although in Liberty's eyes Isabelle had been against the separation, she had been very harsh with Percy. After dismissing Cecil with a wave of her hand in case she lost her nerve, the over-indulgent mother, realising she had raised a spoilt, selfish and self-indulgent son, decided it was time to point out his faults.

'You do realise that you treated her very badly. We had always only wanted what is best for you both, and didn't interfere, even when you lived with us, but you really treated her like a trophy wife, and abused her willing nature. You simply didn't respect her and certainly did not appreciate her for who she is and what she is capable of.'

Percy was fully aware of this. Since his sister had died he had always felt the pressure to do the right thing, earn oodles of dosh to keep the old family seat from crumbling and find a wife to breed with. He had managed the earning oodles bit, but as far as a wife and children were concerned, he really just wanted to have fun. When he met Liberty she was so stunning that he had instantly fallen in lust, and he realised that she would be an asset to his family. He had thought that she would toe the line, enjoy the lifestyle he could give her, and be there when he needed her. When exactly it became more of an 'I don't want anyone else to have this gorgeous creature' situation he wasn't sure, but he knew in his gut that before his wedding day, he was fooling himself if he thought that a family life was for him. But because he couldn't bear the idea of Liberty being with someone else, he married her anyway, made her 'his'. However, since she had left him, he had realised how good she was for his business, how many of his colleagues said he was crazy to let her go.

He had enjoyed affairs throughout their relationship, before and after marriage. It made him feel naughty, a sort of childish release to take the pressure and responsibility away from real life. Perhaps a psychologist could have a field day with him, but Percy was essentially a control freak. He liked his perfect life, his perfect wife, and to feel adored by beautiful women. It was his right as a red-blooded male. He loved to own beautiful things; his art collection was probably the only thing that pleased him completely. He owned it, could look at and admire it. No one else could touch it or see it if he chose; he would spend hours locked in his private study gazing at his Pissarro. Now his pride had been sorely knocked. If he met one more person who asked him 'How on earth could you let her go, she was so lovely, beautiful and clever, what man in his right mind would do anything to jeopardise what you had?', he would scream. She was just so bloody perfect. Although, come to think about it, she always forgot to pick up the dry cleaning and banged on at him to stop smoking cigars and drinking so much whisky in case it stopped their chances of having a baby. Who wanted babies, anyway? They stopped you going out, and when you could, it was mess and noise everywhere; you had to get rid of the Bentley and put up with sticky fingerprints everywhere, and more to the point, Liberty would have had a new love, no time for him.

Percy had started his last affair when Liberty got serious about IVF. He had read somewhere that the more sex you had, the less potent your sperm, so he figured if he screwed Ginny senseless often enough then he might not produce the goods for Liberty. Ginny had then become far too demanding, as all the best mistresses do. She wanted him to leave his wife and move in. All his own fault; he had given her most of Cartier's stock over the past six months and she figured if they married he would give her the rest, and the family jewels, too.

Percy sat strumming his fingers on his desk. Should he phone Liberty back? Did she now want him back, the silly cow? Just because everyone else thought she was perfect and so bloody lovely. Hadn't she spent the last three years going on about babies, never listening to what HE wanted? Surely it was more worthwhile to spend millions on a chalet in Gstaad rather than on IVF, and a lot more bloody fun. Why couldn't she just shut up, look after him and forget about anyone else? She had given up asking for animals very early in their cohabiting bliss – a pug, for God's sake, just because her mother always had them. What made her think he would walk around looking like a big ponce with a smelly flat-nosed dog on a lead? What would his friends think? Dogs were for shooting, and therefore kept outside – preferably in Scotland.

Oh well, if she wanted to come back it would save on a housekeeper and it would be on his terms – no more baby talk – and she should come and work in his department in the family bank. Then he could keep an eye on her – or even better, not work at all. He would explain that he wasn't ready for a family yet. If she was so desperate to come home, she would have to lump it.

He had also been mortified to be turned out of the Villa San Michele in Florence. The dago prat of a manager had manhandled him out of the place in front of guests and then charged him for the experience (unknown to Liberty, all charges for the room had in fact been sent to Percy, along with a letter explaining he wouldn't be welcome back).

Bloody Italians, only good for pinching bottoms and handbags. After cancelling what was meant to be their trip to Italy, he had managed to offload Ginny, saying that if he had wanted a new wife he would have chosen someone years younger. This insult had obviously hit home, as when he had recently bumped into her at a party (her husband was a colleague from another bank) she had had a rather bad facelift and her lips looked as though she had been punched in the mouth. Neither of which detracted from her huge boobs, which had pressed him against her in the first place, but made her look far too needy and insecure. This was something that Liberty would never suffer from. Damn her, why was she so irritatingly lovely?

He picked up the phone, having decided to have her back. His parents were going to be thrilled after all.

'Hello, Liberty. Percy. Yes, of course it's me. I just missed your call. I see you came home to pick up your stuff. When are you coming back?'

'I'm not. I'm sorry to have just left like that, or rather made you leave. It was a dreadful time to find out about your affair. You realise I was pregnant, don't you? We have no need to speak. I won't be asking for anything financially.'

'I should bloody well think not, you stupid bitch,' roared Percy down the phone, so loudly that Dijon ran behind Deirdre's legs and Custard began to yap and leapt up on to Liberty's lap. 'You dare to try to make a fool of me, you think you are better than me . . .' at which point Percy found himself screaming at his disconnected phone.

'Bugger,' he said, and poured himself a very large glass of Scotch.

'That went well,' said Liberty, and promptly burst into tears. Custard licked them away and settled further on to her lap, knowing she had scared the horrid man away and feeling very protective.

'I'm sorry, darling,' said Deirdre, who had also heard the exchange.

'I'm not. The moment he said my name I simply knew I never, ever wanted to see him again, let alone have a relationship with the man. It is all my fault. I feel I have changed so much through the entire IVF process. I really began to think of what I wanted then. It probably made me very selfish,' sobbed Liberty.

'My darling child. It is about time in your twenty-seven years that you thought about what you wanted. It's just such a shame that you didn't know that when you were younger; but then, who does? You are still so young, with a whole new life ahead of you. Let's have a drink and then I'll take you around the village to meet your new neighbours.'

Their first stop was the tea room. Paul was in the front. He served while Gwen warmed teacakes and made pots of builders' tea in the back. As Jonathan had said, neither of them really had any passion for the catering side. When they moved to the village from South London there were rumours about a scandal involving Paul and a pupil at the school he had taught at. This, if true, had forced his retirement in his early fifties. They wanted to get to know people, and the best way was to take over the tea room. Jonathan had willingly given the tenancy, thinking they were people who wanted to help in the community, and their friendly faces would be so useful for the elderly in the village, with the tea room a place where the lonely could go for a chat. Unfortunately, the rosy-faced Gwen was usually pushed into the kitchen by the bullying Paul, who wanted to leer at the young girls who helped serve, and gossip about all the locals. He had an ally in the doctor's receptionist, Miss Scally. She would come in for her lunch break and, just within the laws of discretion and doctor's confidentiality, through nods and carefully worded sentences, she would let Paul know of any unfortunate who may have chatted too loudly in the waiting room. She loved nothing better than hearing the girls from the council estate come in for the morning-after pill. None of them could ever work out how Paul knew to ask them, 'Good night in Brighton on Saturday, was it?' whilst putting their Coke on the table with a lecherous sideways look.

Paul greeted Deirdre with polite coldness. While his wife

had been thrilled that Deirdre had offered to bake their cakes, Paul hated the fact that their tea room had been so popular since the arrival of apple galette and freshly baked croissants – not because of the increase in income, which was of course welcome, but because of how all the villagers praised Deirdre and said how fabulous it was that someone so well known would bother to help such a little place as this. Paul was the kind of person who wanted a lot while doing very little to get it. Right now, although the café was quiet, he told Sarah, who had been helping Gwen clean the kitchen down, to serve the women while he went back to the till to do paperwork (though actually he was planning to read a copy of *Hello!* that had been left by a previous customer). He therefore was thoroughly fed up when Deirdre said, 'Actually, Paul, we are here to chat to you and Gwen. This is my daughter, Liberty. I believe Jonathan has spoken to you about her.'

Paul looked at Liberty for the first time. 'Oh, yes, hello my dear, what can I get you? Gwen – GWEN! Come here NOW! Get this lovely lady whatever she wants, on the house, of course.'

A bit rich, thought Liberty, as the cakes had already been provided at no cost by her mother. Liberty had a strange effect on men at the best of times, but old lechers like Paul seemed to turn into jelly under her gaze. True enough, he flapped about, smoothed his comb-over repeatedly, sat down and then stood up again.

'Sit down, Paul,' said Gwen as she arrived, as patiently as a wife with a flirt for a husband can. 'Hello, my dear girl, so glad to meet you at last. Deirdre has told us so much about you. We are thrilled you may be moving here.' She placed tea in front of them in chunky, grey-white mugs.

'Thank you,' said Liberty. 'I think I may well be, but I don't want to tread on any toes. My idea was to set up a café, and I would only be doing so if, as Jonathan says, you were thinking of giving up this place.'

'Well,' said Gwen, 'as much as we love it, it's been five years now and the years take their toll. Our daughter Nicky and her husband have just had their first baby, and we would love to see more of them, and it would be nice to have a holiday once in a while.'

'Yes, dear,' followed Paul, 'but money doesn't grow on trees. I thought you could take Gwen on as an assistant?' This was directed at Liberty, although he didn't look at her.

Relieved that she wouldn't have the ghastly Paul around, but amazed that a husband would volunteer his obviously surprised wife who had just said she would like a holiday, and seemingly did all the work in here, Liberty said that yes, she would be needing help, but only if Gwen would be happy about that. Paul, instead of Gwen, replied that of course she would, and hadn't she been nagging him about needing to make friends at the bingo club and getting out more? He was the one who had worked hard in an inner city school while she just raised their children. It was about time he enjoyed his retirement. Liberty thought it best to leave this line of conversation, and asked them more general questions about how much of their business was local and how much from tourists.

'Well, most of the tourists tend to eat at the stately homes they visit around here, those that have cafés, anyway, and there are quite a few tea rooms in the surrounding villages.' *Surely a reason for improving this place*, thought Liberty, but said nothing. She would have to nose around the competition, and try to get an agreement with local tours to bring groups to her place en route to the stately homes and open gardens.

They chatted about local suppliers. The couple seemed to have little knowledge of them, only using the local cash and carry, and after managing a few sips of the muck that passed as tea Deirdre excused them both, saying they must get on, and that they would love to have Gwen over to discuss what she would like to do on another day.

Liberty told them that her plan would be to open in late

spring, ready for the start of the holiday season. With that, they left and sauntered over the green back to The Nuttery.

'Odd couple, but every village needs a gossip, and Gwen is a sweetie. She just needs to get out from under Paul's feet,' said Deirdre.

Liberty agreed. 'I can see your point about them featuring in *Midsomer Murders,* and perhaps that was why I readily agreed to her working for me. But I'm not sure she wants to work, and if I'm honest, I'm not sure I could cope with Paul sitting in my café, taking up a table day after day, as he strikes me as a lazy so-and-so who would delight in free meals, which he would no doubt persuade Gwen to slide to him when I wasn't looking. So I'm not sure she's the right person to assist me.'

Deirdre suggested that they should wait and see. 'Who knows, she may have killed him by then and we won't have to worry!'

18

As they crossed the green, they were passed by Miss Scally, wobbling along on her bicycle on her way for lunch at the tea room. She had a pointy face like a witch, a too large nose and scraped back steel-grey hair and not a scrap of make-up. Hers was the kind of face that frightened children and stopped hypochondriacs from making too many extra appointments with the doctor. She turned and smiled at them with one side of her mouth, a smile that had no intention of reaching her eyes, and said, 'Hello, lovely day when you have the time to enjoy it', implying that she worked far too hard, and off she wobbled, ready for a good bitch with Paul, whom she knew hated the elegant Deirdre and hoped now also hated the far too beautiful daughter.

'Cow,' said Deirdre. 'Dr Brown is a lovely man. God knows she must be good at her job, as I'm sure she flew into the village on a broomstick. All she does is moan, gossip with Paul and make anyone who dares to get sick and ask her for an appointment feel awful.'

As they walked they giggled about how funny villages were, and Deirdre said she still loved the place, and then asked Liberty if she would like to help with her class that afternoon – bored housewives wanting new repertoires for their dull dinner parties. 'They always phone up saying they want to learn to cook more elaborate dishes, when what they really want is to meet other bored housewives and talk about Botox and boast that their husbands earn more than anyone else in the room. They only want simple things to cook so they can spend more time getting ready, which may be sensible – but then why not just buy a cookery book! I used to teach the cordon bleu method; now I feel like Delia Smith telling them to try instant mash and tinned mince.'

'No, do you really do that?'

'No, of course not, but I may as well. It's really strange; the more cookery shows there are on television, the less people seem to want to cook. Nigella makes everyone want to look like her and have a one hundred thousand pound kitchen to work in. Jamie encourages enthusiasm for eating his type of food, but it's directed at an age group who will be working their butts off and want to go for a drink after work, not get home and make a "pukka suppa" for their friends.' Liberty smiled at her mother's use of slang, the words so unwilling to drop off her tongue she made them sound like unpleasant smells.

'I think I enjoy teaching the children more. As I don't really need the income from the bored housewife brigade, I may give up advertising these afternoon classes.'

'Who is coming today?'

'A small group of six women, down from London. They are staying at the Hotel du Vin in Tunbridge Wells, and as far as I can gather their husbands are shooting somewhere and they want something to do. Spa day yesterday; today, learn to bake a new cake, that sort of thing.'

'I think I'll give it a miss, if you don't mind. I want to check out some of the competition. I also need to contact my solicitor just in case I can buy Duck End, and contracts have to be drawn up for the old butcher's shop. It's all so exciting! It must be fate. I thought I would be trawling the country for months looking for the right location, and it's here under your nose. You won't mind my being so close, will you?'

Liberty looked worried; she hadn't thought of her mother's toes, and now she seemed to be treading on them.

'Don't be silly!' Deirdre turned and smiled warmly at her daughter. 'It's a dream come true for any parent; in fact, I'm almost sad you have to move out. It's been lovely having you home these few days.'

They hugged, and then before either of them started weeping mascara on the other's shoulder, they parted.

'Lots to do! I'll be back for drinks before we go to Jonathan's,' called Liberty as she raced to her car, unwilling to show her mother how ridiculously emotional she had become. She had never been fond of dramatic emotional outbursts, and now she could barely drink a cup of tea without thinking how pretty the colour was and tears welling up as she embraced the beauty of the world. *I'm pathetic*, she told herself, but it made her smile.

She spent a useful afternoon visiting busy tea rooms, some in towns and villages, some located at the many houses and gardens open to the public. There were quite a few National Trust properties, and these especially seemed to have made an effort to improve the quality of their produce. They varied considerably, most selling fairly good scones and cakes, and fairly good tea and coffee. Liberty felt she had a niche for her type of food, which would include excellent tea and coffee, a good selection of savouries for breakfast and lunch and afternoon teas, along with breads and pastries. She understood that most tourists were happy to be passed off with fairly good, something that was just a tummy filler before the next ramble or stately home. But she wanted to attract the real foodie. If tourists thought paying for good quality was unnecessary, then they could go elsewhere; she would be happy feeding people who appreciated good food. She was aware, however, that it would take a while to bring these customers in and to build up a reputation. She must work out a budget for advertising, and check out the local newspapers and magazines.

Liberty then spent a quarter of an hour on the phone with her solicitor in London. She sat in Deirdre's office, Dijon and Custard at her feet, feeling like a stranger. She no longer knew the woman she had been only a few months ago. When Rebecca Knowles-Giles, her solicitor, said she would forward all her papers and her will to the new solicitor she had chosen in Tunbridge Wells for convenience, and wished her good luck for the future, she felt another string being cut from her previous life. No going back now. She then phoned the estate agent Jonathan had mentioned and asked whether he had heard from the Smythes, the people who were selling Duck End.

'Yes,' said Tim Beakes, the agent. 'I think it might be a mistake to show an interest in the property before it actually goes on the market. They want a million and three quarters, quite a lot for that house. I phoned a chum of mine at Savills, and he agreed one and a quarter is more realistic.'

'Right, thank you. Once you have spoken to them and they put it on the market, offer one and a quarter as soon as you can. I can exchange in a week. No offers. See what they say.'

As much as Liberty desperately wanted Duck End, she wasn't going to be taken for a fool. She knew, thanks to Jonathan, the Smythes had already bought in Marbella, and they must know the market was iffy. She hoped they would be pleased to be rid of it, and crossed her fingers and all her toes then said a little prayer.

Her watch and her need for a glass of wine told her it was six o'clock. With the thought that Deirdre must finish her class soon, she ran upstairs to freshen up in readiness for supper at Jonathan's. Knowing it would be a simple kitchen meal, Liberty showered and slipped on a warm pair of velvet jeans, over-the-knee boots and a pale grey cashmere sweater that made her green eyes sparkle and glow. She also grabbed a pashmina, remembering that if you were further than a metre away from either the Aga or fireplace, Denhelm was freezing. Her hot shower and blow-dry would keep her going.

As she descended the staircase, mulling over the events of her extraordinary day – Percy, house buying, tea room planning – she tingled with excitement and nerves, not sure which was more prevalent. Trying not to think of Percy, she concentrated on Duck End, which at the moment was more on her mind than the tea room. She had concentrated for so long on food, menus and worrying whether she would be able to succeed in business, that now she felt like nesting. She had never had her own home; in fact, thinking about it, she had never lived alone, apart from her time in halls at uni. Now she felt able to bask in the excitement of her first home. She couldn't wait to get J-T down to have a look, and she must start thinking of furnishings. It excited her to think of making a comfortable, hopefully beautiful and cosy home that she could retreat to when all got too much in the café or to wallow in the bath on her days off, which she was realising would be few and far between.

If she got the cottage sorted, then she could concentrate on the café; she was already organised enough to know how she wanted that to look, and what equipment she would need, thanks to her father's many lists. Through previous research and Alain's excellent help she knew where she was going for the industrial cooker, fridges and other equipment, and with no need of any loan from a bank she had created a business plan that would remain for her eyes only: what she hoped to turn over in the first five years, and where she saw herself going. She didn't want to begin to think of failure, but at least this way only she would know if she hadn't reached her targets. She also knew that she wanted to use some of Deirdre's walled kitchen garden produce, and she hoped to discuss the possibility of using some of Denhelm's acreage for a small allotment, maybe even extending this to keeping a few chickens for eggs. Anyway, she was more excited in the expectation of hearing all about Savannah, Grahame and Edmund. Stuffed shirt that he was at the age of twelve, she wondered what he had turned into.

As she entered the kitchen she snorted with laughter. What on earth? There were six women and her mother standing round the big scrubbed table. Not a jot of food to be seen and none of the normal aromas of baking could be detected. Instead, they were all holding cocktail shakers and standing beside Martini glasses. From the glazed, giggling state of them they had already tasted a few.

'Darling! Do come in,' said Deirdre, 'we are now trying out an espresso Martini.'

'Yes, we are,' chimed a very attractive brunette, about Liberty's age. 'We have drunk one with a twist, one chocolate and something else which I forget.'

'A dirty one,' screeched another well-dressed woman, and they all burst into fits of laughter.

'I believe you,' replied Liberty, gazing at the bottles, olives and cut lemons lying on several chopping boards. 'And exactly what have you got on your faces?' They all looked rather like sticky ghosts.

'Well, Denise here went to a spa yesterday, and her beautician said that honey and egg white were as good and effective as any face mask, so we used the whites for that and the yolks for a much-needed prairie oyster,' said Deirdre with a laugh. 'Come on, do try one. The girls weren't at all interested in cooking. Their husbands had booked them in for a session to get them out of their hair, so I thought we may as well just have fun. Go on, try the chocolate Martini,' she insisted, thrusting a glass of dark brown goo into Liberty's hand.

'Oh. Well . . . maybe, but can I have a lemon one?' *If you can't beat 'em, join 'em*, she thought.

An hour later she was feeling relieved that she would not be spending her days like Denise and her friends. Obviously all married to successful, work crazy City types like Percy, they seemed only to be able to chat about the latest fashion collections, who was the best doctor to go to for Botox, eye or bottom lifts and fillers, then Pilates and how they would simply die if they had the children at home while they were so busy fundraising and socialising with their husbands. There was simply not enough time in the day, and summer holidays were only made bearable with pony club to keep the little darlings away, and how much they were dreading the annual ski trip with or without the children, because although wearing real fur was de rigeur in Gstaad, what if they had red paint thrown over them at the airport? One luscious, raven-haired, size eight beauty was even saying she was sending on the jet in advance with her luggage.

As Deirdre and Liberty shovelled them into a taxi with only ten minutes to spare before they were expected for supper, Liberty asked her mother how on earth anyone could end up so very spoiled and so miserable at the same time?

'It's the path you were on, my dear,' replied Deirdre. 'But I think I managed to cheer them up a little!'

'Well, thank God I got out in time,' was all Liberty could say, with deep sincerity.

As Deirdre shot around, feeding the dogs, combing her hair quickly before the kitchen mirror and sweeping lipstick over her mouth, Liberty was amazed at how her mother stayed so effortlessly elegant. With a quick dusting of Laura Mercier powder and a squirt of No. 5, she was ready. Well, almost. Liberty brushed the excess powder off her shoulders and reminded her to take her apron off before Deirdre added a thick knitted jacket to her neat black trousers and crisp white shirt that amazingly hadn't suffered under the chocolate Martinis.

'Right,' she commanded, 'you drive, it's only fifty metres before we turn up the drive.'

As they hurtled up the driveway, thankfully unpotholed – Liberty hated to be late – she gazed up at the unlit house. It was a beautiful building, part medieval hall, part Edwardian grandeur, that all seemed somehow to blend effortlessly. The house had been loved by its occupants down the ages, and it showed. But there were no lamps blazing their way up the drive, no lights in the window. Rather horrid, considering they had been invited.

19

Liberty could picture the house only because she had spent so much time there as a child.

'What a shame,' she said to Deirdre, slowing the car to a crawl. 'Are they in dire financial straits?'

'What do you mean?'

'No lights. Makes the house look cold and unfriendly. It should be blazing with light. As it is, we can hardly see it in the dusk.'

'Oh, Jonathan is a born again eco-warrior under Edmund's influence. Ed runs some venture capital company that pioneers energy, incinerators and wind turbines. I don't remember exactly, they become so dull when they start banging on about the subject that I usually switch my brain off. The roof of this place now looks like an experiment from NASA, it's full of glass panels and twirling sticks. You are lucky not to be here during daylight. Jonathan would have had you up there on the roof, explaining how much energy he saves and how much the electricity grid pays him for the stuff he produces. I highly recommend you don't mention it. It's boring. Talking of Edmund, though – I noticed this morning you asked after the other two, Gray and Savannah, but you didn't ask after Edmund. He may be a bit uptight, but that was rude.'

Feeling suitably chastised, Liberty apologised, and realised she didn't know why she hadn't mentioned his name. But Deirdre's Martini-addled brain had moved on.

'Do you think I should give up my cookery classes? It was fun this afternoon, but now you are here, with all your grand plans, I think maybe I should do something else.'

'Well,' responded Liberty, 'you haven't written a book since Dad left.'

'Great idea.'

'Maybe they will have you back on TV.' Deirdre had provided competition to Delia Smith on the airwaves during the early 1980s.

'I don't think they would want an old wrinkly on TV; not good for viewing figures.'

Hum, thought her daughter, having just witnessed Deirdre pull herself together physically and mentally after drinking quite a quantity of vodka. Now she was a vision of old world elegance. Liberty thought she would compete rather well with the Hairy Bikers and a sucking, licking Nigella.

They parked at the back by the kitchen door – well, the door that led to a network of corridors and eventually reached the family rooms. There was only one feeble energy-saving bulb to light their way through the gloom of the cold November night.

Mrs Goodman opened the door to their knocking, and they stepped inside. Liberty was not surprised to find it chilly.

'How lovely to see you again, my child,' said Mrs Goodman. Never one to embrace inappropriately, she simply rubbed her hands together in pleasure and led them along the corridor to a toasty warm kitchen. A huge Aga, probably one of the originals, stood against one wall as Liberty remembered it, but she then realised that the dogs, cats and Jonathan were not hugging it and saw they had opened up the chimney on the other side of the kitchen and a roaring log fire was crackling away. Three cocker spaniels and a fat tabby were lying contentedly as close to the fender as they dared on an old warm rug. In the typical style of Lutyens, who had been chief architect in the remodelling of 1920, there was a single long table in the kitchen to hold most utensils and condiments, as well as enough room to seat ten in comfort. Piles of papers, recipes and photographs adorned shelves, as did large copper pans kept in perfect, gleaming condition by Mrs Goodman.

'How simply lovely!' exclaimed Liberty, gratefully admiring the fire. You could only get away with this in such a large room, but the pleasing warmth it gave off enabled her to remove her thick coat and pashmina. She remembered times of sneaking down to the kitchen when she stayed at Denhelm as a child, and even sharing a bed with Savannah. They had sometimes been frozen during the night, and after a day's hunting they would creep downstairs, where Mrs Goodman would be busy catering for the crowds of adults enjoying the hunt ball upstairs, helped only by a few local girls. She would make them steaming mugs of cocoa and wrap them in blankets. Thus warmed, the two girls would often steal up to the main landing and peer through the banisters to watch endless black-tied men and scarlet-coated huntsmen mingling with ladies in beautiful frocks, and they would wonder how people could dress in such thin clothes when it was so freezing cold. If they had delved under the skirts of many of the ladies who had attended balls at Denhelm in earlier times, they would have glimpsed long johns and thick vests, while the poor uninitiated simply shivered or danced nonstop. After the young girls had accidentally disturbed two of the guests in the library who were definitely not reading books, they decided this must be the best way to keep warm when you were grown-ups.

Just then Jonathan came into the kitchen, his shirt sleeves rolled up above his elbows, oblivious to the chill of the rest of the house as only someone brought up in that environment can be.

'Thought I saw your car arriving,' he growled. 'I expected you to be on Deirdre's time, and at least half an hour late. What a good influence you must be,' he continued as he kissed them both. 'Now, what would you like?'

'Um, coffee, I think, and then a glass of red,' said Deirdre.

'Oh dear, another housewives' class? You really must give

them up, you have so much more to offer. Stick with the children – at least they are willing to learn about food and they don't get you bladdered every time!'

'Jonathan!' exclaimed Deirdre. 'I am not bladdered, as you put it. I would just like a coffee and no judgement, thank you.' But she said it with a wide smile as she saw Jonathan winking at her daughter.

Once they were all settled at the kitchen table, a big dish of Mrs Goodman's game pâté and a tray of toast and home-made pickles before them, Jonathan asked Liberty what impression she had formed of both the butcher's shop and Duck End.

'I still love them both. But the agent thought the Smythes might be a problem.' She explained how they were going to ask over the odds for the house.

'I am sure they will come round with a little persuasion. Neville wants my advice on investing in a racehorse, which could help. And if all else fails, I happen to know one of my stable lasses caught him with an estate worker in the Big Barn, so a little blackmail may hurry things along.'

'Oh my God, you can't mean it!' shrieked Liberty.

'The blackmail? Not seriously, of course, but I could just drop it casually into the conversation, if you know what I mean,' twinkled Jonathan. 'Funny how these things make a difference to negotiations sometimes.'

Mrs Goodman then produced a delicious supper of cauliflower soup and cheese straws, followed by pheasant casserole and mash. There was hardly any room for pear and quince crumble with lashings of thick cream, but they all managed it somehow!

'Yummy, a taste of my childhood,' said Liberty, wiping her mouth with a large monogrammed napkin.

'It would be,' responded Deirdre. 'You spent more time here than you did at home!'

'Well, I could say that you and Dad were always working, but really I just loved it here with Savvy. What news of her? I have been dying to find out all about her.'

Jonathan sighed. 'I emailed to let her know you were here, and she wants your email address. She would love to meet up with you, and is planning a trip back home in December.'

'What is her husband like? Khalid, isn't it?'

'Very wealthy; otherwise, not sure really. He owns racehorses, so we get to see them over here in the season. I wasn't keen for her to move to the Middle East, but you know Savannah, when she puts her mind to something . . .'

After leaving her final school in Lausanne in a flurry of scandal, something to do with a lesser royal from one or other European family, Savannah had run away and married a French count. Alexandre had been the perfect French gentleman, and he adored Savannah. Sadly, he also adored women in general. Savannah loved to feel exclusively worshipped, probably something to do with her lack of a mother and a doting father, so the moment she had found Alexandre in bed with the chambermaid she decided that simply being a countess was not, after all, sufficient for her, and she returned home for a brief while.

Her elder brother Edmund had been so admonishing, however, that at the first opportunity and proposal she was off again, this time with a duke. 'They lived somewhere up north,' explained Jonathan. 'I didn't have an opportunity to find out exactly where because by the time we were invited to stay she had discovered him in flagrante with one of his tenants – not a female – so she left hurriedly and quietly. It was after some do involving Elton John. She stayed in London for a while with one of her school friends, who introduced her to Khalid bin Wazir. As you probably remember, she throws herself into any of her passions heart and soul, so she read up on customs, Islam, the Middle East, then converted to Islam and married him. We went out to the Gulf for the wedding and Edmund thought it may be the best thing to happen to her. Grahame and I are not sure. I think she may be a bit of a stubborn, spoiled brat, but she is my own darling little girl and I hate her being stuck out in a country full of sand but empty of her friends and family. She is such a social butterfly – or she used to be. She had both her children quite quickly. Little Sasha and Hussein are just delightful. They are eight and six, and I would love to see more of them all. The biggest surprise to everyone is how well she has taken to motherhood. She simply adores her children. She even gave up riding while she was pregnant, although from what she tells us Sasha now has her own pony and Hussein is strapped in a basket on the front of Savannah's horse!'

'So she has some freedom, then?' Liberty asked.

'Well, yes, but I think she pretty much lives in the desert. Edmund thinks that when she finally masters Arabic she will get bored again and look to the next project. I think differently; she seems to genuinely love this chap, and he appears to be a decent sort. And anyway, now she has the children she has calmed down and feels more settled. I just wish it wasn't so far away, that's all. I have invited them for Christmas, together with Edmund and Grahame.'

'And what news of the two of them? Are they married?' Liberty said this with some lightness in her voice. Edmund, she couldn't care less about – pompous stick-in-the-mud, he probably had some goody two shoes perfect wife and two perfect children – but Grahame, the beautiful Grahame . . .

While Savannah and Liberty had run riot over the Denhelm Estate in their childhood, Liberty and all the other girls who visited had childhood crushes on Grahame. With his white-blond curls, grey and yellow cat's eyes and dark olive skin, he had the perfect combination of his dark father and his fair mother. Grahame had always charmed both adults and children. He also had a winsome way about him. From the moment he was born, he was a natural charmer who won everyone over as he never stopped smiling. And then, as he grew older, he was always kind and sweet and ready to help, and sorted out arguments between his friends and said the right thing at exactly the right time.

Into his teens, he always had the prettiest girlfriends on his arm, and many mothers invited him to their daughters' coming-of-age parties in the hope that he would turn into the perfect husband.

However, Liberty, and as far as she was aware only Liberty, knew the truth. One weekend exeat she had raced excitedly down to the stables to look for Savannah – as usual after only the briefest kiss for her mother – and off with the dogs she went, as she knew the estate so well. She took the shortcut across the fields from her mother's house. They had inserted a gate in the back wall after one escapade when both Liberty and Savannah fell and broke their wrists while climbing along a branch of the old walnut tree in an attempt to get over the wall.

As Liberty raced through the formal gardens, her eye had been drawn to movement at the edge of the yew maze. Curious and thinking it could be Savannah, she ran lightly towards the maze. She heard heart-wrenching sobs coming from the other side of the hedge. She scrabbled underneath it – she had never mastered the way through – and discovered Gray crying his eyes out in a very un-Gray-like way. So shocked at seeing her boy-god upset and unsmiling, all Liberty could think of doing was to hug him. She let him weep on her shoulder for a good ten unspeaking minutes, after which the shuddering calmed and he started to breathe more easily. She was reminded of her pony when she found its companion Shetland dead in front of them, tangled in barbed wire and ripped to pieces by badgers and foxes. It was traumatic for both her and the pony to see the horrific result.

Liberty wondered if it was something to do with his mother. Had he found some memento that had reminded him of her? Her silence enabled him to talk, and it all came out – how he had always known he was gay, but could never give his father the shock or his brother the satisfaction of failure.

Ever since his teens Gray had wanted to go into politics; his personality suited the profession perfectly and his credentials as second son of an ancient English line of aristocrats and his Eton education stood him in great stead to join the Conservative Party. But this was the 1980s. Scandal was rocking the party the whole time. To do well, he knew he could never, ever, be himself. So what was he to do?

Liberty was shocked. She was twelve years old, had heard the word gay and in theory knew what it meant, but this man was her god! She loved him; she was going to marry him when she grew up. This couldn't be happening! *Pull yourself together*, she had told herself silently. Old beyond her years since her parents' separation, she could only think *this is my friend and he needs my help*. She soothed him as best she could. She had no idea what his family would think, so she didn't mention them to him. Vaguely hoping it would be a passing phase and the two of them were really meant to be together one day, she said, 'Well, if politics are so important to you, concentrate on that and see if you can leave your private life for a while.'

Being only twelve, Liberty didn't quite understand about urges and hormones, but because she said it in such a simple and matter-of-fact way, it made perfect sense to the loyal, decisive Gray.

'Right! Concentrate on the career, that's it, old girl, that's what I will do,' he replied. Liberty looked at him wiping his nose on a lace handkerchief.

'Your mascara has run,' she said with a giggle. The New Romantics seemed to have enabled a lot of feminine men to express themselves rather better than in previous decades.

'Thanks, duck,' he said, 'but you really can't repeat any of this to anyone, anyone at all.'

Glad to have this one thing between the two of them, Liberty knew she would carry his secret to the grave, and she told him that if he got her out of the maze and to the stables she would never mention the conversation again.

Savannah never asked why Liberty stopped gazing at Gray from the top of their tree house, or trying to persuade her to ride past him and his friends rowing on the lake. She simply assumed Liberty had another crush. And anyway, he was only her boring brother!

Gray had since made it up the ranks of the Conservative Party. He was given a job in the Cabinet when the new administration came in, and was welcomed as a peacemaker, a genuine hard worker who made sure to continue his work on behalf of his constituents, promising they would go on having weekly dustbin collections. At the same time he offered incentives to install incinerators in brownfield sites and the energy created from these was provided by a private electricity company to local factories at good rates. He also gave the local police the confidence to clip youngsters around their ears for small offences, and parents, encouraged by this, helped to keep the children off the streets. Most towns and villages in his constituency had installed board parks and youth clubs. People from the community held fundraising events, which were hugely helped by the attendance of Gray's famous and glamorous friends. He was simply so popular that no one questioned how he got to know Elton and David, and the crowds that went along with them gave generously.

So Gray had been the one member of the de Weatherby family that Liberty had been able to keep tabs on. Although, since he left home, they had not spoken much.

Liberty wondered if Grahame had since married, but Jonathan simply said, 'No, neither Ed nor Gray have married yet, but it's more normal for boys to live a little before settling down, and anyway, Savannah has married enough times for all of us! Ed lives and works in the City, but he is hoping to start working full-time down here. He is part of a very exciting company developing alternative sources for power production. He helps on the financial side, and they are looking to set up offices out of London, to save money. I thought they should use some of the rooms here, maybe even try some of their experiments on this house. Have I told you about our heating system? Saves a bloody fortune!'

'Um, right,' piped up a dozing Deirdre, made sleepy by good food, the warmth from the fire and the rather excellent claret

Jonathan had served with supper. 'I think we had better be off home now. It's late and Liberty needs to get started early.'

'Do I?'

'Well, you better had – I don't want you under my feet, cramping my style forever, you know, and we have equipment to buy, not to mention decorators, electricians and other workmen to hound.'

'Yes, of course,' replied Liberty meekly. 'Well, Jonathan, you had better let me see a copy of the tenancy agreement. We should keep things formal, and above board. And please let me have Savannah's email address,' she yelled over her shoulder as her mother propelled her down the chilly corridor back to the car.

'And you call me rude! You hypocrite!' she admonished her mother as they crawled down the drive, unable to see much through a frozen windscreen (Liberty was too cold to wait for the windscreen to defrost before setting off).

'I promise you, you don't want him starting on his eco ramble at this time of night,' replied Deirdre, her eyes hazy, 'especially not after a few drinks.'

20

Liberty smiled to herself in her bathroom mirror as she prepared for bed. She had seen the way Jonathan gazed at her mother, and wondered if there had ever been anything between them. Although Deirdre had been devastated by her divorce, she had enjoyed several flings since, only to end them when things grew serious. She had told Liberty that all she really missed was someone to go to parties with or out to dinner. It was very hard to be on your own after years of marriage and to walk into a room of people without someone at your side; even if you didn't see them for the rest of the evening, it was nice to know there was someone there who could catch your eye and smile – or laugh when they saw you were stuck with a bore. Liberty hoped her mother could find someone, but knew she had never really got over her love for Alain.

She mused about her own life; would she ever be brave enough to enter into a new relationship? She had made such a mess of the last one, she doubted if she would trust her judgement again, and Percy had been her only man since her late teens. *I'd better concentrate on getting the business up and running rather than on men*, Liberty thought to herself. She happily climbed into bed, to dream of vast steaming lines of freshly baked bread and pastries being eaten by happy customers, who thankfully this time did not turn into an angry Percy bearing down on her, as had happened in some fearsome nightmares recently.

Of course, life never takes the path you expect. The next day Liberty went over to the old butcher's to meet a shopfitter and joiner she had contacted through Jonathan. He was going to put in shelves and cupboards along the sides of the room in the style of old dressers, and she wanted to get some measurements of the kitchen and check what, if any, of the existing equipment she could use. While she was fumbling with icy fingers for the key Jonathan had given her, a deep voice with a strong southern Irish accent queried, 'Liberty James?'

With those two words Fred Townsend made her name sound like the sexiest thing on earth, a bit like butter melting over the edge of a hot crumpet. Liberty turned to see a tall, broad-shouldered, dark-haired, blue-eyed Adonis standing behind her. Despite the cold of the morning he was wearing a light T-shirt and jeans, albeit with a pair of heavy hobnailed boots. *Crumpet indeed!* she thought with a giggle.

'Yes?' said Liberty, blushing furiously as she realised she had been staring at his chest, which bulged with muscle in an attractive, healthy sort of way. Fred's blue eyes twinkled; he was fully aware of the effect he had on most women, and thrilled that this beauty was not immune to his charms.

'I'm Fred,' he said by way of introduction.

'I thought I was meeting a Malcolm Nesbitt?' queried Liberty.

'Not sure who he is, but I'm the local blacksmith and farrier. Mr de Weatherby said you would be wanting a new sign for the shop. I was checking out his hunters yesterday, and I have a quiet week. So I thought I would pop up and see if you might be interested.'

'Well, yes, I suppose so, no time like the present. I was going to get everything else sorted first, but we may as well be prepared, and if you really are free at the moment . . .'

Just then a small man in dusty overalls clambered out of a red van. 'Ah, that must be Malcolm now. Look, I really need to concentrate on how to fit out the shop today. Why don't you let me know where you work, and I'll call you later?' Liberty suggested. She was also thinking she could put on some make-up and tidy her hair before seeing him again. Her thick Puffa jacket and furry hat with ear flaps was not the best outfit, really.

Fred gave her directions, which made her feel silly, as he simply pointed to the other side of the green and said 'That cottage with FORGE and BLACKSMITH and all the hanging baskets outside' and with a ravishing smile said he looked forward to seeing her again, adding, 'If you think you can find me!' Feeling like an idiot – how could she have not known there was a forge in the village? – she watched him amble casually over the grass with admiration, before remembering the man patiently waiting beside her.

While Malcolm Nesbitt was not such a beauty to look at, he was a master carpenter, and Liberty spent a useful morning deciding on shelving and display units that would eventually look as though they had been there forever. Malcolm had fabulous ideas of his own, suggesting her cakes should be displayed on shelving looking like a cross between an old pharmacy and a French patisserie, that there should be lots of dark wood and glass, with shelves to hold large glass containers full of biscuits for coffee, home-made marshmallows in pretty colours, and the candied fruits dipped in chocolate that Liberty planned to sell. He also came up with the idea of deep drawers in the cupboards for easy access to plates, cups and saucers and teapots. And he made sure she knew to send dimensions of cafetières and chocolate pots so he could accommodate those.

Did she need tables and chairs? He knew of a great barn in a nearby village where lots of unmatched chairs, tables and other bits and bobs were collected together, all of very good quality, usually from house clearance sales, and he could repair anything. Liberty thought this style would go well with her theme of vintage French, and took the address down. She also needed to find a good source of vintage china, pretty coffee and teacups and large platters for serving food, along with cake stands. Malcolm gave her the number of a dealer in West Sussex, who specialised in the growing market of 'shabby chic'. He knew they bought up lots of pretty vintage teacups and saucers, but warned that prices these days were always high. Liberty knew she had to be practical; if her father's experience was anything to go by, lots of the china would be disappearing with the customers, but she wanted things to be pretty and just right. He suggested she trawl all the second-hand shops in the area and get a mismatched selection. He was very useful, knowledgeable, and deferential enough to be easy to work with. Liberty was happy to give him a deposit, after agreeing on a price and letting him start as soon as possible.

She walked back to collect her car and drove the few miles to Flatfield to look at the chairs. She found the barn easily, which was situated off the road leading to the little village, as a large board was placed by the side of the road: 'Antiques, second-hand furniture and more! By appointment.' She bumped down the un-surfaced driveway and peered up at the old wooden barn, with its beautiful peg tile roof. Only one little door, carved into the much bigger double doors which once let the animals in, gave any indication that this was anything but a large cowshed.

I don't have an appointment, maybe I should get one, Liberty thought, as it looked a little intimidating. She phoned the number on the board and told the gruff voice on the other end she was looking for several tables and lots of chairs, and could she make an appointment for that morning?

'I suppose. What time?' came the rude reply.

'I'm outside. So now?'

A long sigh, and then, 'I'll meet you at the door.' Down went the receiver.

'Oh well, it's worth a look.' Liberty parked a little nervously. The large woman who opened the door looked at her as though they had never spoken. 'Yes?' she asked.

'Liberty James. We just chatted on the phone.' Although 'chatting' was hardly the word to describe their brief exchange, Liberty was determined to be friendly. 'Can I come in and have a look round?'

'Come in, then. It's really my husband's place, but he's not here,' said the woman. 'I don't know prices and what else he has apart from what's out here, but have a look.' And with that she locked the door behind Liberty and walked as fast as her fat legs could carry her back to what Liberty assumed was the private accommodation. Grateful to be left alone, if a little alarmed at being shut in, Liberty gazed around the vast room, which was thankfully well lit, as there were no windows. Crammed to the corners with furniture, it was a fabulous display of different styles, ages and woods. There were hundreds of chairs, numerous benches and decorative pews, and many tables varying in size – highly polished or waxed and obviously lovingly maintained and restored. There were some heavy oak carver chairs which Liberty instantly wanted, but for her own home, and a massive oak table, made seemingly from one huge piece of wood in an arts and crafts style she would love as a kitchen table; it reminded her of a small version of the one at Denhelm. She wandered about, squeezing between tables, making notes and taking measurements. If the prices were right, she would have no problem finding everything she wanted right here, but only if Mrs Gruff and Grumpy's husband returned. And how was she going to get out?

Having had a really good look around, she tentatively called out, 'I'll be off, then,' and tried to open the door. No key, and definitely locked. *Great*, she thought, *what have I got myself into now? Just when I thought I had found a complete poppet with Malcolm, he sends me down the road to slave traders about to box me up with furniture and ship me off to Africa to end my days serving as mistress to some war lord. OK, calm down, imagination. I shall sit and wait a while.*

Just then a key was placed in the lock from the outside, and a very jolly looking man entered. No one would have put them together as husband and wife. She was large, lumbering and downright rude; he, tall, willowy with smile lines firmly engraved down his face, which he was demonstrating well now, beaming at Liberty.

'Hello! What have we here? Come to look at my etchings?' With that he burst into laughter and winked at her.

'I thought I might have the wrong end of the stick – your wife didn't . . .'

Philip Buffington, passionate furniture restorer and collector, stopped her there. 'Ah, yes, Decca has never shown much of an interest, and poor thing hates intrusions, shall we say? Or could I just be honest and tell you she thinks she wasted her life on a promising young doctor who turned to his hobby to earn little but satisfying money. She can't understand why I won't sell to anyone who doesn't appreciate what they are buying.' (*Hence the vast stock*, thought Liberty). 'Anyway, enough about me; you must be Miss James. Malcolm rang and said you may be popping in, but unfortunately I was already at a house sale. Complete waste of time, I might add, so had to leave you to look around and remain in Decca's capable hands.'

They were both laughing now, Liberty feeling very much at ease. She explained to him that she was in the process of taking on the tenancy of the old butcher's in Littlehurst, and also hoping to buy Duck End, the beautiful house next door. Both of which would need furnishing.

His eyes lit up. 'Righty-ho, but first things first – I'm freezing!'

Soon after they were wandering around the barn with steaming cups of terrible but toe-warming coffee, while Philip pointed out pieces here and there. Liberty was getting very excited; she needed small but sturdy chairs and tables for the café but most importantly, the tables must not wobble and the chairs must be comfortable, or could be made so with cushions.

She had already put stickers on a Windsor chair for her kitchen and a high-backed settle for her hall. Philip promised he would look at some smaller things at auctions he was going to over the next few weeks. If he found anything, he would call her and she could decide whether he should bid.

He reminded her of Lovejoy, getting through life by the skin of his teeth, charming his way out of corners and no doubt debts too. She gave him a page of her diary with her mobile phone number scribbled down. 'Let me know, but I will call you anyway when I have signed the contracts. Duck End will be lots of fun to furnish, but I have promised myself not to be too disappointed if I don't get it.'

He replied with a wink that was obviously second nature. 'Don't you worry, my lovely, those stickers will stay until your call. I think those pieces will be happy with your bottom on them!' With that, her faith in human nature firmly restored, she bid him goodbye and returned to her car.

21

The next few weeks were a whirl of tenancy documents, sawdust, and flying around the county looking at furniture, china and linens. Liberty was thrilled with Malcolm's work. He had tongued and grooved the walls, to be painted in soft colours. The café looked rustic and the woodwork went well with the beams, which were now sandblasted back to the bare wood, making the room lighter.

Deirdre was planning a party to welcome Liberty officially to the village. She knew from having a check-up at Dr Brown's that Miss Scally's tongue and imagination had been at work. Gossip was whirling that Liberty had returned after abandoning her poor husband and varying amounts of children after some scandal at Radley Bank. This all started after a small piece in the back of the business section of *The Sunday Telegraph*. (Miss Scally obviously had little more to do on a Sunday than read the papers backwards, even the bits that most people put straight in the recycling.) The piece claimed that established private Radley Bank had decided to close its Berlin office now that Percy Cholmondly-Radley had taken over as managing director and had decided the bank was over-extended. Nothing more, nothing less, but Miss Scally and Paul at the tea room were convinced between them it must mean he had to cut his working hours after being deserted by his wife. Had they only looked within the society pages of the same Sunday paper, they might have thought it was really because Percy was spending more time in the casinos of Vegas and Monte Carlo with one girl after another, and had decided work could take a back seat. At the same time as he was awarded his managing directorship, Percy was having something of a mid-life crisis.

Liberty had received divorce papers. There was nothing nice about Percy now. He had requested a divorce on the grounds of her unreasonable behaviour, demanding that all property previously belonging to the Cholmondly-Radley family be returned. The only item she had of theirs was her engagement ring, but these papers would be in the public domain, and any nosy journalist prompted by Percy could gain the impression that Liberty had legged it with the family heirlooms.

Liberty just wanted it over so she could get on with her life. However, she didn't sign the papers; as much as she still blamed herself for bumbling into the unsuitable marriage, and felt guilty towards Percy for messing him and his family around, she didn't feel that she could end it now, for some reason. She tucked the papers under her bed, for want of a better place, to contemplate later. Her mother, curious at this response, imagined it was a head in the sand reaction, and that Liberty would work out what she wanted in her own time. Although some of Deirdre's concerns had been swept aside by Percy's lawyer's statement that, as Liberty was not claiming financial support from his client, his client would not seek likewise, she was terrified her daughter might decide to go back to her old life, but she kept her thoughts to herself.

Liberty had sent Mrs Stickybunns a birthday card and received the very sad news by way of a return note that Cecil was seriously ill with cancer and he and Isabelle had retreated to Anstley Hall in an attempt to cope with the horrors of chemotherapy through lots of fresh air. The dutiful son had not been seen, and Isabelle had been nursing Cecil on her own, refusing outside help as she knew her husband was too proud for that. Mrs Stickybunns wrote she was sure Mrs CR was doing too much, but for the time being they were coping and she would keep Liberty informed. She reassured Liberty that Isabelle still thought very fondly of her daughter-in-law, and they would love to see her if she was ever passing.

Liberty had been putting off Deirdre's plans of a party, not feeling in a celebratory mood. She felt awful about Cecil, and not having heard about Duck End, the only positive note was that the tenancy agreement had been signed by her and Jonathan. The old butcher's was officially hers.

When Neville and Sabrina Smythe, the owners of Duck End, had suddenly returned to the village, Liberty thought it was to help the sale along, but they had simply come to supervise the removal of all their ghastly furniture. Zebra skins and gold urns were seen being loaded into the van, followed by the shiny new suits of armour and a full-sized stuffed bear which Liberty couldn't believe she had missed. At least there must be good storage, she giggled with Deirdre, as it had been hiding!

Sarah had in the meantime moved into The Nuttery. Deirdre had insisted on this when one evening Sarah had gone home only to find the house locked. She ran to the pub to see Tom her husband and Dilys the barmaid openly snogging. If Sarah hadn't minded this, Deirdre wouldn't have interfered, but she was distraught, as were the children, whose school friends were now singing songs about the lovers:

Tom and Dilys, in the hay

One kiss, two kisses; they'll be married by May.

It wasn't fair on the young children. So Sarah, Jack and Amber moved into spare rooms. Deirdre enjoyed the extra help and Liberty enjoyed the company of a young person. Sarah had great ideas for the café and was encouraging Liberty to forget about thoughts of European pastries and concentrate on old local recipes and tarts brought up to date.

'It'll keep the locals happy, and don't forget the children. If you welcome families, your café will be full of grateful parents and their kids, eager not to battle over meal times at home.'

Liberty had almost resigned herself to not getting Duck End, and living above the shop, when she noticed the pretty cottage in the property section of *Country Life*. Over a cup of coffee with Jonathan he explained that, despite his own encouragement and the estate agent's insistence that hers was a very good offer, the Smythes were being greedy, probably because they had spent such a huge amount of money on the property. They had employed a London firm of interior designers with exceptional talent who charged a fortune for recreating a perfect country home, replacing all the wattle and daub fronting the walls. This, by the time they had kitted out the kitchen, bathrooms and gym, had cost as much as the original house. Liberty was therefore holding out no hope, especially after Jonathan had used his star card and mentioned to Neville about his misdemeanour, only for Neville simply to roar with laughter.

'My wife was also in the stable! You dirty bugger, didn't know you were into watching!' he said. And with that he laughed all the way back to London.

However, by the end of November the Smythes had obviously realised the housing market was as active as Ann Widdecombe on *Strictly*, and they reluctantly decided to accept Liberty's offer.

When the agent phoned with the good news, Liberty and Sarah danced round the kitchen. The dogs picked up the happiness vibes and trailed behind, expecting treats to follow. Dijon waddled, but he was dancing inside. Despite it being only ten o'clock in the morning, Deirdre opened a very special bottle of vintage champagne.

'Mother! This is from your wedding! Thank you so much!' said Liberty as she gulped and enjoyed the fine bubbles and instant headiness the golden liquid gave her, something to do with the time of day and the adrenalin. 'Wowee, my new home!'

Deirdre was thrilled to open the bottle she had originally been saving for her and Alain's fiftieth anniversary celebrations. Her own daughter in the village! She was happier than a dog with a bone.

Liberty surprised herself at how thrilled she was with the prospect of moving into the cottage. She promptly emailed J-T and told him to drop everything and come and stay. She needed his eye and encouragement. 'If I want to open the café early next year, I need to get the house sorted so I can concentrate fully on the business. J-T will help everything go smoothly and know where I can find the things I need.'

Her mother, who had simply gathered and inherited bits and bobs throughout her life, and if any space was left, filled it with flowers and dogs, couldn't quite understand why anyone might need help furnishing a home.

'Don't forget,' said Liberty, 'I'm starting with nothing. I really have to put all my efforts into the café. I don't need to be driving all over the country looking at duvets, fabrics and flooring.'

Sarah, who had been born in a two-up two-down which she shared not only with her parents but also, by the time she left to marry at seventeen, five brothers and sisters, thought it unimaginably grand to be able to summon help to decorate, and until Liberty explained about J-T, was wildly excited about a man coming to stay.

'Well, at least it means I am over Tom!' she laughed. 'I will miss you so much when you leave, Liberty.'

'It's been great fun being back here for a while, and being so well looked after, but I will be only just across the green. And I hate to burst your bubble, but J-T is gayer than pink meringues.'

'I will miss you too, of course,' added Deirdre, 'and now you must let me get on with planning the party.'

Deirdre was an excellent party planner. In the days of helping Alain with publicity she had thrown some infamous dos, usually enlisting the help of her great pal Paloma, who knew everyone who was anyone. This was to be no exception. Despite Liberty's protestations that it was only to include the locals – 'I need to know all the faces, friendly and unfriendly' – Deirdre also wanted it to be a celebration of Liberty's homecoming and new business and a huge excuse for opening up the house she had lived in alone for too many years, and which had for a few short weeks been filled again with laughter, noise and family. She also knew that Liberty was going to need some national press interest to get newcomers coming to the café until it established its own reputation. Remembering how much Paloma had helped Liberty during the summer, and knowing her restaurant could be left in the capable hands of the manager Vevetine, she phoned her friend and got, instead, Claude. After a brief catch-up, she told him of her plan and Claude said Paloma would be thrilled to help. Could they come and stay the week before? It would be so good to see how Liberty was settling in, and to look round the café. He also had good news. His girlfriend Evangeline was pregnant and despite his almost hippy upbringing they would be getting married in the new year, so more reason for celebration! It was settled that the three of them would come to the party – the more Gallic glamour the better.

Meanwhile, Deirdre phoned Jonathan. She knew he was organising a hunt ball shortly before Christmas, and wondered whether her party should be held before or after that.

'Why not as a New Year's bash?' he enquired. 'Everyone wants something different. I only hope it isn't too late to organise marquees and so forth.'

'And of course,' continued Deirdre, writing notes as she spoke, 'you WILL persuade your three youngies to come along, won't you? Liberty would be so thrilled.'

'It looks as though the entire tribe will be here for Christmas for the first time in years, so I will attempt to imprison them until after New Year's Eve. Anything else I can do?'

And so the party arrangements began.

22

J-T arrived to be greeted by a flurry of organising. Liberty had taken over her mother's morning room; recipes vied for space with lists of equipment ordered or needed, pictures of chairs, tables coming from auction rooms, piles of linen, samples for napkins and tablecloths.

Custard was using the latter as a makeshift bed and was delighted when J-T crouched down next to her to have a cuddle.

'How adorable! And I thought Frenchies were the only dogs for me nowadays!' he spluttered, as Custard licked his face, ever hopeful for crumbs. 'How's it all going?'

'All organised,' said Liberty. 'Café kitchen's being fitted as we speak, and my star of a carpenter has made a super job of the café itself. We will go and have a look with Mother after coffee. Come and see her, she will be so excited to have you here again.'

Deirdre was surrounded by even more pieces of paper. She was having a whale of a time in her office. 'How I love parties!' she exclaimed to J-T.

'And how simply divine to see you, Mother Deirdre. You are as glamorous as ever,' exclaimed J-T, giving lots of air kisses and a huge hug to his surrogate mother. (His parents had been less than thrilled at his coming out, so his university summers had been spent with Bob at The Nuttery, welcomed by Deirdre, who treated their boyish enthusiasm as she would a pair of Labrador puppies who would have made about as much mess, their sexual preference being of little importance to her.)

'Drink first, or are you being dragged over to Duck End by

my impatient daughter?' Deirdre said laughingly. 'She is like a child in a sweet shop – new home, new business.'

'I would kill for a Bloody Mary. Those trains have plastic sandwiches and tins of beer; not sufficient substance for a growing boy,' he said with a grin.

Over a jug of well-chilled Bloody Marys and cheese straws they caught up with news. Bob was working hard, and Liberty picked up that all was not a bed of roses for J-T at the moment. Maybe that was why he had been so willing to drop everything and come for a prolonged stay. His always cheery, rosy face was a little thinner than normal. 'Too much partying, my dear,' he explained, dismissing her fears. 'Bobbie is so busy and I get fed up staying in on my own. He loves what he does, but we need time together, too. The dogs even barked when he came home the other night. They had forgotten he lives with me.'

'Why don't you get him down here for a while? I insist he has a break, and anyway he only needs to come over Christmas.'

'My goodness,' chortled J-T, 'that would be fabulous, wouldn't it? Can we really? Can the dogs come too?'

'Of course, darling,' responded Deirdre enthusiastically, 'the more the merrier. Paloma and Claude will be here, and as Sarah and her terrors will be at her parents for the holidays there will be plenty of room.'

'Right,' said Liberty in her best organising voice. 'Before we get stuck into another jug, can I drag you along to show you the old butcher's place?'

'If you must,' grumbled J-T, 'but then I want to hear all the gossip and the update on Piggy Percy.'

They arrived at the now almost completed café, and Liberty proudly ushered him inside. J-T stood quietly for a few moments and then gave his considered view.

'It's hardly The Ivy, darling . . . but it's fabulous. Very you.'

Liberty hugged him. 'Thank you. I really needed your approval.'

The large room had been transformed. The huge flagstones

were gleaming after being steam-cleaned by Sarah; the cream painted walls were almost covered by oil and water colour paintings framed in different gilt and woods. Landscapes, portraits and animals gave a cosy atmosphere.

'The wiring is in place for most of the lighting,' explained Liberty, 'but we need to get the right balance of being able to see well enough to serve customers without blinding them, and at the same time creating a cosy atmosphere.'

J-T nodded, adding, 'Getting the lighting right can make or break a place,' then, with a smile and a sideways glance at his now anxious friend, 'but I can help with that, darling!'

The shelves were covered with masses of vintage teapots, cups, saucers and jugs, to be used both for decoration and storage. Pretty ornamental glass jars, ready to hold biscotti, shortbreads and different coloured home-made marshmallows gleamed on the top shelf. The large counter made from walnut and glass would display cakes and pastries and was rather high, separating the kitchen door from the restaurant, so nobody would have to sit being constantly passed by staff coming and going. Liberty had found a settle at Philip's warehouse where customers could sit quietly and read a newspaper without being disturbed.

The beamed ceiling was painted white and the large windows ensured a light look. They were dressed with a simple but pretty embroidered fabric in grey and red to add a splash of colour. Any problems with too much light in the summer would be taken care of by wooden shutters, neatly tucked back when not in use.

The friends continued into the kitchen, which, although small, now contained every piece of equipment that Liberty would need. As she was planning on doing all the cooking herself, space would be no problem.

'I'm waiting to bring the rest of the furniture in until after the health inspector has visited,' she explained.

'It's going to be absolutely fab,' said J-T, clearly impressed.

'The only other thing we are waiting for is the coffee machine, which will sit here, to the left of the cake counter. I'm still tasting different beans. Mother and I haven't slept for two weeks as we are sampling so many. We think Milano, but we have to try each one, and we'll need different ones in the morning and evening. Our own house blend of tea is being compiled by Fortnum and Mason. We went there to mix them to our taste, and I had the best time. I also managed to find the china for my house at the same time . . .'

'Oh, darling,' said J-T, 'take a breath. I do realise you are living and breathing furnishings and fittings at the mo, but your passion needs to last.'

'Yes, but it's so exciting. While we were fitting out the kitchen we were going to insert a horribly expensive water filter but the water board sent someone to check out the well at the back, and the water is the same as Jonathan's, so couldn't be improved on.' Jonathan, in the 1980s, had plugged into the bottled water business and sold the spring water that spouted up from below his land. 'We also found a local miller who stone grinds the wheat and spelt; it makes such a difference and it's so fresh.'

'Darling, you are telling all this to the wrong person. As long as a cocktail and a canapé match my outfit I don't really care what it tastes like!'

'Oh, come on, you eat at top restaurants all the time.'

'Only to be seen there. We gays live on vodka and fresh air. It's surprising that the supermodels don't copy us, really. Talking of vodka, show me your cottage and then I want to check out that quaint pub, it looks too English to be true. I'm sure it's either ghastly and modern inside or a Tardis to the fifties.'

Liberty had been avoiding the pub as she didn't want to upset Sarah by chatting to Dilys the barmaid. But she agreed to have a drink – just a quick one – and then to check back in at her mother's house to see how the party planning was getting on.

23

J-T was charmed by Duck End, which looked so much better now it was emptied of tasteless treasures, although the Smythes had left all of the dreadful curtains, so blowsy they swamped the pretty windows and took most of the light. Liberty made J-T shout with laughter when she told him about the suits of armour and the stuffed bear.

With the honesty of a true friend, J-T said that his usual modern-with-a-twist style would suit the house, but she was better off choosing comfortable, homely things, more like her mother would have. 'You sort of need to fill it with things that look as though you have always had them, lots of pretty prints and ornaments, and I think the walls lend themselves to fabric and trims.'

'You can help me there. I need everything and then some. I forgot I even need tea towels, duvets and silverware, let alone furniture.'

'Lamps, lots of lamps,' counselled J-T, 'to give a soft light in the evenings. Apart from the kitchen and bathrooms, you don't want overhead lighting. Let's make it as pretty as you! It's a dream, and although you say the Smythes had no taste, I have to love their en suite with antique mirrored glass panels on the walls – not that your beauty needs enhancing, my dear, but they would make an elephant's arse look good with the soft glow they create. Not sure about the gold taps, though; they may have to go!'

He pushed open the plush pink taffeta drapes in the master bedroom. They were trimmed with purple satin bows, which gave an air of Marie Antoinette crossed with Lady Gaga. 'I bet they had Pomeranian dogs, too,' he said with a giggle, and then gasped as he saw the beautiful garden down below. The Smythes had employed a gardening firm to design the layout, simply because the firm had won a gold medal at Chelsea the year they moved in.

The garden was a perfect rectangle, set out into different zones. Formal box hedging bordered beds filled in summer with a riot of violet, white and green. At the moment they contained only rosemary and winter pansies, which gave some colour, but the clever paving and design made the winter garden look neat. The Smythes had needed low maintenance, as they had no idea about gardening and were too mean to employ a gardener when they were not in residence. This suited Liberty as she needed to devote all her time to the café. From the first-floor window it was easy to see how the different sections of the garden could look in summer, planted out with grasses to wave in the summer wind, and Michaelmas daisies intermixed with echinacea for autumn colour. It waited to burst into life with careful planting and some inspiration. Fruit trees lined the south-facing back wall, bark glowed from the Tibetan cherry tree, and there was a clump of moonbeam birches gleaming even in the dull winter sunlight. As yet unseen, thousands of bulbs had been planted to give colour from January onwards – snowdrops, iris, tulips and others – ready to burst through and provide a bright contrast to the stone of the paths and the walls.

'Wow!' said J-T excitedly. 'That will be a wonderful place for parties in summer. Count us in!' He had been making notes on his iPad as they walked around the house, and now said they had better go to the pub as Liberty would need a stiff drink when she heard the recommended budget.

He was pleasantly surprised by The Acorn. Very old-fashioned, dark-beamed and low-ceilinged, with a long bar curving through what once must have been two rooms, now divided only by a roaring fire. There was a mix of furniture; tiny tables almost impossible to eat at and a large trestle table along one wall where people had to sit together if they wanted a meal, but lots of comfortable old wooden chairs on the ancient flags.

There were a few locals standing at the bar. No sign of Tom, but the ever-smiling Dilys burst out of the back kitchen, ready to help. 'What can I get you, my darlin's?' she asked in her broad country accent.

Dilys was impossible to dislike. Her bright chestnut eyes twinkled out of a round rosy face, surrounded by dark curls. Her plump, curvy figure was always displayed at its best; plunging necklines and short skirts were finished off with punishing heels, never flats, probably to enable her to see over the bar, as at five feet nothing she was tiny. She made up for her size by always smiling, and was famous for being cheerful in the dreadful floods of a few years ago, when she served sandwiches and pints of warm beer to the emergency services when the power was off for three days. They had eventually resorted to cooking over the open fire and encouraged everyone to help with the village clean-up, followed by a party in the pub.

Officially, Dilys had the licence and Harold ran the place, but it was so popular because of Dilys's personality. They served simple food in a basket, sandwiches and home-made pies supplied by Deirdre, and there was also a good ploughman's to be found at lunchtimes. Takeaway fish and chips could be bought at weekends, and everything was supplemented by local bitter, cider and red and white wine, depending on which bottle had most recently been opened. They would never make their fortune, but they knew their market, and by sticking to their guns they attracted a wide customer base from local villages, where people were upset that their own pubs, in difficulty because of the smoking ban and drink-drive laws, were trying the gastro thing to boost takings. Some villages now had a weekend taxi fund or a designated driver, so between them they could get happily tanked while being served by a friendly barmaid after a hard week on the farm or in the office.

Liberty ordered two halves of local bitter, but J-T asked Dilys for a shot of vodka to accompany it, which of course delighted the barmaid.

'What brings you to these parts?' she asked, recognising London clothes and envying Liberty's cashmere clothing and effortless chic.

'I'm Liberty, Deirdre's daughter.'

Dilys didn't even blink. 'Oh! That's you opening the café, hey? Do we get a discount as locals? Be good to have a decent place to go to on my day off. So pleased you took Sarah in, she and Tom have been so miserable for ages. I'm doing my best to cheer him up.'

Liberty found she could hold no grudge against the tiny woman, who smiled and twinkled as much as Mrs Tiggy-Winkle. How could she judge another married couple's relationship? She decided she already liked the morally loose Dilys. She was tempted to ask what Harold made of things, but was pre-empted by Dilys saying that what with Harold away in Thailand the whole time, her bed needed a spot of warming, and with a gurgling laugh and a wipe of the bar she tottered back into the kitchen to heat the deep fryer.

J-T and Liberty, aware of the locals observing them, found a table in the corner. 'Good God, it's not half bad!' exclaimed J-T, and christened his drink the J-T cocktail. 'She seems a bit of a sport.'

'Yes, but I do feel for Sarah. She's one of the world's workers. Probably had too little time for fun before she had children. Tom, her husband, always did have a bit of a roving eye, but he used to focus it out of the village. I think it all came to a head when the kids at school started teasing hers.'

'Nothing worse than mean children,' said an all-too-knowing J-T, who had been happy to be labelled gay at a young age, much to the annoyance of his peers at school, who had done their best to tease and beat it out of him.

Their meal was accompanied by happy discussion of the

interior decoration plans for Duck End. As they left, Dilys called out, 'We've heard a rumour about your party at New Year's! Harold will be back by then. Your mother always makes our mince pies for Christmas; we serve them before the midnight church service.' Liberty had a feeling she would be making them herself this year, as her mother was not as forgiving as she was.

'What a cheek that woman has,' said Deirdre as they reported what Dilys had said. 'She assumes she will get an invitation. If I do ask them, we will have to ask Tom and Sarah too, and then what will happen?'

Everyone jumped at the same moment. They had not realised Sarah had just entered the room. 'Don't worry about me,' she said, bending down to scratch Dijon behind his ears. 'I had best go to see him anyway. Can't go on living here forever, can I?'

That evening they experimented with party cocktails. J-T mixed a variety in the blender. 'What we need is a get-up-and-go cocktail. Not enough to annihilate the locals, which only ends up with swimming in lakes and paramedics, but something to jolly up the proceedings after Christmas has exhausted everyone.'

'I'm not sure that two parts vodka and one part tequila is where to start, then!' objected Liberty as she watched J-T pour generous measures. 'Maybe a take on mulled wine?'

'Yuck,' said J-T and Deirdre simultaneously. 'No, think about it,' continued Deirdre, 'one measure of a spirit and then maybe some spice such as ginger ale and then top it up with some orange or grapefruit.'

'I see where you are going,' said J-T, 'but do try this one, it'll blow your knickers off.'

Half an hour later Jonathan walked into a kitchen fuggy with Deirdre and J-T's cigarette smoke and a giggling Liberty dressed in a maid's outfit that might have looked perfectly decent on a woman of average height, but on her, with her hair piled up, endless legs and a bursting cleavage, it looked rather more erotic than would be good for most of her customers' hearts. J-T was commenting on how unfair to the human race it was that after months of baking and sampling cakes, she only seemed to put weight on her bust. Deirdre screamed with laughter.

'Do people really use that word bust nowadays?'

'I don't know,' said Jonathan, swiftly entering into the party spirit, 'my grandmother definitely had a bust, we used to put our drinks on it when she took her nap after lunch. But I haven't seen one since.'

He gulped out of a glass he found on the worktop, not realising it was neat vodka, ready for the next mixing. 'Jeez,' he whispered between choking, 'what's been going on?'

'Not much party planning, I'm afraid,' explained Deirdre. 'We only managed to decide: no peacocks.'

'Apart from me,' spluttered J-T. 'And then we turned to what Liberty should wear in her café, and, God knows why, Deirdre remembered she had a maid's outfit.'

Jonathan then made a mock bow to each in turn while handing out invitations to his party. 'Savannah and Khalid are definitely coming,' he informed them.

'Hooray!' shouted Liberty, now swathed in a large cashmere dressing gown. 'Will they be able to stay on until the mew year?'

'That's the plan, especially if you mean NEW year!' Liberty had the grace to blush, realising she must be a little intoxicated. Jonathan went on, 'She is so excited to see you again, and can't wait to introduce you to the children. Mrs Goodman is cleaning out the attic of all the old toys, and opening up the nursery.'

'Do they have a nanny?'

'I believe they have everything. A nanny for each child, a cook, maids, a chauffeur. Savannah isn't allowed to drive. Nothing about the law there; it's Khalid's wish that she doesn't.'

'What a blessing to other road users,' said Deirdre, remembering the screech of brakes that used to be Savannah's calling card.

Liberty collected loaves of bread, cheeses and charcuterie from the pantry in the hope of warding off hangovers while she and J-T agreed that parties in the country were always so much more exciting than those in town. 'Probably because the ones we go to are in such beautiful houses,' commented J-T.

'Not mine,' said Jonathan. 'It will be filled with moth-eaten hunting jackets and ancient frocks. Don't forget to put your thermals on underneath. It's bloody cold in that house, whatever we do to warm it through.'

'But people love to wear their best,' said Liberty, 'and we are so looking forward to it.'

24

A dark cloud of hangover somewhat oppressed the mood of the party organisers the following day. Liberty served frequent coffees to her mother and J-T, who were busy trying to address envelopes. They had chosen pale green ones to match the printed invitations from Smithson's. J-T discovered he had buttoned his shirt askew, and Deirdre realised that her top and tailing was somewhat squint.

After lots of coffee, a big breakfast and eventually a strong Bloody Mary as nothing else worked, J-T and Deirdre perked up.

'Let's go and shop,' suggested J-T. 'It's what I do best, and I'm certainly not doing justice to these envelopes – my handwriting looks as though it's written by a drunk.'

Liberty smiled and said, 'I cannot fathom why.' Sticking his tongue out at his unfeeling friend he said he would run over to the cottage to take some measurements. 'And let's go suss out the antique shops in Tunbridge Wells, then we can have lunch.'

'I think hangover shopping sounds great,' replied Liberty. 'But we don't want twelve tallboys just because you think the name amusing,' she said, giggling. She was beginning to feel normal again.

Liberty drove, as she hadn't had a drink since the evening before.

On the way, J-T was busy on his iPad, and found out there was an open sale at a renowned auction house that afternoon. 'We didn't miss a preview as it sounds like a one-off; worth a look, though.' They had decided to lunch at Thackeray's restaurant on Deirdre's recommendation – an excellent one, as it turned out. They ordered from the set menu and enjoyed eating in the old building that was once home to William Thackeray, and had for many years been Alain's closest geographical competitor.

J-T studied the auction catalogue on his iPad throughout the meal, and as Liberty pointed out over her glass of Pellegrino, he seemed remarkably competent despite the two bottles of Pouilly-Fumé he and Deirdre had indulged in. He made a mark against something, and said, ignoring Liberty's remark, 'These sales are funny. The dealers come along in the hope of finding a missed treasure, some of them for a possible profit, and there are people like us who know what we like but rely on the auction house's honesty, and there are the sweet old ladies who have fallen for something they could never afford but want to see it and stay in the hope it will go for a fiver and look fabulous in their cottage.'

'What about the wealthy ones?'

'They rely mostly on decorators and designers like me. But the really, really wealthy, of course, are after investment pieces, and only go to specialist sales, or more likely have someone to bid for them. Apparently, there are vast warehouses in China stuffed to the roofs with Chippendale furniture and Bordeaux wines that will never see the light of day, but sit and make money by merely existing. Decades ago the Yanks were buying the stuff, now it's the Chinese. And by the way, darling,' J-T added, smirking at Liberty, 'if I couldn't work competently with a good skinful inside me, I wouldn't be able to cope with most of my clients. I hope you aren't going to turn all virtuous on me now!'

Deirdre smiled into her coffee but Liberty was somewhat cautious about letting J-T loose with their bidding card.

They were outbid on the bookcase Liberty had wanted. Obviously, someone somewhere knew something about it, as it was a phone bid that won the piece at twelve times the reserve price, after a long battle with a Kirstie Allsopp lookalike standing at the back. But Liberty came away with a charming leggy mahogany dining table, shining like a conker with a patina you could see your face in. It had been loved and used, and could seat eight with ease.

She hated the 'matching' chairs that someone had placed with it, so refrained from bidding for them, but she fell instantly in love with a grandfather clock, so she ignored J-T's pleas to wait for a specialist to advise her before buying such a piece. When the sharply dressed Allsopp lookalike, who was eying her sideways, told her the workings were not the originals and offered to take it off her hands, Liberty suspected there was something special about it, and replied, 'Thank you, but no, I just fell in love at first sight.'

J-T nudged her in the ribs and said, 'You must have got something there. I told you that you didn't need me!' But his pride was salvaged when she bought a fabulous tallboy for the bedroom and a few side tables under his guidance.

'Right, job well done – now back home,' said Liberty when she had paid and given the delivery men directions and told them she would meet them at the cottage door first thing the following morning.

'What fun!' said Deirdre, feeling envious at the purchases. 'Maybe I should redo my house.'

'No!' shouted J-T and Liberty simultaneously. 'It's perfect, and it's absolutely you,' said Liberty, 'and you are not allowed to improve on it, because you can't.'

'Although,' put in J-T, unable to resist, 'I could show you some fabric samples you might like to jazz up your morning room, and the dining room is a little dated.'

Liberty scowled at him, but drove them home, happily excited to think of her very own grandfather clock ticking in the hall. It would bring the cottage to life. Then she fell to musing, as the other two slept, that there was really no point in filling a home with fabulous things if she was working all hours, and there was nobody else to see them. But she followed this with a mental kick in the shins and reminded herself that at last she had her own home, somewhere she loved, in a village she adored. She knew her home would welcome her back at the end of a hard day's work with a hot bath and cocoa if that's what she felt like. No point worrying now, she had made her bed; now she would buy one . . .

Deirdre was only pretending to sleep, realising she knew exactly what to get Liberty for Christmas, now only two weeks away.

J-T snored away, but in his dreams he measured, brought in decorators, placed furniture in Duck End as it arrived and made a lovely home for his friend.

Over the next few days, Liberty sketched catering kitchen designs which J-T softened and domesticated, and the result was a mix of steel, walnut and soft green paintwork. The old gym in the basement was to be a huge pantry and storeroom, with a laundry section at the back. There would also be a wine fridge in a corner. 'Very important,' agreed J-T and Deirdre. J-T got on with work; he completed the ground floor designs, which combined greens and gold and cleverly took the eye from the window to the garden and back into the house. Soft raspberry accents added warmth along with dark furniture and a mix of old and new paintings collected from various junk shops and art dealers. Liberty loved to mix styles.

She was thrilled with all the ideas, and the bits and pieces they found on shopping expeditions up to London and down through West Sussex; and although eager to move in to Duck End, was quite pleased her bed would only be delivered in mid January along with all J-T's soft furnishings, giving her the excuse to remain in her mother's house and avoid the insecurity of stepping into the unknown. She feared loneliness but knew that once she opened the café she wouldn't have time to notice she was alone, and something in her relished that.

The café itself was almost finished. She was pleased with her pretty, mismatched floral crockery combined with Provençal patterning for a happy balance of femininity and modern luxury.

She certainly didn't want to frighten away male customers, who tended to order more food than women, by offering only flowery china teacups. She was hoping to use different styles for different people. She read in *Restaurant* magazine that a Scandinavian café had hit on the idea of giving their customers their favourite cutlery and cup. The owners found that many people still used a special cup or knife at home, and by making them feel exclusive, repeat business had gone up tenfold.

J-T was still badgering her to think of a new name. 'You really cannot keep calling it the old butcher's!' But Liberty couldn't think of anything, until one morning Deirdre called to her, and J-T suddenly screamed out, 'that's it! You are brilliant!' Kissing a bemused Deirdre on the nose he ran into Liberty's bedroom, ignoring the fact she was half naked, and announced, 'Now you have to introduce me to the gorgeous blacksmith, and you have your new name: LIBERTEAS.'

'That's my name, you idiot,' Liberty countered as she dressed hastily, but smiling she asked what he meant. 'Well, Liberty sounds a bit like tea at the end, and it's your name. Use that one word, it will be memorable – think about it!' And with that he bounded out of the room as though he had just solved world poverty.

25

Just before Jonathan's party, on a frosty morning when Liberty was frantically shopping online for Christmas food, she realised that she wanted not only to buy a new party frock for herself, but also some sort of gift for Savannah's children, as she had missed their christenings, or whatever ceremony they had in their Muslim country. She didn't want to search for either online, so she set off for the London train. As she stood stamping her booted feet on the platform, a deep Irish voice warmed her soul by saying softly, 'So you couldn't find me, then?'

She turned and once again found herself looking into the twinkling eyes of Fred the blacksmith. After stammering a few excuses she mentally shook herself and pulled herself together. He really was utterly gorgeous. What on earth was he doing hiding in a forge in the middle of deepest Sussex? She emerged from her thoughts and realised he was asking her where she was off to. 'Not running back to town, surely?' But he spoke with laughter in both his eyes and his voice.

'That's it, can't stand the country a day longer!'

They sat together in the train and for the first time in her life Liberty didn't mind her private travelling space being invaded. They chatted happily into the suburbs of the city, he telling her about coming over from Tipperary to work for a famous racehorse trainer, when aged eighteen he fell on a gallop and broke his back. All dreams of being a national hunt jockey were washed away in minutes of writhing agony. During his prolonged recovery, to strengthen his upper body he became apprenticed to the blacksmith who served the yard. He still desperately wanted to be close to his beloved horses and to prove himself worthy, so he worked hard for his mentor and saviour Dick Bumble. 'Yes,' he said, laughing, 'that really was his name.'

When Mr Bumble retired a few years ago he had left his forge and all the equipment to Fred, much to his son's annoyance, especially as the business was called Bumble and Sons. Fred laughed as he recounted to Liberty with a wide smile that he had always tried to persuade Dick to drum up more business by changing the name, and putting in a bit of advertising. Fred had returned from a holiday in Mexico with T-shirts from a bar called Dick's Halfway Inn. This made everyone in the village roar with laughter, but sadly Dick Bumble was a traditionalist who didn't care tuppence for making chandeliers for the rich and providing luxury goods.

Dick retired, happy in the knowledge that Fred would work hard and enjoy modernising the forge with his hanging baskets and whatever else was in fashion. For his part, Fred had no wish at all to leave and head back to Ireland. He felt blessed to be given such an opportunity from such an amazing man.

'And what of his son?' enquired Liberty, genuinely impressed by Fred's story.

'Oh, a good smack on the chin sorted him out,' he replied, and for the first time Liberty saw no smile as he spoke. He asked little about her, and she surmised that he had heard enough from village gossip so didn't need to question her. She did find it strangely attractive that this man should be happy to talk, but ask no nosy questions about what she had done in the past. She had been blinded by a pair of twinkling turquoise eyes and a hot body so was unaware of Fred's blatant flirting and teasing. At Paddington, he said, 'Will you be here all day?'

'I was planning to get the four-thirty back.'

'You don't fancy having some dinner together and staying in town, then?'

Liberty blushed and then realised she might be assuming far too much.

'You don't mean . . .?'

'Well, yes, I do mean. You are a very attractive young lady, and I would be silly to miss an opportunity like this.'

'Oh, I don't know . . .' She stumbled with her words.

'There you go again, Miss James. Nobody would think you were a high-flying career woman. I'll leave you to your shopping, then. Meet me before Christmas and I'll have some ideas drawn up for your sign, and I think J-T's idea for the name is a good one. Once your customers meet you, they won't forget your name in a hurry.' And with that he ambled away, inadequately dressed for the weather in T-shirt and jeans that managed to show off his long legs and lean but muscular body well.

Bother, I am obviously really out of practice at this, thought Liberty, almost feeling steam coming out of her ears.

Liberty enjoyed a very busy day's shopping on Sloane Street, where she somehow ended up at La Perla for sexy underwear – now what had made her do that? She fell exhausted into her first-class seat on the return train, laden down with bags from Hermès, D&G, Harvey Nicks, Roland Mouret (a dress for the New Year's Eve bash) and Ralph Lauren (for the hunt ball). She had also ordered from Dragons of Walton Street a vast toy chest for Savannah's children, to be embossed with their names and delivered full of toys for Christmas.

Pleased with her success, Liberty enjoyed the scenery as the train sped south. She giggled as she remembered her conversation with Fred, and blushed like a schoolgirl as she thought of his body. She was looking forward to their next meeting.

She thought briefly of taking J-T along to the forge as chaperone, but knew that in the face of such beauty he would be no help at all, and would no doubt flirt uncontrollably himself.

'Well, hello there, stranger!'

Liberty's eyes flew open, knowing immediately who was standing in front of her, and then, dammit, she blushed again, imagining he knew she had been thinking of him. Determined not to stammer and stutter, Liberty said shortly, 'I thought you were staying in London?'

'Only if you were, my dear girl.' Bizarrely, Fred was now wearing a shirt and tie and was holding a box labelled Thomas Pink. When she asked him to sit down, he replied that he didn't have a first-class ticket, but he sat anyway.

'Why didn't you explain that you should have been in first class this morning?' he asked.

Liberty was admiring the way the pale green and blue checks of his shirt brought out the turquoise of his eyes. His hair had been slicked back, taming the dark waves, and he smelled of expensive aftershave.

'Why did you wear a T-shirt and jeans to town, and yet you are all dressed up now?' she asked. 'Most people would do it the other way round.'

'Well, you never know who you might bump into and have to impress on a journey,' he said and laughed, then ordered two gin and tonics from the trolley lady, together with two bags of crisps.

Liberty gladly slurped the warm drink but haughtily exclaimed, 'How can you eat such muck?' as he tore open a bag of prawn cocktail flavoured crisps.

'Loved them since I was a kid at school. Actually, it was the only thing I did love about school, and after years of working to be a jockey I still have a soft spot for them,' he replied, demolishing the last crumb and starting on the second bag.

He's even beautiful when he smells of those disgusting crisps, thought Liberty after a second gin.

'So, will you come round this evening and take a look at some of my ideas? My dentist was very late so I had lots of time for sketching.'

'Why see a dentist in town?' she asked.

'Another legacy from riding. Most of my real teeth were knocked out in the fall, so I have to see a top man, otherwise I'd end up with dentures dropping out and a mouth like a horse's.'

As he whipped back his head and roared with laughter he displayed what looked like a perfect set of straight white teeth. Liberty didn't even pick up on his arrogance and vanity. She just basked in his beauty.

'Why can't I see your sketches now?'

'I've only drawn them in my small book. Give me an hour and I'll have them in ink on a large pad. Anyway, what's wrong with you coming back to my place? We've plenty more to talk about.' And he gave her a deep stare.

When Liberty arrived home, all in a fluster, Deirdre asked her whatever the matter was.

'I'm going to see some sketches of my café sign, and I have nothing to wear,' she replied.

As Deirdre watched her daughter bending further into her wardrobe, bottom sticking out, flinging clothes at Dijon who lay on the floor nearby, she said, 'Mm, the divine Fred, I assume. Enjoy.' She crept downstairs to confide in J-T, and although neither wanted Liberty to be hurt, they agreed it would be good for her to have some fun. J-T choked on his vodka while being shown a photo in the village newsletter advertising The Blacksmith, one of Fred himself, stripped to the waist, hammer in hand, sweat dripping down his – was that oiled? – torso.

'I am definitely going with her,' said J-T excitedly. 'I have just got to see that in the flesh!'

'No, you are not!' said Liberty, coming into the kitchen wearing tight black trousers, long black boots, black cashmere polo neck, her hair scraped back.

'Are you going to burgle him or seduce him?' shouted J-T as she walked to the door.

'Piss off, I just don't want to look obvious,' was her reply.

'How ambiguous can obvious be?' said Deirdre, but she and J-T were both delighted that Liberty was up to flirting again.

She was surprised, as she walked round the green to The Blacksmith, that she could see no lights shining from Fred's windows, but suddenly the door of the pub flew open and out came the man himself carrying four bottles of wine under his arms.

'Sorry,' he called to her, 'had to stop and have a drink. Realised I didn't have anything to offer you at the cottage.' He was struggling to open the door, so Liberty took the bottles from under his right arm, not sure whether she was pleased he had bothered or appalled that she might have to drink all four before having the courage to kiss a new man – or was that presumptuous?

Fred put on some lights. The Rayburn warmed the small, messy kitchen.

'Sorry,' he said again, 'but Sarah doesn't do until Monday.' He seemed uncomfortable, completely different from the over-confident young man she had met previously; he was repeatedly pushing his strong hands through his thick hair, and shifting from one foot to the other, as though nervous in his own home.

God, she thought, *and it's only Tuesday*. She looked round at the pile of dirty crockery and empty tins littering the work surfaces. He wiped a chair and told her to sit while he poured some drinks. Liberty remained standing and surprised him by saying, 'I'd really like to see the forge.' Suddenly, his eyes lit up, and he reverted to his old twinkling self.

'It may be a little chilly – the fire's out – but I would love for you to see it.' Helping her back into her coat, and carrying her glass of wine, he led her outside.

They had to walk through his courtyard garden filled with pots of dead plants, a small rickety table with an overflowing ashtray as its only decor, all well lit by an unflattering security light. Built into one wall of the courtyard was a set of solid and imposing metal gates that Fred set about unlocking, and upon opening revealed the barn that contained the forge, fronted by an immaculate brick-paved terrace. There were several beautiful old oak barrels filled with winter pansies and rosemary. They stood guard proudly at either side of the barn doors, and beside each was a neat pile of discarded horseshoes and an exquisite sign swinging off an iron bar, of a blacksmith shoeing a shire horse.

'I guess that is the sort of thing you will be wanting,' said Fred, his Irish accent warming her chilly bones as he noticed her gaze at the sign, 'but without the horse or the blacksmith – unless you want to include me as a fixture . . .' Liberty let this slide, but she blushed into her pashmina.

The interior of the barn was immaculate. All the tools hung neatly from a forged pole, all ash from the fire was tidily swept and examples of his work – hanging baskets, plant supports and fire irons – stood along the walls and hung from the giant beams.

Her appreciation of the pride he took in his work must have been obvious from her expression, for he said, in a serious voice, 'This is where I spend most of my time. I'm not house-proud, but I am very, very forge-proud.' Taking a long drink from his can of beer he told her he loved what he did and hoped she would be pleased with any work she commissioned from him.

They were now, despite the residual heat from the fire, freezing, and he suggested they went back indoors.

'Not exactly what you are used to,' he said, looking gloomily around.

'No, but much impressed by your forge,' replied Liberty sincerely, 'and it doesn't matter in the slightest, so now let's look at your etchings!'

This broke the ice, and they both burst out laughing. The drawings were surprisingly excellent. Much more detailed than Liberty had imagined; in fact, she had had her doubts that he had done any at all, and had thought this was simply a ruse to lure her into his cottage. Fred pulled up a chair, perhaps unnecessarily close, and went through them. Some were just a name in block print hanging from a pole.

'I've called it The Old Butcher's, as I didn't know if you were going to change to Liberteas? But I have to agree with your friend, it doesn't exactly sound good for a café.'

'No, but it'll do until I decide, and you seem to have come up with lovely ideas.'

The drawings had a narrow black border. There was one with the outline of a loaf of bread and wine glasses. Another had a sheaf of corn. The final one, which Liberty knew at once was the one she wanted, was a simple knife and fork crossed over a spoon in the centre of a broad black border, with the name hung independently beneath them so it would swing separately.

'That's it!' she exclaimed delightedly. 'Simple, but with style. And having seen your hanging baskets, can you make four for me, with brackets for the wall hangings? And if the brackets could have the cutlery outline, could I include them somehow in the logo?'

'Logo, hey? That sounds chichi! Yes, of course I can.'

'And if you don't mind, I will use it on the menus and my website.'

'What the divil!' he said, reverting to an Irish brogue in his enthusiasm, 'and do I get the copyright or what?'

She ignored this, and explained, 'I'm planning to open by Easter. No point earlier in the year. Can you get the things done by then?'

'Well, I am busy, what with it being the hunting season and all, but for you, no problem. You will have to let me know the proper name, obviously, as that is the bit that will take the most time, but I can get on with the rest in any free time I have.'

He rose to fill her glass, but, unsure whether she could stomach the ghastly sweet white, Liberty said she was fine and should be going. Fred looked round from opening another can of beer and asked, 'What can I do to persuade you to stay?' As he leaned back against the worktop, his beautiful rugged hands spread against the wooden surface, and he smiled at her. Liberty thought: not much! 'Maybe I could rustle us up some supper and find out more about you. Not often I get a beautiful woman on her own in my kitchen.'

So obvious was his meaning, and so cheesy, anyone else would have made it seem sleazy, but as Fred was so self-assured and good-looking, he just made spending more time in his company a pleasurable delight.

'Only if you open the red, as it might be more palatable,' she countered. 'Do you cook?'

Fred looked hurt. 'Is the wine that bad? I hadn't been expecting to entertain, and didn't have time to shop, sorry. And to be blunt, I should take you to eat at the pub – dogs have been known to turn their noses up at my food, but I'm excellent company, and I'm sure Dilys won't gossip too much.'

At this, Liberty blanched and said, 'Why don't you let me knock you up an omelette? You must have some eggs, and maybe some cheese?'

'Have a look in the fridge. I just need to wash.'

As she rummaged around and started to do some washing up to clear a space, Liberty wondered what on earth he was doing. Housework, perhaps? She found some ham and some eggs and some salt and pepper, a few rather squashy tomatoes, ancient garlic, a couple of onions and a chilli. *Well, gosh, culinary excellence aside, I can do something with these*, she thought, and rustled up some huevos rancheros. She divided it on to two plates, and then realised Fred had still not returned. She called his name, and then went into the sitting room, from which a narrow set of stairs led to the first floor. After calling once more, she thought she could hear his voice upstairs. Curiosity got the better of her, and she mounted the first step.

'I thanked you for the shirt already,' she heard, 'but I wasn't going to sit around looking like your toy boy while you shopped, I just got bored. If you want to see me next week let me know, my precious, but I have needs too, and watching you spend your husband's money isn't one of them.'

As she backed down to the sitting room, Liberty thought, *Yuck*. So that was it. Let down by his weekly, was he? So he had decided she could fill in for his regular. What had she been thinking? She put all the supper on to one plate. As she was drying the other one he came back into the kitchen, smiling broadly and apologising for taking so long freshening up. Liberty smiled just as widely and said she had made his supper, but she was sorry, she had to leave.

'Thanks again for the designs; I will be in touch with the name.'

So saying, she grabbed her bag and stamped off before he could smile sexily at her again and persuade her to stay.

'What a bloody idiot I am,' she muttered to herself, frosty air spurting out of her mouth. 'I must look like a fool.' She let herself into the warm comfort of The Nuttery and was greeted by an excited, snuffling Custard. She picked up the little dog and cuddled her close. 'You need to go on a diet and I need to get a life,' she said aloud.

'What on earth was I thinking?' complained Liberty as she plonked herself on the sofa next to Deirdre. 'Why did you let me go?' Enjoying the comfort of a Diptyque-scented sitting room, a clean glass of decent wine and a dog on her lap, Liberty wondered if she was a little spoilt.

'Oh, darling,' replied her mother. 'We thought you needed fun and maybe a bit of slap and tickle. He's such a tart, I know, but a kind one nonetheless. I don't think any of the local girls are unaware of his charms. Just look at how many houses use his signs! They are practically his calling cards!'

'And your mother is trying to pep up your love life,' added J-T.

'You don't look right,' said Liberty, noticing for the first time that J-T was holding a handkerchief and twisting it round his fingers. What was going on? 'Anything the matter between you and Bob?' She was instantly concerned.

'He is such a workaholic, and now says he can't possibly get away before Christmas, and doesn't want to come to some silly hunt ball anyway. I miss him so very much, and he was going to bring the boys down here too,' wept J-T.

Custard took this to mean she wasn't up to replacing the two

French bulldogs and leapt off Liberty and up on to his lap to remind him how gorgeous she was.

'Yes, yes, I know how lovely you are, darling,' J-T told her as he cuddled the wagging ball of fluffy pug, 'but I do so miss my family.'

'Oh, sweetie,' responded Liberty, going to him and giving him as tight a hug as she could with Custard competing for the space. 'We are all sorted here for the time being. Go back to London tomorrow and catch up with Bob. Get him to take you out on the town. I'm sure he misses you hugely.'

'No,' wailed J-T, 'that's exactly the problem. I just suggested that to him, and he told me he didn't need the distraction and I would just get in the way. We used to do everything together, and now all he does is work, and he doesn't need me. I'm going to bed. I'll feel better after some beauty sleep!'

And off he swept, carrying Custard upstairs with him for warmth and much needed attention.

'Humph,' said Deirdre quietly. 'I just feel that Bob's success is overshadowing J-T for the first time; tricky situation. He has always been the star and the centre of attention, so it's going to be difficult for him, but he should be pleased that Bob is making such a name for himself.'

Liberty had thought the same thing, and felt terrible for her old friend.

'It's as though Bob's had a baby and has no time for J-T,' she said quietly. 'Thank goodness Bob is a little more grounded than – as much as I love him – the spoiled brat upstairs. Maybe I should call him, get a feel of things at his end.'

'No, no, leave well alone. If life has taught me anything, it's to stay out of other people's relationships!' Ignoring Liberty's 'I can't believe you just said that' look, she said, 'Let me make us some supper, and you can tell me about your close shave with the village *enfant terrible*.'

26

The evening of Jonathan's hunt ball finally arrived. The village people were in great spirits. Most of them were either involved in the hunt or were tenants of Denhelm Estate, and the gossip was of nothing else. Those who couldn't afford new ballgowns often borrowed one another's from the previous year so they could wear something different.

Everyone was feeling Christmassy too. The lights had already been lit on the trees surrounding the green, and a vast Norwegian fir, donated by Jonathan, of course, from his plantation, had been hoisted in the centre. Traditionally it was decorated by children from the local school, and this year Deirdre had helped them make large gingerbread men and had iced them in red and green. Wide red ribbons were laced around the tree, and electric candles lit up the branches. Pretty white lights twinkled from the old cottages, Father Christmases climbed on the roofs, reindeer stood on the front lawns and nativity scenes blazed from the windows of the sky-blue painted estate houses.

'I don't see how they can afford the electricity!' exclaimed Deirdre. 'It must cost a fortune to light them up. Jonathan will erect a wind turbine for them if they are not careful.'

The Nuttery had been stunningly decorated by Deirdre and J-T. Gold satin bows graced every picture frame. Branches of holly and yew engulfed the mantelpieces. An all red, green and gold tree stood in the hall, although it was rather bare on the bottom branches as the dogs had eaten the baubles and baked goodies.

'I always forget to leave the lower bits empty,' said Deirdre, laughing as Dijon coughed up a red bow and a partly digested ginger biscuit.

The Nuttery party had been invited to Denhelm Park for cocktails before the ball so they could meet the family from the Middle East and catch up with their friends. Custard seemed to approve of Liberty's ballgown hanging in her bedroom, and managed, by means of frantic scrabbling, to dislodge some of the beads from the shimmering gold satin hem, which was now shredded. 'Aaaagh' went up the scream when Liberty emerged from her bathroom, and then in keeping with her lovely nature, she giggled and picked up the adoring dog.

'Are you feeling left out?' she asked, as Custard licked at the carefully applied make-up on her face. 'Why don't you come too? Jonathan's hounds are kept outside, and you could be their hot water bottle.'

Liberty had planned to wear thick stockings under her floor-length dress, with boots. She realised she would have to do something to prevent beads shimmying over the floor, because doubtless someone would skid on them and sue the estate for negligence. 'What a world we live in,' she muttered. She went downstairs in her underwear, relaxed in her mother's over-heated house. She found the sewing box, complete with the button tin she had played with as a baby. Having collected the needle, thread and scissors, she was bending over to close the sewing basket when she heard 'bloody hell' behind her, and a thump. She ran to the French doors, and there, on the frosty terrace, lay a handsome man wearing hunting pink. She immediately recognised the crumpled face as that of Edmund, Jonathan's elder son. She opened the doors to a blast of freezing air, which reminded her she was wearing nothing more than a gold La Perla slip that barely covered her bottom.

'Edmund, what a lovely surprise. What exactly are you doing?' she queried.

'Pa sent me to get you all. He reminded me how late your

mother can be, and he was insistent you all come up to the park before the ball people turned up.'

Only Edmund could give a lengthy explanation to a freezing woman without standing up!

'Most kind of you,' she chattered, 'but what are you doing lying on the terrace?'

'Oh, tripped,' he spluttered, making it sound like a silly question, but he got to his feet in a surprisingly athletic way and said, 'I'd better come in before you catch your death.'

Treating me like a baby, as always, thought Liberty, and offered him a whisky before scooting upstairs to repair her gown and get dressed. She yelled to the others that Edmund was in the sitting room waiting for them, and slid into her gold ballgown, hoping nobody would notice the shredded fabric on the hem, or the beads and sequins scattering around the carpet. *Perhaps they will all come off before we get there*. The colour of the fabric set off her loose brown hair, and showed off her narrow shoulders with fine, barely-there straps. Quickly pulling on her Jimmy Choo knee-length boots, which made her well over six feet tall, and grabbing her fur wrap, she carefully made her way downstairs, not wanting to fall and let Edmund know how clumsy she could be. As she entered the sitting room she realised why he had tripped. The sewing basket was kept on the lower shelf of the bookcase facing the French doors. *Oh my God, he must have come up to the doors, looked through before knocking and got a full view of my bottom and goodness knows what else!*

The blush spread up from her toes, over her body, and to her face; whereupon she did the only thing possible and burst out laughing.

Edmund, who thought he had fully recovered from viewing the most beautiful pair of legs, topped by a well-trimmed muff and peach-like bottom, was just getting used to the breathtaking vision before him when it laughed. *Why do women turn out to be so confusing?* he thought. *Bloody Pa, why send me? Gray and Savvie are the ones who adore her so, silly girl.*

Liberty only saw the now older but still scary Edmund.

'It's so lovely to see you again after all this time,' she said politely, straightening her expression. 'I'm so sorry you had to see me in my undressed state. I am rather embarrassed about it, which is why I can't stop laughing. But it's all Custard's fault, really.'

'Oh, what has the dog got to do with anything?' he barked, and, still unsure whether he could stand safely, he gazed intently into his whisky glass.

Edmund de Weatherby was what most people would describe as a stuffed shirt. Beneath the shirt lay a beautiful body and face, but it was hidden by the weight of the world that seemed to sit heavily on his shoulders. He was twelve when his mother died giving birth to Savannah, his loveable and wonderfully unruly sister. He had spent the previous eleven years being the eldest child, adored for five years as the son and heir, born less than a year after his parents' marriage. For six of those he was also the older brother to the delicate but handsome Grahame, who was born on an Easter Sunday (not the Easter Bunny and chocolate that Edmund had hoped would pop from his mummy's tummy). The arrival of his brother meant he was suddenly dropped from the pedestal of one and only; now it was always 'Oh, do be careful with the baby', and having to help the grown-ups instead of getting his own way. But he adored his brother, and when his mother died he took to making cups of tea laced with brandy for his father, and he looked after the family as best he could, together with Mrs Goodman. His father fell into a black hole when his wife died, so Edmund tried to fill it, while not understanding it at all. When Jonathan awoke one day a year after his wife had died and realised he had three healthy children, an estate that needed to be run and a duty to his dead wife to take care of it all, he did his best to live a full life again. But that year took its toll on Edmund, and turned him into the serious teenager whom Liberty had poked fun at on her visits to the park.

Dark, like his mother, he had chestnut eyes with flecks of yellow and a slightly too large nose which prevented him from looking too impossibly handsome. When he did smile it lit up the room, partly because it was so unexpected and partly because he looked so vulnerable then. He also more resembled, at those times, his siblings, who had become professional smilers.

When Edmund was appointed head boy at Eton, his father had been overwhelmed with pride, and had since then admired his son and agreed to anything he wanted. Not that Edmund had ever done anything to make his father worry. He emerged from Cambridge with a first in English literature and the adoration of most of the girls, one of whom he had dated for much of his three years there. But he moved on to his career in the City, which absorbed his interest and time, and this, combined with his interest in the environment, had recently caused a rupture with his latest squeeze as she couldn't stand waiting for him evening after boring evening. He had recently founded a new company, an investment bank that supported environmentally minded commercial ventures. He was aware that one day he would take over Denhelm Park and the estate, but he wanted to make his own mark first. Green Venture Capital Holdings had recently been written up in the *Financial Times* as 'the most independent-minded, forward-looking entrepreneurial success in the new century. Edmund de Weatherby is far sighted, and advises companies to forget about Now, and to think of Tomorrow. His mantra is: "Don't line your own pockets until those of others are full, and your company is making a profit."'

Edmund loved coming home. Apart from proving to himself that he could make a go of things in the real world, he loved nothing more than riding out with his father over their land, surveying the East Sussex countryside. He would sit by the Aga while Mrs Goodman fussed over him and made him feel like a boy again by cooking her nursery food for him – the only meals he had ever truly enjoyed. He might dine in top restaurants in the City, but nothing tickled his taste buds any more; it was all fancy fashion to him.

He lived in his father's old tweeds and sweaters whenever he returned, while at work his suits were of the finest Savile Row tailoring. Beauty and fashion were Gray and Savvie's thing; Edmund appreciated beauty when he was confronted by it, but he didn't crave it for himself.

However, looking at Liberty like a golden vision before him, hair gleaming around her shoulders, with only a narrow diamond necklace setting off her throat, he was completely mesmerised. What had happened to the silly, lanky kid who used to hang around and do daft things with Savannah, he wanted to know. He didn't like being so out of control of his emotions; it was a new sensation for him. Lust and love swamped him like a tidal wave. He couldn't even listen to what she was saying, which was just as well, as she was apologising for displaying herself earlier, and explaining that her mother would be down soon.

Liberty felt like a scolded schoolgirl again, and remembered the days when Edmund would shout at her and Savannah for taking out Jonathan's prize hunter for a mad gallop, or dressing up some of the hounds in Christmas antlers as a joke just before they were collected for the hunt.

Edmund had thought he was grown-up and sophisticated, but suddenly he wasn't sure.

Thankfully, at that moment Deirdre emerged, an advertisement for the 1948 New Look. Her classic black Dior gown had mid-length sleeves, a cinched waist and multiple petticoats to give a full skirt above Cuban heels. She wore long gloves and bright red lipstick.

'You look stunning, Mrs James,' murmured Edmund, rising swiftly to kiss her on both cheeks.

Why didn't he say that to me? thought Liberty petulantly.

'Stop sulking, and pour the poor boy another drink,' said

Deirdre, thinking Liberty's mood was caused by her obviously torn gown.

Liberty told herself to stop being selfish. 'We only need to wait for J-T now,' she explained to Edmund, as she handed him a whisky and her mother a Martini. 'I told him to wear really warm clothes, but as style matters so much to him he is probably knitting himself a vest from a rare Himalayan mountain goat, or something.'

'Oh, don't worry about that,' replied Edmund. 'Pa has really turned up the heating. Khalid and Savvie arrived this morning and even she hasn't complained.'

'I suppose I can always remove layers,' said Deirdre, shattering the illusion of effortless glamour.

As Edmund had not asked who or what J-T was, Liberty assumed that Jonathan must have told him the story of what she was now doing, and J-T's part in it. But although Edmund knew her marriage had broken up, he hadn't been informed of the house guest's background. J-T entered the room, looking the ideal model of how a gentleman should dress in a dinner jacket. Edmund scowled.

'How do you do?' he said in his plummy voice, and held out his hand to the elegant man before him, expecting an American accent to respond (no Englishman looks that good in a DJ). The limp, dry handshake and the camp voice saying 'Good evening, Handsome', wiped the scowl from Edmund's face, and it lit up with his rare smile. *Oh, he isn't Liberty's new boyfriend after all*, he thought, mightily relieved.

Liberty just stopped herself from gasping. *Oh, poor Jonathan, maybe that explains why Ed has never married. My God, he must be gay too*, she thought. She saved the situation by suggesting they drove to the park before Jonathan sent out a search party.

27

Mrs Goodman had made Jonathan immensely proud. She had arranged with the head gardener to grow indoor flowers in the hothouse for the occasion, and these were now gracing the huge entrance hall. There was a mix of holly, ivy and white roses against the walls. The heady scent of stephanotis hung sweetly in the air, and mingled happily with the smell of wood smoke, while richly perfumed potted bay trees sat on each step of the wide, curved staircase that led up to the open galleried landing. Ivy and red ribbons wound up the oak banisters and huge garlands of yew and holly, tied in swags, hung from the ancient beams. Tall candelabras topped with flickering white candles, added to the best bit – it was very warm!

'Liberty! Oh my God, are you here? Where are you?' called a voice from the gallery over their heads. 'Oh my, just take a look at you!' screamed Savannah, who now appeared at the top of the stairs. She was wearing what looked like a man's tuxedo; however, it was perfectly tailored to her petite frame, and in deep navy velvet. It was cinched at the waist with a wide satin bow in the same colour, softening the otherwise masculine outfit. It just about hid her modesty, especially from her guests' vantage point down below. Her perfect, tanned skin glowed from the exotic, scented Arabian oils that she had applied after her bath, and her blonde hair shone like a moonbeam. She ran down to meet Liberty, clinging to the sturdy banisters as she was wearing incredibly high gold Louboutin heels. She had no need of make-up, except for black kohl around her eyes, and mascara.

At the same moment they both screamed out, 'You haven't

changed a bit!' Then they fell into each other's arms, and now Liberty was happy to feel like a schoolgirl again. They asked each other so many questions, but neither was able to hear the other as they were both talking at once. As they wandered around the hall, holding hands and taking frequent glances at each other, gaoping that neither had aged, and asking how had they left it for so long, they slipped into their old friendship without hesitation. It was obvious to onlookers that they were good friends, desperate to fill in the gap created by years of separation.

Liberty had not realised until this moment just how much she had missed her childhood friend. They had formerly been like sisters, and that closeness returned instantly. They arrived eventually at the long oak table, swathed in a linen cloth embroidered round the edges with dark holly leaves that was serving as a bar for the evening. A very handsome Arab man approached, and took Liberty's hand.

'Darling,' said Savannah, 'this is my husband, Khalid.'

Khalid made a bowing motion and lifted her hand, although he did not kiss it. 'I am very pleased to make your acquaintance, Liberty; Savannah has told me of some of your more tame adventures. I look forward to hearing more!'

Liberty gazed at the tall, beautiful, olive-skinned Khalid, and was strangely reminded of Edmund. He had sadness in his eyes and a haughty, hooded look: a cross between the eagle on *The Muppet Show* and Cary Grant. Before Liberty could respond with more than 'It's lovely to see Savannah again, and to meet you', her friend had grown impatient, as was her nature, and she shooed Khalid away, saying, 'I told you I would want to be alone with Liberty. Please understand, I haven't been home for over a year, and I haven't seen Liberty for goodness knows how long.'

Khalid took her rudeness in his stride and went to fetch drinks.

'So, tell all about ghastly Percy,' said Savannah, turning to

Liberty, who, feeling a little uncomfortable, raised her eyebrow. Savannah mouthed 'message understood'. When Khalid returned with their champagne, she gave his hand a squeeze and said, 'Thanks, dearest.' This, however, seemed to surprise Khalid, and his brows flew up as a brief smile flickered on his lips. He hovered momentarily, trying in vain to cover up his wife's cleavage; her outfit revealed most of her sternum.

'Don't bother, dear, it's not as though I have got anything in that department, and we are not in the Middle East now,' she assured him. *Extraordinary*, thought Liberty, *same old Savannah. Marriage hasn't mellowed her, then!*

Khalid, obviously a diplomat at heart, simply said, 'I am going to help your father, please do excuse me.'

Savannah led Liberty to a Knole sofa in a corner of the hall, and as they sat down they both resumed talking at the same time, Savannah once more enquiring about Percy, and Liberty winning with, 'Tell me about Khalid. How did you meet him? How did you end up in the Middle East? Where are the children? I'm dying to meet them both.'

'Oh, they are fabulous, really sweet. And where are yours? Or don't you have any?'

The look on Liberty's face told her friend everything, and with the knowledge and understanding that only your nearest and dearest can have, Savannah immediately changed tack.

'Little Sasha is eight, and a mermaid; blonde hair, like mine, but lovely olive skin. Always saying she wants to be a pony. Rather like me. Hussein is a heartbreaker. Just six, dark like his father, and thankfully with his brains, too. You must come for lunch tomorrow, so you can see them; are you Christmassing here? Oh, Pa,' she yelled across the hall, 'are they Christmassing here with us?'

'No, darling girl,' came the reply, 'they have their own lives to live, you know.'

Deirdre, who was standing with him, helpfully piped up. 'We have guests for Christmas, so too many of us.'

'Don't be so silly, you must, I have to spend as much time with you as I can.' Savannah grasped Liberty's hand, and all her sadness suddenly travelled through Liberty's body, sending involuntary shivers down her spine.

'Let's talk about everything tomorrow,' she said, hugging Savannah. 'Tonight, let's just have fun. Talking of which . . .' And she related the circumstances of Edmund seeing her again for the first time in years, and his subsequent fall. They were still laughing as the first guests arrived.

Jonathan had been master, or joint master, of the hunt for thirty-five years. He was an organised person, and had no qualms about maintaining his hounds despite the hunting ban. It gave employment to a number of people in the village, and kept several elderly people busy when there were puppies to bring on. So, despite his advancing age, and because he was good at it, he kept the position and was glad to have it.

He had held the hunt ball annually since taking over Denhelm Park and estate when his father Montgomery died, so most people knew the form and one another. All but a few had ignored the promise of warmth and arrived in floor-length gowns, old furs and long cloaks, with various forms of woollen comforters underneath. The castle soon filled with the old county set, younger huntsmen and their partners, and splashes of hunting pink merged with the multi-coloured frocks. Very few wore black. Khalid and J-T's dinner jackets stood out from the crowd, as the local men who didn't hunt were mostly dressed in dark suits. They were taking comfort in each other's company, because the local females would have made mincemeat of them otherwise – despite Khalid's large wedding ring and J-T announcing to anyone who would listen that he was the only gay in the village.

Everyone enjoyed Jonathan's lavish hosting skills; there were apparently limitless bottles of champagne, whisky and wines in well-filled crystal glasses that sparkled in the candlelight.

Eventually a piper marched through the door into the large

medieval hall which served as a ballroom. In homage to his Scottish mother, Jonathan always started the dancing with a few reels. Jonathan and Deirdre stood at the head of a line and twirled to Strip the Willow, and everyone joined in as they realised what fun it was. It was also a good way to work up an appetite.

Mrs Goodman and her team had created the usual magnificent spread of platters groaning with local cheeses, pâtés, hams and salads. Deirdre and Liberty had baked endless loaves of walnut and fig bread. There were tureens of cauliflower and cheddar soup with cheddar-crusted straws to dunk. A haunch of venison lay ready to be carved by the brave and ravenous, accompanied by bowls of chips fried from various root vegetables. On a side table sat traditional puddings – Mrs Goodman's speciality trifle, apple pies and jugs of custard. Liberty was so pleased she hadn't brought the canine version, as she envisioned Custard jumping inside one of the large jugs and licking it clean before starting on the sausage rolls.

The food was being laid out in the dining room, which was nearly as big as the hall. When in Edwardian times the house was redesigned for modern living, a row of barns, formerly entered from the exterior, had been merged with the house by newly built but artificially aged connecting passageways. The result was an eclectic yet surprisingly cosy house for its size. It also created potential for lots of mischief in hidden corners and cupboards, and was a perfect party house.

Young girls and boys from the village serving as waiters for the evening stood by in black uniforms, ready to hand out plates, knowing that when the revellers had eaten their fill, Jonathan was always kind enough to let them join in. Meanwhile, Mrs Goodman still slaved away in the kitchen, stirring the kedgeree that would be served to stragglers, family and drunken revellers to sober them up in the early hours.

Many of the guests had assumed for years that Deirdre and Jonathan were partners, and this suited them both, as they loved a good party, but without having to be chatted up and then let down by interested but uninteresting people. Deirdre could hear old Widow Tankard shouting in Jonathan's ear as he marched her surprisingly energetic body round the floor to the Gay Gordons. 'Fancy meeting for a bit of what-to?' she was asking loudly. Deirdre giggled to herself, relieved for Jonathan that the music hadn't suddenly stopped at that moment. Polite as ever, Jonathan simply carried on dancing and muttered a platitude in Lady Tankard's ear, something that made her smile and nod in agreement and look at him in a sorrowful way. *Something to do with his wife, I suppose*, she thought.

Suddenly, Khalid was at her side. As he gently guided her around the floor to a Scottish waltz, she was surprised at his knowledge of Western dancing.

'Gordonstoun School,' he remarked simply, answering her unspoken question.

He is a dark one, thought Deirdre, not referring in the slightest to the colour of his skin. There was a menace in his expression, handsome though he was, that made him look like the perfect baddie in a Bond film. She had already heard from Jonathan that he was an excellent horseman and a ruthless businessman. He bred racehorses simply because he could afford to; but then, everyone in racing knew how much money was needed to breed success. His impassive face had not yet shown her a flicker of emotion. *You wouldn't want to cross him in the boardroom, OR the bedroom*, she thought.

Deirdre squeaked as Khalid grasped her shoulder so firmly she winced in pain. She followed his eyes and saw Savannah chatting animatedly to a very handsome man in a heavenly dark grey suit, with matching shirt and tie.

'Gray!' she burst out, at which point the vice-like grip was mercifully released. Without waiting for an apology, Deirdre said, 'Do let's go and join them. I haven't seen Grahame for so long.' They left the dance floor. Taking drinks from a passing tray – water for Khalid and champagne for Deirdre – they went over to the reunited siblings. Khalid noticed the finger marks he had left on the older woman's shoulder, but his maddening wife had been pushing his limits further and further recently; he would apologise later. Khalid was not sure if coming to England had been such a good idea after all.

'Darling,' sparkled Savannah as they approached. 'Gray, meet my husband at last! Khalid, my brother Grahame, who is the hardest working Member of Parliament this side of Scotland.'

Grahame and Khalid shook hands, and because both were experts in pleasantries and small talk they managed to hold a conversation while Deirdre and Savannah embraced.

'I'm sorry I raced off with your daughter earlier,' said Savannah, who was extremely fond of Deirdre. 'It was rude not to greet you, but I have been so excited since Pa told me she was going to be here. We have both been terrible at keeping in contact, but it now feels as though we are back where we belong.'

'How do you like living in Abu Dhabi?' asked Deirdre.

'Mm, well, we'll see,' mumbled Savannah ominously. 'Tell me about you. Are you still running those fabulous cookery classes? I must get the children to come along. I'm a no-hoper in the kitchen, and at home all the meals are prepared by the kitchen staff. I'm sure the children think that food appears as if by magic. In fact, I'm not sure if they have ever seen a kitchen!'

'We will have to change that, then,' said Deirdre. 'Has Jonathan told you Liberty is opening a café in the village?'

'He mentioned it, but I need to hear all the details. Liberty is coming to lunch with me and the children tomorrow, and she's not leaving till I catch up with all her news.'

'Will you be staying for New Year's Eve? I do hope you come to our party at The Nuttery.'

'We aren't sure about that yet,' said Khalid, taking his wife's arm and marching her off to a corner, where they appeared to start a very animated conversation.

'Don't like him at all,' whispered Gray to Deirdre. 'Something dark and brooding going on in that handsome head of his.' Then his beautiful, cherubic face lit up as he smiled at her and embraced her warmly. 'So very good to see you.'

He had been close to the older woman for years, as she was a regular visitor to his father's home. He often asked her advice, having no wife to consult. As every Member of Parliament knows, their partners play an invaluable role. They clear troubled, undecided minds, balance arguments, listen to endless prepared speeches, offer advice when needed and stay quiet at the right time.

Deirdre had offered him an ear many times. She agreed with most of Gray's policies, and had a knack of softening his very factual speeches, which helped people stay interested and listen rather than drift off in boredom. This had honed his skills as an MP. He had inherited his father's feeling of duty to care for the common man. There had been speculation as to why he had never married, but as he was so handsome there were many volunteers who offered to be his partner for parties and meetings and so people simply assumed he would eventually make his choice and marry when the time was right. No hurry for a man, is there, they thought. Although rumours of his sexuality had circulated for many years, nobody had dared ask, and his popularity with journalists – he always made sure to keep them on side, as he knew how invaluable their support could be – had kept him out of the gossip columns. His constituents would be devastated to lose the one MP who really seemed to care for their well-being and always did his best to help; 'no matter too small', as the sign in his office declared. Therefore, if there was a scandal to be found in his personal life, which didn't affect his work, they weren't going to look for it.

On his part, Grahame had only been involved romantically with a few men since that fateful day with Liberty in the maze. He found it hard to trust people he met in bars; you never knew who was trying to set you up, and the internet dating sites were impossible to police. He would love Liberty forever for keeping his secret. So sure was he that she would never divulge his mess of a life to anyone, that he was never suspicious when Deirdre invited him for supper and placed him next to a single man at the table. Deirdre was a bright woman and had plenty of experience of the world, but felt no need to ask. She did wonder why he didn't tell his family, but understood that in his profession, you had to remain, on the surface, at least, as 'Boden' as possible: two point five children, a dog and at least one holiday in the British Isles every year summed up the expected personal life of a country MP. She never mentioned it to Jonathan, thinking it none of her business, and simply assumed, rightly, that his silence was more to do with the unforgiving and hypocritical nature of the British public.

Liberty was having a fabulous time, meeting the guzzling, the good, the boring and the brilliant from the neighbouring estates, and local people too. Surprisingly, she found she had missed parties and people and fleetingly wondered if immersing herself in the country was the right thing to do, but she realised it was probably only so much fun when done occasionally. As she was introduced to people from diverse backgrounds, she noticed that most reactions to the news of her opening a café were the same. Most of the villagers assumed it to be for tourists; they all politely said how clever to be a cook, and smiled when she started to explain her idea of a small French-style café-cum-patisserie, selling fresh local produce, simply cooked from a small set menu du jour along with home-made pastries, breads and cakes to either eat in or take away. After the first few pairs of eyes glazed over she decided she was either impossibly boring or people simply had no interest.

What was it in this country? You mentioned bread in France and the whole room would butt in with ideas for flavour, types of meal, shapes, the best boulangerie to buy it in. Here, as long as your stomach was full, everything else was of scant concern. She was learning simply to say she was staying with her mother while between jobs, and doing up a cottage in the village. Now that sparked their interest, indeed it did. How much had she paid, where did she find her builder, how difficult was it to get a decent plumber? *Property prices and animals; that is how to make small talk in England*, Liberty thought, smiling to herself.

As if in acknowledgment of this discovery, she could see J-T handing out business cards. He was in his element; unlimited vodka, dancing and party frocks, and he could stay up all night. He had no idea how to dance a Scottish reel but relished the attention he was receiving while trying. Thankfully for his chosen partners, the disc jockey was setting up his stand and soon J-T, along with the rest of the very merry partygoers, were bopping along to Rihanna and The Black Eyed Peas.

Midnight came and passed; the hunting horn blew out and Jonathan took his place at the head of the stairs to make a brief speech. He thanked all the helpers, the horses, the hounds and the brave people who rode them. He looked forward to seeing them all on Denhelm's wild lawn to either support or join the Boxing Day hunt.

Then all the helpers were 'raffled'. Whoever had the same ticket number 'bought' them for a day. The pretty girls were busy swapping tickets so they all got taken out for dinner by the person of their choice, and the older ones just took it in good part, and usually managed to have their logs chopped or their lawns mown. Unfortunately, one year poor Charlie Tracksthwaite had been bought by Lady Tankard and made to dig dandelions out of her one acre lawn by hand. He counted two thousand and five by the end of the day, and from then on he had refused to take part.

Savannah and Liberty had found each other again.

'Come upstairs a mo,' said Savannah to her friend quietly. 'I need the loo and to powder my nose.'

As they entered Savannah's bedroom, Liberty let out a shriek of laughter at the sight of two very white bottoms wriggling under the bed covers.

'Out, now!' shouted Savannah sternly, and the two young lovers scuttled out, red-faced and grabbing clothes.

'I'm sure that was Karin. She can't be more than seventeen, and her mother would be distraught. She makes goat's cheese and is trying to be a success at it,' said Liberty, frowning.

'Well, I'm certain that I was up to the same at that age, and snogging in a four poster has to be more glamorous than being up to your elbows in stinky goat's cheese,' hooted Savannah, and they both dissolved in mirth. 'Oh,' she said, once they calmed down again, 'it's so good to see you again, after all this time. Oh look, can you help me with these sheets? I don't think Khalid would appreciate red wine stains and heaven knows what else on these.'

They remade the bed, happily chatting all the while as though it was the most normal thing to be doing at one thirty in the morning. Liberty could still sense an odd underlying sadness in her friend, but this was masked by her ever-smiling face as she talked about her obviously adored offspring.

The door opened and Khalid's head popped round.

'Oh, there you are. I wish you goodnight,' he said and left quickly. Savannah's mouth made a perfect O as Liberty turned to look at her quizzically.

'I thought he would be in here with you?'

'So did I. Obviously did something wrong. Oh, bollocks to men, let's go and see if Mrs Goodman has disappeared under a mound of drunken teenagers on the hunt for some stodge. I'm ravenous.'

Her elegant, if too skinny, figure indicated little interest in food, and indeed she was someone who ate to live rather than the other way round. Liberty was now certain that things were not plain sailing between her and Khalid, but decided it should wait until their lunch the next – or was it now later this – day when they could talk openly. Mrs Goodman was always excellent at feeding the children, as she still called them, and knew exactly what was needed.

The candles were almost burned down as they descended the staircase, but the low wicks were flickering romantically as many of the guests took their leave. Residual heat from the large number of people had kept the house as warm as promised, although as the icy air blew in through the front door, Jonathan was encouraging the stragglers into the drawing room where the fire still blazed.

J-T was ensconced in a comfortable armchair, chatting animatedly to an aspidistra.

'Come on, you,' said Liberty, hauling him to his feet. 'You need Mrs Goodman too.'

They tumbled downstairs to the kitchen where they found Edmund and Gray already tucking into plates of fried bread and kidneys.

'Most of the kedgeree was demolished, but there's a little in the warming drawer, if you would like, dears,' said Mrs Goodman as she enthusiastically threw more bacon on the griddle, as though it was 9 a.m. on a Sunday morning, rather than 2 a.m. after a very long evening. Her cheeks glowed. She was in her element, and this was always her favourite part of the night, when the family and others came down to tell her of the comings and goings upstairs. Her eyes sparkled as she listened to news of Mr and Mrs Stewart, divorced for five years and discovered beneath the dining table, entwined and reunited. And new whipper-in James Otter had run the pack of hounds through the Great Hall and out through the French windows, where they were met by a bunch of anti-hunt demonstrators, mostly vegetarian pot smokers, who on seeing the dogs coming towards them had to clear hedges and race down the drive faster than some of the horses. 'I don't think I've ever seen stoned kids sober up so fast,' Gray said, laughing.

'Don't they realise we are now drag hunting?' asked Savannah, at which point J-T's interest perked up.

'Did I miss the drag show?' he enquired of his plate.

'Oh, dear.' Mrs Goodman shook her head. 'That will make the papers.' She handed Liberty a plate of steaming kedgeree.

'Heaven! Thank you so much,' said Liberty, and putting down the plate, she hugged the housekeeper. 'You have done such a fantastic job; I can't believe how much I have enjoyed myself.'

She pulled out the chair next to Edmund and turned to him.

'Hi, where have you been all night?'

'We can't all be social butterflies,' said Edmund with a scowl as he clattered his knife and fork together, stood up and stalked out of the room.

'What's wrong with Lord High and Mighty?' asked Savannah through a mouthful of apple and blackberry crumble with lashings of custard on top. 'He just skulked in the library all night, although even he usually enjoys a party.'

Jonathan had just entered the kitchen, and explained what was going on.

'I've asked him to take over the running of this place, as I intend to retire. I have told him it will be a challenge.'

'What?!!!' was the collective cry from round the table.

'Why, are you dying?' came the less than helpful question from a gradually sobering up J-T. The sobering part had been helped by Mrs Goodman popping spoonfuls of mashed potato into his mouth, but the lack of tact was his alone.

'No,' replied Jonathan, 'not immediately, but I just think it's time. He has to do it at some point, and he needs to apply himself, dedicate himself to Denhelm. And I think I need a change of direction – to travel, read. Enjoy myself.'

'What brought this on?' asked Savannah. 'I have just come home, and you want to go away?'

'But you will go back to Abu Dhabi soon, and you may as well know I have just proposed to Deirdre, and she has turned me down, so I need to get away. I might even visit you!'

At this point everyone stopped eating and stared.

'Can someone please fill me in?' asked Liberty, feeling she was in a whirlwind.

Gray took control. As a Member of Parliament he was used to dealing with drunken, disorderly questions and knew that someone had to take charge before the situation became maudlin.

'Everyone. Bed. Now. We'll talk more in the morning,' he said in a voice that defied argument. 'Let's all meet here at midday after we've had some shuteye.'

As they filed silently out, Deirdre muttered, 'I thought we weren't going to mention it.'

Liberty had been looking forward to the usual post-party gossip, her favourite part – who did what, who did who, so on and so forth. She had also been hoping to curl up on Savannah's bed for a chat before leaving, so was a little annoyed to be hustled out of the house.

'Bloody hell, it's cold out here,' said J-T unnecessarily, hoping to prevent Liberty's criticism of his drinking, as they huffed and puffed their way down the drive. 'He clearly loves you,' he said to Deirdre, as the three of them linked arms for warmth.

'Yes, dear,' she replied, her breath showing white as they approached the village street lighting. 'Jonathan did propose, but I think it was more something to say at an awkward pause than a moment of passion.'

'He clearly loves you,' repeated J-T as they entered the house. 'Did I say that already?'

'Yes, but nice to hear it again, dear.' Deirdre was secretly pleased that J-T was more drunk than she – most unusual – and also to have escaped from Denhelm. She couldn't think what had got into Jonathan, her stalwart and very unromantically involved friend. She felt sad that it must mean he was feeling lonely again. He hadn't proposed for a couple of years now. 'Jonathan will be pleased in the morning when he sobers up; come on, I'll make us all cocoa.'

'He didn't seem drunk to me,' replied J-T, thoughtfully taking himself upstairs.

'Nobody would seem drunk to you!' chimed Deirdre and

Liberty in unison at his retreating figure stumbling up the stairs. His only reply came in the form of a particular finger held above his head.

The dogs looked up sleepily, but had no inclination to be put out in the cold, so didn't even bother to shuffle over and find out if it had been a doggy bag sort of party.

Liberty took off her boots and wriggled her toes into the sleeping dogs' fur; better than any hot water bottle.

'Now, are you going to tell me about Jonathan, or do I have to use torture?'

Deirdre smiled as she put two mugs of cocoa on the table, adding hefty slugs of rum to them.

'He is a dear friend, and for many years we have sort of hosted his parties together. After a few too many he gets a little wistful and starts looking at me with puppy dog eyes. I think that because the family are around, and the grandchildren, too, this year he is feeling a little more emotional than usual. Don't forget, his wife died on Christmas Eve so it's a tough time for him.'

Liberty knew this well, as Savannah had always held her birthday party on 24th June. No one was allowed to mention so much as a happy birthday on Christmas Eve.

'But I have to say I was shocked doubly this year. He has seemed so much more together, less lonely recently, and when he proposed to me in the library, I was taken aback. However, as I was giving my usual speech, letting him down gently, there was a cough from the wing chair by the fire. Edmund had been there the whole time, and heard everything. His father must be feeling embarrassed, that's the only explanation I can think of for his harsh words to Edmund. Normally you have to light a fire under the man to get him to criticise his children.'

'Typical bloody reaction from Edmund. How dare he stay quiet and let you talk about something so personal?' huffed Liberty.

'Darling, I think you will find he knows as well as I do that his father will never love anyone as much as Helena.'

'But what about you? Do you love him? Jonathan, I mean of course. I didn't even know you had a relationship . . .'

'We haven't, not that sort. It's all sort of unsaid and undone. It would ruin our friendship, and I really value that. Anyway,' said Deirdre, smiling, 'I'm not sure I could bear to share my bed with anyone again, all that hair and toothpaste in the bathroom, and his house is so cold, and if I'm honest, there's no spark, it would be like sleeping with my teddy bear. Having sex with my teddy bear! That sounds wrong – come back J-T!' she yelled at the door. 'I feel too drunk without you.'

'I think there must be enough left of the night for a little beauty sleep before we head back to the park tomorrow,' Deirdre declared. 'We should be planning our own Christmas feast, but there seem to be lots of undercurrents going on. Savannah doesn't look happy, for one thing. I think you may be in demand as an ear to bend, my dear. And I do believe we will find Jonathan looking rather relieved when we see him again.'

28

Liberty got up early. She was unable to sleep as she couldn't stop worrying about her mother. Did she love Jonathan or not? Did she really yearn to marry the charming gentleman with the perfect manners, and maybe refused him because she had to stay and look after her useless daughter who had returned home? And Savannah. She was clearly not happy, and although Liberty knew her well enough to understand anything could become a drama with her, she had gained the impression her oldest friend was intensely unhappy. Liberty decided to clear her head by taking the dogs out and then making breakfast for the two sleeping beauties, hoping they might be awake by the time she got back.

She headed downstairs to the kitchen and on the way switched on all the twinkly fairy lights strung around the house and on the Christmas tree. Liberty loved the days that ran up to Christmas almost more than the day itself; the anticipation and the fresh smell of pine around the house. Her mother refused to decorate more than a week before the big day, saying that, 'If it's done too early, it loses its magic.' The first rays of the sun were sliding between the curtains and crisp frost on the lawn was sparkling as she drew them back. This was indeed why she loved living back in Littlehurst.

She knocked up a batch of bread dough from her mother's starter, kept alive in the fridge with frequent additions of rye flour and potato, then put bacon and sausages in the Aga to cook slowly, and hoped to find some field mushrooms on her walk that could line their stomachs ready for a busy day.

Custard snuffled happily along the hedgerows as she collected a few mushrooms clinging to life under the blackthorn, together with some rosemary that was just surviving. Dijon had stayed in the garden, unwilling to venture further in case his legs gave way. 'You poor thing,' said Liberty sadly as she tickled him under the chin when she returned.

Deirdre and J-T had both shuffled into the kitchen, lured by the smell of cooking bacon, and Deirdre had managed to press some pink grapefruit juice without splashing her crushed velvet dressing gown.

'You must sleep in a vacuum or something,' grumbled J-T. 'I had to go through six face packs to look this bad, and you two look as fresh as daisies.' He glared at them from behind a vast pair of Prada sunglasses, not so much to keep the light out as to protect onlookers from the red-rimmed swollen eyes behind.

'Good genes, and a lot less booze than you, young man,' said Deirdre, chuckling as she handed him a glass of Prosecco and grapefruit. 'Chin chin!'

Liberty piled the breakfast on to platters along with the freshly baked bread; her mother had found the dough proving and put it in the Aga. None of them had eaten much the night before and this, along with the lack of sleep, had made them all ravenous. Liberty piled marmalade, bacon and a poached egg on a slice of bread, sprinkled them with fried rosemary and handed the plate to J-T. 'Can you manage a knife and fork or shall I feed you?' she asked.

'I can't manage anything,' came his pathetic reply.

'EAT!' commanded his hosts in unison.

'Bollocks!' exclaimed J-T as he struggled with his fork and a shaky hand. As some of the food found his mouth his expletives became more enthusiastic. 'Bugger me! Is this the best thing ever?' he asked. 'Oh my God, why haven't you given me this before? You must put it on your menu as "Hangover Heaven".'

'It's only because you feel so dreadful,' said Liberty as she enjoyed her own, but she did think he could have a point for Sunday mornings.

The dogs were feeling left out as the humans devoured the lot. Custard was given only a rasher of bacon and half a sausage, and Deirdre coddled Dijon an egg.

'He seems off form this morning. Maybe I'll get Mr Night the vet to come out later.' Dijon trembled visibly. 'It's OK, dear old thing. We'll take care of you.' And Deirdre took herself upstairs to dress before she broke down and cried.

Restored to vitality thanks to the hair of the dog and a good breakfast, they all set off to Denhelm Park. Arriving promptly at noon they let themselves in the back door. Mrs Goodman had obviously been working hard. You couldn't tell there had been a party the previous evening. All the candles had been replaced with poinsettias, and the ribbons, candles and baubles had been put back on the Christmas tree in the hall that had been danced round. The air hung with the scent of fresh flowers and all trace of cigar and cigarette smoke had disappeared.

They found the family in the kitchen. Mrs Goodman was clearing the detritus from a late breakfast, and preparing a fore rib of beef for later. She hadn't been able to do a 'proper roast' for ages; the huge joint, complete with a mottling of beautiful yellow fat, looked as though it would feed twenty.

'Raised on our farm,' said The Lord of the Manor as he wandered in. Jonathan was indeed looking both relieved and rather sheepish towards his dear friend. He hugged her close and whispered 'thank you'. Gray and Edmund were chatting about some government scare. Liberty crossed to where Savannah sat huddled by the Aga, despite the toasty warm kitchen, clutching a black coffee that looked distinctly cold and untouched.

'Hello, darling,' she said, brightening at the sight of her old friend. 'Come up with me to meet the children. They are putting on jodhpurs, desperate for Grandpa to take them out cubbing and, although I have explained that it is the wrong time of year, they have grown up with bedtime stories of their mother and her friend riding around Denhelm, and want to see if it is as beautiful as I have led them to believe; I'm not sure the English weather will impress them much though.'

As they climbed the stairs, Liberty told her not to worry and that children, as far as she knew, never seemed to notice the cold, and then she asked where Khalid was. Down in the kitchen, Deirdre was quizzing Jonathan on the same subject.

'Gone. Flew back to Abu Dhabi this morning. Just left a note. Must have been at the crack of dawn, as even Mrs G missed him. He didn't say goodbye . . .' And her big blue eyes clouded with tears.

As Savannah cleaned herself up to greet the children, Liberty admired some painting on the wall, and suddenly realised she was gazing up at Edmund. Blushing for no apparent reason, she returned to Savannah's bedroom where she was getting dressed and asked the question she was already dreading the answer to. 'Will you have to leave?'

'No, I think it will be best if the children and I stay on here for a while. They need to get to know Pa, and I need to think, but now is not the time to talk,' she whispered as two beautiful children, dressed head to toe in tiny tweed, looking like a Ralph Lauren advertisement, raced screaming with excitement from their bedroom. Liberty was appalled at herself for feeling pleased her friend would be staying; she had missed her so, but she knew in her heart she would have to persuade her to go back to Abu Dhabi, where she and the children belonged.

'Mummy, Mummy, where's Grandpa? He promised, he promised!' cried the children, and they both tumbled around Savannah's feet like tiger cubs playing. Riding before they could walk, they had loved hearing stories from a young age of their mother hunting before breakfast, galloping over the beautiful English countryside with her best friend Liberty beside her. They would lunch beside the lake on sandwiches and pies Deirdre had tucked into bags that hung from their saddles, returning home as the light faded. As Savannah's children had so far only known a country where the temperature rarely fell below twenty-five degrees during the day, and consisted mostly of sand, they expected English riding to be done round a grassy racetrack as seen on TV with their parents. They were still unable to believe how green everything was in England, even in the depth of winter.

'Come on!' said Savannah, suddenly excited herself. 'Why don't you join us?'

'What fun!' cried Liberty. 'Can I borrow boots and a hat?'

They clattered downstairs, the children racing ahead, both adorable in their animated state. It was contagious. When Savannah told the kitchen of their plan, Mrs Goodman was left standing alone while the rest of them traipsed towards the stables – a glorious quadrangle of boxes filled with hunters and thoroughbreds that Jonathan bred from and rode.

The stable boys got to work and tacked up ponies for the children. While they were preparing to mount, larger horses were made ready for the grown-ups.

Gray and Edmund kept their horses stabled at Denhelm, and were soon walking slowly across the quadrangle, big grins on their faces. Deirdre was competent enough on a walking armchair of a steed. J-T, who had never been closer to a horse than a high street betting shop, was put on old Nesbit, who had lived at Denhelm for as long as anyone could remember, and could carry anyone safely. He would happily walk through a crowd throwing bricks without flinching.

'He must have been a police horse once upon a time, but we can't remember,' explained Jonathan, as he helped J-T into the saddle. 'Just hold his mane, and he will follow us.'

J-T looked rather unhappy, but didn't say anything. Dressed in Gucci trainers, designer jeans and a bright pink cashmere blazer and turtleneck, he made everyone smile – but they admired his spirit. He was visibly shaking, but as no one had any idea whether it was from nerves or hangover, they left him to find out the thrill of riding on such a stunning day. He was indeed doing some admiring, but it was of his own reflection as he allowed the horse to wander past a window while he surreptitiously took a swig of vodka from a hip flask.

He kept sneaking glances at Gray, wondering why Jonathan's younger son had not spoken to him yesterday. Now, with a fairly clear head, and 'gaydar' back in action, the reason became apparent. He took in the cherubic beauty astride a strong chestnut horse, and he wondered why Liberty had not warned him of Gray's sexuality. He would ask her if he was fortunate enough to return safely to the stables.

Edmund sat atop a spirited grey, looking as stern and solemn as ever, but he gave himself away by lovingly pulling his mount's ears and whispering sweet nothings into her neck. He always enjoyed riding out with his father, but today somehow felt like an adventure as they all set out, trying to keep the children in check as they cantered along and happily jumped over logs and low hedges.

'Don't worry,' said Jonathan to Deirdre and J-T. 'We will go through gates.'

The low winter sun warmed their backs as they followed the children at a more sedate pace, forming the perfect English scene, hot breath coming from the horses' nostrils into the cold air.

Deirdre, Jonathan and J-T slowly rode along together, saddle leather creaking happily, while the others grew accustomed to their mounts and the more accomplished and brazen enjoyed the gallops and open fields. Liberty had wondered if she would remember what to do, but once up, she felt as happy on a horse as in the kitchen, and she asked herself why she had ever stopped riding. Edmund glanced over to where Liberty and Savannah were chattering away like starlings, only stopping to call the children back or ask if they were OK. Liberty's hair streamed out from beneath her helmet. It was never a clothing item to flatter, but the two young women carried it with aplomb. Their cheeks rosy from the frosty air and their eyes sparkling, it could have been twenty years ago, thought Edmund. Liberty could feel his critical gaze upon her, and wondered why he made her feel like a dizzy schoolgirl again. She had met Gray the previous evening as a woman, but would always feel like a silly child when Edmund was around. Perhaps he made everyone feel like that?

Savannah was telling her all about life in Abu Dhabi; the initial excitement, followed by the realisation that Western women were mostly seen as tasteless, brash whores – sadly often true in the expat communities. She found the life there so different: glamorous and exciting, especially in the racing community, but she soon discovered that women were not expected to be involved or seen out of the home alone. She thought Khalid had only got to know her because she let slip when she first met him that her father was great friends with Henry Herbert, the famous trainer. He thought she might be able to help him get introduced to the British racing circle; difficult to enter and even harder to be accepted by.

They both adored their children, but after a while realised their lives were so separate. He became increasingly possessive; not, thought Liberty, a trait that Savannah would find easy to deal with, as she was nothing if not a free spirit. Savannah also told her of the long, empty days with nothing to do, as she wasn't allowed to work, and Khalid had insisted upon a fully staffed house. She had spent most of her days riding, and then became great friends with a psychotherapist who had gradually pulled out all her insecurities, none of which she had been aware of before.

'She told me I had spent all my life running away from my birth. A load of it was trash, but I could see something in it. I suppose I had always felt to blame for Mummy's death. Pa never blamed me intentionally, but in angry moments when we were children Gray and Ed used to say if it weren't for me, Ma would still be here. I know they didn't mean it really, but still, I felt it deep inside me somewhere. That's why I had always run away.

The more I thought about it, the sillier it seemed to be away from the place I really love. I spent all my time telling the children about my home, and how I grew up, and how magical it was back here. You saw how excited they were this morning. Well, in Abu Dhabi, Khalid started asking me to stop talking about England, said they were his children and should be brought up as true Arabs, which of course is right, but it made me miss home even more. Eventually, I persuaded him they needed to know their grandpa and uncles, and reluctantly he agreed we could come for Christmas. But as soon as we arrived, he announced we should make the most of it as it would definitely not become a regular thing. I asked if we could travel with him when he comes for a race, and he said he had plans to send them away to school – Paris, then Switzerland – and when I said that's not for years, he said they were booked for next spring.

'I went mad. They really are my life, and I told him he had no right, which of course is exactly what he does have. I told him I wanted a divorce. I thought he would fight tooth and nail. Arab men really think they own you. But it seems as though he has just abandoned us here. I don't know what to tell the children. They will be devastated. And yet, look at them. What a place to grow up!'

Liberty regarded the two youngsters, laughing as they trotted around their uncles. Happiness glowed from them. But having been through it herself, she was only too aware of the pain they faced if their parents were to separate, especially to different countries.

'I'm sure you can come to some arrangement. He will realise how much he misses you all, and you can persuade him to let you come home more often.'

'But I really hate it there!' Savannah cried with surprising force. 'I only realised how trapped I felt as I stepped off the plane. Here I can wear what I like, say what I like, talk to men or women. He was in a bad mood last night because of my outfit. I mean, really! I've spent the past eight years covered from wrist to ankle whenever we went out. One bit of cleavage and you would have thought I was Lady Godiva.'

'Aren't you running again?' asked Liberty softly. 'And think of the children.'

'They are all I do think about! You wouldn't understand, but since I had both of them I just don't think of anything else. What people should do before they marry is ask not what do you want from your marriage, but how do you want your children to be brought up. If only I had known that Khalid is from the 'be seen but not heard, and send them off to boarding school' train of thought, I would never have dreamt of having babies with him.'

Liberty brushed off the hurt she felt from her friend's selfish comment about not understanding. She knew Savannah had not meant it personally, and didn't realise herself how much Liberty would love to be in the position of battling with Percy over children's rights.

They now concentrated on keeping the children in check, otherwise, as Gray laughingly pointed out, 'They might end up in Wales.' He, especially, was really enjoying the feeling of freedom.

'Such a dazzling day,' called out Deirdre as her mare galloped past them. Liberty wondered what was causing her mother to be so carefree, as she was not the most confident of riders normally.

It really was one of those days that made you think there could be no evil in the world. The sun, low in the sky, glinted off frozen puddles and lit up the branches of the ancient oaks, beautiful in their simplicity. Without their clothing of leaves they looked like sculptures set on the hill.

They managed to encourage the children to turn in a wide circle, giving them the illusion of freedom without letting them know they were now headed home.

'Do stay for supper,' Jonathan implored Deirdre as they clattered into the quadrangle. 'Mrs Goodman will have enough for us all.'

'Yes, do,' echoed Savannah and Gray. Edmund had already

handed his reins to one of the stable boys and was stalking back to the house.

Sasha and Hussein were dragging Liberty by her hands towards the house. She looked over her shoulder at J-T, who was dismounting slowly and carefully. 'Can you walk?' she called.

'My God! What have I done to my arse?'

Not wanting him to make crude references to his anatomy in front of the children she smiled warmly and told him how impressed she was with his riding, and he limped towards them.

Much as they wanted to go home and laze in hot baths, Liberty was needed to inspect the children's bedrooms and the toys Grandpa had filled their indoor treehouse with – his excitement at becoming a grandfather had led him to great extravagance and he had arranged with his forester a brilliant, magical construction from ancient twisted rhododendron branches and beech flooring, which filled a spare room in the house. It was like something out of Hogwarts and *The Hobbit* combined. The children's happiness was so contagious that Savannah, Liberty and Gray ended up having a tea party with teddy bears, a complete set of My Little Ponies, which they had to remember the names of, and a large pink rabbit, all squeezed into the child-friendly chairs, which had also been made by the forester. Meanwhile, J-T lounged on a comfortable sofa on the landing and rubbed his thighs.

Deirdre and Jonathan found themselves alone in the drawing room, standing warming their rears in front of the log fire. Jonathan coughed and said, 'I do hope things haven't changed between us. I value your friendship more than you could know, and as much as I think we could make a great team, I do understand your reason for not wanting to take me in, so to speak. I would also like to apologise for Edmund. I don't know what the matter is with him. You didn't say anything to him when he was at The Nuttery, did you? I know how you like to stick your oar in. He seems distant. I only hope he isn't thinking of refusing to take over the estate.'

'Why do you want to retire now?' asked Deirdre. 'You love your position in the community. Everyone holds you in such high regard. I can't believe you want to pass on all the responsibility to Ed now.'

'No, but I have seen so many problems when it's left until death. A child who has struggled to make his own way in life knows, nonetheless, that this huge responsibility will be landed on his shoulders eventually, and it still comes as a great shock when it's done earlier rather than later, but if the parent dies, it's almost impossible. And it's not helped by everyone in the neighbourhood hating change. I think if I gradually give him the responsibility now, I can be here to guide and assist, hopefully not hinder, be the buffer between the staff and Ed, introduce him to all the villagers and try to lessen the shock of it all happening at once.'

It made sense, although Deirdre just couldn't imagine the grumpy, stern Edmund ever being as popular on the estate as his father, who had such a knack of making everyone feel like his friend no matter what their background or breeding. Her first meeting with Jonathan was a prime example. When she and Alain had first set up home in Littlehurst, Deirdre delighted in creating her dream cottage garden. She had seen the beautiful Denhelm Park from her bedroom window, its driveway banked by primroses, violets and bluebells. *Well, where better to start?* she thought to herself. *No one will miss a few of each*. Every day for a week, she took her trowel and a shoulder bag for a walk down the drive. Looking around first, she would occasionally bend down, dig up a few of the prettiest specimens with good roots, and pop them into her bag. Quickly scuffing her shoes over the soil so the gap didn't show, she then casually strolled back to her garden and planted the stolen goodies.

Cowslips! she thought excitedly one sunny day. Getting to work with her trowel, she forgot to look around first, and gasped as she felt a hand on her shoulder. Blushing furiously, she quickly stood up, tearing her new tie-died maxi skirt with her heel (despite now being a DIY expert, gardener and country dweller, she hated wellies or flats). A pair of twinkling blue eyes in a carefree, unlined face met her own. The eyes belonged to a man in a tweed jacket, plus fours and brogues. *Not the gardener*, she thought rapidly.

'Um, I was just, um, oh bugger, stealing flowers.'

'Yes, I've been watching you all week. Should I set the hounds on you?' asked Twinkly-blue eyes.

'Oh, gosh, please don't have me arrested. I just wanted to make my humble home look as pretty as this. My husband will be so cross. He's trying to open a new hotel and restaurant, and it would scupper all his chances if I am caught stealing. Will I go to prison for long? My friend Paloma spent a week in prison for stealing a loaf of bread . . .'

'Well, now that I know your life history, do you want to include favourite colour and dress size, or would you rather come and have a sherry and meet my wife? She planted all these a couple of years ago, when she deigned to join me in this pile. I think she stole them from the banks leading up to Sissinghurst!'

And so Deirdre met Jonathan, and a lifelong friendship began. Both of them were so newly in love with their spouses that there was never any of the usual bother – apart from a basic acknowledgement of the other's attractiveness and friendly nature – of needing to flirt or charm, other than in a spontaneous way.

Deirdre was introduced to the lovely free spirit that was Helena, Jonathan's wife, and found herself promising not to take any more plants, which was appreciated. She offered to replace the ones she had taken, which was not. She invited her new-found friends to supper just as soon as Alain had time off work. And so the four of them became firm friends.

Deirdre felt that Gray must have been the obvious choice as Jonathan's heir, but his father stood by the eldest son rule and knew that with a few years of help and perhaps a good wife,

Edmund would manage the estate and its various businesses well.

'What about girlfriends?' she asked Jonathan. 'Is there a wonderful girl in Edmund's life who might be a potential wife?'

'Not that I know of. I think both boys have such a halo around the memory of their mother that no girl has lived up to her. That's the problem when you lose someone too early. No memories of bad times. You just remember what was perfect.'

As if on cue, at that moment Edmund walked in, followed by Mrs Goodman and a tray of drinks. Edmund seemed to have taken a good look in the mirror and a happy pill, as he strode up to Deirdre and gave her a huge hug. She was so shocked that she did her usual thing and burst out laughing, which broke the ice.

'I'm so sorry I was rude last night,' he said. 'I didn't mean to be. Pa had shocked me by informing me that my life as I know it is over, and I have to take on this great heap of responsibility, and I think that hearing you two may marry was one shock too many.' He didn't add that his feelings for Liberty had also jolted him with fright and excitement. She had spent the day ignoring him, and he was aware he had been avoiding her, so it was hardly her fault she had barely said a word to him. It reminded him of being an awkward schoolboy; always so confident around his classmates, but belittled by his laughing sister and her friend. Maybe he had always loved Liberty? *Goddamn, you sound like a pathetic chick lit character! Pull yourself together*, he told himself sternly.

Pleased that things were now sorted out between the three of them, and his eldest was indeed a human being, Jonathan poured drinks.

Deirdre waited for half an hour before phoning Sarah to ask her to let the dogs out and turn the lights on.

'So what did you say?' asked Sarah, breathless with excitement.

'About what?'

'When he asked you to marry him, of course. I've been waiting to hear all day.'

Deirdre wondered how this piece of information could have got out, but soon untangled the story. Mrs Goodman had phoned the butcher at the farm shop with her Christmas order that morning. He was one of Jonathan's tenants. His wife had probably answered the phone, and no doubt the two had chatted for a while about the hunt ball as they were great friends. Mrs G would never gossip on purpose, but once the information slipped out she would have asked her friend not to mention it to anyone, which meant it was already all round the village, and had reached the ears of Miss Scally, who passed on the news to Sarah when she cleaned the doctor's surgery. So Deirdre had to be quite succinct when she told Sarah that no, she would not be the next chatelaine of the park, and thanked her for looking after the dogs.

J-T ambled into Savannah's bedroom, and they caught up with Liberty's marriage and its break-up while she was in the bathroom. Savannah had been aware of Liberty losing her sense of smell and taste, but had always assumed it would have returned.

'It's strange,' she said, when she had heard most of the story. 'I always imagined Liberty doing something with food. With Deirdre and Alain as parents, it was inevitable. I'm so pleased things are finally working out for her. Must be fabulous to have such a passion,' she continued wistfully.

As Liberty emerged from the bathroom she could tell she was the topic of conversation and laughed at her friends on the bed.

'OK, what have I missed? Have you married me off? Sorted out my life? Decided on a proper career for me to prevent me from opening a café in a village in Middle of Nowhere?'

'Actually, we think it's brilliant, and I am sure I could help you,' said Savannah.

Leaving J-T to make use of the bathroom and its toiletries, Liberty asked Savannah what she meant as they went downstairs.

'As you know, I am considering not returning to Abu Dhabi, and maybe I could help you in the café? If you use those two pillocks who run the tea room, it will be a disaster. You want a totally professional establishment and it's going to be impossible to find staff who know the right knife and fork, let alone what a properly made trifle is, or whatever it is you chefs make around here. I don't need the money, and so you can trust me completely with the till. AND, it would be such fun!'

Liberty agreed with her friend that it would certainly be exciting to work together, and she knew she had been worried about finding help. It would be tremendous to have a well-educated person as front of house. In France it was such a respected job, and people had to train for it. In England, waitressing was always seen as a step to something better, and therefore was rarely something people took pride in, other than in top restaurants.

She was also aware, however, that this was Savannah's latest, and therefore her best ever, idea. After a few months the novelty would wear off and she would flit to the next one. This was simply her nature; but to have that help for the first few months, or even weeks, could be invaluable.

Grasping her dear friend's hand, Liberty said, 'Firstly, I want in no way to encourage you to stay here rather than to return to Abu Dhabi. I think you need to make that decision entirely on your own for the sake of your family. But if you decide to stay, then I will love for you to come and work with me, for as long as you can bear dealing with the public.'

'Hooray!' was all Savannah replied, and although Liberty too felt delighted, her heart sank a little as she realised her friend had decided her marriage was over. They chatted for a while, until Deirdre came to get them. They walked into the drawing room, where the three handsome de Weatherby men turned from the fireplace. What a trio; all tall, one blond cherub and two dark and swarthy. They looked as glamorous as a modern-day *Downton Abbey* cast.

Edmund immediately carried on talking to Grahame about what, as a Member of Parliament, he could do to encourage more land to be set aside for wind turbines.

'A few acres of turbines would power most of Sussex,' he said. 'We could be the forerunners in the country.'

Gray smiled sweetly at Liberty before turning to discuss the subject with his brother. *God, Ed is so rude*, thought Liberty. *No one would imagine he is Jonathan's son.* Then Jonathan handed her a pink gin and she forgot to think about it further.

'I didn't realise people still drank such things,' said Deirdre. 'Mmm, delicious, just what the doctor ordered. Talking of which, Mrs G says supper is at eight.' As J-T and the children joined them, they all sat to enjoy catching up on lost years and fond memories.

29

Waking up the next day was tough. Liberty had slept soundly for once. Deirdre, never at her best in the morning, had struggled to let the dogs out and screamed at her hangover to go away. She had a booking, her last before Christmas; the children from the local housing estate, which was a close of fairly pretty cottages near the river, were coming to make biscuits and mince pies. She had to be on alert and sparkling form for them. Although most had the latest iPod and smartphone, they all lacked direction and most, family too. Not one of the fifteen children seemed to have a happy home. Three fathers were in the clink for some crime or other; one, she believed, was even in for murder. The rest were barely seen, if around at all. Most of the children seemed to have suffered one or other tragedy in their lives, and she loved to mother them and to fuss. Despite their almost kamikaze lack of discipline or respect they all knew to be well-mannered and polite to Deirdre, as she gave them a few hours of hope that there could be happiness and warmth in their futures.

Deirdre shouted to Liberty and J-T to get up, then she forced croissants and home-made black cherry jam on them, followed by gallons of dark coffee. She reminded J-T he needed to finish off all party lists and table plans.

'We must decide if we are going to join the Christmas festivities at Denhelm, or just do the day here. Bob and Paloma, together with her son Claude and Evangeline, his fiancée, will be arriving the day after tomorrow, and we have their rooms to prepare and food to organise.'

Mother and daughter spent a stressful morning making pastry

for the mince pies and wrapping small presents. Each of the children would have a stocking all to themselves to take home and open on Christmas morning. Deirdre was aware that, sadly, most of them didn't expect one from their parents.

They filled old walking socks with clementines, little home-made biscuits, sugared mice and almonds, small toys for the younger ones and books for the older children. Deirdre knew that even young teenagers loved to have little presents to open on Christmas morning, and sometimes the old-fashioned things were still best. Just having something for themselves gave them a sense of feeling special.

The two women decorated the kitchen as much as they could, having bought lots of festive things from Jane Asher online. Sprinkles, sparkles, edible glitter and little people made out of sugar decorated a cake that everyone would share after the class.

The youngsters rushed in with snow in their hair, adding to the feeling of the impending festival. Soon the kitchen was full of boys with their hands in jars of mincemeat, with 'I'll be making mincemeat out of you, tosser' being bandied around the room.

The girls all seemed too quiet, too made up and too grown up. The boys, on the other hand, all seemed immature, clinging on to a half-invented childhood, perhaps. Soon they were all smiling, however, as some good, some bad and some burned cakes and biscuits were brought from the oven.

One boy, Clarence, whose mother was from Zimbabwe (nobody in the village was sure if she was in the country legally, despite Miss Scally's investigations), had shown real talent from the outset. He hardly spoke apart from answering questions about food, but was quick to learn and took instruction well. He had quickly picked up most of the easy recipes, so Deirdre would challenge him to harder tasks on his own. He showed a genuine interest in cooking, especially baking, but whenever Deirdre offered him extra lessons (free of charge) he made an excuse. Deirdre discovered that most of his spare time was taken up with caring for his two baby sisters while his mother found work here and there working at the village shop or at the farm shop when they needed help.

Clarence had not been making mince pies with the others. Unbeknownst to all, he had found an old-fashioned, round plum pudding mould. He had wanted to impress Deirdre, and thank her by making one of the puddings he had seen in the old story books picked up by his mother in the charity shop. In the old illustrations, Christmas puddings were always round, with icing and a sprig of holly on top. However, nobody had informed him that such a pudding needed steaming for three hours, so when he realised he couldn't make it, he changed direction.

He selected chocolate, cream, vanilla and cinnamon from the pantry. Deirdre had noticed he was up to something, but knowing that trust was something important to these children she let him get on with his task, and indicated to Liberty to do the same unless he asked for help. Clarence was pleased Liberty was around as he could ask her advice without telling Deirdre what he was doing. She loved to help and told him what a good idea it was. Therefore, when their time was up, the kitchen table scrubbed clean and all the happy, if floury, children showing what they had made, both women waited with bated breath as Clarence proudly carried his offering to the table.

As he whisked off the cloche that Liberty had found for him, he said, 'Ta-raaaa!' Even the loudest child fell silent. On a white platter, surrounded by a ring of holly, was a small football of shiny, tempered chocolate. Its peak was crowned with a perfect circle of marzipan, finished off with green sugar holly and red sugar berries.

As he cracked open the ball with a silver spoon they could see the rum- and vanilla-laced Chantilly cream within. All the children leapt at it, grabbing a delicate piece of chocolate and scooping up the cream with it.

'Delicious!' announced Deirdre. 'Far too much rum, though,' she said, giggling. She then declared that she would serve one just the same as Christmas pudding. 'Well done!'

Clarence glowed under the praise, and more so from that of his contemporaries, who were all telling him he 'should be the next Jamie Oliver, mate!' and slapping him on the back. He realised most were enjoying the rum content, and he felt happier than he could remember.

They were handed their stockings with instructions not to open them before Christmas morning. Deirdre held Clarence's arm to make sure he was the last to leave, and as he stepped out of the door she handed him her own edition of *Larousse Gastronomique*. She had written on the flyleaf: *I hope this encourages your passion. My best, D. James.*

Deirdre hugged him and told him to have a merry Christmas, and to think again about the extra lessons. She told him he could bring his younger siblings, if that would help? Clarence thanked her, but his awkward race out of the door made her realise that she may not be able to persuade him.

Just then, Sarah arrived to clean and dropped a clanger with the news she was expecting a baby.

'My congratulations,' said Deirdre sarcastically, and then, in response to Liberty's glare, who was shocked at her mother's blatant disapproval, 'Why don't we let Liberty clear up? She needs the practice for her café. I must hear all about this. Come through to the sitting room.'

As Liberty wiped and swept, her thoughts annoyingly kept returning towards Edmund. Like cats, women often find themselves drawn to men who show little or no interest. His handsome face hung in her mind like an adored family portrait. So memorable. He had only ever scowled at her and told her off for being silly, but she had also seen such tenderness when he played with his niece and nephew. What was she thinking, she asked herself. He clearly had no interest in her. She tried to clear her mind, which didn't work, so she concentrated her thoughts on Savannah. She was concerned for her friend. Was Khalid so bad she could consider taking his children from him? She loved her friend, and would do anything for her, but she felt she couldn't condone taking children away not only from their father, but also from their place of birth. On the spur of the moment, she phoned her.

'Hello,' blubbed a nasal voice.

'Hi, Savvie, it's me, Liberty. What's wrong?'

'Can you come over?'

'Be there in five.'

And grabbing a coat she shouted to her mother that she was off to Denhelm Park.

When she arrived there was a police car standing by the front door. Liberty cut her engine and ran up the steps, leaving her car door wide open.

'Savvie, Savvie, where are you?'

'In there,' said Gray from the doorway. He was nursing a brandy.

The parlour was a small, comfortable sitting room, cosy in raspberry and gold. That evening, those were the only colours in the room. Jonathan and Edmund sat either side of Savannah, whose smeary eyes had the appearance of someone who had run out of tears.

A policewoman was taking notes. A younger policeman stood uneasily shifting from one foot to the other.

When Jonathan introduced Liberty to Detective Inspector Alice Groom and Constable Trump, a fleeting realisation of the unfortunate name was followed by unimaginable terror. She raised her eyebrows to Savannah, who could only open and close her mouth silently.

Jonathan took charge, and in a quiet but commanding voice addressed the inspector.

'I think Savannah should now try to rest. She can call you if she remembers anything else. Would that be all right, Inspector? The doctor has given her tranquilisers to help her sleep.' He rose, clearly to show the two investigating officers out.

'Yes, yes, of course.' Alice Groom had a strong local accent, but looked efficient in a neat black suit, hair scraped back into a chignon as though she wasn't yet ready to be out of uniform. Her eyes were bright and intelligent and she asked Liberty why she was there.

As Jonathan and Mrs Goodman led Savannah from the room, Edmund became the man in charge. Liberty just had a chance to squeeze her friend's hand in passing but received no pressure in return.

'DI Groom,' said Edmund, 'this is Liberty James, who lives in the village. A very good friend of my sister. She has only met Khalid once, but may have some insight regarding the situation.'

Liberty wanted to ask 'What situation?', but Edmund's efficient, calm tones kept her silent.

Inspector Groom sighed. She turned to Liberty. 'We believe Mr bin Wazir has kidnapped his children and has returned with them to Abu Dhabi.'

Liberty collapsed into the chair that luckily stood behind her.

'Oh God, no! When, where, how?'

'We believe that although Mr bin Wazir said he left the country the day before yesterday, he actually went to London to book airline tickets for himself and the two children, at the time hiring a chauffeur and bodyguard. Late last night or in the early hours of this morning he, possibly with some help, entered the house, persuaded the children to go with him and simply left.'

'How did he get in?' demanded Liberty.

'The bloody doors are never locked here,' said Edmund stonily. 'Bloody Pa even announced as much when Khalid asked about locking up for the night after the ball. We all thought he was worried about the bundles of cash he travels with. He must have been planning this all along.'

'What about the airports? Can he be stopped?'

'It's too late. He took them to Gatwick, boarded a private jet to Paris, and on to a flight that left France at six this morning. Savannah phoned the police the moment she went to wake the children and found their beds empty. The first question the police asked when they found their father was a foreign national was whether she had their passports. Khalid had taken them from the safe in Pa's study.' Edmund spoke quietly but with obvious emotion in his voice.

'I don't understand,' said Liberty. 'Jonathan would never have given the passports to Khalid.'

'No,' explained Edmund, 'but he left the safe open after getting some of Ma's jewellery out for Savvie. Khalid must have realised that when she was dressing and snuck down. And it wasn't noticed until now.' His voice broke and he turned away. 'Wait till I get my hands on him. He has misused Pa's hospitality.' He was clearly shaken and upset by his inability to do anything.

Gray and Jonathan returned to the room, and Edmund rounded on Gray immediately.

'Any luck with your lot at the Foreign Office?' he asked.

'I hadn't wanted to come in while Savvie was here,' said Gray. 'All I can glean from the ambassador in Abu Dhabi is that legally a woman does have rights, but when she is a foreign national these are simply ignored. It will take a lot more than a good lawyer to get the children back.'

It must be awful to have good contacts and still be so impotent, Liberty thought.

'I will of course do whatever I can,' said Grahame. 'If Khalid takes the children back home, then we will at least know where they are. The ambassador reckons Khalid is unlikely to prevent Savannah from returning to her home, so maybe she will just have to follow them. That would be the best scenario. If, however, he has taken them to an unknown location, we may have problems contacting them.'

'Let's not think the worst,' said DCI Groom. 'We will of course do what we can to find them as quickly as possible. If Mrs bin Wazir can at least speak to them on the phone she will feel better, and then we can take it from there.'

The inspector rose to leave. Taking the uncomfortable constable with her, she asked them to update her with any fresh information if and when they received any. As the door closed,

Edmund pointed out, 'Surely it should be she who contacts us?' But they were all too stunned to really care.

Liberty asked if she should go to Savannah. Jonathan said she was dozing, but added, 'Maybe you could get some things and sit with her? She may need someone in the night and as much as we all adore her, a woman may be best?'

'Of course, of course,' said Liberty. 'I'll go home, fetch some night things and sleep in her bed with her. I'll be as quick as I can.'

'I'll come down to The Nuttery with you,' said Edmund. 'I can explain things to Deirdre while you pack. I need to bloody do something. Those gorgeous kids, they don't deserve this, and as difficult as we all know Savannah can be, she certainly doesn't either.'

All three men had remained calm, but as she hugged Jonathan, Liberty could feel the trembling tension inside him. 'It'll be fine, it has to be,' she said, knowing the words were as ineffective as putting a sticking plaster on a broken leg.

Edmund drove Liberty's car to The Nuttery, where they found Deirdre happily gossiping with J-T about Sarah's stupidity, despite all her sweetness, for having a baby with the cheating Tom.

Only someone who had a child of her own could understand what Savannah was going through, and Deirdre's heart went out to the young woman. As she raced back downstairs with her weekend bag in her hand, Liberty heard her mother saying, 'We would come, but I feel we would be no help, but do let us know if there is any news.'

'If you can think of anything at all, please call at once. I have to pick up Bob the day after tomorrow, and then collect Paloma, Claude and Evangeline,' J-T was explaining. 'But I am free tomorrow and will do anything to help.'

'Oh, I'm so sorry, I was meant to fetch them from Heathrow!' cried Liberty, wringing her hands.

'Don't worry,' replied J-T, glad to feel a little useful. 'If I can borrow a car, I can drive to London, load up Bob and the dogs, and then scoop up the French mob on my way back. No problem at all.' He could be calm and efficient if the circumstances demanded and there was nothing to laugh about. And he had enjoyed Savannah's company so wanted to help.

Liberty gave him a big thank-you hug, kissed her mother and then returned to the park with Edmund. It now looked dark and gloomy despite, for once, having most of the interior lights blazing. As if reading her mind Edmund said that he always thought Denhelm Park was as much part of the family as the family part of the park.

'It really looks upset, doesn't it?' he asked.

My God, thought Liberty. *That's probably the most emotive thing he has ever said*. She agreed, and asked him what he had thought of Khalid.

'Not sure. Pa always approves of anyone involved with horses, but when Savvie got to know him we had some background checks done. Nothing substantial, but rumours of his mistreatment of some animals and dirty business dealings abounded. Nothing you could put your finger on, but I know we always felt a little uneasy about him. Such a shame for Pa. He was revelling in being a grandfather – it was the happiest I remember seeing him, having them all here. Now it's going to be the most terrible Christmas, and we've had some.'

Liberty felt tears welling up as she thought how frightful that Christmas must have been, when their mother died on its eve. How had they coped? She couldn't imagine life without Deirdre holding the fort.

After checking on Savannah, who was asleep, Liberty found Mrs Goodman making sandwiches and pots of tea in the kitchen.

'I don't think anyone is drinking that!' said Grahame, as she put a third pot on the table.

'Well, I have to do something,' she wobbled, and blew her nose on a tea towel.

Gray hugged her close and guided her gently towards the back stairs. 'Bed,' he instructed her. 'Lots to do tomorrow.'

Liberty couldn't remember ever seeing any of them crying

before. Even when immersed in grief after his wife died, Jonathan had always kept his tears private, and Mrs Goodman was always able to cope. One year, after a large party, she announced that she would need a week off to recover from her hysterectomy.

'Of course,' Jonathan had agreed. 'When is it? Can I drive you to the hospital?'

'Oh no, dear, don't worry,' she had replied. 'It was yesterday, but I had to make sure you were looked after.'

Jonathan now disappeared into his study, loaded with guilt for leaving the safe and the doors open. Edmund, Gray and Liberty sat looking at the mound of untouched sandwiches.

'What can we do?' asked Liberty.

'I'm trying my best,' replied Gray. 'But the Middle East is tricky with things like this. The father's rights always take precedence, especially, as I said before, with a foreign wife.'

'They must be home by now,' said Edmund, 'but we will leave Savannah to sleep the night through before we get her to phone. Perhaps we should ask Pa to speak to Khalid, and try to gather a true picture of the situation.'

As Liberty climbed into bed beside her friend she realised just how lucky she had been, and also how small and insignificant life was without children. 'I don't care if I can't have my own, just bring Savannah together with her two little ones,' she prayed and she turned onto her side to wait the night out and watch over her old friend.

Liberty must have fallen asleep; she was woken by a dreadful scream. As she mentally shook herself and remembered where she was, she instinctively reached out to hold Savannah. Finding the bed empty, she awoke properly, leapt off the bed and out into the corridor.

Knowing where Savannah would be, she ran along the landing to the children's bedroom. Savannah was lying on Sasha's bed, holding her little pink cuddly pony.

'My babies,' she wailed, as Liberty flung her arms round her.

'Know one thing,' she said to her friend as calmly as she could. 'Khalid loves those children and wouldn't hurt a hair on their heads. We will find them, we will sort this out, and we are all here to help you; we love you and you must try to be strong for Sasha and Hussein, who probably believe they are on a huge adventure, and would hate to think of you upset.' And she stroked Savannah's heaving shoulders and smoothed her forehead. Slowly, slowly, the trembling woman calmed, but her always-thin body was exhausted.

After what could have been a minute or hours, Liberty said there was little point in trying to get back to sleep. 'Let's dress and I'll make some coffee.' She had to help Savannah put on clothes and wash her face. She gently wrapped her in warm layers, knowing that with shock you always feel horribly cold. Guiding her downstairs to the kitchen and placing her in a comfortable chair in front of the Aga, Liberty set about making a strong pot of coffee.

The moment she placed two mugs of sweet black liquid on the table, the troops arrived. Jonathan, who had not been to bed, but had spent hours phoning his Middle Eastern friends met through horse racing, was first in, then Edmund and Gray. Mrs Goodman appeared soon, checked the coffee bubbling on the hot plate and began to make breakfast.

'Darling, you must eat,' Jonathan instructed Savannah. 'You will need your strength today.' She managed a few forkfuls of scrambled egg and a piece of dry toast.

'I have been able to contact John Oxx, one of the Aga Khan's trainers,' Jonathan informed the group. 'He knows Khalid well, and he told me Khalid has a house near the track in Dubai – did you know that?' Savannah nodded. 'But more interestingly, he recently bought a house in Paris.'

This really startled his daughter. 'Why do you think that is interesting? Or relevant?'

'Well, maybe he booked them on a flight to Abu Dhabi but plans to be elsewhere. We will see.'

'You said he wanted to send the children to European schools,' followed up Liberty. 'Perhaps the house in Paris is something to do with that?'

'I am going to dial up the house in Abu Dhabi,' said Jonathan, frowning. 'I think you, Savvie, should be with me, but not speak to Khalid. We need to be calm with him.'

'I just want to talk to the children,' wailed Savannah.

'We will try our best.'

Nobody expected Khalid to answer the phone, despite Savannah giving Jonathan his private number, so Jonathan was startled when, after the second ring, his voice came down the line.

'Yes, 'allo?'

'Khalid, do you have the children?' Now was not the time for small talk.

'Yes, of course. They belong here.'

'What about Savannah?' asked Jonathan.

'She belongs here too, but she made it clear to me she was going to stay with you. I didn't want to make a fuss and scene so I thought the best thing was to leave and bring the children with me.'

'Didn't you ever think of consulting your wife, the mother of your children?' Jonathan's face reddened as he stood up angrily. Edmund took a pace towards him and made calm-down gestures with his hands. Jonathan collected himself and simply asked, 'So what now?'

Khalid said, 'If she wants to be with the children, she can come home. If not, she can stay with you and forget about them. Let me know.' And he put the phone down.

'Well, at least we know where they are,' said Jonathan.

'But you didn't speak to them,' cried Savannah. 'And I wouldn't be with them if he sends them away to school.'

'I think once we have talked this through you should speak to him yourself, but best not to get angry or say something in haste. I'm amazed at how emotional I got, and you are feisty at the best of times.'

Savannah was already calmer, knowing where her children

were, and she took herself back to her room, needing to be alone to clear her head.

Liberty returned to The Nuttery after getting her things, as she knew how much had to be done before her mother's house guests arrived. After enquiring about Savannah, and checking that all was being done to reunite the family, Deirdre filled her in with the latest developments at that end.

'J-T has left to pick up all and sundry. Hope there's sufficient room in the car! And Sarah talked to me about her pregnancy. An accident, apparently, not that I believe that! Tom wants her to have an abortion. Says another mouth would put too much strain on their finances, but she insists on keeping it, even if it means he leaves her again. The two older children will cope, I'm sure, but it's a shame to divide the family, and how can she work with a little one in tow? I've told her I think she is silly, but I know that doesn't help. What will the poor girl do?'

'I've been thinking,' replied Liberty. 'I will move out of here, get out from under your feet, otherwise I may lose the confidence I have built up to get on with the café. I will need Sarah to help, and she can earn as much as possible before the baby arrives. There will be unpacking and cleaning, and just having an extra hand will help me no end.'

'Oh that's great for a pregnant woman – exhaust herself before the birth,' huffed Deirdre, 'but it could certainly help the money situation. I may let her stay on living here while she gets on her feet. And it could be fun to have a new baby in the house. But Tom may come round to wanting it.'

'He seems to have been very attentive since she went back to him,' said Liberty.

'Yes! Too bloody attentive, apparently!' Deirdre said with a laugh, but then they remembered the horrid situation at the park, and fell into their own thoughts.

30

Two days to go until Christmas. In preparation for the arrival of the French guests, Deirdre and Liberty had made a simple supper of parsnip and chestnut soup, walnut bread, a salad and a platter of local cheeses to pick at. There was also a salted caramel chocolate torte to be served in front of the fire when they arrived, along with freshly baked scones, damson jam and clotted cream.

Liberty was torn between excitement at seeing her godmother and sadness at losing Savannah, who had decided to return to Abu Dhabi. It had only been a few months since the magical time in France, but so much had changed in her life since she had left Percy in Florence. She felt sad that she wouldn't be helped by Savannah in the café; it had sounded fun, although it had seemed a bit of a dream. *Things can't be that perfect*, thought Liberty, *and we could have been a disaster together. Maybe I do need a man in my life*. She grinned, and phoned Fred, the blacksmith with the roving eye.

'Well, hello young lady! Happy Christmas to you.' He was shouting, as the furnace was blasting away. 'Are you phoning to take me out for a drink?'

'Um, yes . . . no . . .' *Oh, why do I have to be so flustered? He's a flirt, a slut, just too bloody good-looking!* she thought, pleased he couldn't see her furious blushes. 'I have decided that J-T was right, and I'm going to be self-indulgent and call the café LIBERTEAS, so now you can get on with the sign.'

'So,' he replied, and she could hear his smile, 'should I change the motif to one of the outline of a sexy lady, then?'

Liberty snorted with laughter and said, 'I think we may be mistaken for a knocking shop if you did, but thank you for the compliment!'

'Of course, me darlin', just pulling your leg – and a very beautiful pair of those you have too. Sure you don't want that drink?'

'Quite sure,' said Liberty, giggling, 'but I think Mother has invited you along with the rest of the village for New Year's Eve, so we can have a drink then.' She put the phone down, amazed that anyone could be so forward, but he had cheered her up.

Liberty raced up to Denhelm to say her goodbyes to Savannah, who was being pragmatic.

'I need to be with my children, simple as that. I realise I was being selfish, just because I have been homesick, and I have no right to mess the darlings around.' She flapped her hands at Liberty as she could see that her dear friend was going to interrupt with platitudes about her being completely unselfish and a fantastic person. 'I am fully aware, despite what many think, of my faults. Selfish is probably number one, and rash decision-making number two. I have to grow up, take my responsibilities seriously, and commit myself to the life I chose to follow with Khalid. I do love him, and I think I must give it a go.'

Although she wasn't sure if Savannah would be saying any of this if the children were still with her, Liberty felt nothing but pride for the woman. It was true that people thought she was a flake, just out for a good time, and this had been the case in the past, but Liberty had seen Savannah with her children, and seen the responsible mother she had become.

'Just don't let him clip your lovely wings too much,' she said as they embraced in a warm hug. Savannah was crying quietly, but calmly, and said it was down to nerves. 'I'll be back, with bells on!' she declared. And Liberty knew she would.

By the time Liberty returned to The Nuttery, Paloma was ensconced in the kitchen, glass of wine in her hand, having been picked up by J-T along with Evangeline and Claude, and a quiet Bob. Many hugs and kisses and don't-you-look-wells later, they settled in the sitting room. Bob and J-T were sitting close together, a French bulldog on each lap, which made the eating of cake and the drinking of champagne rather difficult.

'It's no wonder you guys stay so slim,' remarked Paloma as she noticed both men were feeding more to the dogs than themselves.

'Oh, I have missed you three boys so much!' exclaimed J-T. Bob was asking about Duck End, and whether it was fit for purpose now. 'I have been putting in so many hours at the gallery, I need you home to help,' he said to J-T, who pouted and stated, 'If that is all you want me for . . .'

Liberty couldn't be bothered with their catty chat as she had the blooming, beautiful Evangeline to get to know. Claude was clearly madly in love, his eyes never leaving hers, and he kept jumping up to plump cushions and get glasses of water.

'We are to be married soon after the baby arrives,' explained the petite, clear-skinned woman, her bump barely showing beneath a tidy blue trouser suit with a cleverly positioned long scarf that fell to mid thigh to disguise any thickening of her waist. Her hair was almost black and cut in a neat bob, her chestnut eyes were rimmed with impossibly long lashes that needed no mascara, and a rosebud mouth gave her the look of a chic china doll.

'My parents will never forgive me, having a baby out of wedlock. I had wanted to get my figure back first, but for peace of mind we have promised to marry as soon as I feel able, so the baby can be baptised in Claude's name and they won't think I am going straight to hell!'

'Your English is better than mine!' remarked Liberty.

'Oh, I was educated in an international school. My father is American.'

'And this torte is better than your father's!' exclaimed Paloma to Liberty. 'Your baking is obviously coming on.'

'The British seem to be having a love affair with salt and sweet, so I thought it worth a try,' replied Liberty, blushing with pleasure.

Paloma suggested they went to take a look at Liberty's new house after she had unpacked.

'That may take some time,' whispered J-T as she walked upstairs. 'We had to put her steamer trunk on the roof!'

'You would have thought it was an elephant, the fuss you made!' said Bob, and they grumbled happily to each other as J-T showed him to their room.

You are definitely in love, thought Liberty about Claude as they chatted, Evangeline having gone for a bath and a nap. She noted the puppy dog longing had left his face, and he could for the first time in her memory look her straight in the eye without blushing.

'Evangeline is so gorgeous. You must be so happy. Where are you living?'

'Maman let me build a little cottage in the grounds, and that is progressing. Meanwhile, we are renting in town. Paloma wants to help with the *bébé* when it arrives, and Evangeline is keen to get back to work. She manages a yachting lease company.'

Only in St Tropez, thought Liberty.

'She will be able to work a lot from home, but Maman will be a great help. And I have started working on a new collection of pottery and sculpture. I sold a few last summer and realised how much people are willing to pay, so I dumped the photography and now I am taking commissions from wealthy Russians. I have one for a missile sculpture a fellow wants in his mansion. Can you imagine? He already has a real one – he says it's decommissioned – in the middle of a fountain in his garden!' And they both laughed.

They walked across the green to Duck End. Paloma was draped in fur. The beautiful dusting of snow had given way to a true English winter, dull and misty, so by the time they arrived at the cottage she looked like a polar bear that had gone swimming for seals; beautiful, but somewhat damp.

Liberty had left the Aga and the heating on low so everything was warm and welcoming. After admiring J-T's choice of furnishings, Paloma said with typical bluntness, 'It's very you, but it desperately needs to be lived in. You are stalling, my dear.'

'It feels so safe at Mother's,' explained Liberty. 'I have needed that and we seem to have been busy, but I have said I will move over here early in January, so don't worry.'

'I am not worried at all; I just want to make sure you are going to take the independence leap. You are teetering, not sure whether to jump, and you will be so proud of yourself once you take that step. And what of the café? Have you organised help? Deirdre mentioned some ghastly couple in the village.'

Liberty explained that although Gwen was a treasure, her husband was a liability, and then she mentioned Savannah's predicament.

Paloma, on hearing how dreadful Christmas would be at Denhelm without the guests of honour, exploded. 'Can you imagine? The toys nestling beneath the tree, waiting for the children, the empty seats at the dining table? No! We must do something!' She suggested that the entire de Weatherby clan, including Mrs Goodman, should come to The Nuttery for Christmas Day. On telling Deirdre, who thought it a fantastic idea, the three women set off for the park. Jonathan, however, deemed it a ridiculous plan; he assured them Mrs Goodman had already ordered the turkey.

'Turkey? Never!' protested Paloma.

Deirdre said she would talk to Mrs G. 'And you need to get out of the house on Christmas Day,' she commanded. 'It's no good moping about Savannah and the grandchildren not being here. You can still ride out in the morning and come along early in the afternoon. We will play silly games, open presents, eat too much – all the things you do here, but without the ghosts.'

Liberty gasped at her mother's bluntness, and waited for a

growl from Jonathan. It didn't come. Jonathan glared at her mother for a moment, looking as though he intended to bite her arms off, but simply said, 'If you can persuade Mrs Goodman, then we will come.' And he retired to the library, knowing that Mrs Goodman would never hear of such a thing. He hated to upset her, and anyway, she would be so much better at saying no to Deirdre Steamroller than he was. He was therefore amazed when she agreed to the change in their ritual.

'It will be lovely for me,' she explained. 'I won't have to do a thing, they say.'

'But Mrs G, you have never asked for time off at Christmas, and you always said after Mr G died you preferred to spend the time here, rather than with your family.'

'But not this year. No good looking at the children's presents unopened under the tree. It will be good for us all to do something different.' Mrs Goodman would never before have entertained the idea of allowing the Christmas celebrations to be arranged by anyone but herself. She had in fact been working like a dervish for the last few weeks to get everything ready: cakes, puddings, turkey ordered from the farm shop, along with all the veg and cheeses. But now, with the children gone and no certainty they would be seen in the country again, she felt it would be a fantastic plan to spend Christmas Day at The Nuttery.

Jonathan kept to his word, and spoke to Gray and Edmund, expecting a battle. 'Good idea, Pa,' they both said. And that was that.

31

Christmas Eve morning: rain without but warmth and good cheer within. The house party stood in their dressing gowns round the tree in the hall after being roused from their beds by an over-excited Deirdre, leaving the dogs eating mince pies in the dog room. They sang 'we wish you a Merry Christmas' and handed each other a present.

'How can this be?' asked J-T. 'I was always told I had to wait until Christmas Day!'

'Not in this house,' explained Deirdre. 'We used to hand one round in the evening, but it's usually chaos, serving out drinks to people who call round, getting to Mass, etcetera, so we changed it. And Liberty's may suffocate if left in there any longer!'

As Liberty took the box from her mother, she was told to be very careful. She noticed it was moving and shuffling around. Liberty looked worried. 'I thought you were joking about the suffocating!'

'Go on, hurry up. She's been in there for five minutes already,' said Deirdre. Everyone's eyes were drawn to the box, their own presents forgotten. Liberty lifted the lid.

Looking up at her, sitting on a tiny sheepskin mat was an adorable pug puppy. The puppy did what pugs do best, and snuffled and reached her tiny paws up to balance on the rim of the box, as if to say 'Here I am, get me out and cuddle me'. Her bottom was wiggling frantically as her tail was wagging so hard.

Deirdre was watching Liberty's reaction closely, prepared to take the pug as her own if she had got her wires crossed. She said cautiously, 'Every person needs a dog, every house needs a dog, and so here's yours, if you will have her.'

Liberty scooped up the tiny fawn puppy from the box and was immediately licked around her neck. Deirdre breathed again. From the expression on Liberty's face, she knew it was love at first sight.

'She's perfect. So tiny, and – ooh –so wet!' she squeaked.

'I've had her in my bedroom since yesterday. She's twelve weeks old, and she seems to want to go out, but it's all been a bit too exciting.'

'But Mother, I can't have a puppy. I'm opening a café!'

'Well, I am two steps away, I can help. And you can keep her in a basket behind the counter.'

'Oh, yes, Health and Safety would love that!' But Deirdre was right, and Liberty had already fallen for the little dog's charms. She took her outside for a leg stretch and the little dog snuffled around, with Feran and Bulli, who had been let out earlier, yapping at her heels.

'They will be fine,' said Bob, who had followed in hot pursuit. 'They are just excited to have all this fresh country air. They love their London park, but you can't compete with this.'

True enough, the French bulldogs left the new addition alone and raced off after an imaginary rabbit.

'How are you, Bob?' asked Liberty. 'We haven't had a chance to chat since you came down. I'm so pleased you are here.'

'I do so miss the silly fool, no matter what we say to each other. He is my soul mate. And I can't get over how you have changed,' he said, giving her a huge hug. 'Power suit gone, casual in cashmere – and J-T was right, you really are glowing! I thought bakers were meant to be fat, jolly people, but you look just the same but with rosy cheeks – oh, and bigger boobs.'

'Thanks.' Liberty smiled and playfully punched him on the arm. 'What on earth am I meant to do with this one?' And she scooped up the wriggling pug. 'Mother has the silliest ideas.'

'Yes, I see that. But I got those two at the maddest time, just as work was really taking off. It was tricky at first, and being on your own, it may not be an easy time, but if you can make the effort she will be house-trained and obedient quickly, and suddenly you will wonder how you survived without her! There is nothing quite like the relationship you have with your first dog.'

'Not in a café!' wailed Liberty.

'I thought a dog was an essential part of a pub?'

'An Alsatian, maybe, but a pug?'

'Come on inside,' said Bob, laughing then whistling to his dogs. 'I'm starving, and I haven't stopped eating since I arrived.'

'It's all the lovely country air,' she said as they went in.

For lunch there was a French onion soup, a soufflé made with Sussex Crumble cheese and a green salad. This was followed by a dried fruit salad that had been soaking overnight in cider, cinnamon and vanilla, and walnut tuiles.

Liberty ate little; most of lunch was spent crawling around the floor with the puppy. 'I refuse to call her Holly or Ivy,' she retorted. 'I'm going to live at Duck End so she can be Teal. A pretty name for a beautiful girl.' The little dog promptly ran to lick her nose, obviously liking the choice of name. 'Come on, I'll make you some scrambled egg.'

'Well, I'm gobsmacked!' announced J-T. 'I thought she would insist that *you* kept her,' he confided to Deirdre.

'Yes, but she needs something to care for when she is home alone. Oh, I will miss her dreadfully! I have loved having her here.'

Leaving the puppy to snuggle up to Dijon, the other dogs took their owners for a long walk. If an American tour had passed by in a coach, they would have thought they were looking at a combined advertisement for Barbour and Fendi.

Claude and Evangeline looked blissfully in love.

'I can barely do my coat up, but at least the bump keeps me warm,' joked Evangeline.

'My first photo for the mantelpiece,' said Liberty, running ahead to take photos of the couple.

'There will be lots more after the party. We have two photographers coming and no doubt the press will send some paparazzi,' said Deirdre.

'Who on earth have you invited to warrant paps?' asked Liberty. 'What happened to introducing me to the village?'

'Well, you met that lot at Jonathan's, so Paloma sent invitation cards to all the old set. Terence Macready is coming with his entourage.' He had been as big as the Rolling Stones were in their heyday. 'Then there's Camille DuPont, the most successful and beautiful French actress, and Mark Chailey, the PR guru, to name a few. And all of us, of course! We need to get you into the press, so we must drop a few mentions that an excellent new café will shortly be opening right here in the village.'

'Mother!' shouted Liberty in horror. 'It's not a Michelin-starred restaurant! Wrong sort of press!' But she giggled over her mother's enthusiasm. 'Your lovely friends from the old days eat in fine places with foie gras and caviar; they won't be coming for tea and scones!'

'A little publicity never hurt anyone,' said Paloma, looking embarrassed. It had been her idea.

'And of course it will be the first time that Alain and Deirdre have been together since their split. The famous restaurateur comes to support his daughter's venture,' said Claude.

Deirdre and Liberty stopped in their tracks and turned on Paloma.

'What have you done?'

'Oh, he said he was alone, and would love to come.'

'But surely he's working?'

'I think he's coming after work, but you can ask him tomorrow when he gets here.'

'Whaaaat?' they both screamed.

'He decided to join us for Christmas when he closes after lunch. He's leaving his team to cope with hotel guests.'

Deirdre was apoplectic. 'Why didn't you ask me?'

'Oh, come on,' said Paloma, 'everyone should be happy and get on together at Christmas. It will be wonderful.'

'OK, so next time we hold a party we will ask Claude's father for a cosy chit-chat. You won't mind?' asked Liberty through gritted teeth. She had her arm linked through Paloma's, so was unable to see the strange expression flicker over the older woman's face. 'Mother will now be in a total flap.'

'Not at all,' answered her godmother. 'Don't you see she still loves him?'

'Maybe so, but I think Dad has burned his bridges there, and he will probably thoughtlessly have some nineteen-year-old in tow.'

That evening they enjoyed light nibbles of oysters, tiny toads-in-the-hole and a cheese plate while Claude played Christmas carols at the baby grand piano, throwing in the occasional Noël Coward medley. Candles twinkled on the Christmas tree, and the fire crackled in the grate. Jonathan collected them for a quick sing-song and mince pie in the pub before Midnight Mass, and Liberty gave him a tight hug, reflecting that his daughter's departure was the only fly in their wonderful ointment. He looked tired and grey, but he brightened when he witnessed the merry scene inside. After quick introductions they wrapped up warmly and stamped off into the night.

Everything feels magical on Christmas Eve, and that night the stars twinkled to match their mood. The North Star shone as brightly as it should, and they all imagined shepherds out watching their flocks, although J-T was more inclined to imagine Santa Claus flying through the sky.

The pub was filled to bursting. People who were not seen inside either the pub or the church for the rest of the year milled around, making new friends and catching up with old ones. A few youngsters, already tipsy, were scuffling outside and being told to calm down by Harold, the seldom-seen publican.

'Welcome, boys!' yelled Dilys, excited to see the handsome Grahame and Edmund, and wide-eyed at Claude's Gallic beauty. She allowed them to queue-barge, but no one minded as Jonathan completed the round (as she knew he would) by shouting, 'Drinks on me. Merry Christmas, everyone!'

A huge cheer went up, and then Dilys squeezed her way round with a vast platter of mince pies.

'I wouldn't if I were you.' She winked at Grahame. 'Liberty's have all been scoffed. These are the cash and carry's, and by the looks on those faces, not as good by far.'

Grahame let his pie drop back on the plate and sidled over to Liberty.

'What are we going to do about Savannah?' he asked. 'Pa seems to be going out of his mind with worry. He's been holed up in his study since she left. I feel so helpless, as the Foreign Office has been useless. They don't want to interfere in any domestic dealings in case it upsets trade negotiations going on at the moment, as far as I can tell.'

'Have you spoken to Savannah since she went back?'

'Briefly. Ed had a good chat, and Pa has spoken to her. She sounds calm but a little desperate. Apparently, she is not allowed to leave the house unless chaperoned by one of his private bodyguards.'

'Did she find out what the house in Paris is for?' asked Liberty.

'No, but she thinks that if Khalid is looking for a base in Europe it may just be for business reasons. I have people attempting to find out if there are planning applications in, or any suspect comings and goings.'

'Do try to enjoy yourself between times,' Liberty said, squeezing his arm.

'Will do what I can,' replied Grahame with a wry smile.

Edmund was chatting to Paloma, explaining that he was about to take over the running of the Denhelm Estate.

'What does that involve?' she asked, a twinkle in her eye. 'Yelling at servants and kicking dogs?'

Before he could bluster and get upset, and inform her that the estate ran five separate businesses, all profit-making, Deirdre interrupted and told Paloma not to tease. Paloma thought to herself that if only he relaxed he would be a heartbreaker. It hadn't escaped her attention that his eyes kept wandering to where Liberty stood glowing beneath the soft pub lights.

'Right, time to go,' instructed Jonathan, who as always was reading the first lesson.

When they arrived at the church, his small family group entered the boxed pew at the front, together with Deirdre and her party, as there was otherwise only standing space left in the packed building. Liberty found herself in-between Edmund and Paloma, and despite having plenty of room, Paloma kept shuffling into Liberty, making her move closer to Edmund. He started as though burnt, and Liberty smiled and whispered not to worry, she wouldn't bite, as she looked up at his face.

It was a jolly service. Despite knowing well that this was the only time he would see the majority of the faces until the following year, the vicar was a showman, and enjoyed himself immensely. His sermon was short and positive, just in case it encouraged a few more visits in the coming months.

Jonathan read beautifully. His clipped vowels rang out over the speakers, and the flickering candles hid the haunted look in his eyes. Liberty noticed the fresh flowers beneath the plaque in the side chapel that read: 'Helena de Weatherby. Wife and Mother. 1946–1974. Much missed.'

As they filed up the aisle for Communion there were a few tuts as people noticed Deirdre had brought Dijon in with her, but the tutting turned to laughter as Dijon waddled up to the Communion knee rest and sat on it. She figured it was probably his last Christmas and he needed all the help he could get. The vicar looked bemused for a moment, then shrugged his shoulders and intoned, 'The body of Christ', and popped a wafer into Dijon's mouth, thinking as he did so that he might get some front page publicity in the *Parish News*.

'Let's move to the country,' said Bob to J-T as they disgorged into the night.

'Oh, yes, and by the second of January you will be desperate for the city lights and disappear,' replied J-T, as Bob kissed him warmly, to the shock and delight of the villagers standing around.

There goes my front page, thought the vicar. Miss Scally was probably already writing her objections, about how the standard of village life had fallen, so he made sure to go and shake the boys' hands and suggest they might like to attend morning service too.

'I think we will be busy making cocktails by then, but thank you for a lovely service,' said J-T, laughing.

On their way back to The Nuttery Deirdre said to Jonathan, 'I'm so pleased you are coming tomorrow. Where is Mrs Goodman?'

'Oh, she wanted an early night, and she will go to the service tomorrow morning. But she is no doubt making us a hearty meal for our return in case the roast duck we ate earlier wasn't enough!' he said. 'See you at eleven. Happy Christmas.'

Standing in the garden, encouraging the puppy to wee, Liberty looked up at the stars and wished that everyone would have a happy time, and that Savannah was doing all right. Then she whispered, 'And I know I am being selfish, but please make my venture a success.'

She told Teal she would feel a bit silly if it all failed, and then assured her Father Christmas wouldn't come if she didn't wee.

32

Father Christmas did come. Waking next morning everyone had a miniature tree, complete with lights, at the bottom of their bed. Underneath were sweets, toys and hand-made biscuits, together with a Thermos jug of coffee and another with hot milk.

The puppy found the biscuits first, but Liberty didn't mind, as she felt blissfully happy, despite the nagging thought in the back of her brain that such happiness should be shared with a man. *Oh well, dogs, husbands – much alike, really*, she thought as Teal tugged the trailing belt of her dressing gown and it fell open. Going downstairs to let the puppy out, she thought, *I'm certainly not phoning Percy to say Happy Christmas.* But she did wonder what he would be doing, and reminded herself to call his parents later. She had sent them gifts, together with a long letter telling them what she had been up to, and saying that she hoped Cecil was responding to the treatment. She had also sent Mrs Stickybunns a huge Christmas cactus, remembering how she loved them.

A couple of hours later, the kitchen was a hive of activity, the women happily working alongside each other. Deirdre was laying out a side of wild smoked salmon on a cedar plank, Liberty was making potato pancakes to accompany it, and Paloma was making a dill, horseradish and sour cream sauce. Evangeline had offered her assistance, but Paloma saw she was a little nauseous and sent her off to relax. Nobody was to be allowed in the dining room until Christmas lunch was served late in the afternoon as the table had been laid already, but there was room in the kitchen for breakfast. They set out freshly baked lemon cakes and croissants, preserves and pitchers of champagne mixed with blood orange juice, to drink with coffee and hot chocolate.

While the others ate and chatted, Liberty coated small local goat's cheeses in crushed walnuts for frying later to go on a beetroot salad. This would be followed by roast beef, roast potatoes, parmesan parsnips and purple sprouting broccoli. Dessert would be a port and blackberry jelly, and a 'Clarence' pudding, which Deirdre had made as promised, as she thought it celebratory yet light after such a big meal. She had coated it in edible gold leaf. A whole Stilton was ready on the sideboard for anyone greedy enough to manage it.

'I can't imagine how Jonathan must be feeling,' said Deirdre. 'He was so looking forward to the sound of children tearing into their presents and demanding to go for a ride.'

'Well, then,' replied Paloma, 'it's good he is coming here. Tell me about you and he – has he proposed again this year?'

Deirdre guffawed and said her friend knew too much.

'Ah, but did you say yes this time?'

'Don't be silly, darling. Anyway, with Alain turning up I don't need any more complications. More bubbly, anyone?' It was clear she didn't want to pursue this line of conversation.

Evangeline, who so far had abstained completely, enjoyed a much diluted glass of champagne, and requested a ginger biscuit.

'I either had too much caviar last night or too much fun,' she explained. 'The baby is wriggling around like crazy.'

'Sit down, and we will bring you anything you need,' ordered Paloma. 'Honestly, whatever was I thinking, my first grandchild, to bring you to this madhouse? But you aren't born yet, of course.'

At that moment there was a scuffle and a shuffle as the dogs raced to the front door. Through the glass panels all they could see were the four legs of a horse and one of the rider's.

'Happy Christmas!' yelled Edmund as they flung open the door. One of his twice-yearly smiles transformed his face.

'You are somewhat early,' said Deirdre. 'Anything wrong?'

'I was riding home through the village and noticed the door of Duck End was open and nobody came when I called. I wasn't sure if you knew.'

'No, I didn't,' replied Liberty, looking worried. 'I'll grab my coat.' She followed Edmund across the green.

'You hold Badger while I investigate,' instructed Edmund, handing Liberty the reins. 'Don't you come inside.'

She waited a good ten minutes for him to re-emerge. When he did, he shrugged his shoulders and said, 'All seems fine. You should be more careful. Even at Christmas people could load all these antiques in minutes and be off, given the chance.'

'I am sure I wouldn't have left the door open,' countered Liberty. 'You have to turn the key to close it from the outside. I'll go in and take a look myself.'

'If you must, but I did check thoroughly.' Edmund felt she was being a little ungrateful. 'I had better get home and see to Badger, not to mention change my clothes,' said Edmund. 'Nice place you have, by the way. You have excellent taste.'

As she walked through the house, it seemed to be the perfectly furnished home she had been creating for the past few weeks, but it felt different, somehow. She couldn't put her finger on anything, but something was definitely odd. Walking slowly back to The Nuttery, she kept trying to remember if she had locked the door properly after taking Paloma round. Had she been careless?

'Everything OK?' asked Deirdre.

'Yes, I think so. Nice of Edmund to bother. He could have just assumed I was in there. I'm not sure I thanked him, but he makes me feel so useless!'

'Maybe he wanted a nose at where you are going to live,' suggested Paloma.

'What for? It's not an estate cottage.'

'Perhaps he has more of a personal interest?'

'An interest in making my life more difficult, no doubt. I hope he won't put up the rent on the old butcher's shop before I've even opened.'

'"LIBERTEAS" is its name, and it will be so successful you will be able to buy him out in five years' time,' stated Paloma with such sincerity Liberty wanted to believe her.

The two brothers walked in shortly after that, carrying an assortment of packages. Mrs Goodman followed, her head barely visible behind a glass bowl containing a trifle decorated with hundreds and thousands.

'Mr de Weatherby mustn't go without his Christmas trifle,' she explained to anyone listening, and then in a lower voice said to Deirdre, 'I'm trying to get him to eat more and it's always been his favourite. I hope you don't mind.'

Deirdre hugged the little housekeeper, and helped her place it safely in the pantry.

As they spread their presents around the tree, Edmund explained these included the children's ones.

'We needed to get them out of the house,' he said. 'Pa is getting maudlin. He really seems to have taken this hard. He thinks they will be shipped off to school and he will never see them again. I keep trying to explain that if they are in Switzerland, it will be far easier to hop over there for weekends than going to Abu Dhabi.'

'Yes,' said Gray, 'but I've heard some pretty gruesome stories of separated parents or estranged grandparents getting to the school gates only to be turned away, as the school has been instructed "no visitors". You can imagine, some of these children come from ludicrously wealthy or famous families, or their parents might be top government officials, and there could be a kidnap risk, so schools have to be really careful.'

'Yes, well, thank you, Gray, for that cheery note. Pa will be here in a minute, so we'd best change the subject.' Edmund glared at his younger brother.

Taking matters into her own paws, Teal at that moment chose to wee all over Edmund's hand-made shoes. Liberty blushed with embarrassment and hurried the puppy outside while J-T poured a glass of vintage champagne and thrust it into Edmund's hands to distract him.

Paloma and Deirdre got the giggles and ineffectually tried to mop up the puddle with tiny lace handkerchiefs left out for the canapés.

'Sweet puppy, huh?' said Grahame, elbowing Edmund with a grin. He knew his brother saw no point in lapdogs, but he too had noticed the way Ed had been gazing at Liberty, and how he had gasped when she came into the room before poor Teal relieved herself.

'Dogs should be kept outside and used for hunting, shooting and herding sheep,' huffed Edmund, 'not for sitting on laps, especially dogs with big eyes who look as though they have just run into a wall.'

'Oh, Grumpy Dumpy,' jibed Deirdre, clinking glasses with him. 'I promise, five minutes with a pug and you will be converted. Here, have a house-trained one.' And she handed him Custard for a leg warmer. The dog nestled happily on his lap and waited for crumbs from the canapés to fall.

Jonathan then arrived and told them he had spoken with Savannah and the children, who had, in spite of the fact that Muslims don't observe Christmas, enjoyed Christmas stockings, the excuse being that Father Christmas couldn't possibly be seen as a Christian.

'They are all going to the races. I think Savvie is trying to convince her husband she can be a good wife, and conform.'

J-T had taken over as host, as Deirdre was chatting happily to Paloma and Jonathan. Noticing how he kept everyone's glass topped up, Liberty said to him, 'You know, if you ever wanted to, you could run an excellent hotel. You and Bob could open one in Tunbridge Wells and send everyone to eat at my place.'

'Sorry? You can't seriously expect us to leave London, can you?' said Bob, cutting across J-T. 'My gallery is really taking off, and J-T has clients lined up for months – if he ever returns to work, that is.' He sounded very uppity, and Liberty was surprised at his over-the-top reaction.

'It may give you more time together,' she tried.

'The only reason,' Bob reminded her tautly, 'that we have spent so much time apart recently, is because J-T came down here to help you. Actually, we may have needed some time apart, but he will return after the New Year and I am sure he will be glad to be back in town.'

Liberty remembered Bob as the soft squidgy one who burst into tears at the sight of a limping dog. Where had this tough businessman come from, she wondered as she retrieved scallops baked in their shells with a touch of rosemary and butter from the Aga. She topped them with a tiny spoonful of chestnut and Jerusalem artichoke purée and placed them on a platter with lemon wedges. Another platter bore the smoked salmon; yet another was laden with tiny soft boiled quails' eggs sprinkled with sumac and sesame seeds. The women walked round the room serving the goodies, and hoped everyone would remain sufficiently sober until the Christmas feast was served.

After all the presents had been opened, marvelled over and tidied away, a round of charades ensued. It was a one-sided game, as Bob and Mrs Goodman, thanks to their relative sobriety, got most of them quickly. Mrs G blushed as she guessed Paloma was trying to act out *The Joy of Sex*, only to be told it was *Watership Down*.

'Oh, no! I was hopping like a rabbit and trying to act "down"!' Paloma cried, then screamed with laughter.

Even Edmund relaxed after a few glasses of champagne. He sidled up to Liberty and complimented her on the canapés, then asked her what she thought to achieve with her café. He enjoyed watching her green eyes light up with passion as she talked about giving everyone the chance to experience good local food, simply cooked, alongside beautiful pastries and bread. She had been experimenting with a recipe for a walnut and poppy seed gateau, filled with fresh damson conserve and whipped cream.

'It's got to be a winter winner, with a steaming mug of cocoa made with cream and grated black chocolate,' she told him.

He surprised himself by replying, 'I am now going to be a local, so you can experiment on me.'

Liberty said that as her landlord he was welcome to come and check out her produce any time, and then she reddened as she realised the double meaning of what she had said.

Jonathan, Edmund and Gray had given her an old silver sugar shaker as a present.

'It may need to be kept under the counter, but as you serve people you can always dust things at the last minute,' said Mrs Goodman, who had thought of the gift. 'It's the little things that make the difference. I have put a fine mesh inside the top, which you can't see from the outside, so that if you fill it with icing sugar, it will sift it as it comes out. I made the assumption that you will be using so much that it will not have time to clump up much,' said the practical older lady.

As Liberty thanked Edmund for the immensely thoughtful gift she felt a little embarrassed that she had only given him stiff white linen handkerchiefs embroidered with E. d. W.

'It was the only thing I knew you might use,' she explained, not adding that when she had found them she had thought they were as stiff and colourless as he was. He was such a confusing person, one moment so formal and the next so thoughtful. She watched him stroking Custard, covering his beautiful dark grey suit in fine white hair. Custard was looking up at him adoringly; Edmund had indeed been converted.

'So, what were they bred for, exactly?' he asked.

'Well, to be companion dogs for the monks in Tibet, supposedly,' said Deirdre. 'Probably kept them warm, too. But they are so loving, and they have no jealousy at all, so they adore whoever is loving them at that moment.'

'No problems with aggression, I suppose, with a mouth like that,' said Edmund. 'Couldn't get a purchase on anything. But you are becoming beautiful to me,' he added, putting the dog on his shoulder, and Custard took the opportunity to prove him wrong by swiping a mouthful of macadamias from the bowl behind him.

Goodness, maybe Ed has had too much to drink! thought Liberty, who was watching this conversation closely.

Claude and Evangeline were giggling as they attempted to explain a game which involved a rolled-up newspaper in a bucket and a person reciting a rhyme while stirring the paper in the bucket. Once they stopped they ran towards some poor seated person, who, if they were paying any attention, jumped up and ran if they didn't want to be hit with the paper, which was why the game was called 'whackums'. Everyone laughed uproariously as Claude leapt at Bob, fell over Dijon, and ran around the room with the two bulldogs following and looking anxious as Claude pursued their master.

Paloma and Jonathan were ensconced in the big sofa by the window, chatting happily. Mrs Goodman, whom nobody could bring themselves to call Jane, and who couldn't bear to be idle, went to the kitchen with Deirdre to finish the preparations. Potatoes went into the Aga to be roasted in beef fat, followed by parsnips coated in polenta and parmesan and lots of black pepper. The gravy stock bubbled merrily, a red wine reduction waiting for the beef juices.

Mrs Goodman started visibly at a loud knock at the back door. A black face peered in.

'Clarence! A very merry Christmas to you!' said Deirdre, and the housekeeper relaxed. 'Have a drink?'

'No, thank you, Mrs James, I just wanted to thank you for my present and to give you mine.'

He shuffled uncomfortably and explained, 'I am sorry to disturb you. We eat at midday, so I thought you would too, for some reason.'

'Don't worry, come and look. We made your pudding.' And Deirdre showed him into the walk-in pantry where she was keeping a chocolate bombe, now called Bombe Clarence, cool enough to stay firm, but unrefrigerated so it didn't lose its shine. She pointed out the edible gold leaf decorating the top, and the crystallised rose petals she had set on to the chocolate while it was still sufficiently tacky.

'So now it looks the part too,' said Clarence, really overcome by the sight of the bombe. 'I didn't think of doing that.'

'You were the one who came up with the idea – and don't forget, I have been doing this kind of thing since way before you were born. I am very proud of you.' He beamed at the compliment, and said he was going home to study his cookery book, and looked forward to next year's class on 6th January.

'Oh, do come to our New Year's party,' said Deirdre as he left.

'Thank you, but I think I am babysitting that evening, as Mum wants to go out, but if I can I will.' So saying, he stepped carefully down the path, then stopped and ran back. 'Sorry, Mrs James, here is your present – nearly forgot.' And thrusting something at her, he turned and raced off.

Mrs Goodman asked Deirdre, 'Are you sure you can trust him? He is coloured, after all.'

Liberty, who had come into the kitchen to see what was going on, raised her eyebrows to her mother, amazed that a sweet softie like Mrs Goodman would come out with something so racist.

'Oh, yes,' replied Deirdre, 'we make sure to notify the police each time he comes, just in case.' Mrs Goodman was unsure if her leg was being pulled, so took a large swallow of sherry.

'What did he give you?' Liberty asked as Deirdre undid the SpongeBob SquarePants wrapping paper, which he must have got to wrap his siblings' presents in. Deirdre gasped, as lying in her hands was something very precious. Clarence had made a little scrapbook of photographs he had found on the internet of Deirdre's days on television, her books and photographs of her in the kitchen at The Nuttery, looking over the children's shoulders while she instructed them. All of these were surrounded by handwritten recipes copied down by Clarence from her books over the years. At the back was an inscription: *To Mrs James. Thank you for inspiring me and believing in me. Here are my favourite recipes of yours that I will practise. Happy Christmas, Clarence.*

Liberty thought her mother was going to cry. 'I didn't notice him take photographs. What a dear boy.'

Mrs Goodman took another swig of sherry.

At the sound of the gong, which had been found for the occasion, everyone filed into the dining room and gasped collectively. J-T had been hard at work. Tall vases of white roses, gardenias and trailing stephanotis stood at each corner of the conference pear green walled room. The fire had been lit earlier but was now only smouldering, as nobody wanted to roast while eating; the mantelpiece was groaning with holly, ivy and lots of twinkling white lights in glasses. The heavy velvet curtains in a deep plum colour were drawn back to allow crystal ornaments hanging from the poles on cream velvet ribbons to spin gently, catching the candlelight from large church candles burning in glass hurricane lanterns and other candles which were dotted around the side tables. The dining table itself shimmered with silverware, porcelain collected over the years from different countries, and the light from the multi-coloured Venetian crystal chandelier above.

The sideboard held the huge Baron of veal ready for carving. Accompaniments would be carried in once the toasted goat's cheese in walnuts had been demolished. Jonathan was pouring a fine white wine to accompany the starter, and everyone sat down to pull crackers made by J-T and Deirdre. Each contained a rude joke. Grahame had to read Mrs Goodman's, something about a parrot, a chocolate bar and three not so wise men, but he refused to explain it to her. The women received a miniature silver powder compact each and the men a Mason Pearson comb.

Silly hats were compulsory. Evangeline, who, although educated in an international school, had never experienced crackers before, thought them brilliant, and looked as chic as ever beneath her gold crown. The dogs settled by the fire as they all realised that manners were essential in the dining room, and begging was a no-no. (They were teaching the puppy.) And anyway, leftovers were being created just for them!

Mrs Goodman had forgotten that she rarely drank alcohol, and after her sherry and champagne was now enjoying the perfumed Gewürztraminer. 'I didn't realise wine could be so delicious!' she exclaimed.

Edmund buttered another piece of walnut bread and popped it in her mouth as the plates were cleared.

Jonathan carved the perfectly cooked leg of veal. As it was pink all the way through, Liberty offered to cook a few slices to be well done for Evangeline, who explained that in France, where you were always confident of knowing where the beef came from, you didn't fuss over such things. She was also sweetly excited to be trying parsnips, which they only fed to pigs in France, and the purple sprouting broccoli, which Liberty had cooked quickly with garlic, orange and chestnuts, and which everyone pronounced delicious.

Jonathan stood up, glass of claret in his hand, and stated, 'To the chefs! And may everyone, including my darling Savannah, Hussein and Sasha, have a very happy Christmas.' He then sat down again, rather harder than he meant to.

They all loved the Yorkshires, requested by Evangeline after the toad-in-the-hole last night, individual and as high as their untouched water glasses, seasoned with nutmeg, cloves and bay to give them a festive flavour. Combined with the dark veal jus they were sublime. Although nobody had intended to eat them as it was such a big meal, they still all disappeared.

Claude and Evangeline told everyone their hopes and dreams for the baby. Paloma and Jonathan found they had the same taste in practically everything. Mrs Goodman announced it was amazing that a coloured family lived in the village and yet there was so little crime. Grahame, Patrick and J-T grew animated about a new exhibition of Middle Eastern art in the National Gallery, and discussed the merits of designing a house around your art collection, or do you buy art to suit your home . . .

Deirdre was so thrilled to have such a full and happy houseful she had completely forgotten Alain was meant to be there, so when he walked into the dining room her mouth dropped open, revealing a partially chewed potato.

'Daddy!' Liberty leapt up.

'I thought the free chair was in honour of Savannah,' spluttered Jonathan, as he stood to pump his old friend by the hand. 'You had better catch up quickly.' And he poured Alain's first of many glasses of wine that day. *A bit too friendly*, thought Deirdre, *for someone who keeps proposing to me*, but she smiled gracefully and allowed Alain to kiss her on both cheeks.

'How was your day?' she asked. Alain declared he had already eaten, refused a plate, then picked bits off Deirdre's, having made everyone budge up and insisted he sat at her right hand.

'Oh, the usual mix – people who either through tragedy, misery or lack of anything to say to each other come to my restaurant in the hope that eating out on Christmas Day will restore their happiness. The food entertains them for a while, then they sit back and expect us to lay on a floor show as well! I couldn't bear it; I knew it would be jolly here. We have to open today, but by golly, I would just love to miss it. It's enough to put you off cheffing for life.'

'Oh, I didn't mean that,' he said, turning to Liberty, 'and this veal is incredible. Great idea with the Yorkies, darling.'

Edmund, who was sitting beside Liberty, whispered in her ear, 'I didn't know your parents still saw each other.'

'They haven't for years. Sadly, I think I am to blame for this enforced reunion, although Paloma was the one who invited him.'

'Looks like they are getting on fine.'

'Oh yes, until he remembers he has left his floozy in the car.'

'Do people still use that word?' said Edmund with a laugh, making Liberty relax and laugh too.

'I adore Daddy, but he has hurt Mother so much, I just can't bear it if he ruins a lovely day.'

But he didn't. The laughter reached the roof as he regaled them with anecdotes of his famous guests and their bad manners. If there was a floozy in the car, she was forgotten.

'A couple booked into the hotel, as Mr and Mrs Smith. Then Mr Smith turned up the following week with another "Mrs Smith", only to find he had been seated next to his mistress with her husband on the next table. One of the waitresses became so confused she asked if they would like the tables pulled together, but both couples refused to admit they knew the other!'

Liberty brought out the puddings, put the Stilton on the table, and Alain produced a bottle of vintage port he had been saving 'for a special occasion'.

Mrs Goodman announced she also liked port, and sipped it while eating a bowl of sherry trifle topped with a dollop of rum-laced cream from the chocolate bombe. Then Jonathan and Edmund led her into the sitting room as she started to fall asleep.

'Lovely old thing,' said Alain. 'How old is she, one hundred and two? She has been with you for years!'

'I'm hoping she will stay on when I take over the management of Denhelm,' said Edmund, who together with his father had been updating Alain.

'A young man like you needs to fill that house with a wife and children. Don't you agree?' said Alain, turning to Jonathan. Nobody normally spoke of his unmarried status, so they all looked at Edmund curiously.

'Impossible to find a decent woman capable of running the house in this day and age,' said Edmund, insulting all the women at the table. He had not meant this, but he had no intention of declaring his interest in Liberty, even with a skinful, so he let the statement lie.

'Righty-ho – men to bore each other, smoke cigars and drink more port; women to clear,' announced Alain.

'Taking over as man of the house,' grumbled Deirdre, but she had been surprised at how much she was enjoying his company, and he had cheered Jonathan up no end.

Mrs Goodman woke just as the clearing up was completed. Liberty took coffee and petits fours into the sitting room. J-T and Gray had been decorating the elderly woman as she slept, and she now looked as though a party popper had exploded all over her. She was also wearing a fetching pair of antlers.

'Oh, poor you,' exclaimed Liberty as she handed the housekeeper a mint tea, before racing for her camera.

'Look what I've found!' shouted Bob, who had been rummaging in cupboards. He held up an ancient edition of Trivial Pursuit. 'This will either be fun or start a war. We haven't had the traditional Christmas argument yet, and I can't think of a better way to kick one off. Who'll be in my team?'

They played on, late into the evening. They all enjoyed their Christmas hugely, the dogs content by the fire after their special leftovers, Teal curled up on Liberty's lap, exhausted by weeing in undiscovered corners. Mrs Goodman had fallen asleep again, and eventually, reluctantly, the party drew to a close.

33

The hunt met in front of Denhelm Park on a glistening Boxing Day morning. The anti-hunt crowd had given up and moved on to protest about capitalism, so a very happy fifty or so horses chatted together while their riders, from all walks of life, ate cakes and drank whisky macs.

Mrs Goodman, having had a very good sleep, was back to her best and handed round warm sausage rolls and hot toddies, telling everyone who would listen that they needed to keep their strength up for a long day, no matter if they had over-indulged the night before.

'I'm surprised you are not the size of a house,' muttered a portly old friend to Jonathan. 'My wife insisted on making the roast potatoes with low cholesterol spread yesterday, and she didn't let me have any mince pies this year, and no salt on anything. And I'm still bigger round the tummy than you. I'm taking it that your friendship with Mrs James is nothing to do with her fabulous food?'

Jonathan merely smiled and said they had best mount up as he had to make a brief speech.

He thanked everyone for coming, whether it was to ride or to support, and hoped they would all have a safe and happy day's hunting. He was pleased to spot Deirdre and Paloma walking up the drive, arm in furry arm, surrounded by dogs. He rode over to thank them for such a wonderful Christmas Day, and found himself wondering what it might be like to spend a few months in the south of France. He hadn't been away from Denhelm for more than a few weeks at a time since he inherited the estate from his father, and had never once regretted the challenging and exhausting job of running the companies and bringing them into the twenty-first century. But now, with the reins being handed to Edmund, he found that perhaps he wouldn't miss it too much if he spent time travelling here and there. He told the women he looked forward to seeing them on New Year's Eve, and that if there was anything he could do, just to tell him.

With that, the master blew his horn and the hounds leapt into action, baying and wagging tails as they followed the trail created by two estate workers on a quad bike.

A few reluctant and a few hungover riders waited until they had finished their drinks, but most cantered off behind the master.

'It all looks so perfectly English,' said Bob, as he and J-T watched from their bedroom window, 'like something from an old film. It's hard to believe that both the postmaster and the taxi driver are riding with the county rich – those clothes make them all look like landed gentry.'

'Liberty told me that the hunt donations help to kit out those who can't afford the gear,' said J-T, 'and lots of them borrow horses. Apparently, it's so much a part of the community that many jobs would be lost if there was no hunt. I guess it's the same as us belonging to a gym, or going to a club. It's good to release tension by jumping a two-ton beast over huge hedges, and galloping at twenty miles an hour over boggy ground.'

'Think I'll stick to my kick-boxing, thanks,' replied Bob.

Deirdre had decided, with Paloma's advice, to bring in party organisers ('You will be so much more relaxed and have more time for me!'), so was happy to let them work over the next few days while she enjoyed Paloma's company. Much of the day-to-day cooking had been taken over by Liberty, so she was having a good time. She hadn't minded having Alain to visit at all; in fact, she surprised herself by going over their goodbye in her mind several times. She had put him up in the spare room, despite his protestations that he was fine to drive.

'Oh, yes,' chortled Deirdre, 'you have had more port than Nelson when he had his arm cut off, so to bed. *SPARE* bed!' she called after him as he wobbled off in the direction of her room. He turned, walked back to where she stood on the landing and kissed her, a gentle yet passionate kiss, and one that lingered a little too long; he murmured in her ear that if she needed company she knew where he was. She had been shocked by her own body's betrayal, the heat that flooded through her, the quickening of her heartbeat and the hair-tingling, toe-curling loveliness of a familiar but long-lost connection. She had locked her door from the inside, more to protect her from herself and any night-time wanderings than because she thought Alain might try to enter. He was too much the gentleman . . . goodness, when had she started thinking that again? She turned her romantic thoughts to her adored friend Paloma, and had been thrilled to see the sparkle in the French woman's eye when she caught sight of Jonathan in his hunting pink. Now, that would be interesting.

Claude and Evangeline were returning to France to spend New Year's Eve with her parents. Many tears were shed as they waved their goodbyes.

'Don't leave it too long before you come to see the baby,' said Claude to Liberty. 'I know you will be busy, but we would love you to be godmother.'

This time it was Liberty's turn to cry. She thought they must have asked her because she had no children of her own, but as if reading her mind, Claude said they simply couldn't think of anyone more capable of giving their child advice and a safe place to run to when fed up with its parents!

'You are our only friend with a stable home and a clear mind!' they insisted.

Feeling the house a little empty, Liberty and J-T had persuaded Bob to stay for the party, mostly due to the important guest list, which included an old friend of Deirdre's, a popular pianist and singer, who had several homes dotted around Europe, and who incidentally collected art.

On 30th December the marquee was hoisted into place. The rain poured down and the wind blew all day, but the workmen said they were used to it, as they came in for welcome hot cups of tea and cake. The dance floor was laid, and everyone grew excited.

'I just hope it won't rain tomorrow evening,' said Deirdre to Sarah. 'Lots of people won't go out in bad weather, and the peacocks won't like it one little bit.'

'Mother!' exclaimed Liberty. 'I thought we both agreed – no bloody peacocks!'

Deirdre looked sheepish, but twinkled as she said, 'I just couldn't resist!'

The two preposterous birds had been delivered that morning, and looked unhappy. Deirdre had taken pity on them and put them in the orangery, but their wailing was so horrible that after ten minutes she shooed them into the garden. Once there, they pecked at various plants and tried to display, but they had no tail feathers yet so looked rather silly. A new location meant they thought they were now rivals, but at least it prevented any ideas they might have had of escaping.

'What do we do with them overnight?' asked Liberty. 'They can't be put with the chickens or ducks!' The birds took matters into their own feet and roosted on top of the chimneys, comforted by the heat from below and calling every few minutes. By the next morning even the most peaceful villagers wanted to shoot them, and Deirdre was ready to pluck and roast them over the fire.

'So much for our beauty sleep,' murmured J-T as he descended for a late breakfast. 'The dogs barked every time they crowed, or whatever it is they do, so Bob and I got no sleep whatsoever.'

Nevertheless, the party atmosphere was upon them. The caterers were busy in their kitchen, which they had set up at an amazing rate in a smaller tent, the rain had stopped, and the low winter sun was doing its best to dry the puddles.

Liberty was doing the same indoors. 'I do so love you, Teal, but I can't wait for the day you are trained.' She looked at her mother.

'Don't blame me, darling – it's all part and parcel of having a pet. They are so adorable at that age, so you don't really mind, and she will get there eventually. Keep her in a good routine, and soon she will know it's best to go outside.'

Guests had been instructed to turn up at eight. Deirdre knew the locals would arrive first. Many of the others were booked into nearby hotels, and Terence Macready was even helicoptering in, with kind permission to land on Jonathan's land. In the good old days, Deirdre had held many parties like this, and so had no sweaty palms concerning the 250 or so guests descending for the evening. She had found it always worked to mix people, so each table had a selection of the great, the good, the famous and the local. It was always interesting to see who got on (and who didn't). One year, she remembered, a very well-known film star tried to land a part with a director she sat next to. The man was so delighted to be flirted with and chatted up by the beautiful but brainless young woman he couldn't bring himself to tell her he was the director of an institute, not of films.

As the hosting household beautified themselves upstairs, waiters in smart uniforms readied their trays and poured champagne. The canapés were being laid out. Deirdre and Liberty had tried not to bother the caterers too much, but couldn't resist taking a look in the kitchen. Deirdre knew the locals expected something different and amusing so they could discuss the menu for the coming twelve months. Those used to eating in the best restaurants would be happy with something rather more homely, so she had decided on adventurous canapés followed by sausages and mash piled on to huge platters for the main course. Each table would be presented with its own Desperate Dan platter, sausages sticking out of the mash, and each guest would have his or her own tiny bottle of ketchup and brown sauce. For pudding the adventure revved up again. Each person would have 'A Passionata': one passion fruit panna cotta, one coconut and passion fruit macaroon and one thin slice of dark chocolate tart, topped with passion fruit jelly.

Cooking 550 sausages was fairly easy, and the caterers were relaxed. The previous day they had been hurriedly stuffing partridges with pigeons and foie gras, so they were enjoying themselves. The sausages were from Ted, who would be coming tonight, thrilled that Deirdre had promised to name him on the menu. He was used to people laughing when he told them his name was Ted Pig, and yes, he really was a pig farmer, and so he was looking forward to the comments, and hopefully some orders.

The house began to fill up. Fred the blacksmith was one of the first to arrive. He looked devastatingly handsome in black tie. He would have been the epitome of a Greek god on legs, had his mouth not fallen open in a very un-God-like way when he saw Liberty, who looked ravishing in her Roland Mouret dress that enhanced her tiny waist and showed off her curves and long legs. It was in silvery green, which made her skin gleam and her eyes bewitching. When he recovered, he kissed her on both cheeks and said her sign was coming along nicely. He fished his phone from his pocket and showed her some photographs. She was thrilled with the elegant simplicity, told him so and gave him a huge hug, at which point Edmund walked in. Glowering and glamorous in evening dress, he stalked straight past her to say hello to Paloma. Grahame was not so rude, and waited until Fred let Liberty go before kissing her.

'Hello, Fred,' he said, a little coolly. He remembered finding him in a compromising situation with his sister years before. It had caused a few problems, not least of which was Savannah confiding to Grahame a few weeks afterwards that she was late. Thankfully, this was only a horrible scare, but as Fred had denied any wrongdoing, and rudely claimed it could have been anyone's, Grahame had never forgiven him.

Paloma looked stunning in a Dior dress she had found in a vintage clothes shop in Paris. 'Probably made when I was born, and has aged much better than me,' she told Jonathan laughingly.

'Oh, I don't know about that,' he replied, gazing down at her happy, inclined and unlined face.

From inside the house it looked as though the fireworks had begun early. The photographers had leapt to their feet from the cold ground where they had been waiting for recognisable faces, and they set to work, flashes blitzing every few seconds as cars disgorged business champions, sports personalities and the occasional actor. One surprising face was that of Genevieve a Bois, the ballerina with whom Alain had had a child, Leah, all those years ago, and for whom he had left Deirdre. Paloma had invited her, as Deirdre and Liberty had wanted news of the daughter – wanted to meet her and perhaps get to know her. On her part, Genevieve was stunned by the invitation, and immediately booked first-class tickets for them both. She had kept Leah to herself, infuriated when Alain had refused to follow her to the States for her career. She had become a choreographer but now, faded and unrecognised, she relished any chance to shine, and imagined, incorrectly, that she would be guest of honour, not giving any thought to how her neglected daughter would feel.

Leah was getting out of the car. She looked nothing like Liberty – very blonde, California skinny, wearing a handkerchief of a dress and far too much heavy make-up on her pretty but strained face. She stalked into the house, saw Liberty and asked where the bathrooms were. J-T returned from taking her to the cloakroom, and informed Liberty it was to powder her nose, and not in the old-fashioned way.

Deirdre greeted the retired ballerina, albeit with gritted teeth. 'Gosh, you have changed so much,' was the booming reply she was given. 'England is so behind in facial enhancement, you must come to stay with us in the States, and see my dermatologist.'

Before Deirdre could deck her, Jonathan leapt to the rescue, telling her a queue was building at the door, all freezing as they were being photographed. Deirdre raced off to rescue her guests before they fled and Jonathan introduced Genevieve to Ethan Trickster, a beautiful upcoming actor who would be happy to sleep with his mother if it meant becoming more famous. He was here at his manager's insistence, but he had noticed his manager was in London with some of his more famous clients. He and Genevieve were both preening like the peacocks that were still calling from the chimney tops.

'That bloody woman, how could Alain have seen anything in her?' complained Deirdre to Liberty. She downed a glass of champagne, took a deep breath and vowed to steer clear.

People were starting to move out to the orangery from where the French doors led to a covered walkway that took them to the marquee. Banks of flowers lined the walls of the marquee, making it look like a walled garden rather than a tent, and the tables were adorned with more floristry art, giving a feel of opulence. The dance floor had temporary rugs strewn over it to absorb the chatter and make the atmosphere cosier; they would be rolled back later. A jazz band played in a corner as waitresses moved through the crowd with trays of canapés.

Bob had managed to interest a round-the-world yachtsman in sponsoring a new artist, so would be lost in conversation for hours. J-T and Grahame were becoming drinking partners. Gray always found New Year's Eve tricky. Meanwhile, J-T was fed up with Bob for working rather than partying, so the two lonely gays were getting on famously.

'Another bottle for us, I think,' said Gray, snatching one from an unsuspecting waiter. 'God, I hate New Year's. No matter how much fun the party is, there always seems to be the expectation of something better. It's just another night, but everyone always seems to think it could be a whole new beginning. They don't get it. It will just be the same old shit tomorrow.'

'And there was me thinking you were the happy one in your family,' said J-T, smiling.

'Oh, sorry, it's the cynic in me appearing. Doesn't Liberty

look fabulous?' said Gray, to change the subject. 'I wonder if she is having a fling with that dreadful Fred.'

'Oh, she had a near miss, or that's what she told us,' said J-T. 'What about you? Anyone on the scene?'

Gray looked up at the handsome smiling face and wished he could pour his heart out.

34

The canapés had been demolished. Deirdre managed to find Fred, who helped her force open the downstairs cloakroom door and physically remove Leah, who had decided to stay in there all night.

'Come along, young lady, I want you to meet your half-sister.'

At this, Leah ran back into the cloakroom and threw up the little she had eaten for lunch. *Bloody Paloma, this hasn't been a good idea*, thought Deirdre.

Ballerina and actor were still nose to nose, and had changed table placements so they could continue their burgeoning relationship. Both talked at once, each telling the other how fabulous they were, when really they were describing themselves.

The vicar was trying to have a discussion with a very interesting art history professor, who had worked on bringing the largest ever Leonardo collection to the National Gallery. But Miss Scally kept interrupting, reminding the vicar his sermons had been getting too short, and asking what she should do about Dr Brown, as he seemed so depressed.

Doesn't seem depressed to me, thought the vicar, watching the doctor's familiar crinkled face smile down on Sarah as she chatted animatedly to him.

Dilys the barmaid was trying desperately to entrap Terence Macready the pop star with her cleavage, which he was doing his best not to fall into. He was far too polite to tell her he was still desperately in love with his wife of forty years, and that it was only his publicity team who kept rumours of his affairs and promiscuity going so the media didn't forget about him.

The guests eventually took their seats, and the Ted Pig sausages and mash were brought out, red wine poured and a happy mixture of conversation and music filled the marquee, only occasionally marred by the wail of the peacocks who had decided to make the flower displays in the walkways their supper.

Everyone was tucking into the delicious food, except for Genevieve, who was now trying to calm her weeping daughter while simultaneously flirting with Ethan. This was not easy, as the actor was doing his best to comfort Leah by putting his hand up her tiny skirt. This had the desired effect.

'Hello,' Leah said, finally cracking a smile. 'Please may I have a glass of wine?'

'Trouble there,' said Edmund to Liberty; they had been placed next to each other by Paloma.

'I don't know why Paloma thought it would be a good idea to have them at the party,' replied Liberty after glancing in the direction he was indicating. 'Dad tried to keep in contact with Leah, but Genevieve sent his letters back unopened and refused to take his calls. I'm sure that's why he cancelled coming tonight. He said his sous-chef had come down with something, but I'm not convinced. And he had such a good time at Christmas.'

Once the sausages had been devoured, and the passionata pudding was being picked at by the now very merry crowd, the dance floor was cleared of rugs for the next stage of the evening. The band, who had taken over from the initial musicians, struck up with 'I Gotta Feeling' by The Black Eyed Peas. Deirdre found herself being led by the unusually relaxed and very merry Dr Brown, who whooshed her around the floor and said admiringly as they twirled, 'Fabulous party, great crowd. So nice to be able to meet such a mix of people – reminds one of what's under one's own nose.' Deirdre was wondering what he meant – she hoped he wasn't going to declare his undying love – when his eye caught Sarah's and he waved at her over Deirdre's shoulder.

Hmm, thought Deirdre.

Deirdre felt the evil eye of Miss Scally upon her and asked the doctor, 'How do you cope with such a terror as receptionist and secretary?' She was having to shout to be heard, but thankfully there was so much noise nobody else could hear her.

'She has been a godsend at organising my office and files, and can you imagine the fallout if I fired her? I've been hoping she may retire, but who would take her place?'

Deirdre's mind was still in gear. 'What about Sarah? She will need to work after the baby comes, and she is exhausting herself with cleaning.'

'Lovely girl!' beamed the doctor. 'Not a bad idea, not a bad idea at all . . .' And with that, they gave up trying to talk over the music.

Liberty had surprised herself by enjoying Edmund's company during the meal, but he had quickly taken his leave when Fred bounded over to ask her to dance. As Fred nuzzled into her and tried all his best moves, Liberty wondered what was wrong – she felt no attraction to the Irish hunk now. Maybe it was knowing he was such a tart. But she allowed herself to enjoy his firm, capable body swinging her around the floor.

At ten minutes to midnight Terence Macready, who was really very tired of women trying to seduce him, decided to remove himself from the throng in the only way he knew. Asking the band if they minded, he took the mike and announced he was going to sing them into the new year. One of his most popular tracks had been 'Dancing For the First', a catchy rock number released with the sole purpose of reaching number one for the new year – well, actually, new year in 1979, but with his hips gyrating in his black jeans, bow tie removed, and his dark shirt clinging to his taut midriff, he still looked very much the rock star. His voice was perhaps not as strong as it had once been – too many concerts and too many cigarettes – but it was now softer and more gravelly, which suited this particular band. Originally he had been accompanied by drum rolls and clashing guitars, but now the smoother sound of the bass guitar and saxophone gave the song a real energy and life of its own.

Dammit, thought the quiet Mrs Macready, who had spent the last thirty-five years as the stay-at-home wife and manager. *He sounds so good, we are going to have to re-record and re-release that song. At least it will help with the grandchildren's school fees.*

At the end of the song was a countdown which usually fed into a guitar solo, but had been also used as a lead up to midnight by DJs for the past thirty-five years, and Terence brought the house down when he shouted 'Midnight!'. Fireworks were exploding in the park, welcoming in the new year, and guests raced outside for fresh air and to ooh and aah. As they rushed past the demolished flower displays, the peacocks took exception to the noise and colourful explosions and flew off into the darkness.

Liberty was being kissed and hugged by everyone. She hoped it was not just the drink that was encouraging her enthusiastic welcome to the village. She hugged and kissed back, smiling as she watched Fred snogging a young beauty in a gold-sequinned dress.

'You don't mind?'

She turned to find Edmund standing behind her.

'What? Fred? God, no, he's funny and gorgeous, but a little loose for me where morals are concerned. Oh, Edmund, happy new year.' And she awkwardly kissed him on the cheek; he returned the pressure and hugged her to him. A fizz of energy spun down from her hair to her toes, and wrapped itself cosily round her shoulders where he had placed his arm. Embarrassed that he might be able to sense her excitement, she pulled away from his embrace a little too quickly, and he looked soulfully down at her.

'I had better find Pa to wish him a happy new year,' he excused himself.

Liberty touched her cheek where he had kissed her. She had found herself thinking of his handsome face all too often recently, and now she told herself to get a grip, as he seemed to want to move away from her so quickly. Although, when they chatted at supper, they had so much to say. *He probably has women falling at his feet, and doesn't want to lead another one on*, thought Liberty sadly.

Terence was back at the microphone, the lead singer of the band only too thrilled as the press photographers had managed to enter the marquee and were now snapping away. Great publicity!

Most people were getting a second wind, helped by bottles of champagne generously distributed over the tables for people to help themselves. Steaming coffee pots were also being laid out alongside trays of petits fours, which disappeared quickly. Dijon had forgotten his advanced years and disgraced himself by escaping when Liberty took the puppy out. He had thoughtfully dragged a tray of leftovers – sausages and mash, and pudding left for the disposal bin – to where Custard was waiting. They were found looking fat and guilty by Deirdre, who only said, 'I thought you were meant to be scared of fireworks, but happy new year to you both.'

She was en route to the cloakroom to freshen up when she caught sight, through the sitting room door, of Jonathan and Paloma in a passionate embrace. Steeling herself for a jealous fist to attack her heart, she was surprised that all she felt was delight for two of her oldest friends, and she found her mouth smiling as she reapplied her lipstick.

Hours later cars rolled up the high street to take the guests home. Liberty was feeling a bit flat as she said goodnight to the last few stragglers. She was wondering what had happened to Edmund, Gray and J-T. Jonathan was in the kitchen with Deirdre and Paloma, and Bob had gone to bed after sealing a deal with Terence for three paintings by one of his latest discoveries that Terence had been admiring on Bob's iPad. It had also been agreed, by way of thanks, that J-T would redesign the

Macreadys' flat in London, because Mrs M said it looked like something from the 1970s.

'It's where he still goes to write music, and I do believe it could bring his music into today's world if he is no longer surrounded by wooden standard lamps and Moroccan prayer rugs. He even has a kaftan,' she admitted, laughing, 'but don't say I told you!'

'We all get inspiration from different things,' said Terence, fondly pushing his fingers through her hair. But he had allowed his wife to discuss their project with Bob, as she rarely asked for anything. Bob wondered where the hell J-T had got to, so felt little guilt in offering his work free of charge.

As Liberty rested her danced-out legs by the Aga, Teal on her lap, she asked Jonathan whether Gray and Edmund had gone home.

'I'm not entirely sure,' replied Jonathan. 'I haven't been paying much attention.' He smiled at Paloma, looking like a wolfhound that has just found a huge sofa right by the fire, together with a bowl of Bonios with 'WELCOME' written on it.

I may just be missing Savvie, thought Liberty, who always felt deflated after a party. But it had been such fun. She really felt she had got to know lots of the local people. She had managed to steer clear of Miss Scally, and she had even chatted to Gwen and Paul, the couple who ran the existing tea shop. She had suggested to them that maybe they would like to do some travelling while they could, and enjoy their retirement rather than working all hours. Gwen agreed, saying she had always dreamed of visiting Portugal, and perhaps they could go on a painting holiday. Paul, who preferred lying on a beach pretending to sleep while ogling the topless sunbathers, said he would think about it, but money didn't grow on trees.

'You have a good pension, dear,' sighed Gwen, whose feet, used to running around all day, were now feeling pinched in her party shoes. Liberty felt sorry for Gwen, but she needed energy and vitality, not an exhausted, frustrated housewife, as her front of house. Pleased she hadn't hurt their feelings too much, she wished she could summon Savannah back – that would be such fun. She would work something out.

'I really must go to bed,' announced Deirdre finally. 'Tomorrow we have to round up those bloody peacocks, God knows where they are, and I feel awful about Leah. Did you get to talk to her at all?'

'No. Last I saw of her, she was arguing with her mother about some man. It's sad, but I'm not sure it was the best time to try to unite long-lost sisters!'

Deirdre smiled and said, 'No, I suppose not, but I think you should try again. The poor girl seems lost, and with such a bitch of a mother and an absent father, I'm not surprised! Did you happen to notice Dr Brown talking to Sarah? I think something may start there!'

Liberty sighed. 'Mother, you must stop matchmaking, Sarah has enough problems, not to mention a husband.'

'Yes, true, but she deserves better, and if she could work for him, it would kill two birds, so to speak. However, I have no intention of having voodoo dolls made of me, and finding boiled rabbits on the stove. I'm sure Miss Scally has put off all poor Dr Brown's admirers since his wife died.'

'You could start by addressing him by his first name,' put in Paloma, whose eyes were glazing over with love as she yawned into her camomile tea.

'I had better say goodnight,' said Jonathan, and he rose to leave. Paloma followed him into the hall.

'Lots to talk about in the morning, my darling,' said Deirdre, raising her eyebrow as she bent to kiss Liberty on the forehead. 'Happy new year, my wonderful girl, it's going to be a great one. I love you.'

35

Liberty woke late; not surprising, but annoying for her, as the first day of January was her favourite day of the year. It was an opportunity, Liberty felt, not for resolutions, but for a clean start, especially this year. After dressing quickly, she clutched the still sleepy Teal in her arms and went downstairs, saying in the pug's ear, 'Your first hangover from a late night, honey, but not the last!' She plonked the dog on the lawn, and then pushed Dijon and Custard out too. They still looked very portly after their midnight feast.

The garden was a sight. Glasses littered about, spent firework casings stuck in the hedges – there was even somebody's dress lying on a chair. The organisers would arrange for the marquee to be taken down later, and the caterers would collect the glasses, but she couldn't just leave all the mess, so she wandered round, picking up plates and detritus. After a few minutes she heard a whimpering. Had one of the dogs trodden on a glass, she thought in horror. She looked about only to see J-T, exhausted, red-eyed, sitting on the frozen ground, still in his dress shirt and socks.

'Don't ask!' he wailed.

'Well, you know I'm going to, but you must be chilled to the bone! Have you been out here all night? Go and have a hot shower and get into some warm clothes. I'll put the coffee on.' Liberty helped him up as he was icy cold and could barely stand.

She pushed him up the stairs, terribly worried as to why he was out there in the first place. She called the dogs in and warmed some milk, put a little brandy into a jug, then, just as she poured the coffee she heard shouting and arguing. Recognising Bob's voice, she decided to leave them to it, but was now very concerned. It was fifteen minutes before J-T entered the kitchen, together with Deirdre, who had been woken by the ruckus. He was now fully dressed but barefooted, which startled Liberty, who had only ever seen him impeccably clad. She put coffee before him and added two spoonfuls of sugar. Deirdre added brandy and milk, before helping herself and sitting beside him, wrapping a woollen blanket over his shivering shoulders.

'So tell me, what's happened?'

'It's just awful. Too awful.' They heard a car's engine starting up outside. 'That will be Bob. He's gone,' he said quietly.

'Why and how?' asked Deirdre, remembering J-T had used her car to fetch Bob.

'He called the company driver who had been staying with his family nearby,' J-T explained.

Liberty sat beside him, put her hands around his, and said gently, 'It can't be that bad. Tell us about it. We might be able to help.'

'Oh, it's bad,' he said. 'I've messed up three lives, and have only myself to blame for it. If only there could be another tsunami!'

'I don't understand, what do you mean?' asked Liberty, now desperately worried for her trembling friend.

'You know,' he mumbled, 'the big story that knocks all the others off the front cover.'

'It was only a party,' said Liberty. 'What on earth can have happened?'

'I suggest you run to the shops and fetch the papers,' said Deirdre to her daughter. She was now beginning to comprehend this could be more serious than a mere lovers' scuffle.

Everyone Liberty met while rushing along the street thanked her for such a good evening, but seemed to have an ironic edge to their voice. She was now seriously worried. There was the *Daily Tidings*, stacked up before her in the newsagent's.

Nobody ever admitted to reading it, but everyone did, as it kept the country informed about the latest footballer scandal, who had been sacked from the latest TV reality show, and vegetables that looked like Jesus or Cherie Blair.

Liberty's heart leapt into her mouth as she saw the front cover. Its entirety was taken up with a photograph captioned 'How Much Energy Are You Saving Now?'. The meaning was clear. The photographer must have been right outside, for he had taken a remarkably clear picture of Deirdre's dining room, whose windows faced the village green, despite being set well back from the road and fronted by a high hedge. There, for the entire world to see, was Grahame doing something to J-T's crotch, although it was deliberately blurred.

No, no, impossible! was Liberty's initial thought. And then: *I can't buy all of them!*

Mr Podaski, the newsagent, had not attended the party as he had to be in his shop by five every morning. By now, almost wishing he had, he was watching as Liberty snatched a copy of every newspaper he stocked, and fled. He put them on Deirdre's bill. She rushed home carrying her vast bundle, and into the kitchen, where J-T had been telling Deirdre what had happened between sobs: about getting bladdered with Gray, finding a friend and confidant, but taking it too far and falling into his arms (and obviously other parts, too). He looked up as Liberty came in; a brief flicker of hope washed over his face as he prayed that what he and Gray had feared when they were blinded by the photographer's flash had not been reality. But once he glanced at the front page of the *Daily Tidings* he despaired; there was no denying the magnitude of the coverage.

The first five pages covered the 'story' angle. A journalist who had in fact been hired by a society magazine for the evening had written the story and been only too happy to sell it to the rag, gaining himself a reputation of sorts.

'Are we all fed up with toffee-nosed Members of Parliament telling us to live more moral lives and save the world? Let me

show you how clean, green, Grahame de Weatherby spends his free time.'

The article continued: '*Super eco-champ Grahame de Weatherby, whose lineage dates back to the Norman Conquest, has been campaigning for all of us to put up with wind farms and incinerators in our villages and towns. Maybe this is how the other half keeps warm in winter.*

'*His sordid secret is now out. His boyfriend, interior designer Julian Tracey Jackson–*'

'Tracey!' Liberty exclaimed.

'Not the point, darling, do read on,' said Deirdre.

'No, don't,' sobbed J-T. 'How did they find out who I am?'

He turned on his phone to try and call Bob. He didn't want him to read the article before he had talked to him. They had already had a fight when J-T told him he had done something awful. Bob understood 'awful' to mean 'unfaithful', which to him meant 'unforgiveable'. So he stormed out of the house, little realising how public the situation was.

J-T's phone rang. He said 'no comment' to a reporter before listening to his messages. Most were from his personal assistant, Catherine, who tearfully reported that she had been fooled by someone who called pretending to be a client desperately trying to find where he was, as their sofa had collapsed. She was not the brightest girl and, keen to earn brownie points by working on 1st January, she had thought this must be her first interior design disaster and had given away too much information about his friends and family so the client could find him.

'That means press on the doorstep,' said Deirdre grimly. 'I'll close the curtains at the front. I should have done that last night.'

The women's thoughts turned to Grahame.

'Do you think he's told Jonathan?' said Deirdre. 'Oh, the poor, poor boy.'

Just then Paloma wandered in, eyes sleepy but full of love and happiness, mouthing, 'What a perfect day.' Then she took in the papers strewn over the kitchen table, and the horror-stricken faces, unusual lack of food on the table and said calmly, 'Right, I'll do breakfast, you call Jonathan.'

Paloma and Liberty clucked round J-T, telling him he would get through this. Bob would realise he had made a rash decision. They put eggs before him, and J-T actually smiled at this and said, 'You don't cheer up a gay man by forcing calories on him.' But he took a mouthful of poached egg on toast to be polite.

Deirdre came off the phone and relayed to the others that Jonathan and his sons had been up all night. 'The papers and their journalists are homing in on Gray, no pun intended, as he is the bigger story – sorry J-T, but he is an MP – and they have been arriving in their droves and are camped out up there. Gray has told Edmund and his Pa all they need to know. I'm not sure whether anything would shock Jonathan at the moment, but he sounded horrified the press had caught hold of the story.'

Paloma was pacing. 'Should I go to see him?' she asked Deirdre.

'With all the press outside, I don't think Jonathan would appreciate visitors now. You can always call him and talk, but right now he needs to concentrate on his son.'

Paloma was desperate to comfort her new love, but understood, and felt for the sobbing young man sitting before her.

'Gray hadn't told his family he was gay – he hadn't told anyone,' sobbed J-T. 'And here is me, showing the world! Oh God, what am I going to do? I can't live without Bob, and he has taken Feran and Bulli.'

Thank goodness, was Deirdre's first thought. She hated the yapping duo.

'Talking of which, you two don't seem surprised,' said Paloma, pouring coffee and looking from Liberty to Deirdre.

'I have known for years,' said Liberty. 'Since I was a child, really, but I didn't realise you knew, Mother.'

'I didn't. I just guessed, I suppose. I was always surprised Jonathan didn't suspect, but I think he always hoped to have more grandchildren so maybe he blanked it out.'

Liberty didn't allow her mind to wander towards Edmund. He had filled her dreams all too vividly last night.

'Anyway,' continued Deirdre briskly, 'I don't think it prudent to go over to see them, or for J-T to go anywhere near the house. The press will be all over us, and hopefully there will be a bigger story for them to cover tomorrow.'

Sadly for J-T and Grahame, the following week was a quiet one for news desks, so the photographers and journalists hovered around the village for several days, trying to get a new angle. Most people were loyal to their beloved MP; however, an unnamed source gave a full account of the party with her own additions – it was accepted that Miss Scally was the source – that homosexuality was encouraged at The Nuttery and why did Alain leave Deirdre, after all? This gave Alain the opportunity he had been looking for to phone Deirdre and roar with laughter down the phone that he hoped next time he visited she would be reclining in bed with some 'buxom, rosy-cheeked villager'. Deirdre told him to stop being so frivolous when 'all around is falling apart'. But she felt comforted that he had called.

Four days after the news broke, Liberty announced she was going to move into Duck End, if only to get out of her mother's house and take the press and J-T away from her. Paloma phoned Jonathan to tell him she had to return to France to await the arrival of her grandchild, but she hoped he would visit her soon. Jonathan said he understood, but he was devastated. He had at last found feelings he thought he had buried with his wife, only to be dragged away by his family. Was this a message from Helena? He loved his son, but his timing concerning coming out could have been better. As she thought about J-T's statement that the scandalous story had ruined three lives, Deirdre reflected that there were several more relationships hovering in the balance.

Liberty had wanted J-T to stay a while once she moved, but he said, sensibly, that he had to return to London to try and sort things out with Bob. They may have drifted apart over the past few months, and he had in a moment of drunken insanity given way to his feelings of neglect, but he knew they had something worth fighting for.

Opposition members of Parliament were trying to use the story to discredit Grahame, but his constituents were being surprisingly loyal for such a conservative area, despite many of them having old-fashioned prejudices. They had seen for themselves what a good person and MP he was. He had stood up for their country rights many times, and they had to admit that green energy was the way forward. He had obtained many grants and other monies to rent land for turbines, so now the majority of them had stopped worrying about how their countryside would look and started realising anything that paid for itself had to be good. It saved them money, after all.

Grahame, however, was devastated. One moment of weakness after too much alcohol had brought his lifetime's terror upon him. He had always felt the knowledge of having a homosexual son would be devastating to his father. Jonathan hadn't even blanched when Gray sat him and Edmund down and told them the situation that fateful night after the party, but he knew his Pa was hurt, mostly in memory of his mother, Helena, who would have loved a home full of grandchildren.

Edmund only said, 'Mama would have been proud of you, so don't worry, we'll get through it.' But Gray would like to have heard this from his Pa, too.

Savannah had phoned when she heard the news on the BBC World Service.

'Are you OK, darling?' she asked. But she went on to say that Khalid had been mortified the children had been staying with a gay man, so Gray knew Savannah was even more depressed than before, although she didn't say so.

He had always wanted to make the world a better, happier place, and now he was bringing his family's world down around their ears. He recognised that he had to stand down and disappear from public life, grateful though he was for his constituents' support. When at last he returned home he found a brick had been thrown through a downstairs window with 'HORE' and 'POUF' written on a piece of paper wrapped round it. The typo gave him the chance to smile, but he thought to himself *nothing changes*, as he cleared up the glass.

A knock at the door. He steeled himself to open it. A gaggle of press photographers stood outside. 'What next, Gray?' they asked in unison.

Gray thought for a moment, before giving the dreaded speech he had rehearsed in his head a thousand times in the last few days. 'I have already written to those who need to know, and with great sadness tendered my resignation. There will be a by-election, of course. I thank all those who have supported and stood by me through these difficult days.'

As the photographers clicked away and the journos asked questions, he felt sick to his stomach. He found he couldn't stand there any longer before breaking down. 'That is all I have to say,' was all he could muster before he shut the door on the cruel world, sat down at his computer and quickly wrote emails to those people he professed already to have informed. Once sent, he put his head in his hands and cried his heart out, feeling more alone than ever. *What a bloody waste*, was all he could think, *and what for?* A moment of bliss. At this, he allowed himself a smile. J-T had been gentle, reassuring and kindness personified; he hated to think what was becoming of the one man who had understood, ever.

The response was immediate. 'Gray for Green – vote him back in!'

Nature eventually intervened, providing a bigger news story: dramatic flooding in Bangladesh, over a quarter of a million people feared drowned and many more destined to die from disease.

Gray took this as a message from the gods to do more to help the real world. He had realised over the past few days that he had become increasingly disillusioned by central government workings, and the control held by the European Court over

Middle England constituents who merely wanted to cut a hedge or build an affordable home, only to be told that section nine, paragraph 3.2.11 of the European Diktat stated that no home without triple-glazing (at vast personal cost) could be built unless on a brownfield site, etcetera, etcetera. He was totally fed up with petty fights. He would leave Edmund to wrestle with Denhelm's alternative power research, and volunteer his services to whoever needed his help.

His talents were greedily snapped up by UNESCO, one of whose senior officers was an old school friend and knew how good Gray was at achieving the impossible by sheer persistence. With conflicts springing up around the world, and the global economic situation so dicey, promoting cultural diversity had become increasingly difficult. Grahame was the perfect candidate to get things done. Therefore, much to the regret of his constituents, Gray announced he was off to Bangladesh to attempt to help people far more deserving and needy than those in the UK. He would travel via Abu Dhabi, he added to Jonathan and Edmund, to try and see Savannah.

'I want to see her and the children, check she is OK. I couldn't bear for her to be unhappy for long.'

Jonathan understood his younger son's decision, but was sad to see another of his children disappear off round the world.

'I'll be back. The job is only for a few months and then I will be ready for something here. I just need for everyone to forget what happened.'

'I feel I only just know you now,' said Jonathan, giving his son a hug. 'Maybe I should come with you and see what I can do to help Savvie and the children.'

'I don't think Khalid is going to welcome me with open arms, and he may see you as a threat,' said Gray. 'If I think there's trouble at the mill, albeit the gold-plated mill, I'll let you know.'

He also wrote a heartfelt apology to J-T at his office, not wanting to compromise any reconciliation between him and Bob by sending it to their home. He simply said he was sorry for all the publicity and embarrassment and hoped he and Bob could sort out their differences.

Bob had in fact benefited from the publicity. Headlines such as 'Famous duo in MP's downfall!' meant everyone had heard of The Small Dog Design Company and of his gallery. He was furious with J-T, who had been allowed back into their apartment, but was relegated to the spare bedroom. Bob appreciated that he was working too hard, but J-T had been the one to leave him for a jolly with Liberty. He knew designing the interior for a country cottage would have taken all of one brain cell, and he was perfectly aware that his partner had spent most of the time having fun. Loyalty and fidelity were incredibly important to Bob. He had been humiliated, and wondered if it had been the first time J-T and Gray had been intimate. He seconded the call by opposition MPs for Gray's resignation, but then, with time to mull it over, felt a little sorry for the man. His career would be over, but Bob couldn't believe Gray hadn't told his family earlier that he was gay. There must have been a reason. He thought perhaps he had tried, and was met by Jonathan simply refusing to acknowledge his son's existence any longer, as had happened to Bob. If that was the case, he was truly sorry for the man.

J-T's parents had been desperately angry when he told them in early adolescence, and were initially disgusted with him, but it was at least a reaction, whereas Bob's father had never spoken to him again. Not for twenty-five years, for heaven's sake. Bob felt terrible, thinking of the horrible time Gray must be going through. Every gay person unites in the terror of telling their nearest and dearest. Some parents are surprisingly accepting, despite being seemingly truly conservative in their outlook. J-T's parents had always been so laid-back, having spent most of the 1960s and 1970s caravanning around the world to promote peace and free love. They got stoned regularly and refused to commit to work until dragged kicking and screaming into the real world when a child arrived. Sadly, by the time J-T announced to his parents he was gay, they had morphed into the very people they had spent their formative years rejecting.

Once he settled into a comfortable job as a bank manager, Mr Jackson became as dull as the bank he worked in. He forgot about free love, as he realised very quickly that fitting in and keeping his head down was rewarded by a good salary. Once he had money, a car and a home he was happy to hold on to what he had, thank you very much, and he threw away the kaftans and the caravan. Thankfully, Mrs Jackson had kept some of the atmosphere of free spirit in the home, and she passed on her artistic temperament to J-T.

Bob knew it would take him a long time to forgive his partner, who was working hard and taking the dogs to the park every day without complaining. J-T obviously regretted deeply what had happened, but Bob needed to know his soul mate was serious about being faithful from now on, and wanted to convince him of what they had together. He had even suggested a separation so his eyes could be opened to what a good life they had. But J-T had looked so terrified at this suggestion he backed down, in case the silly boy did something to harm himself.

But both of them were very aware that something was wrong in their relationship.

36

Liberty felt as though she were in the eye of the storm. Her friends all seemed to be having problems and she could do nothing to help. So she concentrated on moving into her cottage and opening her café.

Sad as she was to leave her mother's comfortable home, it was exciting to transport all her belongings into her very own place. This was the first time in her life she had lived alone, apart from halls at university, which didn't count, and she was pleased to have Teal's reassuring furry presence. The little dog helped to explain creaks in the night, and any loneliness was calmed and eased by a lick or a stroke.

The house was beautiful. She loved it, and it really started to feel like home when cooking smells took over from paint ones, filling the house with the aroma of gently simmering coq au vin and a rhubarb tart when Gray came to see her before leaving for Abu Dhabi.

She burst out laughing as he arrived at the door. All she could see was a tall tree in a pot, and a large cardboard box.

'Are you there, Gray? Or is the tree coming in on its own? I didn't stock up on Baby Bio!'

'Your mother told me you needed to fill the place with real stuff, so I've brought my plants for you to plant-sit, and all my old books. Bookshelves without books are ridiculous.'

Liberty had placed a huge order of old and new cookery books with Steve Bainbridge, a friend of her mother's and source of all things bookish in Ludlow, and they would be wending their way to her once he had the titles together. However, she was grateful for the gesture, and said she would certainly look after them until his return. Gray had also brought a bottle of champagne and a delicate, prettily coloured Meissen vase.

'Happy house warming,' he said and gave her a hug, with his now free arms. They left the new additions in the hall for Teal to sniff while Liberty showed him proudly round the house. Once he had admired and clucked in all the right places he asked her if he could have a drink.

'Oh, God! Sorry, my hostessing skills are terrible now I have so much to show off. I'm going to be perfect in the café. I'll show everyone my sparkling pots and pans and forget to feed them!'

'Don't you worry,' said Gray, laughing, as she handed him a chilled glass of Sancerre, the champagne he had given her being too warm to serve. 'Cheers.' He took a sip, nodded in appreciation and said, 'I've never really thanked you, have I?'

'What for? The disastrous New Year's party, or introducing you to J-T?'

Gray shook his head but smiled kindly. 'For keeping my secret. Not many people can do that. And I now recognise, sadly, it would have been better all round if I had been open. Maybe not for my chosen career, but certainly for me and the family. Look at me. I've basically been living in enforced celibacy for the past twenty years.'

Liberty raised a well-groomed brow.

'I don't know about your private life,' she said, 'but no relationships at all?'

'You should have advised me to go into a different profession!'

'Hang it all, I was eleven!' joked Liberty.

'I may not have said anything, but you have held a very special place in my heart, and I thank you now from the bottom of it.'

Liberty had a lump in her throat, and no idea how to respond apart from feeding him, so she did just that.

They sat at the oval table in the kitchen, dishes and a claret jug on the table so they didn't have to get up. Liberty served them both with the juicy wine-rich chicken, mashed potato and a green salad, which she placed on pretty cabbage-shaped side plates. While Gray poured the wine, Liberty asked him what he thought was going to happen regarding Savannah.

'I honestly can't think. I know that girl, and it's impossible to imagine her imprisoned in a home in the middle of a country she respects but dislikes. However, the children have changed her life, and she will do anything to keep them happy and safe and by her side. It was just finding out about the house in Paris that gave me an odd feeling. It just doesn't make sense. Khalid was insistent they made their home in Abu Dhabi, and of course that's where he is from, but it makes me wonder if he is planning to leave Savannah there while he goes off to Paris and the children are in Switzerland. I cannot see whom, if anyone, it would benefit. He loves those children, and he seems to adore Savannah, so why separate them? If Khalid is planning on doing anything that would hurt her, I would like to be up to date with his plans.'

'You had people watching the house, didn't you? Did they give you a clue as to its purpose?' asked Liberty as she spooned another portion of buttery tarragon-infused mash on to his plate to sop up the juices. He had obviously not been eating since New Year, and his once fitted shirt was loose around the gills.

'No, nothing, apart from once in a while a lady goes in and comes out a couple of hours later – God, this is good by the way, any more chicken? We think she must be a maid, but we can't exactly interrogate her without evidence of wrongdoing.'

Liberty dished up the last of the bird on to his proffered plate as she said, 'I suppose not, and I'm sure it's probably just another investment. I'm convinced Savvie doesn't know the half of what his business interests are. What did you think of Khalid as a person rather than your brother-in-law?'

'Well, he seems nice enough – strong views, bright as a button, meant to be amazing on a horse and bloody good-looking, which will have wowed Savannah. He also appears to be a man of the world, so I don't quite understand his rash actions with the children. Unless I'm off the mark entirely, which Pa thinks I am, I believe his love for Savannah and his family made him desperate, thinking he would lose her, so he has tried to trap her. Pa's been asking around his racing buddies, and he has a good, solid reputation in a sport that often harbours cheats, crooks and cruelty. He obviously has a jealous streak, but Savvie, bless her, doesn't exactly help as she is a natural flirt, and I would imagine a chap brought up in the Middle East would find her quite a handful. We had some good chats before the hunt ball about horses and oil reserves. I gather he owns some wells in Saudi Arabia. He even asked about the popularity of renewable energy and said he was thinking of opening a laboratory in one of his refineries to look at the possibility of green alternatives working alongside fossil fuels. I just wonder if seeing Savvie among her own sort at the hunt ball made him think she was going to stay here and not return home.'

Liberty felt exceedingly guilty at that point, as she recalled encouraging her friend to stay and work in the café.

'But your father thinks differently?' she asked, not adding that the thought of true love being behind the kidnap of sorts seemed more like a fairy tale than real life. She cleared the plates, and brought out a rhubarb tarte Tatin and a box of home-made vanilla ice cream.

'My, that looks good,' exclaimed Gray, who had thought himself full to bursting. 'Everyone in the county will be piling on the pounds when you open up shop.'

'I need to practise my puff pastry. I've only just moved in here and the chest freezer is practically full of the stuff,' said Liberty with a laugh. 'I've scented the layers by adding a tiny amount of crushed cardamom into the butter.'

As the warm, crisp, buttery pastry melted on his tongue, counteracted by the sharp and sweet rhubarb, Gray decided he had died and gone to heaven; when he added a little ice cream to his following spoonful, he knew he had.

'I tell you what your trick is,' he mumbled with his mouth full. 'You bring childhood flavours to make the consumer feel safe and then you add a touch of sophistication to surprise and reward. I know you will be a hit, young lady.' He raised his glass of Tokay and made a toast. 'To friends old and new and to both our futures!'

Liberty joined him in the toast, glowing from his compliments about the food, but she felt obliged to ask him if he was sure he was doing the right thing by disappearing off to Bangladesh.

'Major Race has confirmed the job is waiting for me,' said Gray, referring to his old chum. 'And if I had any qualms about leaving here, just reading all the literature I can get my hands on about overseas aid has persuaded me. The money they get quite often simply disappears when it reaches the country, either straight into politicians' silk-lined pockets, which makes me mad enough, or, almost worse, the money that does reach the afflicted areas is distributed amongst those meant to be directly helping the homeless and disease-riddled. They use the funds to escape themselves.'

'I admire you hugely,' said Liberty, 'but we want you back very soon. Let's go into the sitting room. I lit a fire and I had better find Teal – most unusual for her not to be begging.'

The little pug was fast asleep by the ottoman in front of the fire, and there was a puddle on the rug.

'At least she didn't lie in it,' sighed Liberty, as she mopped and rubbed the rug. 'J-T would be thrilled to learn the kilim he tore from Afghan weavers' hands has wound up as a litter tray.'

'He is a nice man,' said Gray sadly. 'I hope he and Bob sort things out, and I must remember not to drink so much whilst being flattered by elegant young men.'

'I think we could all benefit from that,' added Liberty with a giggle as she sat beside him and offered him home-made truffles. Gray looked directly into her eyes, took both of her hands in his and said, 'I may well die if I eat one more mouthful, but let me tell you, it will be worth it.' And with that he popped one into his mouth, letting the soothing, endorphin-releasing dark chocolate cheer him into the night.

The village had enjoyed a little local scandal, but there was a general feeling of relief once the press left. Anyone who felt they needed more gossip was suddenly coming down with a mysterious illness – diagnosed by Dr Brown as nosiness – and were making appointments at the surgery so they could get the latest from Miss Scally. Was Jonathan really giving up Denhelm? Was he selling to a hotel group? Were they all gay? Was his eldest son going to turn his tenants out of their cottages or raise rents sky high so that only holidaymakers could afford them? Were aliens going to land? And so on.

Miss Scally was still upset with Dr Brown that he had danced with everyone but her at the New Year's Eve party, and most especially with Deirdre, and she was spreading the rumour that it was under Deirdre's influence that Jonathan had decided to retire. Unfortunately for Miss Scally, Jethrow, one of the estate gardeners, was sitting in the waiting room listening to her completely fabricated story that Deirdre had persuaded him to sell the estate as she wanted to borrow money from him to encourage the troublesome Clarence and others to cook at her school and open some sort of home for delinquents – the slight truth of this being that after Clarence's success and enthusiasm Deirdre wanted to concentrate on young people rather than bored housewives.

'Lady Muck has probably got her eye on the doctor's surgery as well. Dr Brown is a tenant, you know. Just you wait, soon the village will have no doctors, no pub and no shop, just a chichi tea room selling poncy cakes no one can pronounce.'

Jethrow had heard enough. He was only in there to have his back seen to, as he did regularly. He rose stiffly and went outside to phone Mr de Weatherby. It was the first time he had used his mobile, so it took a few minutes.

Soon afterwards, Jonathan's Land Rover pulled up outside the surgery. Mr de Weatherby himself patted Jethrow on the shoulder, thanked him and told him to wait in the vehicle. He then marched up to the desk.

'Miss Scally, I wish to see Dr Brown NOW,' he said with such quiet, calm authority the receptionist knew she was in trouble.

'I'm sorry, Mr de Weatherby, he's busy, and he has no free appointments all morning.'

The few elderly women in the waiting room concentrated on their ancient *Country Life* magazines, but with their ears and hearing aids on stalks they could hear their landlord telling Miss Scally in no uncertain terms that if she carried on with her malicious and offensive gossip he would happily and personally fling her from her cottage.

'I believe I have been a fair landlord,' he continued. 'While I was custodian of the estate, have I not fixed gutters, painted your cottage every two years, and even had it re-thatched last year? Not once have I raised your rent in the last TEN YEARS,' he said rather more loudly, 'as your parents were loyal workers on my estate. If I hear any more gossip emanating from this surgery, you will find that my eldest son, who is taking over the reins from me, will do exactly as I instruct, and ask you to leave. My son holds this village as close to his heart as I do. If you do as I suggest from now on, he will look after you, as I have always done, and I hope he will be rewarded by kindness and gratitude and loyalty, and no more malicious lies. Talking of which, while I'm here, yes, I am very proud of my younger GAY son (at this word Miss Scally's mouth turned into a cat's bottom) and his future work in Bangladesh with the washed away, disease-ridden starving and homeless. He is not, contrary to your delightful story, retiring to Sri Lanka with a toy boy.'

Miss Scally had not realised that this particular rumour, which she had started after drinking one too many sherries in the pub, had reached his ears.

'Yes, sir,' she muttered. 'Sorry, sir.'

Jonathan turned on his heel and left the now silent waiting room. He was in fact immensely proud of all his children.

Savannah was doing the right thing and standing by her man. Edmund was learning the ropes fast at home and his darling Gray was so much more relaxed and happy now his secret was out. Jonathan wished once again that his beautiful wife were here to tell him what to say. He had never been good at voicing his emotions – boarding school and English heritage to blame for all that – but he did wish he could tell Gray that he still loved him just as much, if not more. Perhaps he would write him a letter.

His thoughts were also with Paloma, the beautiful, exotic Paloma. Could he really be in love again? Should he really fall in love again? He needed to talk to Deirdre, but was that a good idea? After all, a few evenings ago he had proposed to her. At least she had been sensible and realised theirs was friendship and not love, but he still felt guilty about asking her advice on a relationship with someone else, particularly as that someone else was her best friend. Why did life seem to get more complicated the older one got?

He took Deirdre out to lunch in a little restaurant in Bodiam, good enough for Deirdre to appreciate the food, private enough for them to enjoy lunch without any more gossip. They ordered, on recommendation, cheese soufflé and steak and kidney puddings to go with a bottle of claret. She knew what he wanted to talk about, but he chatted about everything but Paloma. Deirdre eventually had to broach the subject herself over coffee and an excellent damson crumble.

'So, my dear, when are you planning to go to France? Paloma obviously adores you, and I think you feel the same. At our time of life you can't let these opportunities slip through your fingers.'

Jonathan, relieved, gasped, flushed and then smirked like a schoolboy. Deirdre realised he was truly smitten, and told him so.

'I'm pleased. I couldn't bear her to be hurt, though. She has dedicated her heart to her son and now he is starting his own family it would be nice for her to have a little of her own happiness.'

'Could I live in France, though? I'm probably more English than a cream tea being devoured by one of your Labradors. I need strong tea from a teapot three times daily. I become unstable if I don't eat roast beef once a week and I wear tweed, for God's sake.'

'You may surprise yourself. They hunt in France, you know. And come on, the food there is incredible. Anyway, Mrs Goodman and I will be here, only a few hours away, to provide tea and scones when required. You may need a wardrobe change for the south of France, though. Tweed shorts are out of the question, but we don't want you turning into Silvio Berlusconi, with a hair weave and a thong on the beach!'

Deirdre screamed with laughter at her own joke, as Jonathan tried to maintain a straight face. He had a good head of hair, thank you very much, and was sure a few linen suits could be rustled up by his tailor. 'Though I'm not sure what thong I would thing,' he lisped, giggling like an idiot, 'maybe "Je t'aime".' When they had recovered from laughing, and Deirdre had stopped snorting unbecomingly, she said, 'I will miss you dreadfully, but I know you will be back to check on Edmund and I'm planning to come out myself once the baby is born. Liberty too, as she will be *marraine*. So go for it – just try to give up the bad jokes!'

37

That night, Deirdre felt a loneliness descend on her for the first time since her divorce. She had always been so busy with cooking, writing or her classes, and had relished the few moments on her own. Now, having given up most of the aforementioned, and without Liberty's presence, she felt a little downhearted after all the excitement of Christmas and the party. *Don't be silly*, she reprimanded herself, as she sidled up to Dijon and Custard by the Aga, eyeing the glass of red in her hand, whilst idly wondering if she should be drinking alone, then reminding herself it was all right as the dogs were there. 'What I need is a project,' she said. 'It's all Liberty's fault. I got used to her laughing, happy face around the house, and now she's gone. I can't interfere with her plans; she must be allowed to do her café on her own. She won't want me bothering her and I mustn't be an interfering parent. But golly, I wish she needed me.'

The dogs appeared to be listening to her every word. They gazed up at her sad face and Custard even bothered to get up and puggle around, trying to lift the moment. Deirdre had never before felt so unneeded. The next minute a gust of cold air blew through the French doors, together with a bouncing puppy, a lot of leaves and a windswept Liberty.

'Oh, Mummy, I am so scared. Am I going to be all right? Will the café work out? Am I doing the right thing? Can I talk you through the menus and ideas? Can you tell me if this tastes right? I've made so many and I want it to be perfect.' And a towering cherry confection was thrust onto the table, complete with a leaf and twig that had landed on it on the way over.

'Do you hate it that I won't leave?' said Liberty, hugging her mother. Deirdre's heart gave a great thump and the lump in her throat stopped her from saying anything. So she merely put her arms tightly around her beautiful daughter, and both felt everything was going to be all right.

After devouring most of the delicious kirsch-soaked cherry chocolate gateau and a pot of coffee, Deirdre said Liberty had nothing to worry about. 'Your competence, imagination and willingness to work hard will do you proud. You deserve to succeed, and with a lot of energy and a bit of luck you will be fine. Did I mention how proud I am of you?'

Relieved, and feeling much more confident, Liberty answered, 'Not today, but it means so much to me that you believe in my abilities, so thank you. Anything about the menus?'

'You don't need to thank me so much, you know it's my pleasure.' But inside Deirdre was glowing with happiness that her daughter still needed her. 'Perhaps think of children's tastes a little. They prefer a little more milk chocolate and a little less booze! Do you have a date in mind yet for the opening?'

'Yes, Easter weekend – open with a bang, or the crack of an egg. And I'm going to get moulds and make chocolate eggs, choux bunnies I can fill with crème pâtissière, and simnel cakes and so on.'

'Great,' replied Deirdre. 'What can I do to help?'

'Well, if I print out a couple of sample menus for the opening and lists of the cakes and breads I'm going to sell, you can let me know what you think – whether it's balanced enough, and so on, and if you think I'm missing something. I also still have the problem of finding an assistant. I can't do all the cooking and serving. That will just result in slow service and grumpy customers. Have you any ideas? I don't want just anybody and I'm not sure I would be very good at interviewing.'

'No,' agreed Deirdre, laughing. 'You would fall for a lame duck sob story and end up employing some homeless layabout and doing twice as much work. However, Sarah is going to be heavily pregnant, and although I know she needs the money, I would wait until she knows what's happening at home. You don't need your staff running off after a few weeks. I'll put my mind to it, darling. Oh, sweetheart, I am so proud of you. You have to be a little scared so that you work hard and make it a success, but a success it will be. The only thing I can think of is your lack of advertising.'

'I was hoping word of mouth would be enough.'

'After a few months it will be, I'm sure, but you need to get people in from day one, build a peak of interest. You need local press interest, and to make vouchers for the papers – offer a free drink with a cake, that sort of thing, or even a free piece of cake if you buy a lunch. That way, you will encourage people to try your baking, which is where you excel. You need the journalists to recommend you, so invite the local rag and *Sussex Magazine* to sample your wares. They can only say no, but I can't imagine any journalist I have met turning their nose up at a free meal.'

Hesitant to sleep with the enemy after Gray's dreadful experience, Liberty balked at this idea.

'My darling girl,' Deirdre assured her, 'journalists exist for a reason. A good write-up can fill your place for months.'

'And a bad one?' asked Liberty.

'That's why you invite them. Know when they are coming – try to have them to your place before you open to the public, and make damn sure everything is perfect. Ask Edmund if you can raid his hothouse for flowers; they always make a place look so homely but cost a fortune if you have to buy them. Buy lots of little jugs and vases in second-hand shops cheaply, and then you won't mind so much when they all go missing. Did I ever tell you about the time a customer tried to steal the tablecloth at your father's restaurant?'

Liberty had heard this story, and many others, over and over, from the time her mother worked alongside her father when they were setting up, but she let her ramble on, happy with her memory. Liberty had, despite being wrapped up in her own panic, noticed her mother's forlorn expression upon her arrival. She was mindful that Jonathan was possibly going away, and she had just left home, even though it was only to a house across the green. So she thought her mother needed cheering up.

Liberty was in fact loving the freedom and the excitement of living alone for the first time in her life. Waking up in her own bed, linens untouched by anyone except herself, and of course Teal, who sometimes forgot herself and jumped on the bed. She enjoyed being able to sleep with the curtains open, seeing the winter sky from her bed with the light of the silver moon reflected in her cheval mirror as it made its nightly journey past her window. Percy had always insisted on a dark bedroom, but if ever he had been away Liberty loved to be woken by the sun in summer, and the winter didn't seem so terrible if she could see thousands of stars. She could make coffee in her smart espresso machine, and choose to eat cake for breakfast if that was what she wanted, which was lucky as she was doing a lot of experimenting. The house was coming alive around her, gradually filling with knick-knacks she found on her trips to markets and antique shops, trips when she was meant to be finding things for the café. She couldn't help spotting things that would be perfect on a bare shelf or in a cubby hole in Duck End.

Philip Buffington had been perfect and found pretty tables, sturdy but elegant, that would withstand hot teapots and children's playful fork-bashing. As he pointed out, a bit of wear on a table made it look loved, and Liberty had decided that after three o'clock, when she would serve afternoon teas, all tables would have linen tablecloths anyway.

Between Philip's hunting and Liberty's measuring, there were now ten tables in the little restaurant, eight seating four, one six and one two. The chairs were a pleasant mismatch, either painted or bare wood but all the same height (with some help from Philip). A beautiful soft leather sofa with chunky arms had been placed in the bay window on one side of the door. Liberty had decided that the hard settle would be more at home in Duck End, and customers' bottoms would stay longer if they were cushioned. An ottoman was conveniently placed for feet or magazines, daily papers and children's books. The long dresser built to fit by Malcolm Nesbitt was filled with flowery teapots and cups of fine china for the ladies' teas. When she opened there would be a selection of finger sandwiches and tartlets, bite-sized sandwiches, tiny scones and petits fours. There would also be plain cream teapots and mugs for the builders' teas, large filled sandwiches, fruit, plain or cheese scones, and cakes.

Liberty had found some tiered cake stands to present the ladies' food on, and her carpenter had created side tables to look like old-fashioned brick carriers to hold the builders' food at the side of their tables. One of her greatest annoyances had always been lack of space on a table. By the time a teapot, milk jug, cups and so on had been placed, there was no room for elbows!

She had placed large decorative jugs and huge glass bonbon jars on the top shelves. She was perfecting her marshmallow technique, so she could fill the jars and present each child with one as they left. Most commercial varieties were all air and no texture; she had flavoured hers with raspberry, blackcurrant and pistachio, and coloured them slightly. One bite made it give just a little before dissolving in a light, chewy way on the tongue, delivering a burst of fresh flavour.

The counter on which her patisserie and cakes would be presented had three shelves. The bottom shelf was for large cakes to be served by the slice, the middle one was for the chocolate and fruit tarts, large and individual, and the top was for eclairs, biscuits and bonbons.

The quiches, sandwiches and tarts for lunches would be prepared in the well-equipped kitchen, along with a soup of the day. Large baskets behind the patisserie counter would hold the artisan loaves. Liberty felt as though she would never sleep again. Baking would have to start around three o'clock in the morning, but she had frozen considerable quantities of pastry and she would keep her freezers stocked as necessary.

She was aware she had got precisely nowhere with her own

kitchen garden, but surrounding the courtyard behind the café were now raised beds and large pots to hold herbs and lavender to be used in the kitchen and scent the air. The old walnut tree had lent a branch for an old-fashioned swing chair, painted cream. J-T had made cushions for it in bright patterns and stripes to disguise sticky finger marks and spillages as much as possible, and the seat would surely be used constantly in the warm months.

The little courtyard had an array of stone-topped tables that could be left out all winter, and the cobbles, although wobbly, took sturdy chairs well enough. Health and Safety had not been too keen, but the inspector admitted it was pretty, so as long as she put up a small sign warning of uneven surfaces, the sue 'em brigade would be deterred.

The cloakroom was beautifully fitted with teal tiles, a large basin set in a Victorian washstand, and a soap dispenser fixed to the wall so it could not be taken by the light-fingered mob.

Lighting had been one of the biggest considerations; the restaurant grew dark in winter at three-thirty. Liberty knew that even the most beautiful food benefited from flattering lighting to enhance the glazes, and each table had a low-wattage lamp above to give diners a chance to see what they were eating and to prevent side glare showing up dust or un-wiped surfaces.

Old-fashioned carriage lanterns made from bronze and glass were to hang on either side of the jauntily coloured emerald gloss door, and her colours of lilac and emerald had been stitched into linen napkins, tea towels and printed on patisserie boxes and bags, depicting the LIBERTEAS logo dreamed up by Fred. J-T had pointed out that one airline had reduced passenger sickness by 80 per cent after it changed the green seat covers for beige ones, but Liberty pointed out her building wouldn't be moving and green looked so smart and fresh.

'Look at Fortnum's, Harrods and Wimbledon – their colours never look shabby. No one refuses strawberries and cream on finals day, while Harrods food hall is a crush on the quietest morning,' she insisted. So he had relented and found a beautiful deep emerald which he linked to a lilac to match the wisteria that would soon be hanging its tresses over the door.

Liberty was thrilled, but now, with only the menus left to perfect, she was becoming increasingly apprehensive. Everyone was full of advice, but she knew she must stick to her guns and not stay with safe food. Dilys at the pub had told her hot dogs and burgers were all the locals wanted, but Liberty had decided that was because it was all they were offered, and that she would do better.

She wanted to do some traditional English dishes, but with a twist. Her toasted teacakes were going to be made with an enriched dough, like a fruit brioche. Her scones would be made with fresh unpasteurised buttermilk from the goat farm down the valley, who were also happy to supply her with cheese and soft curd. The buttermilk added a sharp sweetness to the scones and enhanced their deep, moist, satisfying flavour.

One afternoon she invited her mother over for another tasting session. Deirdre marvelled over the walnut and poppy seed cake filled with kirsch-flavoured cream and black cherry jam. She asked Liberty about a licence.

'You know, darling, a drinks licence. I know you want to concentrate on your cakes and pastries but you will also want to attract people with your savoury tarts – for example, this bacon and thyme and clotted cream tart would taste perfect with a light red wine, and your idea for a daily salad for ladies who lunch is excellent. A walnut-crusted warm goat's cheese salad needs a glass of Gewürztraminer.'

'Oh,' replied Liberty, ' I must apply, it had completely slipped my mind.'

'Look into it. I believe it can take time these days. They look into your criminal past and everything,' her mother told her, laughing.

It took Liberty an entire evening to fill in the paperwork, but when she posted the application she was pleased. One more thing done!

38

The dark days of January dragged on. Layers of snow moulded the Weald into beautiful new shapes, and brought everything to a standstill. Despite the council claiming they were ready for all eventualities, the council spokesperson announced on the local news after an extra centimetre of snow had fallen that there was insufficient grit to go round. Edmund sent the estate workers to clear the roads and pavements around the green, so the elderly could get to the shop. He also offered his Land Rover as a taxi for those who needed the doctor or had other important appointments. He had taken to popping into Duck End almost daily, happy to taste Liberty's cakes and declare them all perfect. He found it calming talking to her about the stresses of his new responsibility, because his father had been extremely popular. He wasn't exactly changing the world, but he had discovered some areas were wasteful and had let go a few staff from the spring water plant after finding three people watching bottles fill.

This had caused a bit of an upset, and strikes were threatened, until Jonathan stepped in and told the estate workers their jobs were safe. It was merely that Edmund had seen a waste of expenditure that could be used in other areas.

Edmund shared his frustration about Jonathan's interference with Liberty. But she assured him it was just because his father was still living there.

'You will naturally defer to him. Wait until he goes off to France. Now, try these arancini.' And she popped the piping hot morsel into his open mouth.

Deirdre, who was sitting nearby on a bar stool, smiled as she watched Edmund swallow the tiny, deep-fried risotto ball with a filling of buffalo mozzarella. They would be excellent on a chicory salad with some parmesan shavings and maybe some fried sage, she advised, and she told Edmund she would have a word with Jonathan regarding his departure for the south of France.

'I don't know why he is prevaricating; he and Paloma hit it off so well.'

'I think he is scared of leaving Denhelm after all these years,' said Edmund, and pronounced the mouthful yummy. Liberty had popped out of the room, and Deirdre smiled at him and said, 'You don't have to say everything is perfect, you know. She likes you anyway.'

Edmund flushed and told her it might be better at Denhelm when the café opened, as Mrs Goodman was fed up with him leaving most of his supper after filling up at Duck End!

'What news of Gray and Savannah?' asked Liberty, rushing back in with Teal close behind.

'Gray couldn't say much, as he was phoning from their home. In fact, he seemed very upbeat, as though Khalid was in the room, although he insisted he was phoning from his bedroom, which by all accounts is a house in the grounds! He said they all seemed blissfully happy and we shouldn't worry. He said that he was all right and everything was going to be OK. Either he was on something or his mind was on Bangladesh, where by all accounts the floods are getting worse. His flight has been cancelled twice.'

'So what will he do until then?'

'Wait at Savvie's until he gets the go-ahead. All flights have been cancelled until the monsoon clears.'

'But you and your Pa must be pleased that Savvie is happy?' said Liberty. 'I don't understand it. I've emailed Gray to give me the full picture, but have yet to hear back and Savvie has not returned my emails either. Do you believe Gray?' Liberty thought back to the conversation she had with Gray just before he left. Had he been right? Was it all true love and just a huge misunderstanding? Why hadn't she heard from either of them?

'Oh, don't be so impatient,' snapped Edmund a little too sharply, still worried about his beloved sister despite Gray's protestations that everything was coming up roses. Nothing was that perfect, was it? He allowed his gaze to rest on Liberty's fair face for a moment too long before continuing more gently, 'He's only been there for a few days, so maybe he's waiting to see more of them together so he can judge the situation better. It does seem he has been forgetting his own worries and playing with the children.'

'That must be lovely for him,' said Liberty wistfully. 'I wondered how Khalid would react to him staying there after Savannah said he was horrified that Gray was gay.'

'Mmm, Gray did mention he was slightly concerned before he arrived, but Khalid was all welcoming and the good host, proudly showing off his stud farm and taking him off into the desert to hunt with his falcons. I can't work out whether Gray has been wowed by Khalid, and is therefore not checking on Savannah, or maybe everything is just wonderful after all? We need to hear from the horse's mouth, and Savannah is keeping shtum for whatever reason. But I do feel a little better after Gray's reassurance. I had better go – I promised to take Mrs G to the farm shop. She can't walk there with these drifts. We would never find the little lady if she fell into one, and the estate would surely revolt on me if anything happened to her! She will be garbed up by now in her galoshes. Thanks for lunch.' And he grinned at Liberty and kissed Deirdre.

'He's got a wee crush on you, young lady,' said Deirdre after he left.

'Don't be silly,' sighed Liberty. 'He's just grown a bit softer, and likes to escape from the angry workers!'

Liberty had a fair amount of free time on her hands now that

LIBERTEAS was all set for its Easter opening. So she decided on a trip to London to catch up with J-T and find out how things were progressing between him and Bob. And she knew she should meet Percy, tell him of her plans and say a real goodbye.

As she sped along, Teal illegally but comfortingly on her lap, she mused how much things had changed in the past eight months. Although she was delighted with her new life, she did miss the excitement of London, and she had so much enjoyed her time living with the CRs. She hoped Cecil was not too unwell; she must visit them.

To lighten the mood, she turned up the volume on her stereo. Lady Gaga almost woke the snoring pug, but then Neil Diamond calmed both driver and passenger.

Bob and J-T lived in Covent Garden, in a charming town house. It was a jewel among converted warehouses and shops. It felt like stumbling on Diagon Alley with Harry Potter. If you were window shopping or looking for one of the many cafés on the narrow street, you could walk past their smart black front door and miss the house completely; but when you knew it was there it appeared so *Ideal Homes* you couldn't resist ringing the bell and standing back to look up at it.

This is exactly what Liberty did, having managed to find a parking spot a few streets away. Teal was doing very well. It was the first time she had displayed her smart harness from Mungo & Maude – cream with black stitching and a matching lead. She trotted happily at Liberty's heel as though, to her, London was no different to the tranquil village of Littlehurst. She loved all the attention from passers-by, as pugs always do. She only disgraced herself once by weeing on a chap's shoe as he smoked a cigarette outside his office. Liberty got away with it as after his initial expletive and move to give the small dog a large kick up the backside the man looked up and saw the beauty on the end of the lead and decided Teal was really a charming little creature. Of course it could wee on his tasselled loafers, beastly uncomfortable things.

Liberty peered at the narrow windows. The house was built of black bricks with white painted sash windows. She hoped everything was all right. At last, a cacophony of yapping indicated that at least the dogs had heard the bell, and would alert J-T. The door was flung open, and she was enveloped in a hug.

'You look well!' they cried simultaneously.

'I expected to find you a shadow of your former self,' explained Liberty as she followed J-T upstairs to the apartment; the ground floor and basement were used for their offices and studio.

'I've been a very good boy: no drinking, cooking for Bob – well, buying in and reheating – and being a very good house husband.'

'Back in the bedroom yet?' she enquired.

'Not permanently, no, but I have been allowed to visit. Bob has been wonderful – he's trying to cut back on work and I'm trying to ignore temptation by not getting tempted in the first place. And how is Gray? I still feel awful for him. He sent a lovely letter, but seeing as Bob and I have managed to hold it together, if only just, he definitely had the short straw.'

'He seemed all right, better than all right, before he left for Bangladesh. I think it was a weight off his shoulders when he finally had to tell his father. Anyway, we can fill each other in over lunch. But I need to leave Teal here with your two, and she probably needs to use your garden first.'

J-T took all the dogs out while Liberty freshened up in the bathroom, all gold leaf and black marble.

'You have redecorated again,' she marvelled as she met J-T downstairs.

'Only because we ordered that suite for one of our clients from an Italian store and they went off it at the last minute. They had paid and it would have been churlish to throw away a hand-made marble washbasin and loo.'

'People really have marble loos?' asked Liberty, laughing. 'I thought it was just meant to look like marble.'

'That is the precise problem with it – nobody thinks it can be real, which instantly makes it appear cheap, despite costing God knows what. We even had to strengthen the floor to put it in!'

'It looks unbelievable,' said Liberty politely, privately thinking that the two tasteful designers had scored a definite miss.

'Where am I to take you, little Country Bumpkin?' asked J-T. 'I thought you may like something a little more lively than you are used to?'

'What I would love is to go to Rules. I have no need for fashionable and busy, I want to catch up with you, and Rules is perfect for warming winter food and good service, and it always feels like home. And we are unlikely to come across anyone we know.'

'Why is that important?' asked J-T, tucking his hand under her arm and steering her along the pavement.

'Not sure, but I am getting twitchy about phoning Percy. I should see him and talk about what we do next.'

They were walking through Covent Garden. J-T stopped and faced her.

'You haven't called him to let him know you are coming?'

'No. I thought I would go round after work.'

'So you haven't heard the gossip, then,' said J-T, pulling Liberty close beside him again, so they could keep warm.

'What gossip? What do you mean?'

'I think we need a drink first.'

They stepped off the busy street into the calm oasis of Rules. It was like going into a bygone era. Smart polished brass, old prints, starched linen on small tables mostly occupied by dark-suited men who looked as though they were used to enjoying the finer things in life. Unusually for the modern day, especially at lunch, most tables bore bottles of wine. The only thing missing was the fug of cigar smoke, otherwise it could have been a gentlemen's club. Specialising in game and fine wines, Rules was reportedly the oldest existing restaurant in London.

Waiters in long white drill aprons took orders and managed to complete a merry dance between the tightly packed tables, serving efficiently and subtly. It was the kind of restaurant where most people had a regular lunch table, but tourists who had heard of its reputation were also eagerly welcomed, despite an eyebrow being raised towards jeans and trainers. They were simply placed away from established clientele and once seated the tablecloths rendered their indiscretions barely visible.

J-T and Liberty were given a table for two in the window. Once each held a glass of Montrachet and had ordered – oysters Rockefeller for J-T followed by rib-eye and chips, venison carpaccio for Liberty followed, disloyally, by teal in a crayfish sauce – Liberty repeated, 'Come on, now. What gossip?'

'It came from Bob, and as you know, he doesn't ever pass on gossip unless it's true.'

J-T was reddening under Liberty's gaze.

'Go on,' she insisted. 'I'm waiting.'

'Um, well, he heard that the wife of a crony of Percy's was expecting a baby.'

'So?'

'Well, um, her husband is well past sixty, and it has been sort of known for some time that Percy has been seen with this lady in, um, well, hotels, sort of thing.'

Liberty's eyes grew ever wider.

'It's his baby?'

J-T was quiet for a few moments. 'It's just gossip, that's all. I don't know any more than that.'

'But who is she?'

'You will have to ask Percy. I just didn't want you popping over to your old place in case she was there or Percy was decorating the nursery.' J-T had meant this as a joke – he couldn't imagine anyone less able to pick up a paintbrush than Percy – but one look at his friend's face told him he had put his perfectly shod foot straight in his mouth. Liberty took a large gulp of wine and waited to feel shock, anger, jealousy or any other emotion.

'Don't tell me your sense of taste has gone again,' jested J-T, still trying to lighten the mood. 'Bad timing would be just the start of it.'

'No,' replied Liberty, 'I just feel sad.'

She found, when her venison arrived, that she had lost her appetite.

Liberty excused herself and almost ran to the ladies', knocking chairs and waiters out of her way in her haste to get there before she broke down. Slamming the door of the cubicle in an unusual display of anger, she sat on the loo seat and burst into great anguished, wretched tears. She felt sick. Her heart was pounding and it took her a while, between sobs, to realize there was also a pounding on the door. Her friend was worried for her.

'Darling girl,' called J-T's voice, 'I'm guessing that's you in there as the news I just gave you couldn't have turned you into the pinch-faced witch crossing her legs out here.' Liberty gasped with shock at her friend's outrageous comment as she heard the outer door slam, but she stopped crying, came out, and allowed J-T to take her in his arms and comfort her.

'I'm sorry, darling,' said J-T, all contrite. 'I shouldn't have said anything.'

'It was a shock, that's all,' said Liberty, trying desperately to pull herself together. Her mother had only just told her that if her night terrors had continued she would not have let her leave The Nuttery. Looks as though they would be returning!

'I don't think I will see Percy after all,' she announced in a small voice, as she let J-T wipe her face and blow her nose like a small child.

'Good idea,' he said as he led her back into the dining room, grinning like the Cheshire cat at the pinch-faced witch, who had either wet herself or used the gents'.

'I shouldn't be surprised, I suppose,' said Liberty back at the table before downing a fresh glass of wine. 'It's really no business of mine.' And she drained J-T's glass. 'Let's change the subject. You asked how Gray was.' And she started to ramble on, filling him in with news of his trip to Abu Dhabi and his impending work in Bangladesh.

J-T watched his friend's beautiful face. The sadness once so prevalent in her eyes had returned, and he felt a pig to have put it there. He was aware she longed for her own baby, but he couldn't let her go to her former home and have the shock of her life. Now he felt horrible and wanted to make it up to her.

'Look, you are not eating, and much more of that wine on an empty stomach will make you go all silly. I would have to join in, and then we would end up in a bar until two in the morning and I will get into trouble and no one wants that to happen . . . again. So I'm going to get the bill and then take you on a gastro tour of the patisseries around here, maybe give you some ideas for your place and tempt your appetite back.'

Liberty looked relieved, and gratefully took J-T's proffered hand. He paid the bill quickly, and scribbled a note down on one of his business cards, throwing it down on pinch-faced witch's table as they left.

'What did you say?' asked Liberty.

'Sorry,' was all J-T answered as he dragged her off, his infectious giggling cheering her up.

Three hours later, and with a notebook covered with scribbling about the benefits of over-cooking pastry so it stayed crisp, and lining pastry cases so they stayed crisp, the need for soya milk and fructose for coffee and tea service and the idea of soft amaretti freshly made each day with sour cherries or candied peel instead of a chocolate to go with an after lunch espresso, Liberty felt both better and hungry again.

They bought strawberry tarts and coffee eclairs from the patisserie close to J-T's house. Noting Liberty's interest, the owner, who had inherited the place from his parents and loved his work, advised, 'A touch of gelatin in the crème pâtissière makes it hold better in the millefeuilles.'

So the day had not been wasted.

'Thank you, my good friend,' said Liberty, feeling satisfied and happy. 'I shall go home, call on Mummy and phone Percy from there with her to support me. By the way, what did you really put in that note?'

J-T got the giggles again. 'I wrote, if she ever needed to sit on the loo crying her eyes out, I hoped the girl outside wouldn't be sighing and checking her manicure and might actually care about another human being.' Liberty smiled sadly at him and told him he had spent too much time in the country.

'I remember crying my eyes out in lots of loos all over the city after doing pregnancy tests. I was never asked if I was OK. Not once.'

They hugged for a long time, then kissed as they realised they would miss each other. J-T surprised her by asking after Edmund.

'Oh, well, I think. Sweet man,' was Liberty's reply, and with that she scooped up Teal and left her friend standing on the street with his two dogs yapping a goodbye, pleased to be rid of the young pretender. J-T's mouth was wide open.

'By God, boys,' he said to the loud-mouthed canines. 'She's going to be all right after all. The girl is in love!' With that he punched the air, looked around, checking no one had witnessed the very un-gay behaviour, and went inside to find Bob.

39

Liberty drove home carefully, mindful of the wine at lunch and her complete confusion over Percy. *He hadn't not wanted children; he just hadn't wanted children with me!* had been Liberty's first reaction. But now, after time to think, she realised she was jumping to conclusions. Was this woman pregnant at all? Or was it just gossip? She was aware that Percy had been attracting a fair amount of attention since his promotion; he seemed to be spending more time out of the office than in it, and the financial papers had been giving him a roasting because of it. Maybe the rumour of a baby was just to discredit him? It was all so difficult. If only Liberty had some facts, she could confront him, but all she had was a bit of gossip and an idea of who the other woman could be. She needed to chat with her mother. She tried to call, but there was no answer.

On reaching Littlehurst, she ignored the comforting lure of her own home and jumping into bed to hide under the covers, and drove straight to her mother's house, letting herself in through the French doors in the kitchen as she knew they would be unlocked. Then she wished she hadn't.

'I thought you were staying in town tonight,' said Deirdre calmly, belying the fact she was standing at the Aga dressed in a floor-length negligee stirring a pan of scrambling eggs. The unsettling part of the picture was the sight of her father standing very close by wearing jeans, a smirk and nothing else, showing off the muscle in his tanned body. He was amazingly fit for a man of seventy-two. He was also holding a rack of toast.

'Mummy, Daddy?' Liberty didn't know where to look, so she

bent down and said hello to Dijon and Custard. They had been snuffling round Teal, who wanted to tell them of her London experiences.

'I decided against it,' she continued. 'Sorry to interrupt. My mistake. Maybe come over for breakfast tomorrow. About nine? I guess I mean both of you.' And with that she grabbed Teal, backed out of the room through the French doors and, forgetting her car, hurried over to her warm house, where she turned on all the lights, sat in the kitchen and burst into tears.

'Have I no idea what is going on in the world?' she asked the wriggling pug who was trying to get up on her lap to comfort her. She couldn't face phoning Percy, so she calmed herself and went upstairs to clean her face of London grime.

There was frenzied yapping from the kitchen as the doorbell rang.

Bugger off, Mummy, thought Liberty, but went to let her in.

'Oh, it's you!' she exclaimed.

'Sorry to be a disappointment,' said Edmund, trying to look offended, but he entered the house nonetheless.

'I didn't mean it like that at all, it's lovely to see you. I've just had a very odd day and was wondering what to do with the rest of it. Please come into the kitchen. I need a glass of wine.'

'I was passing, saw the lights and remembered you were meant to be away. I wanted to check the house. I can leave now that I see you are all right.'

'No, no, please stay.' Liberty realised she really meant it. She needed a friendly face, and his seemed to be getting better every time she glanced at it.

Edmund regarded her pale, almond-shaped face, devoid of make-up, her green eyes glistening and slightly bloodshot from crying. *God, she is heart-rendingly beautiful*, he thought.

At the same time Liberty was thinking: *No make-up and a red nose from crying. I must look a sight.* She handed him a bottle of Riesling from the fridge and he uncorked it, looking at her all the while.

Under his unwavering gaze she went into default mode and asked, 'Can I make you some supper?'

'No,' he replied firmly. 'You pour drinks. I will make supper.'

Liberty burst into shocked laughter, and couldn't stop. It became contagious, so in the end both of them stood in her kitchen, shaking with fits of giggles, tears streaming down their faces. As they wiped their eyes Edmund realised he couldn't remember the last time he had laughed with so much gusto.

'Am I really that funny?' he asked in a mock stuffy voice. 'I have lived on my own, you know, and I can knock up a pretty good omelette.'

'OK, challenge on. Eggs on the side there, cheese in the wine fridge (better temperature). I'll make a salad.'

So they fussed around each other in companionable silence, finding plates and cutlery, breaking eggs, grating cheese, plucking herbs from the pots on the windowsill. In ten minutes they were sitting at the table with a delicious meal.

'Yum,' pronounced Liberty. 'I'm impressed. Not too runny, just right. Funny how you know where everything is in the kitchen.'

'I have sat here often enough watching you,' said Edmund, thinking how fortunate it was that, despite barely taking his eyes off her when she had been baking him endless samples, he had noticed where things were kept.

'One forgets how delicious the simple things are. Utterly delicious. Thank you, thank you,' said Liberty, as she cleaned her plate with sheer delight and a wedge of sourdough bread. 'I feel so much better.'

'So, do you want to talk about it? Or shall I make coffee and tell you that Pa has booked a flight to France?'

'Gosh, love does seem to be in the air,' replied Liberty.

Edmund looked at her strangely, his dark eyes boring into hers, making her unsettled and obliged to explain that she had just walked into an odd situation with her parents.

'It wouldn't have been so strange if they hadn't divorced umpteen years ago, and haven't spoken since.'

'I thought I saw his car up there. So, how do you feel about that?' asked Edmund, removing his gaze from her face and looking instead at his empty plate, relieved and disappointed at the same time that she hadn't been talking about him.

'I'm not sure. I should be delighted, but I hope they know where this is going. I couldn't bear it if he hurt Mother again.'

'They are old and wise enough to know what they are getting into.'

'Old, but maybe not too wise,' said Liberty. After a few glasses of excellent wine, a calming and scrumptious supper and Edmund's strong presence, she suddenly needed to explain the Percy situation. So she cleared the table and he made coffee. As she talked, she realised how comforting it was to discuss her ex-husband with someone who wouldn't take sides or judge. But Edmund's response was surprisingly fierce.

'How dare he not tell you about a baby? He must have known how upset you would be after trying so long for one yourself. But you must get clear facts before saying anything. If it's not true, and you accuse him, he could get quite nasty. From what I have heard of him, he is not the type to let things lie.'

'He's left us alone so far. I expected him to make some snide comment about J-T and Gray when the scandal erupted in the papers. J-T was very surprised he didn't contact the press when it blew up.'

'Oh, that would be because he didn't want his name in the papers any more than it is now. But depending on whose baby it is, he may well not be able to avoid having a juicy little story or two about himself.'

'I have no right to be angry, but I can't stop it hurting. Is it selfish and self-pitying to be jealous of a baby fathered by someone I would have been miserable with? Probably,' Liberty answered her own question, hiding her tear-laden eyes by busying herself looking for chocolates in the fridge and then firing up the espresso machine.

She jumped as a pair of strong arms wrapped around her

from behind. 'Your time will come, I am sure,' said Edmund gruffly into her hair. 'I'm not really sure of the right words to comfort you. If only we could rid the world of selfish arseholes like Percy.' And then he thought, *I am madly in love with this woman, and want to whisk her off to a desert island and give her all the babies she desires*. But he just hugged her until she stopped snuffling. He let her go slowly as she said brightly, 'Coffee's ready.'

There was an awkward moment when she turned round and Edmund was standing very close, only two espresso cups between them. They gazed at each other, both ignorant of the way the other felt, but completely held in the moment by the strong emotions flowing between them. Teal leapt up at Edmund's trouser leg, breaking the spell, and he took the cups and suggested they had coffee by the fire, which he busied himself lighting.

Liberty meanwhile loaded a tray with florentines and pistachio macaroons, chocolates and the coffee, before joining him.

'Any news about your application for a drinks licence?' asked Edmund as he piled red alder logs on the already blazing fire. He thought it best to talk about something neutral, and then was distracted again. 'My word, these macaroons are good. What is it about them?'

'A touch of orange zest and coffee, so they are not too sweet,' replied Liberty, realising she hadn't checked the post. She leapt up and found a pile of junk in the box, together with a large manila envelope containing a single A4 sheet.

'"Dear Mrs James,"' she read. '"Thank you for your recent application to be a licence holder at the above premises. Unfortunately, we cannot by law allow ourselves to grant licences to holders of criminal records. Yours sincerely . . ." What on earth?'

She handed the letter to Edmund, collapsed into a chair and yelled to the gods, 'Could today get any worse?'

'What criminal record do you have?' asked Edmund, as it was the only question he could think of.

'Exactly,' she replied. 'I may have had a few parking tickets over the years, but nothing more.'

'Not even in your debauched youth?'

As Liberty flashed an angry look at him, she realised he was smiling.

'Come on, now, they must have the wrong person. You have to laugh. They either sent you the wrong letter or, horror of horrors, there are two Liberty Jameses out there. So don't panic. Think reasonably. There must be a mistake. We will clear it up on Monday.'

Liberty felt reassured by the use of the word 'we', and started to calm down.

'I could do with a day off,' said Edmund. 'Let's go to your solicitor together and ask him to phone the council.'

'What if it gets into the local press before I've even opened?' asked Liberty, panic rising again. '"Ex-con to open tea rooms in idyllic village." Oh cripes.'

'Come on,' said Edmund for a second time, but very gently. 'First of all, who would release that to the press, and secondly, why would they? This area is screaming out for a decent place to meet and eat. Tell you what. On Monday we will contact the local rags, get them to do a piece on you and your plans, then put a bit of advertising their way before you open. How long to go?'

'Only eight weeks, so it's probably a good idea. That may well stir up some interest. Mother was just telling me that I need to publicise my opening.'

'I will contact Gray by email tomorrow,' Edmund reassured her. 'He had lots of friendly contacts in the local papers. Don't forget, they gave very fair comments when the national red tops were hounding him.'

'Oh, would you?' Liberty breathed a little easier. 'You are clever to think of that.'

Edmund thought his chest would explode. After weeks of feeling utterly useless on the estate, a tiny compliment made him feel like a king.

'Right,' he said briskly, to cover his emotions. 'You get some sleep. Don't forget you need to face your parents in the morning. Come for a ride in the afternoon – that might help clear your mind and blow a few cobwebs away, and you can fill me in.' At Liberty's bemused look, he said, 'I'm meant to keep abreast of all comings and goings in the village!' He did not include that he wanted to make sure she was all right.

'Thank you for everything,' said Liberty as they walked to the door. 'Supper was lovely and I feel terrible to burden you with all my rubbish. I haven't even asked you about the estate and how you are doing. You must think me horrible. I shall make you a deal. Tomorrow, we will talk about your life and how miserable that is, and I will bring lunch.'

Edmund burst out laughing. 'Thanks,' he said ironically.

'Well, you know what I meant,' said Liberty, blushing. 'My crappy life – at least pretend you are having a tough time too!'

They kissed, quickly and formally on both cheeks. Both felt the fire running through their bodies and, ignoring the magnetic pull, leapt apart as if forced to do so. As Edmund walked purposefully down her garden path back to his car, Liberty allowed herself to think, *You have made the day bearable. Thank you.*

As she brushed her teeth and washed her face again, she still basked in the warmth and strength of Edmund's words and body. *Please let tomorrow bring answers, and less parental flesh!* Turning the lights off, and once again mentally thanking J-T for putting all the side lights on composite wall switches, she let her mind drift over the day's events: criminal record, Percy having a baby, Mummy and Daddy playing happy families. *Will I ever sleep?* She curled up under the duvet, the full moon shining on her bed, and for once allowed Teal to jump up and curl up next to her. *I'm sure things could be worse*, she reflected, thinking about Gray in Bangladesh and Savannah possibly imprisoned in Abu Dhabi.

40

After a wretched night's sleep, Liberty rose early, determined things could only get better, and took Teal out for some air. The morning was glorious and, unable to resist its charms, she set off for a romp over the frozen fields of Denhelm, carrying Teal most of the way as she was a little too young to be walking so far. A silhouette in the distance looked handsomely familiar and she made a direct line for the well-muffled Edmund, wondering what he was up to. Reaching him, she shielded the little dog's ears from his expletives.

'Edmund?' said Liberty tentatively. Edmund dropped the long rod he was shoving down a manhole while swearing like a trooper, and said further loud and very rude words again as the rod disappeared into the murk. Turning to face her, his stormy face broke into a huge smile.

'Morning! And you thought you had trouble!' he said with another ear-to-ear grin. 'The pipes have all backed up, probably frozen somewhere, and the kitchen smells like something the dog wouldn't bring in. I had to forcibly remove Mrs Goodman as even if she could cook breakfast in there, I certainly wouldn't be able to keep it down!'

'How and why are you so cheerful, then?' asked Liberty, bemused to see the normally solemn-faced Edmund so happy in adversity.

'At least I feel useful, or I was, but now I seem to have made things worse and will have to call someone out. Bugger.'

Desperate to keep the smile on Edmund's face, Liberty asked

him to join her for breakfast with Alain and Deirdre. 'It would be lovely to have you there,' she said meekly.

'As a buffer between you and your apparently reconciled parents, you mean,' said Edmund laughingly, but he agreed, and said he would be along when he had showered and changed.

Edmund had been grinning for most of the night; even the stench in the kitchen hadn't removed the silly expression from his face. Liberty had made him feel like a man again. She needed him, she trusted him, and after seeing her so vulnerable, he couldn't imagine anything better in life than making sure nothing bad ever happened to her again.

The winter sun shone through the large kitchen window as Liberty returned from walking across the frostbitten fields. Her cheeks were glowing from the cold air and from wondering what today would bring. She was thrilled that Edmund had agreed to come to breakfast. Despite his being able to guess why she had invited him, she hadn't added that she loved having him around full stop.

Liberty was in the mood for uplifting music and found Mozart's 'Piano Concerto No. 16' on her iPod. She enjoyed the happy sound washing over her as she busied herself making potato pancakes, frying black pudding and apple, and slicing smoked eel to give to her parents. Then the phone rang. *Oh, please don't cancel on me, Edmund*, thought Liberty as she reached for the receiver.

'Hello, Liberty, it's Percy.' She almost dropped the receiver. How did he have her home number?

'Hello,' was all she could think of saying, all the previous joy instantly swept away. Why was he phoning?

'Yes, look,' barked Percy, 'I think you will have heard already, but I thought I should tell you myself. Some silly bitch is claiming to be having my baby. All bloody awkward as it's Hugh Cyril's wife.'

Liberty baulked and her stomach clenched, horrified to be reminded of how he spoke of people. She had met the quietly spoken yet attractive Hugh at the bank, and his wife at several parties. She had been a bit of a social climber, but pleasant enough.

'Oh, do you mean Georgina?'

Obviously surprised that Liberty remembered her name, Percy was quiet for a moment. 'Um, humph, yes, her. Anyway, don't put too much thought into it, it's a load of tosh. She just thought I was an easy target when Hugh threw her out and refused to pay her maintenance.'

Liberty couldn't imagine kind Hugh throwing anyone out of his house, except perhaps the former chancellor, for whom he had an unreasonable hatred, or maybe a hatred of having to advise him financially during his time in high office.

'Right,' she said, not sure how to continue. Did she believe him? Did it matter? Then another thought crossed her mind.

'Why did you phone now, I mean, today?'

Long silence. 'I just thought you would have heard by now. Do you think we should get divorce proceedings underway? Be good to have done with the whole shebang. Bye now.' And with that the phone went dead.

Liberty was gazing at the receiver in her hand when she realised the black pudding needed turning and she hadn't put the coffee on. She resisted the urge to cry, as that wouldn't sort out anything. She had so many questions, but she needed to try to be cheerful for her parents so she pushed Percy, divorce and his sorry mess to the back of her mind.

'Morning, darling!' Two cheery voices floated through the kitchen window. Other than in commercial kitchens, Liberty hated extractor fans, and had opened the window to try to vent some frying smells into the frosty air.

'I'll just come and open the door,' she shouted. Dijon and Custard limped and flew in to greet little Teal, then Custard raced around the kitchen to check in case Liberty had left piles of sausages on the floor.

Deirdre and Alain were gazing at each other and looking like a couple of teenage lovers, which made Liberty forget all about Percy and feel sick instead.

'Oh, yuck,' she said, 'now I feel like a child embarrassed at my own parents. Sit on opposite sides of the table, and I'll pour coffee.'

'Oh, we brought champagne, and sloes left over from the gin. Let's have a cocktail – it's time to celebrate!' said Deirdre. Alain was grinning like a schoolboy but saying nothing.

So Liberty tried to be the good daughter, look cheery and manage to splash champagne into flutes with a few of the sloes. She told her parents about the letter from the licensing board, and they agreed with Edmund it must have been a mistake or a mix-up.

'Talking of Edmund, I just met him on a walk, and invited him to join us. I hope you don't mind?'

Liberty hoped it was a rhetorical question as she wasn't sure how much love-struck parenting she could take on her own.

'Told you,' was all Deirdre had to say, and that was directed at Alain, who told her not to interfere. At last finding his voice, he ignored Liberty's puzzled look and advised, as though they had all been discussing the subject, 'Your main idea is to have a daytime patisserie-cum-café, so it's not the end of the world if the licence isn't sorted before you open. If you are going to start advertising, don't mention an alcohol licence until it's up and going, but I'm sure a quick phone call will clear that up.'

Liberty could hear him talking as she served up breakfast, but felt as though she was hovering above the room. Where could Edmund be? She listened and watched as her parents fell upon the food, drank cocktails with gusto and finished off the coffee and tiny almond and pear tartlets.

'If this is anything to go by, you will have happy customers,' said Deirdre and Alain, sounding like nauseating twins.

'Oh, stop it. Just tell me – what is going on with you two?' said Liberty crossly. She had been unable to eat a thing.

Deirdre and Alain looked at each other, and then back at

Liberty. 'If you will allow me, my dear,' said Alain, eyeing Deirdre in a stomach-turning sickly way that was both delightful and horrible to Liberty. 'I knew I had made a terrible mistake the moment I left your mother. I felt I had to stand by Genevieve when she fell pregnant, probably in a selfish way, because I didn't want bad publicity at that time for the restaurant.'

Deirdre opened her mouth to say 'But what about me?' but closed it again. She and Alain had been over it a hundred times in the past forty-eight hours and she was now blissfully happy. 'When I left Genevieve I didn't feel I could impose my selfish self back on the love of my life. I had made my bed and had to lie on it. Girls came and went, but only chosen to be pretty and light-hearted entertainment.'

'Sex, you mean,' said Liberty bluntly.

'Well, yes,' agreed Alain, having the grace to look sheepish. 'But it took your leap of faith – leaving Percy, opening a café – to make me realise that I could change my life too, and correct the wrong I had created. I thought if your mother would have me back . . . I had to give it a go. She has admitted to being fond of me still, and of course would love to have me back,' said Alain with a laugh, his macho side clearly feeling stroked, along with God knew what else.

Liberty turned to her mother. 'Really?'

'Yes, darling. Your father is going to live back here, and, after long discussions and a few disagreements, we have decided to turn the hotel into a school, to help people like Clarence. They can live in and learn at the same time. Applicants will have to prove their desire to learn to cook, combined with either a misspent or unfortunate background, whether their own fault or not. I have introduced Clarence to your father, who agrees that given the right direction he could become our first success.'

'We will find him a job in one of my cronies' hotels or restaurants and get him on his way,' interrupted Alain. 'A sort of upmarket *Fifteen* idea from the brilliant Jamie Oliver.'

Liberty was in a state of confusion – delighted for her

parents, but horribly angry with them at the same time. In fact, the strength of her emotion was rendering her speechless. She loved the idea of a school to help others and thought her parents would do a marvellous job, but she couldn't work out why she was feeling so terrible. Thankfully, at that moment the roar of an engine, screech of brakes and slamming of a car door indicated the arrival of someone who hated to be late. Edmund threw himself through the door, breathless and apologising.

'The sink just exploded. Mrs Goodman was covered in something very unpleasant and I couldn't leave her, and your phone is on the blink,' he said in a rush, by way of explanation. He quickly took in the scene: Alain and Deirdre holding hands, grinning; Liberty looking as though she had been slapped with a dead fish. He also noticed her phone was floating in the sink alongside the frying pan.

'Well, that explains one mystery,' he said, taking command of the situation and removing the now drowned phone. 'Is there any food left?' He knew Liberty could cope with anything if she was feeding people. His question did the trick. Colour slowly flowed back into her face as she made some fresh coffee and rescued the plate she had saved for him from the warming oven of the Aga. Meanwhile, Alain and Deirdre filled Edmund in on their good news and plans for the Dark Horse.

'It all sounds great, and of course I'm thrilled to bits for you both. Congratulations are most certainly in order!' And Edmund raised the glass of champagne that Alain had filled.

Liberty was pacing. 'Are you sure you can live together again?' she asked.

'It's so strange!' Deirdre giggled. 'It's as though we were never apart. Daddy got up and laid the fire this morning.'

'After laying something far better upstairs,' hooted Alain.

'Oh, stop it, you two,' said Liberty, covering her ears.

Deirdre and Alain both rose from their chairs, still smiling like idiots at each other. Deirdre said, 'You haven't said much, darling, are you feeling quite well? Are you not pleased?'

Liberty turned to face the Aga, leant against its warming comfort, and then realised it was no good. Like bile needing to find a release, her anger was encompassing her. The silence grew longer and even Edmund began to feel uncomfortable.

'Darling?' said Alain. 'The correct response would be to hurl yourself at us and kiss us all over, saying congratulations and about bloody time!' Alain was still grinning inanely, like a demented schoolboy who has just been given a balloon, a bowl of water and a bridge to play on. Deirdre, meanwhile, was starting to look a little worried and took a step towards Liberty.

Liberty immediately stretched out her arms in a stay away gesture. 'Pleased? Excited? Congratulations?' she shouted in a strange, strangulated voice. 'You took away my sense of taste and smell and my ability to have a decent relationship. You barely spoke to one another through my teenage years. I had to make the terrible decision of who to choose at Christmas and birthdays. Arguing over the phone, never being able to agree on what school I should go to, what I should do in the holidays. You hardly spoke to one another at my wedding, but both of you insisted on giving speeches, so you would feel even. You had your own table of friends to sit with to make sure there were no scenes. I didn't invite either of you to my graduation as you both made it clear that if the other was going you wouldn't come. You even took my first car back when Daddy, who didn't know BECAUSE YOU DIDN'T TALK, gave me one of his!'

Liberty glared first at her mother, then her father. All the tension of the last few months spilled out of her at last in a huge, bilious purge. Tears streamed down her cheeks.

'You have a daughter, Daddy, my half-sister, who is a complete wreck, growing up without me ever getting to know her. I didn't even meet wife number three. Has she got any children from you? My life was littered with workmates and fellow students asking if I could get them a date with my handsome, playboy father. How do you think that has made me feel over the years?

'And Mother always seemed so depressed and lonely, despite

pretending not to be, which only made it more plainly bloody obvious. I had to put up with all of that, and now I'm meant to be congratulating you both on finally sorting your stupid relationship out?

'Just get out, go and congratulate yourselves to one another. I've got other stuff to worry about.'

'But darling!' began Deirdre, trying another step towards her hysterical daughter.

'Just get out!' screamed Liberty. 'I mean it!'

Alain grabbed Deirdre and said to Liberty, 'We will leave you to calm down. Call us when you are ready to behave like the adult, competent woman you seem to have grown into, despite having such a ghastly family.' With that he swept Deirdre firmly out of the house.

Liberty collapsed on to a kitchen chair, head in hands, where it seemed to be far too often these days, and sobbed.

Edmund shuffled for a while from foot to foot, amazed to have seen such raw emotion pour from the normally controlled and together woman he thought he had got to know. His heart went out to her. He bent towards her, and held her tightly round her shoulders. He leant his head against hers, and kept it there. After a few minutes she seemed to be calming down.

Edmund said gently, 'It's a horrible part of growing up, realising your parents are not only mere human beings, but also just as useless at life as the rest of us.'

Liberty let out a gasp as she realised poor Edmund didn't even have a mother, and she began sobbing again. 'I'm so sorry, I'm being so selfish. I just feel so lost, and in such a silly way. My parents have actually always been a very solid part of my life – Daddy at the restaurant with his roué reputation, Mother at the same stove through the years. It was at least a comfort, even if they were apart, to know exactly where I stood. Now it's all up in the air again. My café is failing before it opens, Percy just asked for a divorce, indicating that my marriage is officially a failure, I can't have children and nobody loves me. Oh, God,

I forgot how selfish and depressing I am!' She gave a final sob, managed a pitiful smile and lifted her head.

'I am so sorry. I am being ridiculous. I think I just needed to get all that out, and now I've made you all damp!'

Edmund looked down at his cashmere sweater that she was ineffectually mopping with her already wet handkerchief.

'Oh, hang on, I'm not sure that is going to work very well. You seem to cry like you do everything – extremely efficiently. The River Thames is running down my front.'

They both smiled at each other, Edmund pleased to have witnessed the raw Liberty, and for her part Liberty was again realising what a kind, forgiving man Edmund was, let alone the fact he hadn't run a mile when she started shouting. She felt like an utter fool. She admired this man and she had just demonstrated what a mess she was.

'You think I was over-reacting?' she asked quietly.

'Maybe just a touch,' he replied gently, and they found themselves laughing uproariously.

When they had calmed down, Edmund suggested they walk over to The Nuttery and wave a white flag. 'They are your parents. They love you, and you are lucky they have finally realised they love each other. Look to the future; don't blame them for the past. You can't change anything that has happened, but you can show them how to help you to recover the stability you always craved. You always told Savannah you thought they should get back together.'

'She told you that?'

'I seem to recall eavesdropping a little in my youth,' admitted Edmund.

'That was a childish dream, fit only for a child,' said Liberty sadly. 'As I grew older it became clear to me that Daddy had only wanted a fling with Genevieve. But she became pregnant, and he felt he had to do the right thing. I think Mother was always so sad because she knew he had thrown their relationship away for something that ended so quickly, and obviously meant so little to him. And their poor daughter – she ended up getting a very short straw.'

'But now your mother has forgiven him,' said Edmund wisely. 'So can't you do the same? Maybe you could try to reconcile with your stepsister, see what you can do for her?'

'I suppose I should do some growing up,' sighed Liberty. 'How come you are so virtuous and sensible?'

Alain and Deirdre were sitting at the kitchen table comforting each other, when they felt they should be celebrating. But as the one person they each loved more than each other was so upset, they couldn't bring themselves to say it didn't matter.

They jumped and Custard barked as there was a tap at the French doors. An umbrella handle with a white tea towel dangling from it was being dramatically waved from side to side by a quivering camellia bush.

Alain threw open the door as his daughter fell out of the bush, still red-eyed from crying, but looking sheepish and clutching a bottle of champagne.

'Can we start again?' she asked, feeling even more ghastly when she saw her white-faced, wretched looking mother. 'Can you forget all those things I said? Or at least forgive? I did but didn't mean them. It's just been such an odd time. I'm thrilled for you both, of course I am. I just think the reality that you have sorted your lives out, while mine is still such a mess, finally sent me a bit doolally.'

'Oh, gorgeous, gorgeous girl,' said Alain, wrapping her tightly in a huge Daddy hug. 'We were terrified we had done the wrong thing by you, and you will always be the most important person to us. So much of what you said is true – your mother and I acknowledge that I am a disgusting cad, and at times we have not been the best parents, but give us a chance, will you?'

Deirdre reached over and they all stood quietly, hugging, for a few moments. Eventually a subtle cough brought them back from their reconciliation. Edmund, too large to climb into the camellia, had been standing behind it, holding another bottle of fizz, unsure whether to run home and leave them to it and relieve himself of soggy jumper and emotional outbursts, neither of which he had experienced much before. But something had held him back, and rooted his feet to the spot. That something now turned and said, 'Poor, dear Edmund, you must think us ridiculous. Come and make a toast. I feel you will be very good at that. My vocabulary seems to be in the intolerant, grumpy, self-centred part of the thesaurus – not a place to find words suited to these two old love birds.'

Edmund indeed made a fine toast to the now happy again couple. They all delighted in drinking to their health, happiness and better luck the second time around.

41

After what seemed an indecent amount of champagne, it was still only midday. Edmund remembered he had pipes to clear and Mrs Goodman to calm; thank goodness his father was still around. He said his farewells, glanced towards his car and wobbled off on foot in the direction of home.

Alain disappeared into the sitting room to make some calls; he was arranging a holiday for himself and Deirdre and wanted to give his girls some time together. Deirdre immediately started to gossip.

'Paloma phoned this morning to say she and Jonathan are planning a trip to Paris to see if they can find anything out about Khalid. Paloma couldn't give two hoots, of course, but she sees an opportunity to shop! They seem to be truly happy. I wouldn't have put them together, but love finds a way and golly, did they both deserve to find happiness. Paloma was funny, though, she said that she always knew Alain and I would work it out in the end.'

'What news of Evangeline and the baby?' asked Liberty.

'No arrival yet, but any day now.'

'I do hope I can get there for the baptism, before LIBERTEAS opens,' said Liberty wistfully, thinking how everyone else was enjoying themselves while she was planning to do nothing but work.

'You know we will hold the fort for you, darling,' confirmed Deirdre. 'You must be impatient to open and get going?'

'Yes, but no point before Easter, as I keep saying to myself and everyone else. As we discussed, I haven't advertised yet. I should get on to that today, but first I need to tell you about my day in London, and why I was in such a state this morning.'

Was it only that morning? So much seemed to have happened. Liberty's mind was pleasantly foggy with all the wine and she felt exhausted, but needed to tell her mother about Percy's request for a divorce, and the possibility that he was going to be a father.

Alain had rejoined them by the end of her story, and he was fuming. 'What the bloody hell does he think he is up to?' His protective streak leapt out and he wanted to strangle the man who had treated his little girl so badly. 'I do agree you should get the divorce sorted – free yourself from him. Why would you be upset about that?'

Liberty blushed and said, 'It just seems so final, like an admission of failure.'

Both Deirdre and Alain could have wept. 'Don't be silly, darling,' said Deirdre. 'Think of it more as a fresh start. Like a new year, it will be the beginning of your next chapter in life.'

Alain told Liberty that she looked terribly tired, and said why didn't she go home to get some rest? Then, looking a little embarrassed, he admitted, 'We have to be going. I'm taking your mother to Le Manoir au Quat'Saisons for a couple of nights!'

'Oh, Alain!' squeaked Deirdre as she threw her arms around his neck, smothering his face with kisses. Reality checked in all of a sudden. 'Who will look after the dogs? I have to pack! Who will drive – we've both had too much booze!' Unable to cope with such excitement, she fell back into her chair again.

'It's OK, sweetheart,' said Alain. 'Sarah is coming to look after the dogs, and I have arranged for a driver so we can both relax, and yes – you need to pack. So go upstairs and find something elegant and something lovely to go underneath for two nights. You will only see the room and the restaurant, so don't worry about other clothes.' He smirked, and then abruptly stopped as he saw the expression on Liberty's face.

'I may well be happy for you both, but I have no need to hear the intimate bits!' she said, giggling. As Deirdre raced upstairs,

Alain told Liberty he wanted to see his old mate Raymond, the chef he most admired for his commitment and hard work as well as his ability to produce exquisite modern and classic food with the best possible ingredients. Alain was prepared to pay his prices as he felt they were deserved, unlike so many of the more expensive restaurants. Sotto voce in Liberty's ear he added that he planned to propose properly, and he left quickly before she could ask any more questions.

Now able to feel elated and excited for her parents, Liberty hoped Deirdre would accept his proposal. Weird as it was, it would, she knew, make her mother very happy if he proposed formally, and that pleased her hugely.

Deciding it was time to go home, she took her champagne glass to the sink and shouted her goodbyes. 'Call me if you need to!' And she took herself back over the green. Letting herself in, she found a large puddle of wee and an upset Teal, who had been hiding under the table during Liberty's outburst and had no idea that everything was sorted out. Picking the lovely dog up and giving her a cuddle, Liberty told her that everything was OK, that she, Liberty, needed to get a life and to clear up the dishes and the floor. As she did so, Liberty continued to chatter to Teal.

'So, my parents have more romance than I do. I think that I am in love with a man who only sees me when I have no make-up on and usually when I am crying. My business may be failing before it opens, due to my apparent criminal record, and my soon to be ex-husband may or may not be having a baby with another woman. Great. Things couldn't be better. Come on, let's go and Skype Savannah to cheer ourselves up.'

As Savannah saw the little pug's face pushed up against the camera she let out a yelp of laughter. 'Hello, my friend,' she said joyfully. 'How's everything in Blighty?'

She and Liberty had a good gossip. The children were still being tutored at home, but Khalid had left soon after Gray. 'Oh, Liberty,' said Savannah, full of emotion, 'it was so good having Gray here for a few days.'

'And are you all right?' asked Liberty, full of concern.

'Well, oddly, yes. Khalid's been lovely, and he has said the children must stay here if that is what I want. All a bit strange, really. He seemed to get on very well with Gray – they kept muttering like best buddies to each other. Khalid seems so much happier here. Gray thought it was the threat of me staying in the UK that made Khalid so strange, and you know better than anyone that I was considering it. But he is being very loving, has asked for my forgiveness, and the children didn't even notice that anything was out of the ordinary – it was just a big adventure to them. He is still very possessive and doesn't like me to phone home too much, that's why I've been out of touch, but, strangely, since my return, I have felt much more as though I belong here and I am making a big effort. I may miss England, but my family is here, so you will just have to come and visit.' She then enquired how things were going with the café and if there was any news of Percy.

After her debriefing, Savannah said, 'If you need me, I can come, it would be fine. Just say the word.'

Liberty felt such a surge of warmth towards her friend that she squeezed Teal too tightly, and the pup squealed and leapt off her lap.

'I know what that means, and I thank you from the bottom of my heart, but you must stay put, at least for the time being. Edmund has been a great support. I really miss you, though; it was lovely to spend those few short hours with you.'

Savannah said the same and that it was such a pity they had lost contact for such a long time. 'We will just have to do our best via Skype and Facebook. Did Edmund tell you that Pa is going off to France soon? So nice for him to be in love again. I sometimes wonder if I have always felt to blame for Ma's death, and now he has found someone to love, I can settle too. Does that sound odd?'

Liberty smiled. 'Only coming from you. I didn't know you had been taking life-coaching lessons,' she joked. 'You never know, maybe you will become the perfect wife and Khalid will be able to trust you enough to let you come and visit!'

Savannah closed her eyes and Liberty immediately regretted saying such a thing as her friend blurted out, 'It would be such a shame if I could never bring the children to Denhelm again.' They moved swiftly on to the subject of Gray.

Both women agreed Gray had done the right thing in resigning his post, but Savannah was furious that Liberty had kept his sexuality a secret. 'I think I was always so self-absorbed in my teenage rebellion phase–'

'Which started when you were about eight,' interrupted Liberty.

'–that I didn't notice my beautiful brother gazing at my boyfriends rather than my girlfriends. He seems to be so much happier now, and this old major friend appears to have taken him in. All sounds ghastly to me, but Gray is good at coping with poverty and sickness. I wouldn't last half an hour myself, let alone a few months.'

'No,' agreed Liberty, thinking of her lovely but spoiled girlfriend. 'You wouldn't. But I'm off for a ride on your old horse with Edmund tomorrow.'

'Oooh, give Black Charmer a kiss on his big nose from me – and the horse as well!' Savannah said with a giggle. 'Is Ed still so severe and gloomy? He seems so negative about taking on the estate. Pa and I thought he would take to it like a duck to water but perhaps we were wrong.'

'Well, I think it's going to take time,' said Liberty. 'I think Jonathan's shoes are a big pair to fill, but Edmund is a hard worker, and he will find his place in time. I'm sure he will love it eventually. Goodness, he has only just found out he has to give up his job, take over Denhelm and cope with me along with the rest of the village, let's give him a chance! Anyway, I had better let you go, give the children a kiss for me. Miss you, call when you can.' And with that she closed her computer and decided to do some baking; it was the only way she knew how to relax these days.

42

Liberty met Edmund at the stables that afternoon. It was another glorious day, low sun giving the promise of spring on its way, sparkling cobwebs in the hedgerows lit up with dew like diamond necklaces, daffodils waving their mustard-yellow heads in the light breeze. They greeted each other fondly, and Liberty apologised again for her outburst. 'It was unnecessary and inappropriate for me to behave like that when you so kindly offered to come and stop me being an idiot, so I'm sorry.'

Edmund reminded her that in no way had he offered to come, but had realised why she wanted him there. Before she could revert back to thinking of him as stuffy old Edmund, he then smiled – gosh, this was an almost daily occurrence now – and said, 'It was my pleasure, and I'm so pleased they are happy. What about you? Was it the alcohol that cheered you up, or are you really OK with the arrangement now?'

Liberty thought for a moment and then replied, 'I love the idea that they are blissfully happy again. I just hope it will have the fairy-tale ending we all hope for.' She then lightened the mood by recounting her conversation with Savannah, and they both remarked on how happy she seemed.

'It's all a bit unreal,' commented Edmund. 'Khalid practically kidnapping the children, and all that horror, and now a few weeks later – bingo, she seems wonderfully content again. I hope it's genuine.'

They mounted, Liberty helped by one of the grooms. She noted that Edmund's reins were merely handed to him, and he had to use the mounting block.

As they sauntered through the park, Edmund told her of his regret that he didn't have people skills. 'Pa always managed to chat with the workers and make them feel like members of the family. I only seem to put their backs up.'

Knowing how gruff and unfriendly she had always thought him, Liberty wasn't surprised. He wasn't the first person a PR consultant would employ, but she just said he should give it time, let them know that he still had the best interests of the estate and its workers at heart, and they would come round eventually. 'Don't forget, most of the employees have worked here all their lives. They were hired and taught by your father or someone on his team. It's different for them now, and they must all be very wary of any changes you make.'

Liberty suddenly remembered Edmund had left before Alain had told her of his plan, and she confided in him that her father was planning to propose to her mother.

'I can't work out if that is far too fast or far too slow!' he said. 'Let's have a gallop and I'll wait for you down at the gate.' And he raced off.

'Bloody cheek!' screamed Liberty, laughing into the wind and kicking Savannah's old hunter into gear. She was convinced she could beat him, and urged her strong, capable mount forward, but Edmund kept his lead and twenty minutes later they brought up their horses for a breather by the river bank.

'A heaving chest and rosy cheeks look well on you,' said Edmund as he patted Black Charmer's strong neck. Liberty gradually blushed as she realised the black horse couldn't have rosy cheeks. Was he talking to her? A heaving chest! She hoped not, and then hoped so with secret delight.

The sunlight was glistening on the emerging buds on the alder trees that signalled an end to the long winter. The birds were calling sweetly and there was that tingle of spring in the air.

'What a perfect day. I don't want it to end,' said Liberty, as they walked back to the stables.

Inspired by the freedom he had just enjoyed on his ride, and by Liberty's company, Edmund uncharacteristically replied immediately, 'OK, let's not end it. I've a yearning to get out of the village. Let's take a jaunt. Get dressed up in your finery. I'm taking you to supper at the best establishment in the area – The Dark Horse, have you heard of it? I happen to know a chap who can get us a last-minute reservation, even on a Sunday night.'

'Or a girl whose father is that chap? Oh, what a good idea! You are clever, it will take our minds off everything, and what with your Pa and my parents, we deserve a bit of fun too!'

She left Edmund to deal with the sour looks from the stable lads, and raced off home to call Alain on his mobile, hoping that she wasn't interrupting . . .

'Oh, no hope, darling, you know us – we're booked a month in advance.' Liberty sighed, but she should have known. Unbeknown to Liberty, her mother was gesturing at Alain's side. Getting the gist of what Liberty was asking, she gave Alain a hefty kick in the shins. Alain spluttered and said, 'I'm sure we will manage something, though – we'll do what is done in these emergencies and put up a spare table for you.'

Alain was eager to do anything he could to please Liberty, but he knew his crack team in the kitchen would be stretched to full limit and the amuse-bouches were waiting to be prepared. But he also knew they would have spares in case of mishap and a fridge full of ingredients, so why not challenge them? Two extra diners. He felt a little guilty about not being there, but he certainly didn't want to leave his beloved's side now. Deirdre had taken the opportunity when he was on the phone to get out of bed at last and he could hear her happily splashing in the vast tub in the bathroom of their beautifully appointed suite. Eager to be in the water with her, he called his second in command and instructed him to move some tables and fit in the one they kept for last-minute VIPs or regular customers they indulged occasionally.

Meanwhile, Liberty was flustered. She thought it might be more relaxing to stay the night, and they could then both enjoy rather more wine, but how would she ask Edmund? In the end she called him and said there were two free rooms on offer. Edmund got the message and said that would be just fine, but privately he regretted the availability of more than one room.

Liberty primped and preened. No matter if Edmund only thought of her as an escape from the estate, she wanted to look her best. Gleaming, oiled, waxed and cleansed she emerged from the bathroom in a cloud of Fleurs d'Oranger by Serge Lutens, much to Teal's disapproval. The little dog looked up at her shimmering owner, and glowered as only a pug can glower, knowing she would be left behind.

'Don't worry, my friend,' said Liberty, picking the pug up and scratching her tummy. Her excitement was catching, and Teal cheered up when told she was going to be looked after by Sarah at Dijon and Custard's house.

As they were going to stay the night, Liberty chose to change into her evening wear on arrival. It would be more comfortable that way on the drive down. She picked a dark green corseted Victoria Beckham dress with little sleeves and an on-the-knee for decency hemline, but with a cleavage-enhancing neckline for Edmund, who just might notice she was a woman and not merely a friend of his sister. Alligator-skin knee-high boots with four-inch heels and pearls for her wrists and ears would keep the outfit smart but not too obvious. *Pearls always make you feel ladylike*, she thought. 'Even though my heart will explode if I don't get to kiss his handsome face soon,' she said with a giggle to nobody in particular as Teal scampered downstairs to puggle round and round by the front door, eager to visit her friends.

Liberty dressed for the journey in slim black trousers, a black polo neck and ballet pumps, and took her Birkin for her overnight things. She had a small bright purple leather Prada clutch for the evening that could hold perfume and lipstick.

Her cheeks glowed from the hairdryer and her eyes had been enlarged with emerald green and violet eyeliner and lashings of black mascara, so she wouldn't have to spend hours in the bathroom once there – something Percy had always criticised her for.

Edmund had said he would pick her up at seven. The journey would only take twenty-five minutes, and as supper was at eight thirty they would have time to settle in and have at least one drink before dinner.

Edmund was early in his eagerness, and driving past the green he caught sight of Liberty racing back home, having dropped off Teal.

'Am I late?' she asked as he got out of the car, resplendent in his dinner shirt, his jacket hanging in the back.

'No, am I overdressed?'

'Oh, no! I thought I would change there, save getting myself crumpled. Is that OK?'

'Good idea. Get your things, then we can be off.'

They drove in companionable silence, listening to Handel on Radio Three. 'Bloody car – marvellous off road, and super comfy, but in true Range Rover spirit something always seems to go wrong. My radio won't tune into anything else. I think it's trying to improve my interest in classical music, which I have to say, is working, although on long journeys it can become soporific unless they are playing a requiem or an opera.'

As they drew closer the car's navigation system told Edmund they had reached their destination. Liberty gave him instructions to arrive safely at the hotel by driving to the bottom of the hill and then taking a sharp left, at which point they could see a large sign saying 'The Dark Horse. Restaurant with Rooms. One Mile. Unmade Track.'

'Blimey, how do people negotiate this after a few too many?' wondered Edmund.

'It's a sign of the restaurant's popularity that people put up with it,' said Liberty as he crawled up the bumpy, potholed track, fringed on either side by thick forest. 'I think it's quirky. Townies see it as an adventure and country people feel they should be able to cope because others do. But it's worth it when you get there.'

Even in the dark, Edmund could appreciate the atmosphere of the place. With the last corner negotiated and the forest cleared, as they drove over a stone humpbacked bridge crossing the stream that lazily meandered through the hotel grounds, they could see the grand old building that housed Alain's pride and joy. It nestled into the hill as though it had grown from the ground up rather than having been built on to it. it was lit by soft floodlights on the outside, and from within the promise of fires and snug rooms peeked out of the windows. It looked tranquil, elegant and very romantic . . .

'Don't be alarmed by the brown bath water – it comes straight from the river,' explained Liberty, feeling excited to be back. 'Shame it's still too cold to have a drink outside,' she reflected. 'It's stunning on a summer's evening with the lavender out and the roses over the walls.'

They parked at the rear and carried their own bags into the hotel. A cosy hall with squashy sofas and roaring fire served as a reception of sorts and Gary, Alain's manager, raced over, full of apologies and horrified they had to carry their own things.

'Don't be silly,' said Liberty as she kissed him and introduced Edmund.

'A drink first?' he suggested.

'I'd like to change my clothes first,' said Liberty, and Edmund agreed. 'Let's put our things in the rooms and then we can relax.'

'Rooms? Rooms?' said Gary with a straight face, looking down at his computer screen, but Liberty noticed the tiny smile threatening to break out.

'Yes, Daddy phoned, I think.'

'No problem,' said Gary, back to his usual professional best and carefully refraining from continuing his little joke. 'I've given you the Garden Rooms, two charming rooms in the west wing. I am sure you will be very comfortable.'

Seeing other guests arriving, Liberty suggested that as she

knew where the rooms were she would take the keys and they could find their way. 'And thank you for fitting us in,' she said, smiling at Gary, pleasure fizzing through her at this unexpected jaunt. She hadn't spent a night here since she was a child.

'Thank you, my dear, and do let me know if I can do anything at all to make your stay more pleasant.'

Opening the door to Edmund's suite, Liberty reflected there would be very little anyone could do to improve their surroundings. The walls of both suites were, as she knew, decorated with birds and plants on silks and linens, and they had massive bathrooms whose tubs sat by the windows so the view could be fully appreciated. A fire twinkled behind a guard in Edmund's sitting room, and a cooler with a bottle of Ruinart Blanc de Blancs sat beside a bowl of fruits. Next to the espresso machine in the corner, a little porcelain bowl held freshly baked buttery shortbread and ginger biscuits.

The half-tester bed was already turned down for the night. No obvious TV, but Liberty showed Edmund how to press the button by the bed, whereupon the mirror on the opposite wall above the fire turned into a flat screen.

'Oh good, I can check the rugby. You go and get changed. Do you want a drink downstairs, or to have the champagne here?'

'Let's have a glass before we go down. We can always take it with us.'

Amazed to find more of the same champagne in her own room, but with an added bowl of the chocolate truffles her father knew she loved, Liberty quickly changed into her dinner dress and retouched her make-up.

Well, well, if we finish both bottles before supper I won't know what I'm doing, she thought. For some reason she wanted to keep her wits about her.

She ate a couple of the truffles, infused with lemon grass, to line her stomach, then knocked on Edmund's door.

As she walked in, he popped the cork and poured the champagne into coupes.

'Baccarat crystal. I'm amazed your father doesn't lose half of his property to guests.'

'Tempting, and he does. But he likes the best! Er, Edmund . . .'

He looked down and realised the glass was overflowing. Liberty raced into the bathroom for towels. Her back view was almost as good as her front, and he had been mightily distracted. She had been so insistent on the two rooms that again he reminded himself there was nothing between them, but gosh, she was a vision. Her dark, shining hair smelled of fresh air and flowers and her creamy skin shone like moonlight as she bent to mop up the spillage. *God, I'm turning into a twit*, thought Edmund.

'Cheers!' they said simultaneously, as they raised their glasses. 'Thank you,' said Liberty. 'Today I'm having the best time possible. This was a lovely idea, although I know my father doesn't do freebies, so do expect a hefty bill!'

'My treat, to say thank you for listening to me banging on about the estate, and good luck with LIBERTEAS. I don't suppose either of us will get much time off in the next few months, so let's enjoy ourselves!'

43

Alain may not have been into freebies, but by the time they made their way down to one of the comfortable drawing rooms, with lots of upright but relaxing chairs and sofas, another huge fire and tables positioned so there was always somewhere for a drink to be placed, Edmund thought whatever it cost would be worth the money. Piles of *Country Life* and *Homes & Gardens* adorned a circular table and pretty jugs of flowers were dotted around. The bookcases were full of a good mix, and there were even photographs in silver frames of Liberty and various family members, including Deirdre and most of the long-term employees; it gave the room an intimate feel, quite removed from the impersonal hotels that Edmund was used to.

Deirdre had influenced the decoration in the early days, and despite the change of carpets, her clever use of bits of furniture with different heights also took away the feel of uniformity. Interesting pictures along the walls, together with gilded mirrors, completed the look of elegant comfort, and the building itself made guests feel as though they were in a smart country house rather than a hotel.

The waiting staff had been taught to move around slowly and fluidly, so their presence was barely felt, but they were attentive enough to notice whose glass needed topping up, and to dispense amuse-bouches to those perusing the menus. Alain had a bizarre pathological hatred of computer script. He kept his fountain pen in his pocket at all times and employed an old lady in the nearby village exclusively to write out the menus every day.

Next door was a bar and an honesty book for guests. It was

a clubby room full of hunting prints and cushions embroidered with an assortment of dogs. Antique golf clubs hung on the walls alongside trophy stag antlers and there were furs on the floor. Checks and tweeds covered the furnishings and the bar itself was a sort of butler's pantry, hand-carved from oak by a craftsman. Liberty showed Edmund round, as most of the other diners had already gone through to one of the two dining rooms. Alain had wanted to keep the feeling of dining in a home, so wouldn't have appreciated one large room full of muttering people. His philosophy was that somehow, in a cosier environment, people were happy to chat away in a more normal manner, Liberty explained to Edmund.

He was enjoying watching her rear view as she showed him proudly round. 'Nothing worse than sitting in a hotel dining room where no one is speaking. It puts one off the food no matter how good it is,' he agreed.

Liberty hadn't had time to feel hungry until now, but after all the fresh air and no food apart from the chocolates since breakfast, she found herself agreeing when Edmund said they should try the tasting menu. 'That way we don't have to regret not choosing what the other has,' he said. 'And I'm terribly old-fashioned and cannot bear it when someone takes food from my plate to try it.'

Liberty smiled as she settled into the chair that Edmund indicated by the fire. 'You sound as though you speak from experience?'

As Edmund made himself comfortable on the sofa at the other side of the inglenook he said uncomfortably, 'I had a dear friend, she was – no, is – lovely, but when things were perhaps going to move a step forward, as it were, I brought her home to meet Pa.' He was looking more and more embarrassed.

'Go on,' encouraged Liberty, sipping her champagne and eager to know what dreaded deed the poor girl had committed.

'We all sat to have supper, and Deborah was getting on well, chatting away and keeping everyone amused. She is very funny, and Pa's friends had all been wowed by her shooting abilities earlier.'

Liberty found herself disliking this girl already and tried hard not to scowl. 'And?' she enquired.

'Well, halfway through one of her stories, she noticed I hadn't eaten my parsnips.' He stopped short as Liberty snorted champagne through her nose, but she waved at him to continue this dramatic tale. 'She picked them up, one by one, with her fingers, and ate them. And she wasn't even sitting next to me! She had to reach across some old crony of Pa's to do it. I had to call an end to the whole thing. When she asked me why, and I told her, she called me a pompous ass and said I was stuck in the previous century.'

Liberty tried hard not to giggle. 'Ahh, the fairy tale; stymied by root vegetables. See, I told you that food and love went together!' And with that she could hold herself together no more, and burst out laughing. 'Oh, poor Edmund,' she gasped as she saw the hawkish glower on his face, 'you really didn't love her – otherwise I'm sure the parsnip misdemeanour would have meant very little. I'm sorry to laugh, but you must see the funny side!' Thankfully, at that moment a diversion was created by the arrival of an amuse-bouche – a tiny square of slow-cooked pork belly garnished with its own crispy skin, and a slice of candied fennel.

'I'm sorry!' said Liberty, wide-eyed, realising she had polished hers off before Edmund had even started his. 'I'm starving!'

'It's lovely to see a lady with an appetite,' he confessed. 'Most of my girlfriends had no interest in food, only in the people who went to restaurants.'

'Apart from parsnips!' Liberty couldn't resist teasing him.

They were lowering the liquid in their bottle of champagne, and chatting away happily, when Amelie, the sommelier, came over to show them the wine list. Liberty asked after her children politely and exchanged pleasantries while Edmund considered.

'Why don't you recommend a wine for us,' asked Edmund,

'as we are having the tasting menu.' At this point Amelie's face broke into a rare smile and she took the wine menu from his hand. 'Very good, sir,' she said and waddled off happily.

'Well done, you are clever,' said Liberty. 'I've never got on with her, as Daddy can't stand her,' she whispered, 'but she knows her stuff, and her husband is from the village. It's terribly difficult to get a top class sommelier to work in the sticks. You will have made her night.'

'It must get terribly boring doing all that study and then to come to an English hotel and always be asked whether a wine she has bought from a particular vineyard is any good. When she gives her advice she is then asked for something cheaper and "maybe by the glass as we are driving".'

'Gosh, I hadn't thought of it like that, I'm sure that's exactly how she feels. Oh, you are clever,' she said for the third time in as many minutes, making Edmund feel top of the class again. 'Isn't this fun? It's so lovely to have a treat when least expected, and especially after the last few days. I feel so relaxed, thank you for suggesting it.' At that moment Gary arrived to take them to their table.

'I feel like a little girl allowed into my father's office, without him being there to tell me not to touch,' said Liberty, her eyes shining.

Edmund just loved her enthusiasm. *She must have eaten here hundreds of times and be quite used to this type of food*, he thought. But she was still going into raptures about their first little case of Stilton foam surrounding a sage and chicken ravioli.

Next came rabbit, a tiny pretend chop, made by sticking a chined rib bone into a piece of tender, moist loin, a miniature quenelle of rillettes and a sautéed kidney.

Then fish. A deconstructed fish stew. One mussel, a lobster claw and a red mullet fillet, with a tiny amount of very strong rich lobster bisque, gently scented with tarragon.

A shallot Tatin, so small that only one perfectly caramelised shallot could fit atop, next to a seared slice of venison and mushroom duxelles with a blackberry port jus, ended the savoury selection.

They had enjoyed a glass of wine with each dish, and now as they rested they realised that although they had eaten a wide variety of dishes, each was so perfectly sized they were happily looking forward to dessert.

Liberty was feeling so happy and relaxed, and a little tipsy. She shocked herself by asking, 'Do you find you miss your mother as much as Savannah says? And are you enjoying running the estate?' without thinking first. They were both taken aback by her bluntness and she said, 'I'm so sorry, that was nosy. Don't answer if you don't want to, I'll be taking food off your plate next and you will have to run for the hills!'

'Gosh, I certainly won't be running anywhere,' said Edmund, and Liberty found herself hoping it was because he liked her, not because he had eaten so much. He took a deep breath and said, 'Two huge questions.' Taking a sip of wine, he thought for a few moments. 'Ma died when I was young. Not too young, so I remember her well, but I had Gray and Savvie to think about. I'm sure you know that Pa went into quite a decline; he could barely function for a year after her death. I think, sadly, I felt angry with her at the beginning for doing that to him. And for leaving me – us – when we were so young. Of course, I didn't realise I was angry at the time, you don't as a child, but I had to grow up pretty fast. Without Mrs Goodman the family would have simply fallen apart. I think I probably became rather too serious; I felt I had to be the man of the house, but my age didn't allow me to achieve that. I lost my childhood and gained an unerring ability to push away those close to me.'

Liberty could feel herself well up; she had spent her youth laughing at the too serious Edmund, but now her heart went out to the little boy who carried the weight of the world on his shoulders. Edmund, whose tongue had been loosened by the wine and the effect Liberty was having on him, carried on. 'Gray's always on at me to chill, and Deborah – parsnip girl, my last paramour – used to call me Scowled. I just threw myself into work, first at school, then uni and setting up my company, which I am so proud of, and now I bloody have to give it all up.'

Liberty looked up at his blazing eyes. It all made sense. He had spent his entire life working hard to achieve something on his own, away from Denhelm and the sad memories, and now he had been called back to live there and take care of it. No wonder he wasn't looking forward to the challenge. He saw the estate as his past, not his future. Edmund, meanwhile, had recovered from his near outburst and went back to reflecting on his mother.

'Pa very rarely spoke of her, so Gray and I would ask Mrs G to tell us stories of what she was like and show us photographs. Pa was furious one day when he caught Savvie looking through her clothes. I'm so pleased he has found Paloma, and maybe some sort of closure. Yes, I've missed having a mother, but many others are in the same boat, and we have a very close family, so in many ways I'm lucky. The estate? We will have to wait and see. I suppose I've always known it would come to me, eventually, and I thought it would somehow fit like an old coat found at the back of the rack after the summer, but I feel very lost at the moment.'

Liberty placed her hand over his to stop him fidgeting with a butter knife. 'I'm sorry to make you think of the past; I was out of turn. I just wanted to know the real you.'

Edmund had stopped fidgeting. His hand was charged with the strange energy he felt when he was around Liberty. 'I've never spoken of such things, and I feel a bore to have done so when we are enjoying such a fine evening. I apologise.'

Their eyes met, and a brief understanding flew between them before they were interrupted by the arrival of a large pistachio soufflé with a spoonful of Liberty's favourite coffee ice cream melting delectably into a hole in the centre. Gary, who had brought over the soufflé, had also been the cupid who instructed the kitchen to make one large pudding rather than individual ones, and he asked sweetly if they would like him to serve or just to leave two spoons. Knowing he was joking but enjoying their moment of closeness, both said, 'Just spoons, please,' and laughed at the delight on Gary's face. The moment of relief had allowed the electricity in the air to settle, and they once again found themselves chattering about more benign subjects.

'Don't you like parsnips, then?' asked Liberty as they placed their spoons in the empty dish, replete but happy. *Edmund grinned – actually grinned!* thought Liberty. *And because he is happy, not because he is fixing drains!*

And then he said, 'I think they may become my favourite vegetable! I have a lot to thank them for.'

The air seemed to have slowly crystallised, their strong emotions freed by alcohol, good company and a general sense of togetherness. Liberty was barely able to utter a word. Her mind was turning in an everlasting circle. *I want this man, but if I say so, and he rejects me, I have lost a great friend. If I don't, and never get the chance again, I'm an idiot.* She certainly didn't need any more food, but suddenly having no idea what to do with her hands made her pop one of the petit fours that had been left with their coffee into her mouth. Why wasn't Edmund saying anything? Did he think her revoltingly greedy? Oh God, she was the new parsnip girl!

Edmund was lost in a world of contentment. As he sat and watched Liberty put another small sweetmeat in her mouth, he mused over people who insisted that when attracted to each other they couldn't eat a thing. If that was the case, he and Liberty loathed each other. But he knew the opposite was true for him. He had never experienced such physical pleasure as when seeing Liberty gently sniff at, nibble, then roll a mouthful round her tongue. She made it the most sensual action.

He had always found other people's eating habits fairly abhorrent, but the enjoyment that Liberty derived from every morsel filled his senses with happiness and his body with longing. In the same way, he loved to watch her working in her kitchen – how she instinctively reached for herbs, flavourings and spices. She seemed to be performing her own ballet, each movement pre-decided upon. She moved as effortlessly as a dancer, every sinew in her body gracefully deployed, as though twisting and stretching from toe to fingertip. She appeared to live and work with every part of herself. This was one of the many things he had come to love about her, and now here she was, obviously full to bursting and trying not to say something. Should he ask her to his suite for a nightcap? If she said no, it would be horribly awkward.

British formality lay between them like a giant oak tree felled in a storm. Liberty was thinking, *God, if I were French, I would have just launched myself on him, and devil may care what happened.*

And Edmund was deliberating, *Goodness me, if I were an Italian, I'd never have brought her down to dinner in the first place.*

This painful, yet delightful, scenario was broken by Gary.

'Miss James, your telephone appears to be ringing.' He handed her the purple clutch bag, which had been placed behind her on the chair.

'Goodness me, I hadn't realised I had put it in there!' said Liberty, blushing furiously. By the time she had scrabbled around for her phone it had stopped ringing, but then Edmund's buzzed in his pocket.

'I don't care if my father does own the place, we will get turned out,' muttered Liberty, knowing that private phones were actively discouraged in the hotel's public rooms.

Edmund looked down at his screen. 'It's Gray,' he said. 'I had better take it. It must be tomorrow already where he is. Hold on a minute.'

Liberty looked at her call register, and the last missed call had been from Grahame. 'Oh, help, it must be an emergency,' was her first reaction. 'But why would he call me first?'

Edmund had left the dining room, and she presumed he

had walked outside to phone Gray. Meanwhile, the few other remaining guests were doing what the British do best: complaining under their breath so she could just hear without catching the details. She looked at them directly and said kindly, 'Sorry, but we were waiting for important news.' After directing a dazzling smile at the male members of the group, who had already noted her long legs and beautiful figure, the grumbling stopped.

Edmund walked briskly towards her. 'That was interesting. I need a brandy.' He was flushed and breathing excitedly.

'What? What? Tell me,' said Liberty.

'Drink first. Two brandies, please,' he ordered, as Gary appeared. Not waiting to ask what type, he returned with a tray holding two glasses of Alain's finest. Edmund took a sip, and then stopped to appreciate the smooth, amber liquid.

'Well. It appears Gray wasn't quite straight – excuse the pun – with us about how he knew this Major Race chap. He is an old flame!'

Liberty looked quizzical. 'What do you mean?'

'He and Gray had a sort of relationship years ago at uni. Anyway, he went off, joined the army, rose up the ranks, and we know Gray's story. The major left the army, left his wife and announced to anyone who would listen that he was gay and proud of it blah, blah, the usual stuff. Children disowned him. He took himself off around the globe to do good for others.

'He contacted Gray after all the press coverage over here covering Gray and J-T. He must have understood what my poor brother was going through. Gray says he is running things over there brilliantly, has got the government trembling in its welly boots and the aid sent to where it was needed most. Anyway, going off the point.

'Gray arrived. Before he could be shipped off into the disaster zone, he and the major apparently started where they had left off so many years ago. Says it's as though they last saw each other yesterday and found love at second sight. The major is going to join him at one of the refugee camps, and is going to get the BBC to cover the flooding and Gray's work to help get aid through. Then, when Gray's work is complete, he is going to stay with the major for the foreseeable future.' Edmund now downed the rest of his brandy, forgetting about appreciation, just needing obliteration.

'Golly, Pa's going to love this. Since Ma died, Pa has been doing everything he can to keep his picture-book model family; all normal, happy and easy-going, hoping we could cope without a maternal figure. And what has he ended up with? One difficult, thrice-married, scandal-ridden daughter living in Abu Dhabi, possibly never to be seen again; one useless, emotionally retarded son and heir, who is managing to ruin the estate before he has even taken over and never married, so no grandson to pass the sinking ship on to; and one gay son who has decided to settle in Bangladesh after bringing shame on the family name and is now about to announce that he is in love with an ex-army major who was saving the world on his own until my family intervened.'

Liberty said calmly, 'I think you are missing the point. It means Gray is really happy, and that is just wonderful.'

'But fuck it,' said Edmund. 'I think I had always hoped he could be my saviour. He would be perfect as custodian of Denhelm. And I was hoping I could get back to my business while he took the helm of my *Titanic*.'

'Oh, don't be so negative,' said Liberty. 'You have only just started out. You are a brilliant businessman, already proven, so just run the bloody estate as YOU see fit and right. It's only because you are paddling about behind your father at the moment that you feel shaky and out of your depth. Go at it in your own way and things will be fine. Wait until he leaves the place; it would be like me trying to take over this hotel and restaurant. My cooking might be OK, but my father has put thirty-five years of his life into it, and things would inevitably change. You need to gain the respect of those around you, and you will only do that if you step out from your father's shadow and make your own mark. Yes, you might well tread on toes on the way, but the workers will learn to respect you if you do that, and trust you, if you show them that your way works. Give them shares in the family business if you like – sort out a profit scheme, set up your own ideas. If they work, and the employees earn more, they will feel more loyalty. You said you wanted to put the land to better use; you could either set up a farm shop or raise rare breeds of pigs or cattle, or train racehorses. I don't know the best way, but you certainly do.'

Edmund looked at Liberty. His jaw jutted out and his eyes grew hard. 'I'm not sure I need to be told what to do by someone who is so scared to get on with what they want. They keep talking about it, but haven't begun it yet.'

Liberty's cheeks flushed scarlet. 'I have to wait for the tourist season before opening! Of course I'm scared, but at least I'm going to give it a go. I don't need to listen to this; I was just trying to put some ideas into your head. Maybe you should call parsnip girl for help. I'm going to bed.'

She managed to rise, take hold of her clutch bag and walk out in a straight line without bursting into tears. Bedroom door firmly shut, dress thrown on the floor, she kicked the very hard bed post and then let herself cry bitterly. 'Bollocks, bollocks and fuck,' she said. 'It was such a lovely evening, what on earth did I screw it up for? More bollocks.'

She got ready for bed. The wonderful food and wine now sat like a brick in her stomach. Why is it that mood dictates your digestion? She splashed her face and pulled herself together. How dare he say she was scared? Of course she bloody was. All alone in the world, with a useless barren body, her only talent was feeding people. She could end her days as a dinner lady at the local school, with baked beans and chips etched on her tombstone. She must make her little café work and prove to them all she was capable.

44

Liberty opened her eyes tentatively. She had not been sleeping, not for hours, but had been lying in bed, unwilling and unable to look upon the day. Feeling as she did, a little hungover with shame at how she had behaved, telling Edmund how to run his business and ruining a perfect evening, she was a little surprised to see a glorious day shining in through the large bay window, encouraging her to believe that spring was truly here. She could discern bird calls through the open window. *How can they sound so damn cheerful?* she thought to herself. *And how do I manage to mess things up time and again?*

She flung back the covers, made herself an espresso on the machine and sipped the steaming cup while nibbling a biscuit. She gazed at the gardens below which stopped at the river; wild flower meadows flanked the croquet lawns, and the daffodil buds were already in evidence. The meadows would look spectacular later in the year when the wild orchids and poppies were flowering. She had often tiptoed through the dewy grasses barefooted, holding a glass of champagne after dinner. She pondered briefly whether Edmund might have left the hotel without her, but she hoped not; she had been over and over the apology she needed to make. After checking her make-up was perfect and her hair shining she found him alone downstairs, eating kippers and drinking coffee. He glanced up from *The Daily Telegraph* he was scowling over and pretending to read, then stood politely.

'I'm so sorry,' he said immediately. 'I turned into a priggish bore last night, most unlike me, and I apologise unreservedly.' In fact, he had been awake until the early hours as well, reeling with his own stupidity. He had felt so happy for Gray and yet he had allowed his own frustration to turn to gloom. He had so wanted to sweep Liberty off her feet. Before taking over Denhelm he had felt he could eventually manage to run it successfully, but now he was all at sea and his confidence was being tossed and turned on the waves. Always sure of himself when it came to his work, he was unused to feeling inadequate – and in this job he had expected his genes to instruct him, instead of which they had downed tools and hidden away. Now he had ruined any chance with Liberty by being a horrible beast, and telling her she was scared, when what she needed was positive reassurance. *Stupid fool I am*, he thought.

Liberty surprised Edmund by sticking to coffee for breakfast. He felt it was an indication of her desperation to get back home, so he quickly finished what he was eating and went to pay the bill.

In reality, she was wondering if she was different from the women he was used to. She had stuffed her face last night, and had talked only of food. She was so selfish, always discussing her own worries, when what he needed was encouragement and support. The journey home was far too slow and silent, the road filled with Monday morning commuters.

With one hand on the door handle as the car came to a halt outside Deirdre's house, Liberty said, 'Please let me pay half the bill. I feel so ashamed of the things I said. You deserve a better friend, but I really enjoyed myself, and thank you.' She got out of the car quickly, leaving Edmund unable to reply, let alone take her in his arms and whisk her off to Denhelm, which is what he wanted to do. He had to prove himself first, get his pride back, and then do the whisking! God, he even thought like a girl . . . what had happened to him? *Love weakens and it hurts*, he decided, as he swung the car through the park gates, *but goodness me, I want to get it right.*

After picking Teal up at The Nuttery, and thanking Sarah for looking after her, Liberty raced back to Duck End, immediately feeling better. The little pug rushed around, obviously just as excited to be back as she was. Liberty loved her home. It enveloped her, and made her feel safe and strong again. How had she ruined such a lovely time?

Teal ran to the sitting room and plonked herself on the sofa while Liberty checked her emails on the computer and realised she hadn't taken Gray's message off her phone.

There was one email from Gray telling her to look on Facebook, another similar one from her mother.

There were photos of Gray and a very handsome, tanned man, with chiselled cheekbones and white-blond hair, or was it grey? She couldn't tell, but it appeared to be brushed back with two hand brushes, in the old-fashioned way, very army. Both men certainly seemed happy. One picture showed them both looking slightly the worse for wear with three dogs, two Dobermans and a Ridgeback, sitting next to them on a garden bench like statues. 'Me in the Garden of Eden,' was Gray's caption. 'Nelson, Spitfire and Radar all send love to everyone who has supported the Bangladesh Raise Aid for Swept Away Food Campaign.'

Liberty then clicked on 'search for Deirdre James'. As she suspected, her mother had no Facebook page, so she tried Alain James. There, alongside a photo of her parents' wedding day, sat Alain's details. Profession: restaurateur. Relationship status: engaged.

'Hooray,' shouted Liberty out loud, so Teal leapt off the sofa to join her and raced round the room. She dialled her mother's mobile, only to learn it was switched off, as always. Almost immediately Liberty heard a knock at the front door and, thinking it was her parents, she rushed to open it, only to find Fred leaning against the frame, looking as naughty and gorgeous as ever.

'Hello, beautiful. I've got something large, solid and awesome to show you. It's in the van.'

'My sign! Yes, of course,' said Liberty, giggling but trying, without success, to ignore the innuendo. Fred had done her proud. Not only was the sign ready to hang from the large iron rod he had already fixed above the door of LIBERTEAS, but he had made six hanging baskets for the front with knives and forks as the supports to do their magic around the courtyard.

'It's wonderful, I love it. Thank you,' Liberty said admiringly. Before she knew what was happening Fred hugged her and told her it was his pleasure, and as she was the only girl who had ever refused him, would she now do him the honour of taking him up to her boudoir? So brazen was his offer, and so firm and beautiful his body, she hesitated before bursting into laughter and saying no, but would a coffee and piece of cake do instead?

'It will do for now, but I will have to bill you in that case,' he said, apparently regretfully. 'So you will have another chance when I bring it round!'

His Irish brogue really was extremely charming, if the man himself was a little rough around the edges. As they walked to the house from his van Edmund drove past, slowed and sped off.

'Bloody prat,' said Fred. 'Sydney the gamekeeper said he's so stuffy you are lucky to get a good morning out of him.' Feeling he had been a little harsh, he followed with, 'Good rider, though.'

After feeding Fred and ushering him out, although not before receiving a kiss planted firmly on her lips, Liberty was wondering whether she should call Edmund to explain. But there was no need; Edmund had been driving round the village waiting for Fred to leave, and now here he was, banging on the front door.

'Sorry to be such an ass yesterday. Of course you don't pay half the bill, or any of it. Despite your damning assessment of your father regarding freebies, there was no bill, and I wouldn't have accepted your request anyway. Can I come in?'

'Oh, yes, of course,' replied Liberty, amazed that he was apologising when she felt it was her fault the evening had gone so wrong.

'I've decided to pull myself together and get on with things,' he said, finding the courage to say what he wanted to relieve himself of. 'Starting with using Denhelm Park to help you. I thought the day before you officially open, we could hold some sort of village fair to celebrate. Put trestle tables out on the green with lots of your cakes and tarts and scones, and so on. Have a few traditional village games – throw the horseshoe, Punch and Judy, stuff like that. Americans love it. It will be almost Easter, so the school children can contribute something, and you can introduce everyone to your food, and at the same time raise money for the Raise Aid for Swept Away Food Fund.'

'What a brilliant idea,' said Liberty, immediately taking it up. 'Too early for the maypole, but we can do everything else – coconut shies, archery, tombola. What fun! Lots of bunting and local stall holders, honey, jams, that sort of thing. Maybe a dog show. Everyone loves that. Scruffiest, prettiest, most like its owner. You are so clever, thank you so much for having such a brilliant idea.'

Edmund immediately felt seven feet taller and able to conquer anything he was challenged with. So what if his workers didn't like him? He had never cared what people thought of him. Why change now?

They sat and wrote some ideas down. Fliers would have to go out very soon, and did he know anyone who could organise perfect weather?

When Deirdre and Alain appeared at the kitchen window Liberty gasped. 'Oh gosh, I forgot to tell you, they got engaged!' She went to kiss and congratulate her parents, who were obviously in no fit state to have driven home. Thank goodness for the driver!

'No, not drunk, darling, just deliriously happy,' insisted Deirdre, 'but what a good idea. Let's open some bubbly.'

Alain watched quizzically as Edmund took a bottle of Ruinart from the fridge. 'Didn't it get drunk last night?' he asked.

'Two bottles and we had wine with supper. Thank you so much, Daddy, it was utterly perfect.'

'I'm glad you enjoyed it,' said Alain, somewhat puzzled that his daughter didn't seem any closer to Edmund. What was wrong with that idiot of a man? How could anyone resist his beautiful girl? Maybe he would put in a bill after all.

'What is your ring like, Mummy?'

'I've never taken it off, you silly girl. But Alain has given me this wonderful necklace.' She pulled back her shirt collar to show a three-strand pearl choker with an emerald drop. On anyone else it would look like costume jewellery, but on Deirdre it glittered and looked regal.

'Wow! That is certainly a piece and a half,' whispered Liberty. 'Are you sure you can afford it, Daddy, as you are shutting the hotel?' And she laughed. 'Talking of hotels, how was the Manoir? I haven't been since my twenty-first birthday.'

'Too bloody lovely. That place never fails to amaze. Raymond's ability to stick with what seems classical, but is always extraordinary food, is the tops.' Alain reeled off what they had eaten and drunk down to the last detail.

'Yes, yes, but I want to hear how you proposed again,' said Liberty.

'Darling,' said Deirdre, 'you know Daddy – never one to shy away from embarrassment. Down on one knee in the middle of dinner, just so I couldn't refuse him. Everyone turned to watch.'

'Presumably so as to see if I could get up again,' roared Alain, totally pleased with himself.

'And they clapped when I accepted. As if I could have turned the old man down!' finished Deirdre.

Edmund told them about Gray's news, and Liberty showed them the Facebook pictures. Love hung in the air. Then Deirdre asked Edmund if he knew when Jonathan was off to France.

'Tomorrow.' His face fell a little. 'He will want to see you all before he goes and said to invite you quietly. He doesn't want a big send-off, so come for a drink tonight about seven? I need to make some arrangements for LIBERTEAS' grand opening, and I have to check some details. Liberty, why don't you fill your parents in about the fair, and I'll get back home.'

Jonathan had packed and was saying goodbye to everyone and

everything, wondering for the hundredth time if he was doing the right thing. Just as he was fondly bidding the sundial he and Helena had placed to celebrate the birth of Edmund farewell, his mobile rang. His face softened as he said, 'Darling, I was just thinking about you!'

'No you were not!' was Paloma's sharp comeback. 'Stop worrying and crying over what you are leaving behind. It will be there when we come back for Liberty's opening or for Deirdre and Alain's wedding. I need you, big man, so be excited, stop moping and get on the damn plane!' With that she put the phone down. She had been rightly terrified that Jonathan was having second or third thoughts. However, her words had the desired effect. Feeling his first ever thrill at leaving his beloved Denhelm, Jonathan quickly went back to the beautiful house, took his bags, and left for an earlier flight, eager to get away, to lose the weight that had pressed down on his shoulders since Helena left him so alone.

The next day was a strange one after Jonathan's unannounced departure. Deirdre and Alain had arrived for farewell drinks, only to be greeted by a weeping Mrs Goodman and an angry Edmund. Deirdre told Edmund his idea for LIBERTEAS' opening was brilliant, and that he would have no problems taking over the helm, but after a quick drink she made her excuses and hurried Alain home.

'Why did we have to leave?' demanded Alain. 'That was damn good whisky he was pouring!'

Deirdre pouted. 'I cannot believe that Jonathan went off without so much as a by-your-leave. I couldn't tell him our news, or wish him well.'

Alain put his arm through hers and chuckled. 'Any lesser man would be jealous. Are you upset he left or upset he left you?'

Deirdre's cheeks flushed a becoming pink. 'I just think he could have said goodbye. And leaving poor Edmund like that! I shall tell Ed that Liberty needs him to help test some recipes tomorrow, get him out of the house. I wonder why they seemed so uncomfortable with each other today, they could barely look at each other! And there was me telling you that they were in love!'

'I don't think you are wrong there, my darling,' said Alain as they continued their walk home, 'but something went askew last night. When I phoned Gary to find out what I owed, he told me that after a good meal, Liberty suddenly left the dining room and disappeared to her room – alone!'

Edmund was delighted to be invited to Liberty's home – any chance to get away from the feeling of wearing a coat two sizes too large. But later that day, on his return to Denhelm, he felt somewhat uncomfortable from eating too many delicate anchovy straws and tiny choux buns filled with a smoked haddock brandade topped with tapenade, and a vast selection of other titbits. He had not known that canapés could be so delicious, and an entire meal (when you ate fifty of them).

He smiled to himself as he remembered the apprehension on Liberty's face each time he popped one of the delicacies into his mouth, as though expecting him suddenly to find something wrong with the light-as-air buttery pastry or drop down dead from some form of instant food poisoning.

The habitual scowl soon returned to his face as he stood in the Grand Hall, looking up and around at his inheritance in a new light. 'All his – all mine,' he muttered to himself. *Curse and buggery*, he thought. He wandered into his father's office. 'No, my office,' he said sternly. 'No, definitely Pa's office,' he confirmed as he looked around at the faded chintzy chairs held together with dog hair and the odd stains he hadn't noticed before. The large library desk, covered in papers, photographs and invoices, screamed 'Jonathan sits here', as did the old uncomfortable wooden chair that he had always used, despite its unforgivingly hard seat, as Helena had given it to him when she moved in.

'My only possession,' she had said as she took over the running of the house with considerable skill, despite growing up in other people's rented manors as her father moved frequently to escape the taxman.

Having lived since childhood in the knowledge that 'one day, my boy, all this will be yours', Edmund expected some epiphany to envelop him, to shout instructions and deliver a job description. He had, for heaven's sake, watched and followed his father for so many years; listening to instructions being given to employees, the annual buildings check being detailed and the crop rotation being listed. The estate seemed to run like clockwork, so why did he have no idea where to start now? He thought fondly of his little office off Pimlico Road; his fussy secretary and her disapproving voice as he left yet another cup of coffee half drunk (she had never worked out how to use his smart espresso machine, and insisted on giving him two spoons of instant as a replacement, in a very small amount of boiling water, which he hated so left untouched).

He knew how to advise large companies how to cut factory emissions, how to reduce their carbon footprint while scooping government grants and how to save pounds on future energy expenditure, but running this house with no occupants except himself and a housekeeper, three tenant farms, a stud, a farm shop, a bottling factory, not to mention the Christmas tree plantation and about 150 tenants in the village left him cold; too many people needing him. The one person he wanted to need him only desired his taste buds. He slumped into a chair, head in hands, and realised he had been secretly hoping his father would find their spring water contained the elixir of youth so he could stay on indefinitely. *Where the hell are you, Pa? How dare you bugger off to enjoy yourself while the girl I love is only interested in how many seeds of cardamom to grind into a Chelsea bun dough. Meanwhile, you find true love with an ancient hippy!*

'Bugger!' he said, and started to decipher some of the mess on and around the desk.

45

The coming village fete to celebrate the opening of LIBERTEAS was creating a wave of excitement and enthusiasm, surging its way through Liberty's family and supporters.

The idea of holding street parties had been joyfully taken up by villagers all over the country, eager to help the royal family celebrate weddings and jubilees. They had come at a time when the British public as a whole were feeling wretched. Money was tight, wars were being fought by brave soldiers, missed sorely by their families back in the UK, news of more deaths were almost an everyday occurrence, and the possibility of a happier and better world seemed further and further away. Streets had been closed off and neighbours had met each other for the first time while planning food, placing bunting and finding trestle tables. Their children had played in the car-free lanes and a happy sense of community had swept the land. Now there was another chance to hold such a celebration. Sarah had already run off to tell her children excitedly, so no doubt the whole village would be aware of the coming event by tea time. However, most of those street parties had been organised a year in advance. Liberty had just four weeks to accomplish the grand opening that was unfurling before her.

She made pots of coffee and poured champagne while her parents added to the list of ideas. Alain thought of baskets filled with pretty loaves of bread to adorn the trestle tables instead of flowers. He knew Paloma would have cheap sources of rustic basketware and could ship some over from France.

'You need to make it look like a television ideal of an English fair. So often they are a let-down. You must think what a tourist would like to see – something from another era, like *Miss Marple* crossed with *The Darling Buds of May*,' he elaborated. 'China pots of tea, linens, scones, cakes, ladies in pretty pinnies – Paloma can send those too, as they still wear them in the south of France. Lots of bunting, striped deck-chairs alongside a few hay bales, lights in trees. You could carry it through to the evening. Talk to the pub – Dilys, is it? See if she would sell beer in plastic cups so people could mill in and out. What about a band? Talk to that Pig chap – you could serve his sausages. Get the cheese people involved, and anyone else who is a local producer, especially those you will want to use for the café. Get them behind the idea so they support you. You will do most of the work, but they will gain from the exposure.

'Don't go the hog roast way, as that is not the food you will be serving. Think more of an English picnic,' he continued, happy to share his skills and ideas with his family. 'Do you remember the scene in *Sense and Sensibility*? The one that Emma Thompson did with that chap, where they organise a brilliant picnic, parasols and hampers in the English countryside? You have the perfect setting right here!'

'Wasn't Edmund clever coming up with the idea?' Liberty exclaimed.

'Yes,' said Deirdre, 'I've noticed how much you love Edmund's ideas!'

Liberty let this comment go, saying, 'It's just so easy as it's his land, so we don't have to ask permission from the council.' Then she asked her mother if she could help with the baking.

'Oh, we will both help,' said Alain. 'In fact, if we get the publicity right we may need more than your kitchen can churn out. It all needs to be spot on, which with patisserie means as fresh as possible. I will arrange for a portable kitchen to come with two extra baking ovens. You don't want fan ovens. Do you have sufficient baking trays? Bread tins and so on?'

'Yes, I've bought loads, and they are all washed and stacked.'

'You have your own tea blend, but you will need filtered water, so we will have to get a large capacity filter. And your milk has to be of exceptional quality. Where are you sourcing it for LIBERTEAS?'

'Daddy! Stop! Remember, you taught me everything I know. I have already been to visit local dairies, sampled them all. I've got raw goat's milk coming from Mrs Bevan at Gateshead Farm for those who like it. Otherwise, non-homogenised organic milk from Burnt House Farm. They have Guernseys; perfect milk for tea and baking. They are also supplying butter, proper buttermilk and cream. I have to use skimmed milk for the coffee machine as it froths better, and some people will ask for it anyway. Burnt House is supplying that too. I'm going to spend my afternoons phoning the local paper. Hopefully they will send a journo for the day, tempted by free food and drink, and I shall put half-page advertisements in from now until D-day asking people to support the fair.'

Edmund had called to say that Eric was keen to show off his hen harrier's talent at rabbit-catching. *Not so sure about that*, thought Liberty. *It could maybe just chase a hare or a cardamom cream bun*. And a couple of Shetland ponies were to be borrowed from the estate where they were used as companions for the more flighty thoroughbreds, to give children rides around the village green.

Edmund also suggested a local family who could give jousting demonstrations, but they eventually agreed that was perhaps a step too far.

Liberty went home and set about writing an advertisement.

LIBERTEAS
YOUR LOCAL PATISSERIE AND PLACE FOR
BREAKFAST AND LUNCH
INVITES YOU TO HELP CELEBRATE
THE ARRIVAL OF SPRING AND THEIR
GRAND OPENING

10 A.M. – LATE
COME AND ENJOY A TASTE OF YOUR LOCAL PRODUCE
COOKED IN A PASSIONATE KITCHEN
FLAVOURS OF YOUR FAVOURITE FOOD
COOKED IN A PROFESSIONAL WAY
USING ONLY THE BEST INGREDIENTS
WE GUARANTEE YOU WILL BE QUEUING FOR OUR OPENING
SATURDAY 20TH MARCH
DOG SHOW: BRING YOUR OWN
ARCHERY • WELLY-THROWING • FALCONRY DEMONSTRATION • MOST INTERESTING TALENT • PONY RIDES • FANCY DRESS • TOMBOLA

The next day, Liberty strolled over the green, feeling enlivened and excited. She let herself in to her mother's house, and was quickly reminded that it was now her parents' home when she found Alain, feet on the table, munching warm soda bread spread with butter and honey.

'Join me, darling?' he enquired.

'No, thanks.'

'You must eat.'

Liberty shrugged off the feeling of annoyance at being told what to do by her newly returned father, and instead asked, 'Is Mummy around?'

'Just walking the dogs. Dijon has had a bad turn, and we've had to call the vet out. She is worried, hence me making soda bread, which she feels too sad to eat, and that makes me sad so I'm eating it to feel better,' finished Alain as he lowered his feet to the floor and looked serious for a moment.

'She got that dog when I left her. I know how much he means to her, and I get the feeling it was my return that has given the poor old thing less reason to stick around.' Alain's stricken face gave away his true feelings, despite his lightness of phrase.

'Oh, Daddy!' Liberty put her arms around him, unused to seeing her charismatic, strong father looking so miserable. 'We don't even know if this is the end. If he's able to go for a walk, he may be fine.'

'I think you will find them in the walled garden. I don't want to impose myself.' And with that Alain put his feet back on the table and tore another piece of soda bread from the loaf.

Liberty spotted her mother sitting on the stone bench where years ago she had sat her daughter down and told her Alain was leaving. Three years later, when the divorce was going through, Deirdre's old dog Grigson had died. To help her get over that and the final rejection, she had gone down to chat with Jonathan, whose bitch had just had a litter. Through her tears she had spied one of the golden bundles jump out of the whelping box and bounce over to her.

Deirdre had thought she could never love again, but her heart immediately melted, and Jonathan let her take the pup home. He never told her that as pick of the litter, Dijon had been promised to the Duke of Speyside, to whom Jonathan supplied his top-quality gun dogs. A crate of vintage port and a promise of lunch at his club had calmed his old friend, and when Jonathan explained it was for Deirdre, and why, the duke had happily agreed that as many puppies from the next litter as he wanted would be his, provided there were no other charming ladies to cheer up at the time. He had met Deirdre already and had been bowled over by her beauty and quiet elegance, and did not bear grudges.

Dijon was lying on his side panting heavily. His eyes looked round as Liberty approached, but his tail gave no customary wag and he seemed unable to lift his head. Deirdre was leaning over her old friend and stroking him gently while whispering loveliness into his almost deaf ears.

Liberty sat next to her mother, a lump in her throat. Unable to think of anything to say, she put her arm around her for a moment, then spread a blanket over her lap. A few moments later Alain brought the vet into the garden. Mr Night was well beloved; he never caused unnecessary worry, and never interfered with an animal unless absolutely necessary. His motto was, 'A dog is strong, sensible and capable of deciding if he is ill. No need for fuss.' But one look at Dijon and he placed his hand on Deirdre's shoulder, which heaved, and she let out a groan.

'He has enjoyed his time with you,' said the vet. 'Now you need to let him go, in peace. It is right and fair. I'll get my things ready while you say your goodbyes.'

Liberty went over to where Mr Night was preparing a syringe. 'Does it have to look so horrid?' she asked.

'We give them an overdose to make it quick. I won't even need to sedate him. Looks as though he has had a brain aneurysm. It's for the best and, hard as it seems, let's not allow him to suffer any longer.'

'Ready, Deirdre?' She nodded but was unable to speak. She knelt beside the great dog, and held his head. 'Goodbye, my faithful friend.' She kissed his furry face. Mr Night was beside her holding the dog's leg steady, and Deirdre reached out her hand. Liberty was going to take it but instead pushed Alain out of his trance towards her. He grabbed Deirdre's hand and knelt beside her. She looked surprised for a moment, and then as the syringe pushed the fatal dose into the vein that led to the golden heart, she crumpled on to him and sobbed.

After a couple of minutes, Alain looked at Mr Night and the vet nodded and said, 'He's gone.' Alain held Deirdre tightly until the tremors stilled, whereupon he said softly that they should pick a special place in the garden. He would lay the dear dog to rest.

Deirdre gave one last backward glance then allowed Alain to lead her to the house.

Liberty had the unpleasant task of helping Mr Night cover Dijon in his favourite blanket and then put him into a black cadaver bag. 'Thank you for being so quick,' she said, unable to think of anything more pleasant to say, as they laid the bag in the shed. She would check with Deirdre later that she really wanted Dijon buried in the garden and not cremated. Mr Night, used to such occasions, was unperturbed and went on his way.

Indoors, the kitchen was empty, so she made herself a cup of tea, then realised she had put hot water in a wine glass and leaf tea in the sink, so poured herself a brandy, grateful for the heat and fire it unleashed in her belly. Alain joined her, explaining he had put Deirdre and Custard into bed, the poor little pug being apparently as upset as her owner. 'Either that, or she is terrified about what might happen to her if she lies still for too long.' A flicker of humour in a sad afternoon.

Pacing the floor, full of sorrow and yet still aware that she must get on with organising, Liberty thought she would call the always-cheerful Paloma, find out about the baby and see if Paloma could help with baskets and linen.

Paloma was delighted to hear from Liberty; from the surrounding noise it appeared she was enjoying a drink somewhere on the Champs-Elysées. 'Sorry, darling, I am standing in the street, waiting for Jonathan. He's been doing some investigating into Khalid while he's here. I'm not sure it will do any good if he interferes, and I can't say it adds to the romantic break, but I think my heart is his, so here I stand.'

'So you are captured to listen to my needs!' said Liberty and explained about the fair.

'Count us in, my love. We won't send the things, we will bring them over ourselves. Jonathan is already missing home, although he won't admit it, and Claude seems to be running my restaurant for me, desperate to escape from demands for back rubs and black pepper ice cream!'

'No baby yet, then?'

'Twenty days late, but she refuses to be induced. Poor Evangeline looks terribly uncomfortable. She is so tiny, with a big baby, but I'm sure it will be fine. Ah, here comes Jonathan. I'll fill him in and get on to organising baskets. Leave it to us. Love you.'

And with those words the exciting sounds of Paris faded away together with the passionate and enthusiastic Paloma. Liberty reflected how curious it was that merely talking to some people made you feel capable, energised and excited. Paloma exuded energy even down the phone. Jonathan was lucky to have her.

46

Paloma's energy obviously extended beyond Liberty. At five in the morning of 6th March, baby Yves was born. A whopping four kilograms. Bonny, smiling and a delight to his exhausted but proud parents.

When Deirdre took the call, it immediately gave her a boost, and she felt a new life had benefited from the space an old soul had vacated. This thought she failed to share with the new *grand-mère* Paloma, who, although she liked dogs, could not understand Deirdre's passion for them.

The James family arranged to fly out en masse to Nice the following weekend for the baptism. Liberty would only stay for one night as she would need to get back to sort out the fair, but Deirdre and Alain thought they would stay for an extra few days with their old friend, Deirdre taking advantage of Alain's reluctance to leave her side and go to work. The restaurant would be open until the end of summer, when it would shut for renovations to turn it into a school.

When Liberty told Edmund of the birth as they met in her kitchen for their now daily coffee and catch-up, he tentatively asked if he could join them, see his Pa and get some sunshine.

'Why, of course, that would be lovely!' exclaimed Liberty. 'I'm sure we can all stay at Paloma's. Bless her, she sounds so excited about Claude's baby, and then refuses to be called "*grand-mère*". Far too ageing! So now everyone is calling her *l'Ancienne*!'

The following Thursday Edmund drove them all to Gatwick, each one invigorated by the baby's birth and the arrival of spring sunshine. Crocuses and daffodils lined the verges after months of greys and browns, and their hearts were lifted.

Alain, true to his word, had buried Dijon in a flower bed at the end of the garden, covered him with narcissi bulbs and bluebells, and placed an order with Fred for an ironwork gazebo in place of a headstone. 'Dijon, faithful companion' would be stamped on a small plaque, and he had ordered a winter jasmine to climb up and over, along with a yellow rose to remember his glossy coat.

Alain was pleased that Yves had arrived to take Deirdre's mind off the loss of her beloved dog, but also that she seemed to take it as right that the dog who had helped her though those lonely years should go now that Alain had returned. He still couldn't believe his luck that his beautiful ex-wife had taken him back to where he had always belonged, and was kicking himself that he had let pride get in the way once he realised his ghastly mistake.

They were searched and scolded by security when Alain was discovered trying to take a pile of cream-laden cardamom lemon buns, his baptism gift, through in his hand luggage. Thankfully, one of the top security chiefs was a major foodie, recognised Alain and, on hearing it was for such an important celebration, allowed them to board, but only after trying one and pronouncing it free of explosives!

'If I ever save enough money to bring my wife to your restaurant, I hope you remember me!' he said. At which Alain scribbled a note and said, 'Use it quickly. I'm closing down in the autumn!' He had given the bemused, work-weary man a voucher for a tasting menu and suite for the night for two people.

'Two freebies in as many nights! Daddy, you are losing your head.' Liberty was finding her father's volte-face rather endearing, if a little odd. She would never have believed he would choose to leave his restaurant unless in a coffin; now he seemed unable to leave Deirdre's side.

'Ah, but darling, love makes you happy, and what else is there, really, in the world?'

They sat in the lounge, drinking champagne, waiting for their flight to be called. As they chatted happily, Liberty told Edmund all about the fabulous place that Paloma called home, and how she had come to be there. 'So she has never caved in and told you who Claude's father is?' Edmund sounded sceptical, whispering to Liberty that there had to be a reason. Liberty didn't care; she was thrilled to be returning to the warmth and excitement of the Riviera and to meet Yves. She had always felt like an older sister to Claude, and now she was an aunt and a godmother!

The flight was short and on time. Edmund helped Liberty with her bag and then went off to arrange the car while Alain and Deirdre waited for their luggage. Deirdre had packed so many presents that they had three suitcases for as many days.

'It is such a lovely time to be on the Riviera,' said Deirdre as they sped in their hire car towards St Tropez. 'Like the perfect English summer's day.' The road was almost empty of traffic, so they made fast progress. Edmund confidently covered the miles, Liberty at his side pointing out road-side stalls, pretty houses and dead cats, while they tried to ignore the cuddled-up love birds in the back. They were reminiscing about their time in St Tropez when they helped Paloma set up on her own. 'She was such a bad cook that one sample of her food and Alain said nothing was to be done, she had to hire a chef!' recalled Deirdre, laughing. 'But she is so entertaining that as front of house she established a reputation that has kept her going. Chefs are banging at the door, eager to work there, and customers are queuing summer after summer.'

Liberty added that the remarkable setting helped, but she couldn't imagine the place without Paloma. However, as they roared up the gravel drive through the wrought-iron gates, always open and completely grown over by the creepers that covered the wall surrounding the property, it was Jonathan who was standing on the steps waiting to greet them, looking as though he had always lived in the south of France. His face was smoothed by love, sea air and lack of responsibility, and he wore a cream linen suit with a pale blue shirt, emphasising his blue eyes, and loafers on his feet with no socks.

'Pa, you've gone native,' said Edmund, as he hugged his father affectionately.

'Come through and meet the star of the show. He's just woken and Evangeline is feeding him on the terrace.' Jonathan seemed very excitable, unable to stand still, and he almost dragged Edmund along, reluctantly waiting while Edmund insisted on helping Liberty.

They walked round the side of the building as they didn't wish to disturb the diners inside. Edmund gasped, Liberty screamed and Deirdre and Alain hugged each other. For sitting alongside the happy mother and babe were Savannah and Khalid, holding hands and gazing into each other's eyes. The children were running around Antoine the gardener's feet and playing tag. Savannah dragged her eyes away from Khalid's, and stood to hug them, and then they all cooed over baby Yves, who, in typical Gallic fashion, was enjoying a good lunch. Evangeline and Claude looked tired, but deliriously happy. It was an idyllic scene. Khalid called the children over, saying it was time for their meal, and he whispered to Savannah she had best fill everyone in on her own while he took the kids inside.

Liberty, waiting impatiently for all the details, picked up a proffered Campari soda and sat next to her old friend.

'Please say this means we can see each other often again! What on earth happened?'

'It's all Pa's doing, really,' explained Savannah. 'When Khalid left at Christmas, I thought he was taking the children and refusing to let them be influenced by the Western lifestyle. I think I had read too many novels and disastrous press reports, and after all my other relationships had ended so badly, I suppose I imagined this one would too. If only I had talked things over with Khalid, I would have realised it was the other way round.

Apparently, he was terrified I wanted to stay in the UK without him, after Christmas. He got in a terrible jealous rage at the party, and thought the only way to hold on to me was to take the children and lure me back, but the whole time he had been planning a different scheme. Realising that life in Abu Dhabi wasn't best suited to me, he had bought a house in Paris, a vast three-storey apartment in the 13th Arrondissement. Gray had been keeping an eye on it, thinking it was for some illicit scheme, but only saw his interior decorator coming and going.

'Khalid thought we could live happily in Paris. He would be able to fly direct to the UAE when he needed, but could conduct most of his business from an office in the apartment, and I could jump on the Eurostar to come home whenever I liked. He booked schools for the children, but when we got all muddled at Christmas he wasn't sure if I would agree even to that, so he didn't mention it at all!

'Pa found out about the house purchase when he and Paloma were in Paris by talking to the concierge, so he phoned Khalid to ask what was going on, which prompted Khalid to break down, tell me how much he didn't want to lose me and could I possibly bear to live out my years in Paris, if he also bought a home on the Riviera for holidays? How could I refuse him?'

They all roared with laughter at the absurdity of Savannah even considering for a moment the idea of refusing such an offer.

'I realised how much I love him,' she continued. 'I just had got it into my head that he must be a beast because those are the only types I've been with before! It's all rather lovely, really. It's like a whole new beginning, and I can't tell you how happy I am – no, we are! He's allowing me to go to some fabulous antique fair next month to buy furniture, but he has employed Nicky Haslam's team to do the house to make it look like an old English home. How sweet is that?' She then followed up with, 'Well, I could hardly employ J-T after his thing with Gray,' misinterpreting Liberty's look of incredulity.

Liberty gazed at her friend, who had softened somehow, as

though acknowledging she was loved had made her relax and be able to love herself. Her eyes glowed and her cheeks seemed fuller and so did her tummy . . . Noticing her friend's glance, Savvie shrieked 'Oh, and I'm pregnant again!' to anyone who wanted to hear. Which they all did, of course.

Khalid poked his head out of an upstairs window. 'We were going to tell everyone together!' He sounded frustrated, but was laughing. 'It seems you have told the whole of France, you loud-mouthed lovely.'

'Goodness me, it must be catching,' said Claude. 'Congratulations to you both.' Khalid waved and shouted that he would be right down.

After chatting for a while longer, the group was catching up with news. Edmund looked like a startled rabbit when Jonathan asked how Denhelm was getting on without him 'Oh, you know, Pa,' he said, trying to make a joke of it. 'All collapsing without its captain!'

Sensing his discomfort, Liberty called over that she should show him around, and took him off to be introduced to Antoine, her gardener tutor. 'Thank you,' said Edmund huskily, when they were out of earshot. 'I don't think this time of joy is the correct moment to share with my father that I'm sinking his prize ship.'

Liberty took his arm. 'You have only been at the helm for a few weeks. He had it for years. He also took it over at a time when he was engulfed in inheritance tax, the land was haemorrhaging money and the Labour government was doing its best to destroy the upper classes. He had nothing to lose; you, on the other hand, have taken over the finished article. It was much easier to start with nothing than to start with everything and every expectation. Give yourself time; remember, you have already started and run a very successful company of your own.' She had done some research into ECOCapital and discovered that, despite many misgivings from larger venture capitalists, Edmund had raised vast amounts of capital and enabled many new ecological ventures to start up. With his clever eye for channelling good ideas, most of them were succeeding, and becoming profitable.

'You need to have the confidence that we all have in you, and Jonathan simply wouldn't have handed the damn thing over if he didn't think you could handle it.'

Edmund hadn't thought of it that way before, and being hundreds of miles away, watching the evening sun shining on the sea in the distance and with the promise of an amusing time away from it all, beside the woman he adored, he felt immediately better. 'You are a kind and loyal friend, thank you,' he said, as Liberty completed her tour of the gardens.

Returning to the merry group on the now chilly terrace, Liberty and Deirdre asked Paloma if they could go to their rooms to change and freshen up.

'Aah,' replied Paloma. 'It's fortunate that your parents have finally realised they should be together, as we will be rather full, what with Savvie and Khalid here. No, no, I won't hear of you staying anywhere else,' she added as Khalid volunteered to take his lot to a hotel. 'But Liberty and Edmund?' this was asked with a somewhat sly look. 'Would you two consider sharing a twin room?'

At both their furious blushes and splutterings, Paloma knew she was on to a good thing, but Deirdre, for once oblivious to others' matchmaking, piped up, 'Liberty can share with me and Alain with Edmund.'

Paloma glared at her friend, who seemed intent on spoiling her plan and replied, 'We are all adults, and they can manage, I am sure. No point in separating the engaged couple.' So two very embarrassed people agreed to share a room, saying it would be just fine. Liberty was grateful she had brought a nightdress, and Edmund was exceedingly pleased Mrs Goodman had packed pyjamas and left out his old teddy bear, which she normally smuggled in.

The baptism was to be held at ten o'clock the following

morning, so would be sandwiched between breakfast and a late lunch.

The domestic arrangements settled, they all sat down for a fabulous supper, while Yves slept in a Moses basket by the table, oblivious to the raucous laughter of friends and family celebrating his life, and Deirdre and Alain's engagement. Rabbit confit was followed by grilled turbot and a dessert of apple tart. After plenty of burgundy and brandy, they all wobbled up to bed.

Edmund used the bathroom first, to allow Liberty to undress, then planned to pretend to be asleep when she came out. However, the vision of the beautiful woman in a silk negligee, her full breasts only hidden by intricate lace, was not conducive to sleep, or even the pretence thereof.

As she sat on the edge of her single bed, she squeezed out some cream on to her hands and started to rub her feet. A hefty chuckle emitted from the lump of duvet in the neighbouring bed.

'What?'

'I'm sorry,' said Edmund, lifting himself on to his elbows, exposing a very 1950s pair of pyjamas buttoned right up to the top, 'but it's funny. I've spent my life fighting off glamorous females, who only wanted me because they knew I was going to inherit a large estate, and the one I've lost my heart to can sit on her bed, comfortably rubbing foot cream in as though nothing could be further from her mind.'

'What did you say?' gasped Liberty.

'Foot cream!' And with that, Edmund rolled over into a fuzzy, brandy-induced slumber, dreaming of a vision in silk cuddling up to Digby, his old teddy.

Liberty sat listening to his gentle snoring. Had he said lost his heart? Really? She lay back, both sobered and startled. Was it the drink? Had he meant it? Was it just the surroundings and all the love in the air? And how dare he say that then go to sleep so easily?

Eventually she fell into a dreamless sleep, hoping that morning would bring clarity. But instead it brought a pot of strong coffee and a demand that she got her lazy ass out of bed as everyone was waiting for breakfast – that was Savannah, of course.

Dressing quickly in a mint-green Yves Saint Laurent suit, she ran downstairs to find them indeed all sitting round hungrily looking at the baskets of pastries. Edmund was sipping a cup of black coffee and avoiding her eyes.

'Sorry to keep you waiting. I took a while to get to sleep, then of course I overdid it.'

'Well, dig in, then we had best be off. Come, sit next to me,' said Savannah, who was holding baby Yves while trying to get her own daughter to drink hot chocolate without dunking her croissant in it.

'It's OK,' said Paloma to her kindly. 'You will find all the children in France do that.'

'See, Mama,' said little Sasha, gazing up at her mother with vast brown eyes. 'I'm already French!'

And the table laughed collectively.

47

The baptism was beautiful – magical, really – and reminded everyone why they should go to church, if only for the ambience. The calm atmosphere and the beautiful altar piece with its Madonna and child, a few offerings left by locals and a couple of flickering candles, made the gathering serene, and even little Yves only gurgled quietly. The open font was the only indication that anything special was taking place; Evangeline and her parents had politely refused Paloma's offer of flowers, saying they would like all attention focused on the ceremony. Infused with the scent of incense, the tiny chapel gave a feeling of grandeur beyond its status, while the sun shone through the small, plain windows, highlighting the fairy dust twinkling through the air. Yves, dressed in generous lengths of lace, waved his chubby arms and chirruped happily at the priest and then at Liberty, his godmother, and Claude's old school chum who was standing as godfather. Blessings and prayers were said, and although some of the congregation spoke no French, it mattered little as it still sounded lyrical and they all knew why they were there.

Once the service had finished, photographs were taken outside under a brilliant blue sky. Locals who had joined the congregation offered their congratulations and prayers, and now wandered off to collect baguettes and stroll around the vegetable market that had been set up in the Place des Lices. Everyone staying at Paloma's gave lifts to those without cars, or those unwilling to drive after what was bound to be a good party. As she went upstairs to change and freshen up, Liberty mulled over the thought that had been nagging at her; Edmund was avoiding her. He had sat right at the back of the chapel, and now was wandering around the gardens with the children rather than going upstairs to their room. But she realised that maybe, just maybe, in a small way he could have meant what he said the previous night. And her cheeks glowed with pleasure.

Meanwhile, Edmund, despite the children's chattering, was turning things round in his mind. How could he have been such an ass? All right, so he had drunk too much, something unusual for him, but it had been such a fun evening. He had been amazed then frustrated that such a glamorous and attractive woman felt so disinclined sexually towards him that she could sit as though on her own and rub cream into her feet instead of, as he had hoped, emerge from the bathroom all scented and fresh with the intention of sitting on his bed and enchanting him. Even rubbing his feet would have been better! But how had he let those rash words escape from his mouth? He knew exactly how. The moment she bent over a foot, he realised he had no hope. If she was so relaxed and able to treat him like a brother while he lay in bed within touching distance of her, it was obvious that nothing could come of his passion for her, and he had simply said what he had to release him from his dream and get it all out of his system.

Instead, in the sober light of day, it had embarrassed her, made him feel like a fool and ruined his chances completely. Worse, it hadn't ended his love for her. In fact, it was increased, as he had almost hoped she would run down to breakfast and announce to her family that she loved him – instead of which, she had merely avoided him. What a mess!

Jonathan could see his eldest son from his bedroom window. 'I'm going into the garden to have a word with Ed, I'll see you at lunch, my love,' he said to a slumbering Paloma, who had just enjoyed the masterful fingers of a very unstuffy Englishman.

'Tell him to get on with it,' she murmured, and Jonathan asked himself what the amazing woman was mumbling about.

How happy she made him, but how confused! He had forgotten what it was like to spend time around a woman's mind; very distracting and not at all practical.

Finding Edmund alone, the children having escaped to the walled garden to build dens, and sipping a Bloody Mary, Jonathan questioned his eldest.

'Is it really that bad?'

'Oh, Pa, you have no idea,' was the reply.

'But I thought it was what you always wanted,' said his father.

Edmund looked up sharply, coming back to his senses. 'Oh, yes, the estate. It's fine. I'm getting the hang of things now, nothing to worry yourself about. I was bound to tread on a few toes. Mrs Goodman always makes me feel better. I've never been great at people skills, and it's really like running a family – quite hard to do when you haven't had experience of that.'

The jigsaw was fitting into place in Jonathan's mind. So that was what the clever woman had meant!

'So, what's your problem? Who's eating your brain out?' he said, sitting next to Edmund on the stone seat. 'Liberty?'

'Is it that obvious?' Jonathan smiled to himself. At least he had got his son to admit it.

'As typical Englishmen, I doubt we would even be having this conversation back home. But I suggest you grab her while you can. I can only say how happy I have been these last weeks. Gray has found what he wants, Savannah is so changed by knowing she is loved, and anyway, it's obvious you are crazy about her!' said Edmund's father, trying to sound wise, but thinking how love indeed changed everything. He had forgotten the strange ability of people, once in love, to love more of everything; life itself bloomed and blossomed through the eyes of the enamoured. Edmund looked at Jonathan: the proud, stiff gentleman, telling him to get a love life. Had the world turned on its head? The thought made him smile, and he felt instantly better.

Family and guests were congregating in the dining room. The restaurant had taken few bookings, apart from regulars arriving to hand over gifts and congratulations for the newly baptised Yves. Liberty was due to fly home after lunch. She was sad to be going but somewhat relieved.

Savannah and Khalid promised to catch the Eurostar over for the fete, and they all talked about Gray's new-found major.

'Do you think he will persuade Gray to stay in Bangladesh?' asked Deirdre.

'I'm not sure,' replied Edmund. 'The major's posting was not permanent, but as he's doing such a good job they keep on extending it, and were grateful for his skills when the floods came – although I am hearing this through Gray, and he would have him able to part the seas and walk on water whilst juggling, so it's hard to tell. I have read a little about him, and have learned he is incredibly bright, top of his year at Sandhurst, and that he was chosen for this kind of work because he never loses his temper. He is very good at keeping calm in unimaginable situations. He was able get one of the top chaps in the Taliban, some heads of government and some UN people around a table, all at the same time, to talk when he was in Afghanistan. Quite something.'

'So he would fit right in here,' said Savannah, laughing.

Liberty had spent most of the day cooing over baby Yves and asking anyone what she should do to be a good godmother. Most people had replied that it meant sending expensive presents, but one elderly lady had wisely said, 'Lead by good example, listen to the child, and above all, notice when the parents are not able to perform to their best, and stand in.' Having said her goodbyes to most, except Edmund, as she was confused and aware that in this highly charged emotional gathering she could embarrass herself, she went upstairs to fetch her bags. The taxi was waiting, and she knew she was cutting it fine to catch the flight back to Gatwick.

The door opened behind her and Edmund walked in. She had her back to him, and breathed in deeply, holding the breath, willing him to say something. He did, but it wasn't what she hoped to hear.

'I'm sorry I laughed last night. It was inappropriate. I had too much to drink and I regret it. I hope you can forgive me.'

She turned, fixing him with her direct gaze. Her heart was pounding with unspoken desire for this handsome, funny, clever man. Could she, by brain waves alone, persuade him to leap at her? The thought that she could do the leaping never crossed her mind; she was very out of practice when it came to romance or lust and her body just felt incapable, her mind unconfident. Edmund drew himself up to his full height and looked at her sternly. Internally, he was searching for the right words, the right thing to do. His body was telling him what he wanted to do. Christ, every cell of his body was screaming at him to take hold of her and kiss her till they could breathe no more. Outwardly, however, he looked as serious and distant as he used to. There was an awkward moment while they both deliberated what to do, then, just as Edmund thought he might as well throw himself at her moisturised feet, Liberty broke the silence.

'Of course I forgive you. It was a fun evening, and we all felt a bit giggly. I'll see you back home.' She grabbed her bag before he could offer to help and half stumbled, half ran out of the room.

'Fuck,' said Edmund.

'Bugger,' said Liberty as the cab sped towards the highway. Feeling as lonely as it was possible to be at that moment, she thought why oh why was she so useless? Now she realised she could have made the first move, but oh, the utter humiliation if he refused her! The tiny amount of confidence she had in herself as a woman couldn't take another knock.

Sarah brought Teal round to her house as soon as she returned. 'I'm sorry, but can I leave Custard with you too? She is missing Dijon, so I don't want to leave her on her own when I go to work.'

'No problem, it will be a pleasure to look after her,' said Liberty, pleased to have her two furry friends to follow her around, snuffling and jolly as always. Something was odd, though. Nothing stood out, but she felt, almost knew, someone had been in the house. She checked the windows and French doors. No sign of a break-in, but she knew there had been more milk in the jug, and the coffee machine had been set to 'cappuccino', something she would only make in the morning. The last coffee she had drunk was during the evening before she left for France. She decided she must have been mistaken, as no one except her mother had keys. Sarah would have told her if she had borrowed them and been in. But something was not right.

Teal spent a while sniffing at the fireplace in the sitting room and then barked at it, which made Liberty smile. 'It's too warm for a fire. Come into the kitchen and sit by the Aga, you silly thing, if you are cold.'

She checked her emails and sent one to Gray, hoping he was well and telling him about the baptism. She attached photos and asked if he had heard about Savannah and Khalid. She also told him of the fete, and the fact that Savannah and Khalid would be coming, also J-T and Bob. J-T had suggested painting the grass on the green pink – now that would make a statement! They would bring the dogs, which Liberty privately thought would only win the yappiest dog class. However, their support was wonderful and their presence would boost numbers. And at the very least, J-T would make an effort for the canine fancy dress.

Savannah had already emailed, with lovely news. She would arrive with the family on the Thursday before the fete, and would willingly help serve food. Liberty giggled as she knew this would result in helping one person to cake and a lot of gossip, but how sweet of her to offer. Gray's news was somewhat more surprising. He and the major, as he referred to him, would be embarking on a long holiday to get away from the horror of the flooding in Bangladesh, when the worst was over and others were in charge. They hoped to stop off in the UK sometime in the summer. Gray was, however, sending some things for her grand opening, as he called it, although he had written that the name sounded a little pornographic! And he wished her well, although he warned the post could be erratic and the parcel might only arrive in time for Christmas, even though he had sent it part of the way on a forces flight. How lovely. She felt her friends remembered her and this made her, albeit momentarily, feel a little less nervous about her first solo venture.

48

The days were flying by. Liberty's mind was awash with excitement one minute, terror the next. Menus, photographs and ideas for cakes scrawled on pieces of paper covered the walls of her kitchen, as though Colefax and Fowler's new range of wallpapers had been taken from cookery books. *Mmm, not a bad idea. Maybe J-T will hire me when the café nosedives*, she thought in a bout of nerves. Pictures of cake stands covered with macaroons and fairy cakes (which she personally hated, but knew were popular with children) were piled on the table. She had taken delivery of her cake tins for the ladies' teas: mini loaf tins for tiny blueberry, ginger and lemon drizzle cakes; tiny flan tins for the most delicate tarts and quiches; she planned to do mini tarte Tatins and mini clafoutis when cherry season arrived, and had found small ceramic dishes that were perfect for both; little Bundt tins for delectable espresso cakes filled with a dark chocolate mousse drizzled with a white chocolate ganache . . . the list went on. Why was everything so cute when in miniature, she wondered? She must leave a set out for Sasha to play with when she came to the park. Liberty knew that she had to be prepared. She only had two days between the fair and her opening.

Advertisements had been placed in all the local papers and the county glossies, and that afternoon a journalist from *Weald Life* was coming to interview her for some editorial above an advertisement before the opening. 'Our next issue comes out on the Tuesday before the opening,' he had said on the phone, 'so if I come now, I can fit it in.'

Liberty wasn't sure; not having opened yet, she was uncertain what the journalist wanted. But he had approached her, emailing and then phoning, quite insistent that he do a piece, as he had heard of her legendary skills. It was only after she had agreed that she wondered how he had heard, but he sounded friendly enough, and all publicity was good, wasn't it? She planned to show him the premises and then give him a slap-up afternoon tea while he conducted the interview, but she wished Edmund was there for some backup. She hadn't seen much of him since his return from France.

She rid herself of any nerves she might have had by losing herself in clouds of flour and sugar. She knew she was happiest when, apron on, washing up, she could smell the aromas wafting out of the gas oven in which she baked her cakes. She decided it was a memory of childhood; walking into her kitchen after school and delightedly sniffing the air, wondering if it was to be apple strudel or chocolate profiteroles that her mother had lovingly prepared, only for Liberty to steal a stash with barely a word of thanks before whisking them down to Savannah, where they would share them with their gypsy friends in the Christmas tree forest, exchanging them for lard buns and rabbit pasties. A psychologist would have a field day with her, telling her she had reverted to what made her happy, and when had this last been? Liberty didn't care to dwell on the fact that it would have been twenty-three years ago.

Teal brought her master back to the present day by reminding her that she needed to be let out. 'Oh, good girl!' exclaimed Liberty, thrilled that at last the little dog was getting the hang of going outside to wee. And it must be a good omen – no puddles for the journalist to stand in! A happy morning was spent making her favourites and putting a great deal of care and attention into the details. She knew it was a male interviewer, so stuck to what Edmund had professed to be the best choices: mini Scotch eggs made with quails' eggs, individual brioches topped with horseradish and local smoked trout, local cheese gougères, and a little Guinness and ginger spice cake soaked in ginger syrup and scented with cardamom and star anise. And her own speciality – the poppy seed walnut sponge filled with damson preserve and whipped cream, which was huge and blowsy and stood beautifully on an Emma Bridgewater cake stand in the centre of the table alongside a basket of fruit, plain and cheese scones, clotted cream and home-made preserves. She had put out pretty yellow checked napkins that were tea towel sized, and her own tea set that she had ordered from Germany – delicate porcelain with a scalloped edge, white with a pea-green trim and gold edging. As her café was not yet open, instead of greeting him in her chosen uniform of long pinny, she dressed in a Chloé shirtwaister and wedges, with a cashmere cardigan, all in palest duck-egg blue. She made sure her hair was shining and Teal wasn't sitting on the table.

Reassuringly, he was on time. A smartly – far too smartly, for a provincial journo – dressed man stood on her doorstep, while a short, rat-faced girl with buck teeth and an angry expression stood next to him holding an ancient camera.

'Jools Middleton,' he boomed confidently, 'and this is Lexi, my photographer. *Weald Life.*'

'Hello,' said Liberty, a little taken aback by the photographer. Her brain was telling her not to be so silly; of course they would want pictures! 'Do please come in. Shall we start with tea or would you like to look at my premises first?'

'Oh, no need. We took a pic as we came past; I'm sure our readers just want to know what you are planning on serving.'

'Oh! All right.' Liberty's stomach made a funny jerking action. For some reason, this did not feel right. Her instinct was screaming at her that something was wrong. She again wished that Edmund was there to put her mind at ease; there was no reason for her to be agitated, but every hair on her neck was standing to attention. She took a breath and said as calmly as she could, 'I'll put the kettle on. Our local water is so good, but it will be filtered in the restaurant to make the perfect cup. What can I offer you? Assam, lapsang souchong, Darjeeling, jasmine, or you may prefer our English tea? We use an everyday brew similar to the Teapigs mix . . .'

'Oh, just PG for us. Thanks, love – anything else would be wasted.' Lexi added that she couldn't stand any of that funny stuff.

'Oh,' said Liberty again, unsure of what else to say. She was trying to promote the extent of her menu, and had been sure the restaurant reviewer would be interested, but maybe he was overworked and underpaid as most journalists were, although that suit told another story. She made a large pot of English breakfast, the closest she had to PG Tips.

'What's that?' asked Lexi, sneering at the silver tea strainer. 'A sieve?'

'It's to keep the tea leaves from migrating into your cup,' explained Liberty, trying to keep the smile off her face, and relaxing a little. 'Do you write all the restaurant reviews?'

'Oh, no,' replied Jools, 'I'm normally financial, but they were short-staffed.' This should have rung alarm bells in both Liberty's ears. The magazine, one of the most respected monthlies in the county, took pride in its restaurant reviews, and they had been keen to write her up, or at least the journalist who had contacted her was. She knew hoteliers and guest houses would leave copies of the magazine around their establishments, so this was important. It was definitely keep calm and carry on time.

Liberty put out all the dishes she had prepared earlier. She had quickly laid another place setting. The table looked beautiful. But before she could offer the savouries, Lexi cut a wide piece from the poppy seed and walnut cake, which was to be served last. It wobbled precariously.

'What is it?' she asked, prodding the golden-flecked sponge with its ground poppy seeds like tiny black speckles of sand, the thick cream mingling with the deep purple of the damson compote.

'That is my speciality. No flour, only ground walnuts and

almonds, lots of butter and eggs. It's filled with fresh cream and my home-made damson jam. The sponge is flavoured with orange zest and I drizzle a light Grand Marnier syrup over the top of each layer once it is baked to keep it moist.'

'Oh, horrid, damsons, aren't they really sour?' Lexi stuck her tongue out and clattered her fork on to the delicate china plate without even trying it. Keeping a fixed smile on her face, Liberty said, 'Maybe something savoury to start with?' She placed a tiny Scotch egg in front of Jools; he shoved it into his mouth and swallowed it, reminding her of Dijon.

'What else?' he said. She put a local blue cheese and cobnut straw on his plate.

'My home-made puff,' she said proudly, adding a miniature Sussex pasty (shortcrust filled with pheasant confit, seasoning and local vegetables). She then deliberated, glanced round the groaning table and pushed a tart filled with oven-dried tomato and prosciutto towards him, together with a tiny twice-baked goat's cheese soufflé topped with a piece of roasted beetroot dressed with cumin-scented honey. All of which he shovelled down his throat without comment. This carried on for a few minutes.

Lexi was by now filing her dirty nails and looking as bored as a schoolgirl on a day trip to the local sewage works. Jools moved on to the sweet items like a cow finding its own roll of silage. *I wonder*, thought Liberty, *if I put Teal's food in front of him, will he eat that too?* But she carried on bravely, placing a delicate spoonful of her marmalade atop clotted cream on one of her single malt fruit scones.

'Mmmm, you can taste the booze!'

Wow! Jools had made a comment! 'I soak the fruit in the whisky for three days, before adding it to my traditional scone mix,' said Liberty, but she knew that her words were falling on deaf ears.

The Guinness spice cake made him emit another 'mmmm', but that was all she going to get. Once he had consumed more calories than his svelte figure would let her believe, Liberty said, 'Do you have any questions? I can show you my menus.' She placed them in front of him, to try to encourage him. 'I'm doing builders' teas, ladies' teas, light lunches, and . . .'

'What about drinks?' he asked suddenly.

'Well, as I said, all sorts of teas, coffees, of course, hot chocolate made from the local milk and Valrhona chocolate.'

'No, what about real drink. You know, booze? People are going to want a glass of wine with their "light lunches".' As he said this he raised his hands and made air quotes with his fingers. This, of all questions, stumped Liberty.

'I haven't thought of a licence yet. I want to get the food established first,' she said, brazening it out and wondering if Jools already knew she had been refused a licence. Indeed, he now answered her unspoken question.

'So, no truth in the rumours you have no licence on account of your criminal record?'

'I have no criminal record, so that would be false,' answered Liberty, feeling she was being interrogated by the police rather than interviewed by a county magazine. She had envisaged a rather Women's Institute sort of afternoon, not Greedy and Rat-Face, the un-comedic duo.

'I think that sums up everything we need to know,' said Jools, standing up.

'But what about opening hours, or my ethos about all local produce, the terroir – the fact that my customers will all taste the food as the air they breathe will have fed it, the soil they walk on will have grown it . . .'

'Yes, yes, I think that is far too fancy for our readers.'

'At least take the menus with you!'

Liberty felt she was behaving in a desperate way, but this was ridiculous. They were leaving. Jools hadn't even taken a pad of paper from his briefcase, let alone a tape recorder. Lexi had taken no photographs of her food, nothing. And all this before she had even opened!

'Don't worry, we have quite enough information!' And with a load belch and a 'Don't mind, do you?', he filled his briefcase with cakes and swept out, followed by Miss Rat-Face, now texting furiously with her perfectly filed nails.

Liberty quietly closed the door behind them and walked back into the kitchen. *Did that really just happen?* she asked herself as she leant back against the Aga for comfort. Teal ran in and scrabbled at her leg, as if saying, 'Didn't I do well? I didn't even come in and bite those horrid people.' As Liberty picked her up she saw that Rat Girl had left her camera behind. She picked it up and ran down the path to the BMW parked on the lane by the green. 'Yes,' she heard Jools saying, 'Yes, all went swimmingly.' Loud laugh. 'Bloody good grub, though, I have to admit.' He was speaking into his mobile, a huge grin on his face, which disappeared as Liberty approached. 'Bye, then.'

'Your photographer left her camera,' said Liberty, holding it out to him.

'Oh. Yes.' And taking it roughly from her he jumped into his car and sped off.

Liberty stood for a moment. She was still lost in thought when Edmund's car appeared at the top of his drive. He was meeting up with some old university friends for a jolly, but as he looked to see if the lane was clear, he saw a forlorn beauty standing alone by her gate, gazing into the distance. He turned the car towards Duck End and pulled over. By the time he had turned the engine off and opened his door, the only change in her appearance was her deeply furrowed brow.

'Is your house on fire?'

Liberty at last seemed to notice his presence, and she moved her head a little to look at him. Her mouth now formed a perfect O.

'Why are you standing out here?'

Edmund was more than a little concerned, any thoughts of his ridiculous behaviour in France now washed into the Med by worry that she had been attacked, Teal had been stolen or a dragon had just run past her house. Liberty seemed completely dumbstruck.

'Time for a drink.' It was a command rather than a question.

Edmund took her arm and led her gently back into the house. She allowed him to guide her to the kitchen and place her on the window seat. There, on the table, were the remains of the disastrous tea, her plate clean and unused, a scattering of crumbs around where Jools had sat, and the vast piece of untouched cake on Lexi's plate. Teal was the only extra decoration, and at last Liberty made a sound. It started with a hiccup, then a gurgle and then she dissolved into full-blown giggles. Witnessing Teal's cream-smothered face, sitting proudly on the Emma Bridgewater cake stand, no cake left, just a very fat ball of fur, was exactly the cure needed to shock Liberty out of her comatose state. Edmund let her giggles turn to tears as he put on the coffee machine and busied himself, removing fat dog, plates and dishes, before asking what the hell had happened.

'Please tell me!' he was now begging, as she had either gone mad or enjoyed afternoon tea on the table with her dog. OK, that would be mad, but he was meant to be on the M25, and he couldn't just leave her. He placed a double espresso and a box of tissues in front of her.

Liberty was gradually getting hold of herself, but then realised how often it was that Edmund had mopped her up, all running mascara and blotchy face. No wonder he didn't love her! Seeing that she was about to start crying again, Edmund tried another tack.

'Liberty,' he boomed. His dark hooded eyes seemed to glow with anger. 'Spit it out or I will have to get your parents!' It was like being scolded by a very attractive headmaster, and it had the desired effect. Liberty stood, walked over to the sink and poured the coffee away. 'I need something stronger, and for once not to look like a drowned rat – no, make that a pigeon,' she added, not wanting to be reminded of rat girl. She ran upstairs, changed into black skinny jeans, long boots and a huge black cashmere jumper that felt like a cuddle. She then used Laura Mercier products to the best of her ability, and returned to the kitchen looking more like Rachel Weisz than Worzel Gummidge.

Edmund had been dressed in a suit and tie, but now the jacket hung companionably on a chair and he had poured them both glasses of Sancerre, after reluctantly calling his friends to say he wouldn't be making it. As she entered the room he gasped at the vision in front of him. His pale grey shirt glowed against his dark skin. The hair on his arms looked as though it needed stroking, but Liberty resisted as she took the proffered glass and started her long explanation.

'These magazines are usually over the top with their praise, as they are just meant to advertise local suppliers and products. I thought it would be a no-brainer. Instead, I feel as though I've had ten rounds with Muhammad Ali, and lost.'

'I'll just make a call,' replied Edmund. Without further comment he left his wine and a stunned Liberty and walked into the garden. Not for the first time he wondered whether someone was attempting to sabotage Liberty's efforts to start a successful new life. He called one of Gray's former secretaries and asked the name and phone number of the editor of *Weald Life*. He then spoke to the plummy editor herself.

'Yes, I had heard of a new tea room opening. Very excited, we are. We are sending a group of WI ladies to give their verdict at the fair, thought it might be fun to do a sort of MasterChef judgement – all in good fun, of course. No, I hadn't phoned to arrange an interview. No, don't use a journalist by the name of Jools. How lovely to be speaking to you, Mr De Weatherby – charmed, I'm sure.'

Edmund was in a dilemma. He didn't want to worry Liberty before he had more facts, but he now knew that someone was definitely trying to sabotage her opening, or at the very least unsettle her. Who was this Jools, then? And was he really a journalist? If so, where from? He returned to the kitchen where he found Liberty, empty glass in hand, Teal on lap.

'I must be overreacting, I'm sorry,' she said. 'And I did notice that you were dressed up. Are you meant to be somewhere?' Her voice, which had been growing stronger, wobbled a bit. The tower of strength grinned down at her, warmth suffusing his hawk-like eyes.

'I don't want you to dwell on this afternoon.' Edmund shook his head firmly as Liberty was about to speak. 'No, not another second. Your food is sublime, the care you take and the love that you pour into it is evident to anyone worthy of commenting on such things, and it will sell, literally like hot cakes. I'm going to take you home and Mrs Goodman will be delighted to cook for you. Bring Teal – it'll be good for you both to get out of here.'

Privately, Edmund had always wondered about the time he had found Liberty's front door open at Christmas. There was something suspicious going on, and he was going to find out what. First things first, though. Get Liberty out of the house.

Once he had Liberty ensconced in the Denhelm kitchen, chattering to Mrs Goodman, who was full of the joys of spring, placing pots of hyacinths and narcissi around the windowsills to fill the rooms with heady scent ('Gets rid of wet dog smell,' she explained), he made a few phone calls and laid his trap.

49

A delicious supper of shepherd's pie, carrots and spring greens was followed by rhubarb crumble and lashings of custard. This expression always made Liberty smile, as it was why her mother had called her pug Custard. She got so fed up with the little creature weeing on her slippers in the early days, she promised her lashings most mornings.

Liberty was feeling much restored. She and Edmund sat in the kitchen playing Scrabble while Mrs Goodman cleared up around them. They finished their wine while they played and then Edmund poured them a glass of his father's excellent port, saying, 'We may as well enjoy the perks.'

She was beginning to relax, especially as both she and Edmund seemed as competitive as each other, both determined to win, by cheating if necessary. So they were soon in fits of giggles as Liberty spelled out journophobia, a fear of journalists, only for Edmund to beat her with teddicide, to murder one's teddy bear.

Edmund's phone rang. He waited a moment before answering, trying to quell his laughter; he knew it wasn't going to be a humorous conversation. Liberty could only hear his side, but it was obviously very serious. 'Right, have you removed the items? Keep them safe. Did you touch them? No? Good. Hopefully there will be fingerprints. Good work, and thanks for doing it at such short notice.'

He turned to Liberty. 'Well,' he said. 'That explains some things.'

'What things?' she asked.

'Nothing you need to know now. We must hope that Sarah isn't as scrupulous with her cleaning as she seems.'

Liberty looked at him as though he had gone mad. 'Have you . . .?'

'Have I what?' asked Edmund, looking distracted but pleased with himself.

'Gone mad. What about Sarah? What has she got to do with anything? Are you trying to distract me so I don't beat you at Scrabble? I may take your word and go and murder your teddy bear if you don't explain!'

Edmund looked quizzically over to where Mrs Goodman was folding sheets before laying them on the Aga.

'Aha!' exclaimed Liberty. 'So you do still have a teddy bear! I shall get him now and torture him until you tell me what is going on!' Laughing, she made a lunge for the kitchen door. Edmund caught her by the backs of her arms, his strong grip surprising and exciting her.

'No you don't, little lady,' he said, smiling while enjoying their close proximity. As he inhaled the scent of her hair, he wondered if she had indeed driven him close to insanity. Mrs Goodman couldn't bear the flying hormones and excused herself for the evening.

'Thank you again for supper,' said Liberty as Edmund reluctantly let go of her so the elderly housekeeper could make her exit.

The moment broken, Edmund remembered why Liberty was there, and the phone call he had received. 'I hope you don't mind, but I have just taken the liberty – ha ha – of having your locks changed. Just a precaution, after having such strange people in the house today. I'd better take you back now. There is someone waiting with your keys.'

'Isn't that a little over the top?'

'No, I don't think so,' replied her earnest friend, knowing it was just the opposite. Edmund had contacted the security firm who had worked at the wind farms he'd had dealings with a while back, when angry Nimbys were attempting to sabotage them, and they had been through Duck End with a fine-tooth comb. Three listening devices were found, including one in the chimney, and one small camera. Terrifying, but at least he had an idea of what had been going on. He didn't want to tell Liberty and unsettle her until he had all the facts, but he was determined she should be able to live securely and safely, and be able to open her café with no further hitches.

Unfortunately for Liberty, one hitch couldn't be undone. *The Saturday Telegraph* magazine restaurant review. Jools turned out to be Julian Middleton, the Jeremy Clarkson of financial journalism, apparently standing in for their regular restaurant critic. He had written the following:

Gastric Bandit!
By Jools Middleton

I may only be a financial journalist, but I think that many years of being wined and dined in the best restaurants by eager managing directors hot for a positive write-up places me in good stead to know a great restaurant from a good one, and a good one from a bad one. This brings me to my latest challenge – foolish to flimsy: LIBERTEAS, a new café opening on 27th March.

It should have a head start. At the helm, Liberty James, daughter of the great foodies Alain James, triple Michelin star holder for the past twenty-five years, and his ex-wife – but soon to be wife again, if rumours are to be believed – Deirdre, baker extraordinaire, TV dynamo, Mediterranean food expert, and, in recent years, a cookery teacher.

Thus forewarned, I delighted in the prospect of a pretty and relaxing journey into the wilds of Sussex to work up my appetite, drooling with thoughts of what this young lady might have learned at her parents' apron strings.

Liberty previously worked in public relations in her ex-husband's family bank, and was very good at it, from what I hear. Perhaps that is where she should have stayed. As her 'café-cum-patisserie-cum-tea room' is not yet open we were invited into her own home to sample what she will be serving. Perhaps a PR stunt? The gloriously named Duck End House is breathtaking, straight out of Homes & Gardens. *Huge Aga in the kitchen, expensive hangings at the windows, and the furniture . . . she obviously had a good divorce lawyer!*

Taken into the kitchen, a film set had been prepared for us. The table groaned with fabulous dainty china, silverware and tiered cake stands, which drowned in cakes, pastries and tarts, from tiny Cornish ('Sussex!' shouted Liberty at the paper) *pastries to miniature cream buns and a vast – what Ms James calls her special – walnut poppy seed cake smothered in cream and cherries* ('Damsons,' groaned Liberty). *All very twee and maybe what the American tourist will be looking for, but a tall hungry man and his photographer wished for beef and Yorkshires after hurtling through all that country air.* ('That must have been gulped through your car window!' cried Liberty to a startled Teal.)

All very pretty, but no substance. That a lady of remarkable breeding can try to rely on her admittedly sexy looks and parents' names saddens me. Sausages and mash and a pint of beer surely will bring smiles to the country yokels who live in such a godforsaken place, but they will have to satisfy their wish for a stiff drink at the local pub, as not only has Ms James forgotten that people might be hungry when they turn up to have 'lunch', but she has been forbidden a drinks licence.

LIBERTEAS by name, Liberty taken. I think this journo will stick to London and decent portions, thank you very much. The entire family will turn out to welcome you at *a free bash on the village green on 25th March, but I will forgo that one. I'll leave the ugly and muddy-booted locals to their own disappointment.*

Liberty was trembling as she put the magazine down. Why had he lied about who he was writing for? How could her career as a chef be over before it had begun? How could she ever show her face in the village?

A loud hammering at the door and simultaneous ringing of the telephone woke her from her dumbstruck stupor. Picking up the phone on the way to the front door she managed a croaked 'Hello?'

'Darling!' It was J-T. 'Great press coverage. How did you get into the *Telegraph* before you have even opened?'

'Shut up, J-T, you obviously haven't even read it yet. Now hold on while I get the door.' Her mother, father and Edmund crowded in. 'I thought it would be you. I've got J-T on the phone – mix yourselves drinks.'

'Hi, still there?' shouted J-T. 'Of course I've read it – what an arsehole! But it's still publicity, and that is what you need. Edmund has been on the phone, and Jools is one of Percy's friends, you know. Chat to Ed, he will fill you in. Call you later. Bye!'

Now thoroughly confused, Liberty looked at Edmund, who was sipping whisky with Alain and Deirdre. 'Ed?' was all she could think of saying.

'He seems to insist on calling me by that name,' said Edmund with a smile as he handed her a drink.

'Come and sit down darling,' said Deirdre, patting the sofa. 'Edmund has some news. Forget yours for the moment. Have you read the *Telegraph* magazine?'

'Have I read the *Telegraph*? Of course I have, and I am bloody done for! How could this have happened? He criticised my food, the locals, me. He claimed to be from the local press. I don't get it,' sobbed Liberty, and she slumped into a chair, head in hands. Edmund's heart went out to her, but he was far too full of news to wallow.

'Listen, I have discovered something that will probably make you even angrier, but it might explain a few things,' began Edmund. Alain removed Liberty's glass of wine, in case it got hurled, and replaced it with a brandied coffee on the table beside her chair. 'Brace yourself, darling,' he said. 'You've had a shock, and you are about to have another one.'

Taking a scalding gulp of the sweet hot liquid, Liberty was able to stop weeping and look up at Edmund. Would anything surprise her now? 'Go on.'

'You remember when I rode past here on Christmas Day and found your front door open?'

'Yes, of course, but what does that have to do with anything? I probably forgot to close it.'

'Wait a minute. It just seemed odd, the open door, and how news seemed to leak out about you applying for a licence and then being refused, and now this journalist . . . Well, I got a team in here to check your place out. They found some listening devices.'

'What!' Liberty jumped up. Deirdre caught her cup and Teal started to bark, picking up unhappy vibes. Liberty gathered up the dog for comfort and started to pace the room, feeling horribly uncomfortable in her own home. 'And I thought someone had been in after I returned from France, but who, and why? Something to do with the previous owners?'

'No, darling, stay calm and listen. Come and sit down, please,' said her mother, worried at how her little girl was going to respond to the news. She had tried to get Alain and Edmund to keep quiet, to sort it out themselves, but they had told her in no uncertain terms that she was going to find out whether she was able to cope or not.

'It's Percy.' Edmund let the statement hang in the air.

'Percy?' asked Liberty, loudly. She set Teal down on the floor. 'Why?'

'We think he has been trying to sabotage you. Correction, we KNOW he has been trying to sabotage your new career. He contacted the licensing board after getting a chum of his to forge documents indicating you had a criminal record, thus preventing them from even considering your application. He has been trying to find out about everything you are up to, even getting a photographer to follow J-T on New Year's Eve to try to discredit your friends and business contacts. I bet even he was shocked with the results of that bit of skulduggery! He has also sent letters to associates down here telling them to stay away from your café, stating that you have been stealing money from his family while his father is ill and that he has been unable to keep control of the family accounts.'

Liberty felt her stomach drop down to her feet. 'I just don't understand. Why would he do that? I thought he had moved on – he's barely been in contact, for heaven's sake! He's got someone else, even had a child . . .'

'We think he is still angry that you left him, and that he can't bear to lose control over you, and so he is trying to make sure your future gets nowhere,' Edmund continued, hating each blow he was dealing her, but knowing it was best out in the open. 'I have people looking into it. The listening devices are evidence, and the document that was forged for him was done by a solicitor friend who thought it was a joke, something to hang on your wall. Now, of course, he is fearful for his job, so is ready to spill the beans to the police. He has already written to the licensing board to retract the statement, and will cooperate fully.'

'What is his name?' asked Liberty.

'Colin Aurmry,' replied Edmund, looking at a small black notebook in front of him.

'Colin! But I spent hours sitting next to that boring little man at dinner parties making polite conversation! I would have considered him an acquaintance!' Liberty was aghast.

'It seems that as soon as he knew it was being used against

you, he was very keen to right the wrong, but he must at the very least be a complete idiot not to have worked out what Percy was up to.'

'What do I do?' Liberty looked at the three anxious pairs of eyes on her. 'No one will come to the fete now, and all the villagers are going to be so angry to be dragged into this. Why did he have to call them ugly?'

'Horrid abuse, and incorrect, for the most part,' said Deirdre. 'Your father pointed out to me that he didn't manage to criticise your food, which would have been a lie, so he found criticism elsewhere – the people, the surroundings and your house. He probably saw Miss Scally leave work. He even makes the fact that you are beautiful sound like a fault.'

'Don't forget, any publicity is good publicity,' Alain piped up.

'That is what J-T said. But it's SO public, and I do think the people around here will take it personally.'

'Don't believe it for one second,' said Alain, shaking his head. 'People in this area of England are made of strong stuff. They will turn up to prove to the world they are civilised enough to enjoy small portions, and put on their make-up. And, of course, mostly to eat free food and enjoy a fete that someone else is paying for and putting on! I can guarantee it. Free food is a bigger pull than you could ever imagine.

'We bumped into Dilys on the way over. She was thrilled the pub was mentioned in the article, and is going to make some of her lethal punch to serve in the evening. She has been on to the local brewery to supply all we will need for the day. The cider chaps from Shepherd's Farm have already spoken to Edmund about putting up a tent. So, you see? It's only going to be good for you. What we need to know now, is what are we going to do about Percy?'

Liberty sat down at last, but was shaking. Deirdre put her arms around her and told Alain to make more coffee. Liberty looked up at the anxious faces. 'Did I tell you about the time J-T and I went to the mews to collect my belongings, and Percy had set up a device to let him see what went on inside the house? I wondered then if he had watched too many late-night films. He must be spending a fortune on Spymaster, or wherever he's getting his gear. I didn't even know he could use a smartphone on his own. He used to get his secretary to work it for him!' They all laughed at this, pleased she was calming down.

Alain filled in some gaps. 'He must have had help. According to Edmund's research, he denied the child was his, and so far has refused a paternity test. Georgina has been welcomed back by her cuckolded husband Hugh, who seems to be treating the child as his own. He has quit working at the bank, and is slandering Percy to anyone who will listen, saying Percy had practically given up going to the office, and that although he is supposed to be caring for his father he is travelling, spending money, gambling – you name it! Percy's parents are not amused, and are threatening to cut him out of their will and sign over their house to the National Trust. Although, I am sorry to say, the NT have informed them that it's just another pile of no outstanding public interest, so they are not keen!'

'Oh, poor Cecil and Isabelle! I must write to them,' said Liberty. 'I feel awful. This is all my doing.'

Deirdre took her hand and said, 'It's your charming nature to take all the blame. But there is only one person at fault here, let's remember that. And it's not you.'

Liberty's parents suggested she join them for lunch, but she needed to think, and sit quietly on her own. Edmund was somewhat miffed that she didn't appreciate his efforts in collecting all the information. He followed Alain and Deirdre to the door, but just as he was about to leave, Liberty put a hand on his sleeve and asked if he could stay for a bit.

'Certainly, I can,' he replied, feeling his heart sing again.

'I just want to thank you. You have been amazing through all of this, and a true friend. Thank you for finding all those horrid things. Do you think they got them all?' She was a little embarrassed at feeling so weak, but it had sullied her home, her haven of peace. It was another part of her life with Percy that was not as she had thought. She was thinking all this while looking up at Edmund's dark, strong, hawk-like face, hoping perhaps he would say she could be more than a friend, or would she just run to the church right now and marry him, or suggest travelling round the world shagging for England and forgetting all these silly people. But he simply looked at her, kissed her on the cheek, said, 'It's been a pleasure to help, my dear,' and left her alone.

Edmund sang a little song as he walked back to his car, his lips burning from kissing her winsome face. Once driving home, however, his face turned to steel and his shoulders clenched with anger. Now to deal with Percy.

50

Liberty phoned J-T and started to tell him the unbelievable news that Percy had been trying to sabotage her, when he stopped her mid-flow.

'Darling, stop. Take a breath and sit down.' He could picture her face as he heard her gulp for air, and imagined her plopping down into one of her overstuffed chairs, quizzical expression on her face and Teal at her feet. He told her that Edmund had given him full details of Percy's revenge already. When Liberty huffed that it was up to her who should know, J-T said, 'Edmund realised it was Percy who encouraged the photographer to get the picture of me and Gray, probably to discredit both of us because we are your friends. My dear, we didn't realise he was so very pissed off, as you hadn't heard from him at all – no solicitor's letters, nothing. This was his plan: to destroy your future if it didn't include him! I can't believe it was he who nearly ruined things between Bob and me. He always claimed to be our friend too, don't forget, and as far as I know, Gray hasn't even met the man! Although, I suppose the fault was mine, as I was the one in the photograph doing the business.'

'Yeeees, quite!' Liberty said with a giggle, pleased to feel a little relief. But then she remembered Percy's horrible words whenever she had managed to get him to have the pair to supper after they were married. 'Bloody poofs' and 'silly fags' were only two of the unpleasant phrases he reserved for them. J-T was the only friend who had stuck by her when Percy was doing his best to rid her of old acquaintances. J-T, unlike her other friends, was not intimidated by the bully. But she didn't want to hurt her friend any more by telling him what Percy had said.

'Bob seems to have taken the news that Percy was behind all of this to mean I'm off the hook completely. He is back to his old warm self, and even treating me as though it wasn't my fault. Although, of course it was. He even agreed to come to your fete with me after I told him Gray wouldn't be there. Can we stay at your place, with the dogs? You wouldn't believe the fancy dress costumes I've got for them!'

Sadly, I probably can, thought Liberty, picturing the two French bulldogs in tutus or worse, but she was thrilled the men would be there to support her. 'I will prepare your rooms, sir!' she said with a laugh. He always made her feel good about herself, and she knew that his presence, along with calm, solid Bob, would be good for her nerves on the day. They said their goodbyes, with J-T promising lots of decorations for the fete.

'Don't forget, I have a showroom full of things, and lots of favours I can pull in. Leave it to me to show you at your best!'

Liberty felt much better, if still a little odd, knowing that Percy or someone attached to him had been in her house. To comfort herself, she decided to cook, which was lucky as she realised she was ravenous. She rootled around in the fridge till she emerged with the makings of a warm walnut-crusted goat's cheese salad.

Thus restored, she sat down to write a lengthy letter to Percy's parents, saying how sorry she was if she had been to blame for Percy going off the rails, and could she help in any way? She also wrote that she was sorry for not visiting them, but had felt unsure of her welcome, and that she hoped Cecil was recovering. She reminded them of her warm feelings towards them both. She felt a horrible gut-twisting sensation, hating the thought of the two kind, generous, warm-hearted people she looked upon as family being hurt and troubled because of her actions.

She then wrote to Georgina, the woman reported to have had Percy's baby. She had never warmed to the glamorous, bosomy wife of Hugh Cyril, a little too socially ambitious to be a true friend, but felt terrible that Percy had denied the baby was his and had now dropped her. Liberty was, in a strange way, curious to meet the baby that could have been hers. Of course she didn't express that feeling, but casually wrote that if she and Hugh were ever in the area they would be welcome at her home.

After a long bath and a wander round the garden, pruning and deadheading early daffodils, Liberty suddenly realised how wrapped up in herself she was being. She hadn't even asked her parents when they were getting married.

'Goodness, they must think me terrible!' And without turning the key in the newly fitted locks, she shot across the green, Teal trotting by her heels.

She let herself in and yelled a loud 'Hello!' as she didn't want to interrupt anything she shouldn't see. In the kitchen, Deirdre and Sarah were clearing dishes.

'Goodness, darling! You look flustered, although I'm not surprised. What's the rush? Someone been to your home again?'

Bugger, thought Liberty, *didn't even shut the door*. But she asked where Alain was to distract her mother from this fact.

'Daddy has at last managed to leave me alone for two minutes and remember he still has a restaurant to run. He's gone to see how things have been going at the hotel without him,' said Deirdre, smiling as she remembered pushing him out of the door. When they were first married, she would have had to lock him in a cage to stop him going to work. 'He's taken Clarence down for a month's work experience. Once we got him to admit he had sold the first edition of *Larousse Gastronomique* I gave him to pay the rent on his mother's cottage (Edmund told us he'd refused to accept the book as payment), Daddy decided to give him a job. He really thinks the lad has talent!'

'Great,' said Liberty. 'I am so pleased things might work out for him. Daddy must think he's good if he is willing to put him to work in his own kitchen. But Mummy–' Liberty went over to her mother and gave the surprised and pleased woman a hug '–how are things going between you and Daddy? I feel awful, I should have been asking about your wedding plans and listening to you going on about new-found love; instead, you have had to cope with all my dramas. Tell me all.'

'Oh, my sweet, we wanted to help you get up and running before planning anything, mostly because we would want you to help with our wedding. Don't worry, we aren't going to dress you up in a ghastly bridesmaid's dress, but would love for you to be part of the day. Daddy thought we ought to use his yacht for the honeymoon, but between you and me, I feel a little uncomfortable celebrating my wedding by sleeping on a bed that has supported so many other women! Dear that he is, he loves his boat, and it would be fun to sail round the Med, end up at Paloma's for a few days and see little Yves, but I think I would feel a little second-hand, if you know what I mean.'

'Mmm, I do. You would spend the whole trip wondering who had been there and done that before – not ideal on honeymoon. Why don't you use one of the other berths?'

'Because I would have to give my reasoning to your father, and he might sell the boat, which would in turn make me miserable, knowing what it means to him. He loves it; it allowed him the freedom he lacked so much of the time, being tied to his kitchen. He had always dreamed of owning one of the luxury yachts that he would watch cruising along the coast when he was working in kitchens in the south of France as a young man. When he visited his accountant to discuss one of his divorce settlements, his accountant said it was a good way of buying and owning something abroad, therefore untouchable if done in the correct way. It gave him the excuse he had always wanted. Named it after you, of course. I was so angry at the time, but now I see how much it means and I would feel weak and pathetic telling him my reason for not wanting to use *Liberty Belle*. It might put a wall up between us.'

'Well, maybe just suggest you redo the interior of the boat before the honeymoon. It is all quite dated, very chintzy, and you could commission a new bed at the same time? Say it's your wedding present to him. He could even design a galley that suits him better than the little one there is at the moment. Make it about him, rather than about you!'

'Great idea, darling,' said Deirdre, smiling. 'Has J-T ever done a boat?'

'Not that I know of, but hell, he would surely love the challenge!'

They poured coffees and sat companionably at the kitchen table when Sarah left.

'What about the service?' asked Liberty. 'I'm sure our vicar is modern enough to marry you, despite it being your second, especially as you are marrying the same person! Or do you intend to have a civil ceremony?'

'Daddy thought we might have an engagement party at The Dark Horse as a combined closing do, and just ask a few friends and family to a church service before a quiet lunch here. We should invite Leah but I'm not sure her mother will allow her to come. Apparently, Genevieve has now had so much plastic surgery she can't open her mouth far enough to eat properly, but that is simply bitchy gossip, and I'm not like that, am I?' said Deirdre with a twinkle in her eye. 'Talking about weddings, have you decided what to do about Percy? He must know you have found the listening devices. And did you contact the Cholmondly-Radleys?'

'I have written to them, and Mrs Stickybunns keeps me up to date in her letters. She says Mr CR is doing well, his carers have left and they have even been on holiday. I feel so awful for them. The strange thing is that Percy always felt such responsibility to the family. He was proud of their coat of arms, history and so on. It's so odd that he now seems to have gone off the rails at his age. There was a piece in *The Mail* that Mrs Stickybunns sent me, reporting on Percy gambling all night in Monte Carlo. He had announced that the first twenty females to apply, if they were attractive enough, could join him on a private jet to fly to Sun City in South Africa, or Sin City as he called it, for a night of gambling and partying. I can't imagine what sorrow that must be causing his parents.'

'Sounds as though he's having far too much fun at other people's expense. I've never been averse to the finer things in life, but when they are just frivolous and wasteful it's horrid. Isn't there anything you can do to rein him in? Vandalise something he really cares about? His car, perhaps?'

'Mother! I didn't know you could be so vindictive, or have such violent thoughts! No, we can't do anything like that, and no, he's never really been passionate about anything at all, apart from his art collection, which I have no claim over.'

Deirdre looked amazed. 'Of course you do! You are married to the man. You could apply for divorce and ask for all the artwork, then when the courts are about to give them to you, you could say to Percy that he could keep them if he treats his family better and goes back to the bank!' Deirdre was thrilled with her idea.

Liberty looked at her mother sternly. 'Even in your and Daddy's worst days of divorce, would you have asked for his restaurant?'

Deirdre's mouth flapped unbecomingly.

'No, I thought not, and I couldn't. It wouldn't sit right on my conscience, so get that out of your mind. Imagine if he said fine? I would end up looking at reminders of my life with him! Believe me, it's bad enough that he's been in my home. I don't want to decorate it with things he loved more than me!'

Deirdre privately thought that she could sell them and reap the rewards, but kept shtum, proud that she had brought her daughter up to be of such good character. Out loud, she said, 'I think it's more to do with investing and making a profit, but good for you, although keep the idea under your hat. Knowing you as I do, you care about Cecil and Isabelle a great deal, and you may need to help them before he lets the bank collapse.'

'Ah, well, I'm sure we can think up some ruse. Do his parents know about the baby? That could create quite a stir, if we knew it was a boy – first born son and heir, and so on.'

Liberty didn't want to dwell on Percy any longer. The last twenty-four hours had made her feel as though he was back in her life, and in a way he was, and always had been; she needed to end that. Talk of divorce made her think she should either sign the papers Percy had sent her, and which had languished under her bed for weeks, or get her papers drawn up to sue him instead. It would be the only way she could feel free, and she wasn't sure why she had been holding off, apart from fear of hurting Isabelle, who had so dearly wished they could work things out. By now she was probably aware that Liberty couldn't live with her son anymore. When she had written to her in-laws, she had told them of the fete and the opening two days later, and hoped they might be able to spare some time and come and see what she was up to.

At eight o'clock, Liberty and Deirdre gave up waiting for Alain to return. 'He is back where he belongs for the time being,' sighed the love-struck older woman. They shared a light supper, while Deirdre quizzed her daughter about preparations for the fete, reminding her, unnecessarily, that it was just around the corner.

Liberty was conquering her nerves by filling the freezer, checking for the umpteenth time that the little restaurant looked just perfect, cleaning it again and again until the windows shone, the china gleamed and the wooden tables developed an antique patina in days. She had ordered flowers from a local girl, and on J-T's suggestion put them in old jam jars decorated with different coloured ribbons. She had told him she needed a way of identifying tables for the benefit of the kitchen and this was his idea. So far she had not heard again from the council about her alcohol licence, but Edmund assured her it would be sorted out, and meanwhile she could charge corkage.

Unbeknown to Liberty, Paloma and Jonathan had asked Alain

if they could raid his cellar for bubbly. They would cover the cost and supply it without charge to customers on the opening day, to get everyone into the swing of things.

J-T arrived with Bob in tow, hugging a new addition: a cat.

'Where are the dogs?' asked Liberty.

'Oh, we had to leave them in the car. They hate her, but we adore her,' said Bob, cuddling the tiny furball. 'A Silver Point Persian. Very rare, horribly expensive, and my anniversary present. But the dogs won't leave her alone, and then she scratches them. Twice in two weeks both dogs have had to visit the vet after Queenie scratched their eyes.'

'Queenie? What a sweet name. Let me hold her, and then you can get the dogs out. Bring them round to the garden entrance.' Liberty giggled as she spied the car with a trailer attached to the back. 'You didn't tell me you've turned into caravanners!' she exclaimed, examining the smart BMW SUV with an ancient Airstream lagging behind it.

'Don't you laugh,' said Bob, wagging his finger at her. 'Believe it or not, it's filled with all the props for your fair. We seem to have searched the entire south of England,' he insisted, looking fondly at J-T, so she understood immediately that J-T had been dragging poor Bob around for her fete. She thanked him and he demurred, continuing, 'J-T and I remembered a holiday we had, invited by some generous clients to their estancia in Uruguay. They lived in Buenos Aires most of the time, and had the most amazing ranch where they kept their polo ponies close to Punta del Este. Lots of smart Argentineans decamp there for the summer. Anyway, while we were there, they invited us for a ride that ended in a picnic. Being Brits, we thought OK, dried sandwiches, and a plastic cup of warm wine if we were lucky . . .' Bob paused to avert an embarrassing incident between his dogs and a passing King Charles spaniel and its owner. He struggled to get the dogs under control and into the back garden.

'Anyway, we turn up at this clearing after an hour too long on horseback.'

'He means the ride took an hour,' put in J-T, joining them after returning the cat to its box.

'An exterior room had been created. Hay bales covered with soft woollen blankets were laid out around kilim rugs. In the background were tall candelabras joined by ribbons and wrapped in greenery. A fire bowl was in the centre of the 'room', and tables had been set here and there so you had somewhere to put your drink. That is where we had the idea of large woollen blankets held together with old polo knee guards. It keeps them looking neat until you need them, and there's a pile of them in the trailer. We asked friends at Windsor Great Park who work for some of the polo lot if they had any spare, and they were happy to give us some of their worn-out ones.

'We figured you would have access to hay bales, but otherwise we've bought and borrowed everything. And we have brought reams of antique French linen to cover the trestle tables.'

Over the next few days, crowds of onlookers appeared on the green, excitedly noting the preparations for the fete. Judging by the number of well-groomed dogs being marched around it on leads, the dog show was going to be a big pull.

Dilys had told Liberty her punch was famous for getting everyone going, and as it was spring she was going to add extra cider. 'I hope a few people will be capable of eating!' said Liberty. But she was pleased people hadn't taken against her after the *Telegraph* article. Fred the blacksmith had offered her his services, with a gleam in his eye, and Liberty had taken him up by asking for a loan of his hanging baskets on stands. These would frame the eating area, and she had planted them with winter pansies and trailing plants, praying for good weather and definitely no frost!

The only edible things in her garden were rosemary and thyme, so she was going to use those in some of the small tarts – seasoned bacon and fennel quiches, and some little cheese and herb choux buns. She was getting there, but would it all come together as she wanted?

51

The day of the fete had arrived at last. It was all hands on deck in Liberty's kitchen, as a bleary-eyed J-T and Bob passed the poor kitten back and forth to keep it out of the way of their dogs and from Liberty, who was struggling between her loyalty to her friends and an intense dislike of cats near food. Deirdre and Alain kept coffee flowing, and Liberty's 'To Do' board now covered most of her already menu-covered walls, with post-it notes in different colours denoting who was to carry out which task. Deirdre frowned when she saw most were turquoise for Liberty, and caused chaos by changing them for others, which ended up with one job being carried out (on paper) by two people. 'Well, at least it's getting done,' was all Deirdre said in her own defence when, in a fit of nerves and frustration, Liberty turned on her and accused her of muddling a day which needed no more muddling!

The weather forecasters had predicted correctly: the sky was clear and the low sun was beginning to warm the chilly morning air. Everyone was feeling entirely positive about the day. Paloma and Jonathan, who had arrived the previous evening, had already been round and, as agreed, had organised the removal of all cars, not only from around the green, but also from the pavement areas in front of the pretty cottages lining the far side. All visitor cars would be directed to the top field of the estate, which was thankfully dry and firm. In the absence of traffic, the village had assumed a Jane Austen era appearance.

People were being divided into two teams: the decorating team and the feeding team. Leading the way on the decorating team were, naturally, J-T and Bob, who chose Khalid and Jonathan for manpower and Savannah to ensure things did not get too over the top. This provoked a snigger from Khalid, and, 'You don't know my wife!' The children hitched themselves to this group and dragged Teal and Custard along with them on leads, wearing pink tutus, gold necklaces and looking like joint winners of the doggie Oscar prize.

'We can't use these! They are incredibly expensive!' said Jonathan, fingering the rugs being dragged out of the trailer.

'It's dry, and they do much worse on photo shoots for magazines. *The World of Interiors* once photographed a $51,000 rug underwater in the Maldives to show off the pretty colours. Don't think we ever got the salt out.' Bob smiled at the memory.

They laid the numerous rugs over the green as a carpet – all slightly different, but all in dark reds and browns. They made the bright spring grass seem even greener.

Three trestle tables were placed nose to nose to create one long serving area. They were then covered with French linens in palest pinks, greys and duck-egg blue that were long enough to touch the ground. Most of them were embroidered with flowers or monogrammed along the edges, and as they fluttered in the breeze the sun bounced off the thread, making it shimmer like fish scales.

Huge hurricane lanterns were filled with lavender and herbs for decoration. Flat wicker baskets were lined with pale green linen napkins to hold the loaves of bread Liberty had been up since three o'clock that morning baking. All these were placed strategically along the tables.

J-T had been resolute in his search for old-fashioned multi-tiered cake stands, and eventually had struck gold. A supporter of every cake stall in Sussex, who had just discovered her husband's affair, put her collection of antique cake stands up for sale on eBay to raise some money for a holiday. There were thirty-five of them. J-T had called her directly and made her an offer that enabled her to fly off to Greece for a yoga retreat.

'Something I've dreamed of doing every time I ironed the bastard's underpants!' she huffed down the phone. 'He bought me one for every wedding anniversary, so good riddance.' J-T knew that Liberty would always be able to use them and felt it was worth cheering up this unappreciated woman.

When these had been placed at intervals along the table, it all started to come together. Savannah had persuaded the children to pick primroses, and the activity had brought people out of their homes to offer more from their gardens. Jonathan and Deirdre shared a smile, remembering how they had met, and encouraged the children to try the driveway up to Denhelm. The vicar was helping Jonathan and Fred to put up the hanging baskets, which were to hang from chunky ironwork posts that stood proudly like ornate lampposts, one at each corner of the rug 'floor', while the vicar's wife sat on a low wall, pretending to read a menu, at the same time surreptitiously admiring the long-limbed Irishman and the way his muscles rippled through his T-shirt. The bunting was connected to each one of the baskets, framing the area to eat and drink.

J-T's workshop girls had made the most exclusive bunting imaginable from offcuts of clients' fabrics, trimmed with beads, ribbons and fancy trims. The metals and crystals in the fabrics sparkled in the morning sunlight.

On cue, Edmund drove up on his small tractor with bales of straw to be placed round the grounds, not only to provide seating and relieve the feet of those visiting the outdoor tea 'room', but also to separate it from the dog-showing arena.

The local archery team were setting up their display, and Godfrey the brewer and his children were organising a table to hold the local beer, which Dilys had kindly agreed could be served. Alain brought out china plates – all bought at junk shops at a total of £50, and so nobody would suffer if a few were broken. Liberty had hated the idea of using plastic, so 200 china cups, saucers, plates and bowls, all of different patterns and sizes, were to be used. The only unsightly object was the generator, needed to provide power to boil water and enable the fairy lights to glow when evening fell. J-T looked at it, aghast. 'The eye will be drawn to it immediately, it has to be covered!' And he set about ignoring all the warnings and laid a priceless wall hanging stolen from Liberty's sitting room over the mechanical eyesore. Liberty had to admit it looked better, but thought she had better watch out for billowing smoke.

Catherine Bevan arrived from Gateshead Farm together with a display of her cheeses. The village was relatively middle class, but she had been having difficulty selling her produce locally. It seemed that people who appreciated the flavour of goat's cheese preferred to source it from further afield, so they could pretend it didn't come from a live, rather smelly animal. Bizarrely, she had secured a contract with a large department store in Paris, and she supplied many local restaurants. When Liberty had tasted it while sourcing her ingredients she couldn't believe it was not sold in local markets; Catherine explained that she had tried and people just didn't seem keen. The packaging was clear but simple: little cellophane tubes of fresh milky cheese plugged with whatever herbs Catherine had at the time. They looked like lollipops, ready to be squeezed and splodged straight on to a plate with no further adornment other than a drizzle of honey and maybe a few more herbs. 'I think you just need a little more exposure,' Liberty had said to the pretty, clear-skinned young woman. 'They really are delicious!'

So Catherine was happily placing wooden crates filled with the little tubes, content in the knowledge that once people had tasted it, they would buy! This was not a way to make money, but she had Liberty's admiration. Alain, who stopped by to sample it, pronounced it fresh, slightly sweet and utterly delicious. 'Just vinegar and goat's curd?' he asked.

'That's right,' said Catherine proudly. 'We let the goats graze on our pastures, which we plant with wild herbs and flowers. We allow the natural taste to come through, and then make it fresh daily.'

'Mmm, heaven, with a glass of Pinot Gris or Graves,' said Alain intently, helping himself to another spoonful.

Soon enough the green looked like the Chelsea Flower Show crossed with *The World of Interiors*. Paloma, Deirdre and Liberty, despite little sleep, and Evangeline, who had managed even less, looked elegant and very glamorous for a country stage. The area was beginning to turn into a scenario from a romantic film. The fruit trees around the green were in blossom early because of the good weather the previous week, and the flowers in the hanging baskets gave the impression that summer was nearly here.

The cakes being brought out added a pungent aroma of spices, vanilla and booze, mingling with sweet fruitfulness.

J-T had rushed to a supermarket to find oils of orange, lavender, rosemary and vanilla, which he now liberally sprinkled on the rugs, and as the sun warmed them they encouraged the atmosphere of a spring day in Provence. People started to emerge from their homes and wandered around, lured by the look of the green and, of course, by greed, despite having just had breakfast.

The flood gates opened just after ten. Cars filled up the car park, the weather and the Easter holidays encouraging attendance. Edmund had coerced, and then ordered, his farm workers to help direct traffic into the parking field, and families were now strolling about, gazing at the cottages, at the duck pond and the lovely setting of LIBERTEAS on the green.

'You're going to need to bring out more food,' said Deirdre helpfully, gazing at a shell-suited family piling their plates high.

'I'll wait a while,' replied Liberty firmly, pouring tea. 'My kitchen is overflowing with food, but I want to spread things out a bit. We have to start with savoury, then move to sweet, just like afternoon tea.' The Shell Suit family were wandering off to sit and munch.

'These are not the sort of people who are going to eat in your restaurant anyway,' decided Deirdre.

'Perhaps not, but if five per cent of the people who have turned up so far come to the restaurant, then we will do all right.'

Edmund effortlessly carried a large tray of brioches and bacon quiches across the green. His groom had quit in a huff when Edmund didn't appreciate a new clip he had given the hunters, and having to muck out and keep his horses fit had improved his physique, if not his mood.

'He should work at the end of a phone, so nobody can see his frowning face,' said Deirdre in a low voice.

Jonathan and Paloma had settled for a rest on a straw bale, next to Evangeline and baby Yves, who was happily licking crème anglaise from his mother's fingers. 'His first solid food!' said Evangeline excitedly.

'Far too young,' said Paloma, ever the protective grandmother, 'but at least he has good taste.'

Jonathan was thinking not only how lucky he was to have Paloma, but how relieved he was that he hadn't married Deirdre, because he would have had to lie and tell her Liberty's baking was not up to her standard. God, this brioche could make grown men weep!

More and more cars were dawdling past the green on their way to the parking field. Liberty was still making tea, in between running back to the kitchen to collect cakes, then cutting them at the tables to make sure they were as fresh as possible, and checking labels went on the food they were meant for, after tiny fingers kept switching them around. The glass cloches over the cakes looked elegant but were almost unnecessary as they kept being taken off when more slices were demanded.

The most popular item was, as she had known it would be, the Victoria sponge, quickly followed by a coffee and walnut cake, but she was also aware that her lemon and poppy seed sponge, filled with crème pâtissière and laced with Grand Marnier and raspberries, was very popular. The tray bakes were flying, especially the cappuccino squares – vanilla sponge with white chocolate chunks, topped with a dark chocolate sponge with chocolate-coated coffee beans. The chocolate brownies had almost gone, thanks to the influx of children. She brought out marmalade cream cake, polenta lemon mint cake, Bath buns, walnut and apple cake made with locally milled rye flour and walnut oil, and topped with a delicate maple syrup cream and chestnut frosting.

Some of the tiered cake stands had been used for more delicate petits fours, which included tiny wild strawberry tarts, lemon sablés, miniature opera gateaux and friands that would be served for ladies' teas. She noticed that several of the ladies who had refused a piece of cake had somehow managed to place quite a few of these on their plates. Exactly as she knew they would. It had always amused her during her London days to observe that friends who proclaimed they were dieting and refused a pudding always managed to eat the biscuit or mass-produced chocolate on the side of their coffee cup. A well made dessert cake could give not only satisfaction but also goodness and nutrition, she thought. She figured if the ladies would eat a few tiny things rather than pounce on a large slice of cake, then she would serve them a good selection. They could have their cake and eat it!

52

Liberty had borrowed an old-fashioned painted gypsy caravan from Edmund, left over from the days when real gypsies lived in the forest. They had given the caravan to Jonathan, partly in thanks for letting them stay, partly because their horse was lame and they had new, motorised, heated vehicles now. Despite the old-world charm, living in an old, leaky wooden box in midwinter was no dream. Jonathan had it restored for the grandchildren to play in, and now, with its door and windows open, it was serving as a safe place to house a deep fat fryer, in which Liberty was cooking light-as-air home-made doughnuts. She had made her enriched brioche dough slightly wetter than normal and flavoured it with nutmeg, cardamom and cinnamon to produce bite-sized delicacies. The one concession to health and safety was a sign pointing out that they would be hot. When J-T laughed and said, 'Of course they will be hot, they have just come out of boiling fat!', Liberty smiled and explained that the bureaucrats had wanted her to put similar signs by the teapots, along with warnings about dog mess, and arrows from the archery, while worries of children falling from the Shetland ponies were keeping them up at night! She said she had demurred over the doughnuts, but had promised the officials that there would be enough people to keep an eye out for rocks falling from the sky or people slipping on the pesky wet grass.

As she fired up the fryer, she pondered her servings. The plan was that each person would receive five in a waxed bag. She scooped them out of the oil and drained them briefly, then they were placed in the bags already containing a mix of sugar and orange zest. When they were handed out she gave two little pots for dunking; in one was a damson compote, in the other a sweetened Jersey cream flavoured with vanilla seeds.

They were flying off the stand, and realising a hot, sweaty face was not the best look for the photographers who would be turning up shortly for the real local paper, Liberty was desperate for a break. She saw her chance as Savannah sauntered over, her figure giving nothing of her pregnancy away. She was glowing and turned heads as usual.

'Darling, these look amazing!' she said, queue-barging. 'But the paps will be here soon. You have had enough bad experience with them recently, and to be frank, you look a sweaty mess. You may be making everyone happy, but you are going to have to sell your body as well,' continued the ever-observant society beauty. 'Let me take over, and you go and mop some of the sweat from your brow!'

Liberty could have wept with gratitude, despite the comment about being a sweaty mess. What it was to have her friend back. 'But you have never even made a sandwich, let alone handled boiling fat!'

'If I can handle two children, I can manage a pot of boiling oil for a while. Give me a demo and I'll be a pro in two shakes. Anyway, with my appetite at the moment, if I make mistakes, I can eat them!'

Feeling incredibly grateful, Liberty gave Savannah a quick lesson. Thankfully, she was a fast learner, so Liberty gave her a hug and told her not to burn herself. Savannah looked at her with a 'do I look that stupid?' expression, then grinned and told her to go and sort herself out. Liberty leapt down from the caravan and started for her house. She stopped suddenly as she spotted three faces in the crowd she wasn't prepared to see.

Edmund was watching her, as always, and saw her expression turn from sweaty and rosy to pale and drawn in a second. Following the line of her gaze, he saw a familiar, predatory face. *Oh, Christ, the bloody man has a nerve*, he thought. He recognised the loathsome journo from when he had swept past him in his car after the horrible visit to Liberty's home. He immediately stalked to where Jools Middleton stood chatting to Mr and Mrs Cholmondly-Radley, whom he didn't recognise.

'What the hell do you think you are you doing here?' he fumed. Liberty ran up behind him.

'Please, Edmund, don't make a fuss. Have you met Mr and Mrs Cholmondly-Radley? Percy's parents,' she hissed.

Edmund's expression changed to one of professional welcome. 'Charmed, I'm sure,' was all he could think of saying, knowing that Liberty had only respect and high regard for the two in-laws, but at the same time wondering how much they knew of the sabotage incident.

'Please, please, calm down,' said Jools. 'Liberty, I wanted to come and apologise. I had no idea it was a personal vendetta against you. Percy had told me you had stolen money from him to set up your café, and I was only being a chum. I thought he was having a hard time of it – you hear all these stories of ghastly ex-wives, stripping their husbands of all their hard-earned money. Christ, my ex took the bloody dogs, despite hating them! I cannot apologise enough, and I want to say that to you in person.' He was indeed looking very sheepish and small under Edmund's glowering expression. 'I really am sorry. If it's any consolation, your baking is quite extraordinary. I take my mother to Sketch for their Michelin-starred afternoon tea, and your food is as good as, if not better.' Liberty flushed even more than her sweaty face would allow, but she was still furious.

'You could do one better, and honour me with a rewrite,' she stuttered. 'It was pure malice. You could have sent me down before I ever opened. I'm surprised you didn't say we had vermin running round the kitchen.'

'Funny you should say that. Percy asked me to write something similar. But after meeting you, I wasn't sure I had the whole story, so left it out.'

Mr and Mrs Cholmondly-Radley were looking from one face to the other, trying to keep up with whatever was going on. They knew Jools, as he had been a school friend of Percy, but hadn't realised he had met Liberty.

'We just wanted to come and wish you luck with your restaurant,' said Mr CR. 'We've had a few problems with Percy recently, and hoped you might have a word with us later.'

'Yes, of course, but I am really, really busy right now.'

Aware that the photographers and journalists should be here by now, Liberty was trying to stay calm. She felt Edmund's gaze on her, and he gave her comfort, despite knowing that for the umpteenth time he was seeing her look her worst. She could see Savannah coping very well, keeping everyone entertained while she fried another batch of tiny doughnuts. Alain and her mother were doing teas, and Dilys had started serving her spring punch, as it was now past midday. The goats and Shetland ponies were so well-behaved, despite a lot of tail pulling and prodding; in fact, everyone seemed to be behaving themselves, even J-T, who had taken it upon himself to judge the dog show, along with the vicar's wife. She could see them having a good gossip over what looked suspiciously like a bottle of Sauvignon Blanc. She desperately wanted to wash her face and at least pull a brush through her hair.

This, however, was not to be. At that very moment, not only did the local *Weald Life* man turn up, but a minibus full of writers from national newspapers drew to a halt in the lane.

Entranced by the sight before them – the green bedecked and bejewelled by sparkly bunting, fancy dressed dogs and children, piles of food and tubs of flowers – the photographers began snapping furiously. Seeing Liberty and Jools talking, they raced over.

'Talking to the enemy, hey, Miss James! What have you got to say now, Jools? Why are you back? Your piece was so bad you couldn't keep away, or are you just keeping the stunning Miss J to yourself?' The reporter who was loudly shouting this out earned a steely glare from Edmund.

'Allow me?' asked Jools. Shrugging her shoulders in resignation, Liberty let him speak.

'It was entirely wrong of me to denounce Miss James's venture in such a manner,' he began. 'I have rarely experienced such fine baking in this country, which, with all the artisan bakers getting themselves on television and on every street corner in Notting Hill, is saying something. And despite my ability to hide it,' he continued, patting his round tummy, 'I enjoy sampling good food.' A titter of amusement went round the reporters. Most of them knew him, and were aware he had invited them to the fete from the depth of his guilt at what he had done. They also knew the size of his tummy was down to a pathological inability to pay for his own meals.

He continued, 'Miss James has managed to recreate what most of us Brits only dream about – a proper old-fashioned fete, with the best local entertainment and produce. I'm sure you will all agree, if every village did this at least once a month, it would do the country good and bring our communities together at the same time. Come on, chaps, have a glass of punch or five, and try some of these cakes. Let a ferret run up your leg and try a spot of archery, but maybe do that before the punch, as it knocks your socks to the sky! The minibus will come for you at five o'clock, so you don't have to worry about driving back, and I hope you not only enjoy yourselves, but give Liberty the very best coverage in your rags.'

'Thank you,' said Liberty, once the photographers had turned away, now realising he had invited the journalists to the fete. 'Have you seen Percy?' she asked quietly.

'No, and when I told him I was pissed off with him for deceiving me, he slammed the phone down. I only found out when your friend Edmund phoned to ask what the hell I was doing writing such a terrible piece on the most gentle, kind, gifted woman to grace the earth.'

Liberty stared at him, not sure if he was joking. As if reading her mind, Jools said, 'No kidding. I mean, the guy is obviously nuts over you, but when I told him that you had done the dirty on a friend of mine, he filled me in on some facts and I felt a complete arse. I don't know what's got into Percy these days. I think his ego has taken a huge knock. After asking around old friends, they all say that they told him the best thing about him was his wife, and they haven't seen much of him since. On that note, I feel I had better warn you that Mr and Mrs CR are going to try to persuade you to have him back, get him on track again. Good to see the old chap on the road to fighting fit once more. Anyway, I am going to grab some of those doughnuts, and then I'm off. Don't want to take all the limelight! Good luck, Miss J, and once again, I'm sorry.'

'Are you OK?' asked Edmund, coming to Liberty's side.

'Fine, I think, but if I don't go and freshen up, I'm going to scare the punters away. Do you think everything is under control? Do I need to bring some more food out?' The question was answered before the words were out of her mouth. Alain arrived at her side, apologising, but the tables were bare and it was time for the second round of savouries. Liberty ran to the kitchen, all thoughts of looking good dissolving into checking on the platters and wooden boards, which she now piled high with delicate tarts made with walnut pastry and filled with spinach and local bacon. Thin, crisp metre-long pizzas, to be cut at the table, were simply adorned with local sheep's cheese, herbs and some of the batch of tomato passata Deirdre had made at the end of summer. Savoury polenta cakes also appeared, flavoured with local mushrooms dried last autumn and topped with a tarragon crème fraiche. Baked risotto balls were filled with butternut squash puree, spiced with amaretti biscuits and mixed with herbs, alongside eggs with a crispy breadcrumb exterior. There were anchovy and cheese straws, and lots of her breads to be cut into wedges and sampled with some of the Burnt House butter and cheese. As Liberty handed platter after huge platter to willing helpers, she realised she was sweaty and un-made-up, run off her feet, but happy. She smiled a million-watt smile and walked back out onto the green ready to feed the hordes. From her hoards.

53

Liberty's one concern was that those who arrived early would eat their fill and then leave. However, the dog show, pony rides and play areas kept the children entertained, while the food stalls and glasses of punch, together with great weather, were enough to stop the adults getting itchy feet. The promise of more free food was always alluring, and amazingly, the same faces seen first thing munching happily on breakfast pastries seemed to be managing lunch, cake and whatever else they could lay their now sticky hands on. Unbelievably, more people were turning up all the time, being directed off the main road via the farm shop. Even the unflappable Dilys had been yelling to her Saturday girl Susie, called in to help, to 'bloody hurry up with more punch', as the reporters were drinking her dry.

Everyone was pitching in. The glamorous Paloma, more used to wafting around in Gucci and a cloud of scent, was cutting bread and encouraging children to try goat's cheese. 'Good for your skin, young lady,' she announced to one very spotty teenager who was turning up her nose and calling it smelly. 'You never see French girls objecting to goat's cheese, and look how beautiful they are.' Paloma knew full well that even in Timbuktu teenage girls got spots, but she held the girl's gaze and indeed, a piece of fresh soft cheese was eventually pushed into her unwilling mouth.

'Oh, when you get past the smell, it's a bit like Philadelphia,' said the girl, her pretty eyes widening in amazement.

'Well, there you go – and so good for you.'

Liberty was now worried she hadn't enough scones ready for the oven. They had counted on more people arriving in the afternoon, but not the crowds now spilling over the green. Deirdre reassured her there would be more than enough – didn't she always over-cater? And anyway, to supplement the afternoon tea scones would be more tiny sandwiches, Victoria, coffee and cobnut sponges, profiteroles, fruit tarts and cider apple cake. 'I can't even remember the other things, so stop worrying,' said her mother, in slight exasperation that Liberty couldn't see what an amazing success it all was. 'If we run out, so be it. I've never seen such appetites, and look at all these happy faces. Darling, you should be so proud of yourself. Look what you have created!'

Liberty took a moment to look up from the list in her left hand, while continuing to cut a cake into neat wedges with her right. She looked over the chattering crowds, mostly standing in groups, clutching plates, cups or glasses; the hay bales covered in cosy groups; children clambering up on to laps to steal another mouthful; dogs ambling round, looking for an unattended offering. Older children had all packed together, playing happily or helping to groom the ponies that were now having a well-earned rest, while the teenagers hung round the punch table. The rosy faces, due either to sun or alcohol, gave an impression of cheeriness and general well-being, and the fluttering bunting, hanging baskets and morris dancers – where the hell had they come from? – were all doing their bit to create the picture-perfect scene.

For the first time that day, Liberty let go of her desperation to make things go perfectly, and she breathed out. Her shoulders relaxed, and she even forgot she still hadn't had time to freshen up. 'Wow!' she squeaked. 'It's going rather well – people are having fun!'

Deirdre smiled and put her arm round her charmingly surprised and very talented daughter. 'Yes, my darling, it's what you might call an absolute roaring success. But if you like, we can simply say it's going rather well, in your delightfully understated way. Your father and I are so proud of you. I think you may get bored with hearing us say that!'

'Never!' announced Liberty, and knowing how much hard work everyone had put into the day, she remarked, 'But the idea was all Edmund's, and I couldn't have done any of it without your help, so thank you.'

Deirdre huffed, poured more tea into proffered cups and said, 'One day, you will have to realise your own talent, that it's something to be proud of, and not give all the dues to others. People help you because they want to be part of what you are creating.' With that she mentioned that the CRs were still hanging around, and asked if they had found an opportunity for a chat.

Liberty, having been so busy, had almost forgotten their presence, but now looked up and into the crowd. There were Cecil and Isabelle, talking to Jonathan and making a fuss over an extravagantly dressed whippet that had been left in his Pierrot costume as he rather liked it, hat and all, and was proudly showing his first position rosette to a smitten Isabelle.

Liberty was thrilled they were enjoying themselves, but after Jools's earlier comment about them being rather keen for her to get back together with Percy she suddenly felt vulnerable and scuttled back to the safety of her kitchen. Her tummy was in knots. Was everyone really enjoying themselves? Was the food good enough? She made the mistake of looking in the kitchen mirror: hair in a bird's nest design and cream down one side of her nose. Very glamorous. There were footsteps coming up the path.

'We know you are busy, and this is probably not a good time, but we need to talk to you. Your cards and letter have been so kind, and you have always been in our hearts.' Mr and Mrs CR stood at the entrance of the kitchen looking nervous, as though they might not be welcome. Cecil, despite the familiar jolly smile, looked a shadow of the stately patrician of his former self. Illness and the upset of his only son's bad behaviour had taken its toll.

Isabelle was commenting on what a charming home Liberty had created, and hoped that they were not overstepping the mark. Unusual nerves for such a socially confident lady. Liberty's heart went out to them both. They had always treated her fairly and generously.

'Of course I have time for you, but could it possibly wait until this evening?' She slipped another tray of scones into the oven, and deftly slid the cooling ones on to a rack. 'It *is* a little hectic.' She hoped they would see she was busy. Her welcoming remarks had made them relax after days of fretting over bothering the dear girl with their problems. They were not used to asking others for help. Now the avalanche had set off downhill, they had to get things off their heaving chests.

Isabelle cleared her throat, another sign of her nerves, and began to speak. 'We have heard that our son, Percy–' Liberty smiled. Which other son would she be talking about? '–has not been, how shall I put it, well, has not been behaving in a respectable way. I once tried to persuade you to return to him, to give the marriage a chance. Now I believe I no longer even want to have him as a son.'

At this, Liberty's head flew up, and instead of gently turning the food mixer on, she pushed the power to full, allowing a cloud of icing sugar to poof out of the bowl and cover her. Entirely. Now resembling a sugar-coated Yeti, she spluttered and asked, 'What on earth would make you say that about your only child? He adores you, and you him. You cannot mean a word of that!'

Cecil looked at her, taking in the snowman now calmly icing the lemon, walnut and cardamom cakes. This capable beauty had been stalked for the last eight months and was still defending her husband. He was confused, and told her so. 'Not only did you move away from him so quickly that we can only guess something terrible happened, but you still fail to ask for a divorce.'

Liberty couldn't tell him that it was because if she did, in her mind it would mean she had failed at her marriage, and also that it always seemed to go hand in hand with asking for money, something she would never do, partly because she knew it was all his family's money, so she clamped her mouth shut. Cecil continued, 'He has now deserted his son. Even a positive paternity test failed to raise his interest.'

'Our grandchild!' wailed Isabelle. 'We cannot ask to see the child, as we are far too embarrassed by Percy's behaviour, and thank goodness the woman's husband took her back. and as far as we can tell, Percy is spending all his money gambling, and on other pleasantries.'

Isabelle was obviously selecting her words with care. 'His friends are very concerned about his drinking, and he hasn't been to the office in the last month. He now tells us it's entirely our fault, as we put too much pressure on him to be the perfect child when his sister died. He says he wants to have the fun he was denied as a child, and do what he damn well wants. Those are his words, not mine.'

Liberty could tell how hurt Isabelle was by her unheard of use of a swear word. But what could she do? What did they want of her? She started to panic, when suddenly help arrived in the heavenly form of her mother. Deirdre ran in and took a plate of scones from the work surface.

'Only forty here – come on, we need more than that.' As she turned to leave, she realised who was standing over the glazed – in expression, and, thanks to the sugar, in the icing sense – Liberty. She screeched to a halt, thankfully not spilling her plateful of scones, and asked if everything was all right.

'Yes, fine, I think – at least, I am about to find out.' Liberty turned to the CRs. 'What do you want from me? I get the impression you are not just here to voice your concerns over Percy to his almost ex-wife.'

'We want it to stop,' said Cecil very firmly. 'And you are the only person with the power to help.'

Deirdre and Liberty's eyebrows shot up in unison, making them look like a comedy duo with perfect timing.

'How?' they asked, again at exactly the same time, which made them smile to one another.

'The only thing Percy ever really cared about was his art,' said Cecil. 'We hoped his passion would spill over to the house and its contents and control of his trust fund, which includes the family property, signed over to him on his twenty-first birthday.'

I didn't know that! thought Liberty.

'We thought about death duties. We were advised by our solicitors, and part of the agreement was that we could expect to continue living in either the London house or the Hall as long as we wished. However, when recently we have criticised his behaviour, he has threatened to turn us out of our own homes.'

'Surely not! Would he do that? Could he?' asked Liberty.

'We aren't so certain any longer,' said Isabelle sadly.

The kitchen was filling up with platters of cakes and scones as Liberty continued to bake, turn out and decorate, and then filled up more as Alain stomped in, missing a wife and shouting, 'Where are those bloody scones?'

Deirdre handed him the plate and another from the table where Liberty was still on autopilot. Alain turned to go, then did a Deirdre and stopped to ask what was going on.

'Anyway,' continued an exasperated Cecil, speaking slowly, as though it was most inconvenient the hosts were trying to serve 350 people food while they wanted a quiet chat, 'the only thing he has ever cared about, as I already said, is his art.'

'Agreed,' said Liberty, surprised that they should easily dismiss their marriage from a list of things Percy might have cared about, but as she knew this to be true she let him continue.

'Well, you are still married to him. You can claim his collection through the divorce courts. His behaviour towards you has been disgraceful. The *Telegraph* journalist agreed to sign an affidavit today to explain how Percy coerced him into writing that dreadful article, and his authority can be cited. You could claim, with our backing, either his art collection or half the properties, money and other belongings. He would never be able to give away the family estate, so he would have to give the art collection, at which point you could say if he just calmed down and went back to work, took care of his baby and made the Cholmondly-Radley name one to be proud of again, you wouldn't take it. The publicity is getting so bad, we are losing long-established clients from the bank; they are worried that any scandal at a bank these days is likely to end up with a banker in gaol and a heap of debts.'

Deirdre, Alain and Liberty looked at one another in amazement. Then burst out laughing.

'Sorry,' said Alain after a few moments. Icing sugar now seemed to fill the air. 'A James family tradition. Laugh in times of stress.' As they tried to calm down, Edmund appeared, took in the situation, the full-to-bursting kitchen piled high with emotions and cakes desperately needed outside, and delegated.

'Alain, Deirdre, get those scones out, now. I'll take the trays of jams and cream.' He then addressed Mr and Mrs Cholmondly-Radley. 'I am under the impression that you would appreciate a moment of Liberty's time. However, this may not be the best opportunity for you to gain her full attention. I would like to invite you to make yourselves comfortable in my home, where my housekeeper will take care of your needs until the evening, when Liberty can join you.'

At the mention of a housekeeper, the CRs rallied. Here was familiar territory. They could cope with that.

'I promise I will be over to see you when all this is cleared, but it may be quite late,' said Liberty.

'That is quite all right, my dear,' said Mrs CR. 'We will be just fine.'

'Mrs Goodman will arrange rooms for you, and a light supper for us all,' said Edmund in a very firm voice. 'I will phone her on our way – my car is just a short walk from here.' Edmund guided the pair out of the kitchen like a gentle sheepdog would corral lost sheep out of a dangerous gully. He turned and winked at Liberty and mouthed, 'See you later.'

Thank God for a masterful man, thought Liberty. She could have kissed him, but because she was aware of her sugared almond exterior, she refrained from chasing after him and got on with the baking, vowing to have a shower before long, by hook or by crook.

Savannah had sold out of her doughnuts, and was now smugly telling Khalid that her first experience of catering had been 'really quite easy. I don't know why people say cooking is hard. And look how happy they all are.' Khalid didn't have the heart to tell his beautiful wife that she looked as though she had been deep fried – all hot and shiny – and was desperately trying to get her to sit and rest instead of leaping about with the over-stimulated children. But as he looked around he could see the happy groups and marvelled that no matter which culture you came from, food could bring everyone together. He also loved watching his beloved wife laughing freely and giggling, chasing Sasha or Hussein as they frolicked around pretending they were ponies, jumping over the bales of hay that hadn't been eaten by the Shetland ponies who were now on the loose as their handler was in the pub.

Dilys was thrilled. Her pub hadn't done so well since the Jubilee weekend. Her punch had been getting stronger and stronger during the day, as Susie had been pouring more booze in, unaware Dilys had already strengthened it. She hadn't been too strict about checking IDs, so several youngsters were looking a little green around the gills. Miss Scally was trying unsuccessfully to force some cake into them to sober them up; not out of the goodness of her own heart, but in an attempt to show the good doctor how caring she could be. This all ended abruptly when a particularly obnoxious redhead from the housing estate was sick over her patent leather shoes.

'Oh, you little bitch!' shouted the receptionist, throwing down the plate of cakes and stamping off as fast as she could with her sensible patent courts sticky and full of vomit. Sadly, unbeknown to her, this was the only part of Miss Scally's do-gooding that the doctor witnessed, and he allowed himself a quiet chuckle.

The morris dancers, having eaten and drunk their fill – they were in fact meant to be half a mile away entertaining the WI, but had decided to stay, much more fun – thought they would now do their bit and began waving bells on sticks and large spotty handkerchiefs. This made everyone who had eaten too much, meaning everyone, feel somewhat energetic. Soon most people were up and dancing, grabbing napkins and tugging flowers from the hanging baskets to wave.

'Goodness,' said Paloma, laughing, 'it looks like a pagan ritual. Are we going to pray to the sun and fire arrows at sunset?'

Jonathan smiled indulgently. He had been pleased to see such a strong crowd, composed both of local people, to whom he diligently chatted, and tourists. So often visitors felt pushed out at such events and tended to stay away. But from what people were saying, out of a combination of loving Deirdre and wanting to support her daughter, and a proud sense that this was their village, the local people were being particularly friendly and welcoming. Besides, so many local producers were being featured and promoted.

Tall candles were lit as the afternoon sun grew weaker and people spilled in and out of the pub, mixing vodka and tonics with delicate cheese straws and olive bread served with platters of cheeses and hams from the local farms. If a village could have feelings, Littlehurst would be bursting with pride.

54

Gwen and Paul from the tea room were the only people from the village who did not show their faces at the fete. This was quite surprising, really, considering the amount of bare flesh on display, with the young girls delighting in the first sunshine of the year. But Paul had realised that instead of being pleased not to be running the tea shop any longer he had become jealous of Liberty's growing popularity and of her aloof beauty at the New Year's Eve party; she had barely been able to talk to him as she hated the derogatory way he treated his wife. He couldn't bear to hear 'Gosh, isn't it going to be lovely to have somewhere decent to eat in the village!' or 'Isn't she lovely?' any longer. Even Miss Scally, who had once been his cohort, was professing to be amazed that such a talented young woman would wish to settle in a small community. She only said this as she believed Liberty would quickly move on to bigger and better things, but it did nothing to smooth Paul's ruffled ego. Not that he had ever worked hard, or much at all, but he would miss the gossip and young flesh on tap at the tea room.

He had felt a little bad telling a strange man where Liberty would be living just before Christmas; possibly not a good idea to chat happily to someone dressed like a cat burglar, but the fifty pound note pressed into his hand took any lasting guilt away. All he could see before him was retirement and being dragged around boring gardens by his uninteresting and ungainly wife. He couldn't bear to sit and watch people enjoying the bewitching Miss James's food, so had decided to take Gwen on her first holiday in thirty years.

They borrowed a caravan and towed it to Blackpool. Gwen sat in a café chewing a very hard rock bun and watched the raindrops coursing down the window, contemplating whether divorce and loneliness would be better than this. Surely anything would be preferable? Paul, meanwhile, was in the bookies watching his safe bet come in last. He tore up his slip and threw it on the floor, ignoring a fiery look from the bookmaker, and wondered if there was any more money to be made from dispensing information on Liberty James. He certainly wouldn't mind getting to know her better . . .

Liberty was feeling exhausted but elated. She had whistled to herself as she turned off her oven and plated up the last food. Taking it out to the happy throng on the green, she wandered among the crowds and was amazed that people still took the new offerings. She was glowing under so much praise, most people saying how delicious it had all been and how excited they were about her café. Some of the more discerning diners had been even more effusive, and delighted in describing to her all the flavours they could detect in the different things they had tasted through the day. Thankfully, Alain had warned her that although she of course knew exactly what she had put in her food, as she had made it, the keener the diners, the more intent they were to tell you what it tasted of. She managed to smile sweetly, say how kind it was for them to notice and repeat over and over, 'I do hope to see you in LIBERTEAS when it opens in two days' time.'

And it was lovely that everyone was being so kind with their praise; she felt truly blessed to have found her premises where she felt so at home already. She looked around for Edmund, and saw him sitting with Savannah and Khalid, both children sleeping at their feet wrapped in polo blankets.

As she made her way towards them, she wondered if she would ever get there, as she felt obliged to stop and chat, thanking the locals for showing up. She asked if they would like to see anything in particular on her menu, and offered a free pot of tea with their first cake in the café. 'It's made us feel like a community again. When is the next fete?' was asked repeatedly. 'What about the August bank holiday?' Liberty was too flattered to worry about future planning, but she did start dreaming about bringing the village together with annual fetes and celebrations.

The vicar proposed she did something for the harvest festival. 'It used to be such a jolly occasion, and the church was as full as at Easter and Christmas. Let's try to bring in the crowds by offering more than the usual pots of jam and oversized pumpkins. Let's do a full-on feast!'

Deirdre was also floating. So many people were asking her to sign their ancient, sticky cookery books; she was almost inspired to write another. She and Alain were constantly being told how proud they must be of their daughter, and wasn't she a chip off the old block?

Savannah, who had been talking babies with Evangeline, was incredibly pleased for her friend, even a little jealous, she was shocked to admit. Maybe she should have a career? And then she burst out laughing, which woke both of her children. She hugged them close, realising that they, along with lots of shopping, could fill her life perfectly.

Deirdre had enlisted her cookery school children to help clear up, and gradually plates were stacked, cups and teapots emptied of their dregs and all taken back to Liberty's house.

'There seem to be very few leftovers,' commented Liberty.

'Oh, I do wonder why!' her father said with a laugh, spotting a child filling a box with slices of sponge cake and her cheeks with Chelsea bun. 'I think several families have been fed for the entire week. I hope they will be hungry enough to come to the café!'

All Liberty wanted to do was have a long, hot soak in the tub, and contemplate the café's opening. But she knew she had to make peace with Isabelle and Cecil and find out what crazy ideas they had been concocting to rein in the wayward Percy. She managed to reach Savannah, who with Khalid was gathering their things and starting to make for home, each carrying a sleepy child.

'Where did Edmund go?' enquired Liberty.

'He has left already. I think he had enough of being told how nice it was to have Pa back in the village!' said Savannah with a little giggle, but not unkindly. 'Poor Ed, he is such a softy at heart, but he just isn't built for placating grumpy villagers and small talk. Anyway, he wanted to check on your in-laws, and didn't like to bother you when you were surrounded by all your new fans. You really have done so well!' And Savannah gave her hand a squeeze, which was about all she could do with Sasha weighing her down.

'Thank you for helping,' said Liberty. 'You and Khalid must be shattered. Please get yourselves and the children home. I need a quick shower and will be up to join you as quickly as I can. We can finish the clearing tomorrow, and Dilys is going to keep the party going when the band starts, so I can leave her in charge now.'

Strolling across to Duck End, she gathered up J-T and Bob along with Teal, who they had been looking after.

'Did you enjoy our country gathering?' she enquired, mostly to Bob, who was usually the last person to be seen at such an event. She was aware he had attended simply to keep an eye on J-T, but hoped he wasn't too bored.

'Bloody brilliant!' was Bob's response. 'Apart from some confusion when I said that Feran and Bulli had come in drag at the dog show – they seemed to think it meant the hounds would chase them, rather than an explanation for dogs dressed as bitches. It was amazing! My dear girl, you have done yourself proud. I can't think of the last time I had so much fun with no vodka involved. People are really interesting. That Fred fellow – now he is a good artist!'

J-T and Liberty exchanged looks and giggled with relief that

Gray hadn't shown up and that Bob genuinely seemed to have had fun.

'You must be exhausted,' said J-T sympathetically. 'Well done, the day was fantastic.'

'Yes. Now I have just got to get myself together for Saturday. And of course, at this very moment Percy has to rear his ugly head again.'

'Well . . .' said Bob. 'I do believe I can help you with that particular subject. But first let's all freshen up, and I will tell you my plans when we get together.'

Liberty looked from Bob to J-T, but J-T shrugged and said, 'I don't know what the man's on about!'

They made their way to her cosy home, filled with the aroma of all the cakes baked earlier and the happy sounds drifting in through the windows from the green.

'Time for you to make yourself presentable and get to Jonathan's,' said J-T as he let the kitten out from her cage, where she had been put for safe-keeping, into a furious scrabble of dogs and fur.

'You mean, to Edmund's house,' said Liberty as she tried desperately to stop the poor kitten from leaping on to the kitchen surface.

'Sorry, so it's Edmund's house now?' asked J-T, in a fit of giggles, grabbing Queenie and kicking the French bulldogs out of the front door. 'I have observed him keeping an eye on you. Rather like a hungry golden eagle setting eyes on a pretty little rabbit.'

'Oh, grow up!' snapped Liberty, whose face was by now an unbecoming scarlet under the sugar, dust and goodness knows what else stuck to her face.

'Sorry, darling,' said J-T, all contrite. He put a comforting arm around her shoulders. 'How lovely to see love blossoming on two unsuspecting trees.'

'Very poetic,' hissed Liberty. 'I need to clean up.'

'There is a smitten, grumpy, hellishly handsome man waiting

to hand you a glass of celebratory champagne at Denhelm Park, and you ought to look more like a human than an iced bun, so get yourself in the shower and we will drive you up.'

At Liberty's surprised look, he explained that Edmund had wanted to throw a little party to celebrate the successful day, and invited them to join Deirdre, Alain and the rest of the mob for supper. *Poor Mrs Goodman*, thought Liberty, but was secretly rather thrilled that Edmund wanted to celebrate. She had barely had time to talk to him, let alone thank him for rescuing her and whisking Isabelle and Cecil away when she needed to work.

All of Liberty's friends and family had noted the presence of Mr and Mrs CR. First of all they wondered why they were there at all, and whispered to one another that for Liberty's sake they hoped Percy was not about to arrive. Then, when Deirdre and Alain had excitedly run out to tell them the CRs wanted Liberty's help to revive the reputation of the bank and prevent their son from doing any more damage, they were even more curious. They had therefore, either because they were Jonathan's family and staying at the park, or because they were Liberty's family and insistent that they needed to be there (Alain and Deirdre) or just insistent (J-T), all wangled an invitation to supper at Denhelm.

Liberty ran upstairs and into the bathroom, neglecting to look in the mirror, knowing her reflection would only horrify. She had spent a day launching her career whilst resembling a cookie monster. She washed her hair twice and spent a little more time than she should on her make-up, knowing the CRs would be well taken care of. Throwing on a navy-blue jersey dress that clung in all the right places and had a flattering boat neck, a pug-coloured cashmere cardigan (bought when she realised how much hair pugs shed) and tugging on a pair of high-heeled dark brown alligator boots, she raced down as Bob and J-T were encouraging the dogs into their beds with a Bonio.

'Don't worry, Queenie has been out and we have left her in our room,' they reassured her. But Liberty was not going to let kitten poo worry her on a night when, despite being bush tired and slightly terrified of what plan the CRs had come up with, she felt like celebrating a day that had gone so well. She also knew she had a lot of thanking to do.

J-T held the door open for her just as the band struck up the introduction of Carly Simon's 'Nobody Does it Better'. As they walked along the garden path, they looked over to the improvised stage on the green and all gasped when they realised it was a clearly pregnant Sarah behind the microphone. When she opened her mouth and started to sing, they stopped walking and listened. It was like liquid glucose; clear, mellow and able to smooth off rough edges. She amazed everyone with her strong, sultry voice. Liberty was smiling as they eventually got into the car and drove off; she had spied the bewitched face of Dr Brown gazing up in surprise and renewed adoration at his cleaning woman.

'Wow!' said J-T. 'Did you know she could sing like that?' he asked as he turned into the driveway, passing Deirdre and Alain and Paloma and Jonathan as they walked along the pretty primrose-festooned drive.

'No,' said Liberty. 'To be honest, I don't think I have even heard her hum before!'

Bob was looking thoughtful, and Liberty asked him what he was thinking. 'Only that I suddenly feel, after spending an eventful Christmas here–' at this point he raised an eyebrow '–and then today, meeting so many interesting people, and having such a good time, that I have been very narrow-minded.'

'NO!' said J-T and Liberty, chortling in unison.

'No, no, let me finish,' said Bob, but not unkindly. He was aware of his previous prejudice against the country set, feeling lost and bewildered by what he saw as a lack of culture when faced with a weekend in the shires. 'It's made me think that J-T's idea of running a boutique B&B is not such a bad one, after all. I could open a gallery down here, and the dogs would love it – and think of what we could afford with the money raised from the Covent Garden pad!'

J-T was open-mouthed at his beloved's sudden rush of enthusiasm about what had been a very sketchy idea, but as they had just pulled up near the front door he had little time to say anything other than, 'Let's talk about this later when we are back at Duck End. This evening has so many eventualities that we may be desperate for an escape, but I'm thrilled you think we have a future!'

He squeezed Bob's hand as they went up the steps. They could hear laughter pealing through the windows. Children were running about in their pyjamas, hotly pursued by Savannah.

'A little too much sugar intake, I fear,' she explained to the arrivals. 'Come on, you two. Time for a story.'

Mrs CR was chatting happily to Jonathan, while Mr CR was puffing out his features and attempting to charm the beautiful Paloma, who was doing her best to appear impressed by the stuffy but kindly old man. Evangeline, having settled little Yves, was sipping a glass of champagne, whispering with Claude and hoping food would be served shortly. Despite the rest of Littlehurst and the surrounding county being full to bursting point, most of Liberty's helpers and friends had been too busy on their feet helping others or looking after wayward children to eat much, or indeed anything, themselves. Therefore, they were all ravenous. Mrs Goodman was working at full speed in the kitchen, thrilled to have a houseful again; she had raided the farm shop and bought a feast.

Edmund came out of the drawing room laden with drinks. His eyes lit up appreciatively when he saw Liberty. 'Come in, you must be completely shattered.'

Liberty, who had felt her stomach flutter when she saw Edmund, and not out of hunger, now felt that she looked tired, and her shoulders drooped a bit, but she gratefully took the offered glass of biscuit-coloured champagne, allowing the cool, delicious bubbles to relax and smooth her nerves about the impending evening.

'How are Isabelle and Cecil?' she asked quietly.

Edmund raised his eyes to the ceiling and whispered, 'Slightly overwrought.' Then, turning to Bob, he continued, 'Good evening, Bob. I hate to tell you, but I may be in need of your expertise this evening.'

Liberty's eyebrows described querying shapes, but Bob replied brightly with a 'righty-ho', hoping Edmund was planning to sell many of the fabulous pictures dotting the walls in order to invest in new ones, bought from him, of course, but knowing in his heart it was more than likely to do with Liberty's in-laws.

'I do believe little pound signs appeared in your eyes just now,' whispered J-T in his ear.

'Oh, shush,' replied Bob, but very fondly.

'I have a feeling in my bones,' continued J-T, 'that Edmund is thinking about Percy and his art collection.'

'That's what I keep wanting to explain to Liberty,' said Bob, but they were interrupted again by Jonathan herding them into the bright summer sitting room, where a reluctant fire twitched in the grate; just enough to add a touch of comfort to the warm evening.

They looked for a place to sit down – all except Liberty, who was buzzing with adrenalin and nervous energy, pacing up and down in the bay.

Edmund took over as chairman. 'I have to apologise, firstly, to Mr and Mrs Cholmondly-Radley, as I am not sure you were expecting such a large audience to hear what you have to say.' This raised a small smile from them both and somewhat broke the ice. 'However, I believe it demonstrates the support and love we all feel for our dear friend Liberty.'

There was a gasp from Savannah, who thought her unemotional brother must have had some sort of stroke to be so verbally demonstrative. Most eyebrows rose, except for J-T's, whose were so Botoxed that they couldn't. Paloma didn't react either, both because of her Botox and because she was of the impression that everyone knew Edmund and Liberty were madly in love and imagined there was soon to be an announcement of a romantic nature. Liberty stopped pacing and looked at Edmund. His dark, brooding eyes met hers directly, and she felt a frisson of excitement shiver down her spine. At that moment she knew this dear man was indeed hers, and she his, but typically, in front of all these people, she could only open and close her mouth like a goldfish, albeit a very pretty one.

Edmund tore his gaze from Liberty's and continued, 'I have been talking with Cecil and Isabelle for most of the afternoon, and it would appear that for the sake of the Radley Bank's reputation, and that of the family, which is perhaps even more important, help is needed to jolt Percy into realising he is damaging more than his liver. They have requested that Liberty make a claim on his Pissarro painting. This is the one possession he loves above any other. It will hopefully get him back under control, and shock him into realising what he is doing.'

'But I don't want his Pissarro! I've never wanted to take anything of his. After all, it was my decision to leave him,' said Liberty, feeling awkward in front of her in-laws, worried they might think this a plan of her making.

'Oh, no, my dear,' piped up Cecil. 'We know you don't. But we feel that if he is told you want it, you could . . . well . . . er . . .' He searched for the correct word. ' . . . persuade him to come back to the bank, thereby reassuring our partners and clients that the bank is worth holding their money in, and then he might take control of himself once again, and as a result rescue what is left of our family name. Perhaps he will even take some interest in our grandchild.' At this point Isabelle gave a somewhat theatrical sob; quite unexpected from such a controlled lady.

Liberty felt a gut-gripping stab of guilt. If only she had been able to give them a grandchild herself, maybe none of this would have happened. She hurried over to her beloved mother-in-law and comforted her, her own tears spilling as the memory of her lost child flooded back. Isabelle managed to pull herself together. She was somewhat muddled as to what had happened to Liberty. She had been told about the miscarriage by a horrified Deirdre, who had phoned her to ask how Percy could have abandoned her daughter in Italy after she had lost her baby. Isabelle had felt guilty since Liberty's visit just after she left Percy. She should have supported the poor girl more. But not knowing the full story, she had felt obliged to encourage her to stand by her son. She had always admired her daughter-in-law for her hard work, generosity of spirit and enthusiasm, and for not trading on her beauty, as so many others had done, making them lazy and complacent.

'Would you allow me to speak?' Bob surprised everyone by standing up. J-T admired his handsome physique as Bob raised himself to his full height, grateful for the Cuban heels that allowed him to reach the mantelpiece. He commanded the attention of all in the room.

'You may be aware that Percy and I struck up a form of friendship through our years in Cambridge, due to our mutual appreciation of art. It almost made him forgive me for being gay! Once in a while he asked me to find him small pictures to have as investment pieces. Sometimes he would sell them straight away, as they had been purchased at well below their value, and sometimes he kept them – usually in the bank's vaults – until they gained sufficient value to be sold. Over a few years this made me realise that although I needed to make money through my own art dealing, I love the pieces I buy and see value in their beauty rather than in their monetary value. Percy, on the other hand, although very knowledgeable, was more interested in making money.

'One day, a few years after coming down from university, he approached me, saying he needed a painting to be authenticated, but on the quiet. When I asked why, he said his aunt needed to sell a piece, but she didn't want the family to find out that she had lost a fair bit of their loot by gambling. Perhaps blindly trusting a friend, I saw the picture, and authenticated an unknown Pissarro. I was so excited I wanted to let him show it before it was sold, and I told him it would encourage a huge amount of interest and draw the big bidders in. To sell on the QT would only arouse suspicion, and lower the price. He assured me he would speak to her and try to do as I said. I heard nothing until I attended a party held at Le Manoir a few months later, only for Liberty to tell me in an unguarded moment that we were not there to celebrate her birthday at all, but rather his new acquisition! By the way, Liberty, Percy was none too pleased you had told me.'

'Yes, I remember!' piped up Liberty. 'I was so surprised he was cross, because I thought he would want to show off to you, of all people, that he had managed this great coup. He had talked of nothing but the Pissarro for the past few weeks, and then he got so angry with me when I mentioned it to you.'

'It was at Le Manoir?' enquired J-T.

'Yes! I believe it was.'

'Uh-huh, explains a lot.'

'Anyway, to continue,' said Bob, drawing the focus back to himself. 'When I asked Percy what had happened and how on earth he had afforded it, he said his aunt had refused to place it on the open market, and he had decided to buy it from her instead, directly, thus cutting out the middlemen and the fees. He said he had given her my estimated price and she was pleased and content to leave it at that. I couldn't very well ask where the money had come from, and he wasn't offering to tell me.'

Isabelle and Cecil were both looking very confused, but Bob went on, 'I believe that he maybe didn't pass on my written estimate or authentication certificate, and I also believe that at that time he wouldn't have had the sort of cash he would need for the picture. I think he may have told the aunt that it wasn't a real Pissarro, and he bought it from her at an absolute knock-down price. All we need to do is go and see the aunt. I didn't question him at the time, not sure why, but if I'm honest I've always been a little scared of the man.' At this he shot a nervous glance at the CRs, but they were still looking dazed and confused. 'But looking back, I feel it may have been, well, somewhat illegal. So, that is my story. What do you all make of it?'

'Very interesting. Very, very interesting,' said Isabelle, slowly coming out of her catatonic state. She took hold of her husband's hand and said, 'Especially as neither I nor my husband has a sister.'

It was Bob's turn to look shocked. 'But I met her in her home. She seemed genuine, and I'm sure it was her apartment in Anstley Hall. It felt right, and she made me tea there.'

'I don't suppose you remember her name, do you?' asked Mr CR.

'Yes, strangely, I do. It's a one-off to see a real Pissarro, and her name was so unbelievable, it was memorable. I remember Percy saying not to laugh when he told me, and that when she married, the family giggled over it for months. It was Mrs Stickybunns.'

'Oh, poor Sticky!' wailed Liberty and Isabelle simultaneously. Cecil, on the other hand, was not thinking about his housekeeper's unusual name; he was growing ever more furious with his son.

'What!' he shouted so loudly that the crystals on the ancient wall sconces shook. 'Are you seriously telling me my son swindled my housekeeper out of hundreds of thousands of pounds?'

'Well, yes, to put it bluntly, I do think it's possible. And it was a good deal more than that,' confirmed Bob, trembling under the full glare of the elderly gentleman, who was now back to his former patrician demeanour, suddenly regaining the strength that chemotherapy had sapped for months.

'Unless perhaps he swindled the bank to get hold of the money, and Mrs Stickybunns has been working for you out of the goodness of her heart, while all the time hoarding her millions under the bed?' suggested J-T, who was enjoying this.

Liberty was now not the only one to be opening and shutting

her mouth like a goldfish. Edmund did the only thing suitable in such a situation: he opened another bottle of Ruinart Blanc de Blancs, and topped up everyone's glass. After a few minutes of absolute silence, the room erupted with talk, everyone shouting over each other and excitedly telling Cecil to call Mrs Stickybunns immediately.

55

At that moment Mrs Goodman sounded the gong for supper, with considerable extra enthusiasm, owing to the amount of noise emerging from the summer sitting room. She was thrilled to have the house full of laughter and jollity again. The children had already snuck down and been given a tray of biscuits and a flask of hot chocolate to take up to their indoor tree house.

Back in the mayhem, Edmund took control. He handed Cecil the telephone and instructed him to phone Mrs Stickybunns, then ran into the kitchen to explain to Mrs Goodman (thank goodness his housekeeper had a sensible name) that they might still need a few minutes, and she scuttled off to put the pea mousse back in its water bath to stay warm, and to cover the resting beef again. She was muttering 'Why do I ever expect to be able to serve on time?' but smiling as she went.

When Edmund returned to the sitting room, Cecil had obeyed the command, and was indeed on the phone. The rest of the room was silent, for once no one ashamed of eavesdropping. Isabelle even had her ear pressed to Cecil's to overhear more clearly, much to her husband's obvious annoyance, as he kept scooting down the sofa, only for her to scoot straight after him, until he was pressed between a chintz arm and a silk one.

'Yes, yes, and did you get the authentication? Oh, righty-ho. So Percy helped you, yes? And what, if you don't mind my asking, did he pay for the very poor fake? Righty-ho, all right, everything in good order in the homestead? Yes, no, not a problem. Just wanted to know. Thank you, see you later. We will be home very late, if at all. Edmund has kindly offered us a bed for the night. Yes, yes, I have my pills. Leave the hall light on, but don't worry about staying up. Right, right. Thank you.' He was trying not to be rude but was obviously desperate to relay her side of the story, and he hung up.

'Well?' All eyes were on him. Isabelle, who despite her husband's best efforts had heard most of the conversation, now resembled a china doll; all colour drained from her face, except for bright pink spots of rouge on her cheeks and a pursed mouth. She took a deep slurp of wine, as did Cecil, before he said, 'Percy . . .' And then he paused, finding it hard to believe, let alone say. 'Percy paid her the grand sum of fifteen hundred pounds for what he said was a very poor fake. Sticky said she had been given the picture by her previous employers when they moved abroad, and couldn't take her with them. She had wanted to join her sister on a cruise, but it was very expensive, and she told Percy she had a painting she thought could raise some holiday money. Knowing he was interested in art works, she asked him to take a look. He told her that although it was probably a waste of time, he wanted an expert to have a look to be sure.' Cecil was breathing heavily. He pressed his thumbs and forefingers into the corners of his eyes as he told them the news. 'She even said, "Dear Percy, so kind of him, so caring, to bother about me." The little bugger, he didn't pass on Bob's assessment.'

The group looked stunned, everyone trying to work out the damage and what it meant to them. Claude was filling Evangeline in on the background of how Bob and Percy and Liberty knew each other, and the circumstances surrounding the extortion. Liberty was feeling nauseous and weak at the knees, realising that the upstanding, decent man she thought Percy was at the time she married him, no matter what he had turned into since, had actually never existed. He had always been a treacherous, deceitful bastard. Did that mean she had no idea of who was decent in the world?

Alain and Deirdre understood what their daughter must be

thinking, and were in turn feeling desperate on her behalf, and incredibly angry towards Percy. Paloma and Jonathan were feeling grateful that their sons were thoughtful, considerate and honest. Edmund's heart went out to Liberty; he wanted to protect her from everything. He took her difficulty as an excuse to go over and hold her.

After a few moments of quiet, it was as though everyone suddenly realised that it was not their feelings that mattered. The only people who mattered were sitting, strangely upright and unseeing, in front of them. Liberty reluctantly let go of Edmund, went over to Isabelle and knelt beside her. Before she could say anything, Isabelle croaked out, 'I suppose we had better start saving if we are to pay poor Sticky the real value of the painting.' She was trying to smile, but her heart had cracked deeply, and was obviously breaking as she had to face what kind of person her son, her own flesh and blood, was.

Edmund took control again. 'Mrs Stickybunns is not the only housekeeper who may have murder on her mind tonight if we don't eat soon!' The room collectively giggled, relieved to break the tension. 'Let's go through, then reconvene when we have fuel in our bellies, and decide what is to be done.'

Jonathan's cheeks went a little pink, not only because he was thrilled to see his son being so authoritative, but also because Paloma's hand found his bottom as they rose to go to supper.

While Liberty and her crew had been feeding the masses, Mrs Goodman had been hard at work. She had been reluctant to join the fete, as it seemed a little incorrect to socialise with one's boss and his future wife. She may only be the housekeeper, but her eyes were wide open. She had therefore spent the day enjoyably raiding the stocks of shops bereft of customers, who were all busy filling their faces in Littlehurst. Florists, delicatessens and the farm shop had all been grateful of her custom on such a quiet day.

The rosewood dining table could hold up to twenty people, but Mrs Goodman had arranged it carefully. The centre was massed with pretty Meissen bowls of white tulips and she had used silverware and huge platters bearing candles and vast displays of pomegranates, white grapes and figs to fill the expanse of white linen tablecloth, so everything looked inviting and homely. Mrs Goodman had always admired the Dowager Duchess of Devonshire for her ambitious table decorations, and wished she could copy the brood hens the duchess had once placed in the centre of the dining table together with a basket of chicks, but on this occasion thought a more traditional route to be best.

Edmund let his father sit at the head of the table, as it would have felt odd to do otherwise. Anyway, he wanted to seat himself next to Liberty and as host, he would have had Isabelle and Deirdre on his right and left. Paloma pouted for a second, but then grinned as she had her darling Claude on one side and the dashing Edmund on the other, and she relished any chance to grill him about Liberty.

Liberty felt Edmund's warm gaze on her back as he held out her chair. The look that had passed between them earlier had pierced the protective cover she had wrapped her heart in. It had allowed her own love to spark, and she now embraced the feeling. There was no holding back; she let the wondrous, warm glow fill her, envelop her whole being. Love was literally lighting her up; her cheeks were flushed a becoming pink and her rosy mouth was set in a permanent smile, something she was aware was not entirely appropriate given the circumstances, but she simply couldn't help herself. She no longer felt hungry. Thoughts of the crazy day they were having, or her café, had disappeared from her mind; she was only aware of Edmund. She knew she loved him absolutely and the look that they had shared in the sitting room had at last made her deeply aware of his feelings for her. Despite the tension and excitement around the table, all she could concentrate on was the electricity passing between their two bodies. Quite inappropriate, she kept telling herself, but when she caught Savannah's eye she was met with a knowing raise of an eyebrow and a smile that spelt mischief and understanding.

'So, where do we go from here?' asked J-T, breaking the silence. There was a long pause, as everyone considered the options. With Mr and Mrs CR at the table, it was difficult to talk freely. Everyone wanted to have a go at Percy, but felt it would be disrespectful to the poor parents. Liberty tried to concentrate on the moment in hand and her in-laws, but failed miserably, grinning up at Edmund's face as he suddenly stood while Mrs Goodman placed wine and starters before them.

'I know we have just shared some shocking news, but come on, we have to raise our glasses and say well done, Liberty!' His eyes did not leave hers as he took a sip. Shivers were sent up and down Liberty's spine, and she didn't dare move a muscle.

Reading her feelings, Edmund interrupted everyone's joint toast as they stood to congratulate her, and said, 'This has been the most extraordinary year. We must congratulate my father, not only on his retirement, but also on his new love, Paloma, whom we welcome to the family. Also, Deirdre and Alain – about bloody time, may I say!'

'Hurrah!' came the collective cry.

Edmund battled on. 'To my darling sister and her crazy husband, who has forgiven us all, we hope, for thinking him a Muslim extremist who would kidnap children and keep our darling sister hostage. It turns out it was a cunning plan to conceive another baby!'

Through the now whooping voices, Edmund continued, 'Talking of which, we must also bless the now probably awake little Yves upstairs. Well done, the two of you, and I apologise for keeping you up so late, as you must be even more exhausted than my darling Liberty.' The room went quiet again as everyone took a large swig of excellent white burgundy, and they looked at one another, expecting him to propose then and there.

Liberty was about to explode, and the rest to dive into their supper, when Edmund came out with a final toast. 'And, to the last two couples we find at our table. First, to Bob and J-T. Thank you, Bob, for your help tonight, and for forgiving Gray and J-T, which enabled you to be here tonight.'

Before Bob could bluster out a 'What the fuck?' Edmund silenced him by quietly saying, 'And a big bravo to Cecil and Isabelle, who have allowed a bunch of strangers into their lives tonight, which I, as a certified stuffed shirt, know is very difficult. Let us help you, you are amongst friends – and welcome!'

Edmund sat as the table erupted with passionate 'hear hears' and clapping from Bob and J-T; even Isabelle and Cecil were smiling. They had found out that the daughter-in-law they thought they had lost was still including them as family. The delectably light pea mousse was now fairly solid, but the brave and the polite were taking forkfuls, most wishing the dogs were beneath the table for titbits, and feeling embarrassed for Mrs Goodman. It had been delicious, but was no longer worth eating. Mrs Goodman had been housekeeper at Denhelm for long enough to understand. Her delight was in looking after the family, making sure there was delicious food if it was needed. She cared not what happened to it. She was so happy that the normally reticent, quiet Edmund was showing the passion and love his mother had passed to him at long last. She cleared the plates, and then went up to see if the children needed more supplies for their camp.

Cecil said firmly, 'I feel I need to offer thanks to you all, especially Edmund, who has made us feel so welcome.' Isabelle, who had been chatting to Jonathan, looked over to her husband with such warmth that the hairs on everyone's necks stood to attention.

But Cecil had more to say. 'We need a lawyer, to find out what can be done via legal routes. If we have a case against Percy, he will have to come back from wherever he is holed up at the moment, and face the board at the bank. We will also have to explain things to Mrs Stickybunns. If she wants to press charges, the ball will be in her court. If she agrees not to go to the police, and if Percy pays her the full value of the painting, he can keep the Pissarro and we just have to hope he will then toe the line, and either come back to the bank or hand in his resignation and separate the family from the business before any more collateral damage is done. However, I very much doubt he will admit his wrongdoing and realise what an ass he has been. I have no idea myself what to say to him. No doubt those will be my waking thoughts for the next few days. Liberty, my dear girl, I leave it up to you to decide how to proceed with the police over the matter of his bugging your home, and I can only apologise on his behalf for the attempted sabotage of the café, but I think we would all agree, based on today's success, he has had little effect.'

Mrs Goodman appeared with a huge wooden board laden with fore rib of beef. She paused for a moment, unsure which Mr de Weatherby should carve, but Edmund came to the rescue and said, 'Pa, you carve. I'm not sure my new-found cake-cutting skills qualify.'

Mrs Goodman shot him a grateful smile, and rushed off to get the parsnip purée, roast potatoes and carrots. As Jonathan passed round thin slices of the perfectly pink beef on warm plates, Liberty dragged her eyes from Edmund and looked about her. She noted most people were slightly confused, as they were having such fun, and everyone was chatting in-between the serious bits, pleased to be there. She could see Bob and J-T in deep discussion, probably about boutique hotels. The looks of love passing between all the couples were rather special, and there was the air of a wedding party.

She then let her eyes fall on Cecil, who was talking to Deirdre about the problems of dogs in town. 'Poo bags! You are arrested unless you carry them, and I'm not sure I could even bend down these days to pick the stuff up. However, we think we may now stay in the country – it's done me the world of good. Isabelle has been an angel, looked after me in a way no wife should have to.' His voice started to quiver, and Liberty hated to see the worry etched on his tired face; he didn't deserve this. She was relieved, in light of the Stickybunns story, that it would not be because she was suing Percy for divorce to try to get him to toe the line, and she immediately reassured him that she would not be sticking – no pun intended – any more dirt to the good name of the family. 'I think he will have no need to bother me. The threat of losing his painting will be sufficient to call him to heel. But I doubt he could pay for it. Would he have to sell the mews house?'

'Surely he would be willing to do that,' replied Cecil. 'Who will approach him?'

'I could,' said Bob as he loaded up his plate. 'I could say I had met Mrs Stickybunns at the fete. If I told him I had discovered he had swindled the old lady, I could speak to him, man to man. That way we would know what attitude he was going to take.'

Liberty suddenly realised she needed to be free of Percy. 'I will sign the divorce papers and send them with you – two birds with one stone!'

Isabelle looked askance at Liberty, who blushed, realising she had possibly enjoyed too much wine, and ignored most of the delicious food, but she was pleased to feel free of guilt at last. She had put off signing the papers, feeling it was an admission of failure, but now it felt as natural as closing a door behind her.

Despite the main topic of conversation being so unpleasant, there was a close feeling around the table. It was as though they were all part of the same family. Khalid, sitting beside Isabelle, was gently telling her how difficult it could be to be brought up as the only, or eldest, son of a prominent family. So much expectation, especially as an only child. 'Maybe it's just been too much for Percy. I have a strong impression he has been leading the life that was thrust upon him, and carrying it out as a duty. When Liberty and he split up it put, I think this is the expression, the cat among the pigeons, and allowed him to do some playing. Perhaps it's out of his system by now, but maybe it is time he resigned his directorship at the bank and found his own path in life.'

'And what will become of Anstley Hall?' asked Isabelle in terror. 'What if he forces us out, or has to sell to pay for the painting?' She had barely touched any food either, but was enjoying the company and feeling of warmth that had been missing from her own family home. 'It's been in my husband's family for hundreds of years. It would break his heart to have to sell it.'

'Dear Mrs Cholmondly-Radley,' said Khalid. 'Times change. We all have to adapt, sometimes for the best, sometimes for our happiness and health. I think it would give you and your husband great peace of mind not to have to worry about the future of a house which has perhaps outlived its purpose.'

Savannah smiled at her husband. How well he understood the problems of a culture, of people trying desperately to cling to a past of apparent safety and continuity, while at the same time attitudes and lifestyle changes had made many of England's grand country houses obsolete. It was an admirable trait of his personality that he had bothered to learn about English heritage and history, although that might have had something to do with being educated at Gordonstoun.

Khalid came from a society where religion and family were intertwined and held more weight than wealth and its trappings, although bizarrely, when wealth was added to the mixture, it was flaunted much more flamboyantly than in England. It had all of its own intricacies, tribal systems and contradictions, but also a long, strong history and ability to hold people together.

Isabelle looked at Khalid in awe. 'I would be asking my husband to give up not only a business that has held his family in their precious home for the past two hundred years, but also the family home.'

'Yes, and then you can go cruising, or on safari!' Khalid quickly changed the suggestion when Isabelle's expression made it clear she would rather spend time playing on a dungheap.

'Well, perhaps not cruising, but tour the Med, stay with Paloma. You should see where she lives, it's magical! Come and stay with Savvie and me in Paris on the way, and then drift slowly to the south of France, and when you get bored with St Tropez, wend your way along the corniche to Italy. When was the last time you holidayed abroad?'

It was a complete mystery to Khalid that the British upper class seemed to prefer vacationing in midge-infested Scotland, or in windy Norfolk, rather than relaxing in warm sunshine.

'I suppose it would be good for Cecil's health, and it would be lovely to see Florence and Venice. The last time I visited Italy was on my honeymoon.'

'There you are!' said Khalid firmly. 'Look to the future. You have been, if you will allow me to suggest, living through your son for a long time. Take the pressure off him, and I think you will find you get to know him better.'

Savannah was telling Liberty across the table that she was going to stay at Denhelm for the weekend at least, and that she could help get LIBERTEAS up and running. 'Please let me help. I'm sure I would be a simply fabulous waitress. Going by today's success, anyway.'

Liberty chortled at her friend's new-found delight in the working environment. 'Very kind of you, darling. Much as it would be fun, I'm not sure I need the distraction. You will do a much better, and more important, job of cheering me up at the end of the day with a glass of wine and a gossip.'

'I can't say I am not desolated,' huffed Savannah. 'But in any case, I am hoping to spend the time with J-T, scouring antique shops looking for bits and pieces for our home. It has vast walls, and cries out for objets d'art, and we have only filled half the rooms with furniture. The interior decorator who darling Khalid hired only papered and painted, knowing I would want to do my own thing once we were installed.'

J-T's eyes lit up as he imagined Khalid's open cheque book. 'Goody,' he said, 'I want to spend lots of time with you, digging the dirt over Liberty's childhood. There must be something very, very naughty about the girl, and I intend to find out what it is!'

Edmund had remained fairly quiet through the meal, but once the pudding had been ignored, and lots of nectar in the form of a delicious Hungarian Tokay had been drunk, he asked Liberty if she would join him for a stroll. They left the others to return to the summer sitting room and enjoy their coffees and the petit fours Mrs Goodman had magicked out of thin air, still determined to get them to eat something. 'It's amazing what you can do with some egg white and a few almonds,' said the blushing Mrs G, but she was very pleased at everyone's compliments. They all apologised for not managing more of the delicious food. *It will do well for lunch tomorrow as a cottage pie*, thought the practical housekeeper as she washed up and observed Edmund and Liberty walking towards the fountain.

'Oh, get on with it, boy!' she shouted into the dishwasher.

56

'What a day!' sighed Liberty. 'And I haven't had the time to thank you properly for all your help. I couldn't have done it without you – goodness, it wouldn't have happened at all, it was your idea in the first place!'

'Of course you could, and you would have. But I'm pleased I was there,' said Edmund, feeling as he always did under her praise; a thousand feet tall and capable of anything. He gently guided her away from the windows or any chance of being observed. They passed the fountain, generously covered in rambling briars and honeysuckle, then turned down a little gravel path that led to the rose garden. 'My mother loved this place,' he said, as they emerged through an archway. The spring evening was scented with honeysuckle and daphne. The deep purple sky, enhanced by the soft lighting under the hedges and beside the pathways, gave everything a magical atmosphere.

Liberty looked up at him. His face was unreadable, dark and set in the habitual scowl she had become so fond of. Who knew the illusion of grumpiness could be so endearing?

He turned and gazed at her, whereupon his expression instantly softened. His eyes crinkled at the edges as he smiled down at her, and suddenly he was the most handsome man on earth again. Liberty knew, no, hoped he had brought her out here to say something of his feelings for her. Her tummy was fluttering around and her head was awash with the idea he was going to declare undying love, then sudden terror in case she was to be submerged in a huge wave of disappointment when she discovered she had her wires crossed and he had no feelings towards her whatsoever.

Edmund, meanwhile, was struggling with his own fear. He knew he was not the most demonstrative of people. Gray once said, when viewing a display of photographs taken during Scott of the Antarctic's expedition, that he didn't think it looked that cold. 'Edmund looks like that on most dates!' However, he knew the time had come to say something, or be still his beating heart forever. He had been pulled to the rose garden, not just to get Liberty away from prying eyes, but also because he drew strength from this place. His mother, who had been very demonstrative, both to her husband and to her children, loved roses, and had created the garden when pregnant with Savannah. There was a lot of love here, and he took strength from his faint memories of happy days helping his mother digging and planting. He didn't know if he was going about it the right way; he had never done this before, but he knew the outcome would change the path of his life dramatically. He summoned up all his courage and said, 'Liberty.'

He stopped as she swung round quickly from where she was lingering by the bower, cheeks flushed and eyes wide. She strolled as casually as she could to his side, so as to see him more clearly, wrapped her pashmina round her shoulders, and in a slightly breathless voice said, 'Edmund?'

He took her cool hand in his and started to speak. 'Just listen to me babble on for a minute. If you think it's all tosh, then ignore me, walk back to the house and leave me here. But let me say this.'

Liberty felt her heart tighten, and all the moisture seemed to have gone from her mouth, so she merely nodded.

Edmund took a huge gulp of air as though he had been underwater for too long, then said, 'When you returned to Littlehurst, when I saw you again after all those years–' Liberty blushed again at the memory of bending over in her underwear, then finding Edmund prostrate on the terrace, but let him continue '–my life changed completely. I wasn't sure what that meant at the time, but now I realise that I fell in love with you immediately. Straight and simple. I've never believed in love at first sight, but that is the only way I can explain it.'

Liberty's heart did a triple somersault and landed back in her chest, bounding around like a crazed jack-in-the-box. She felt intense and complete joy. Her eyes welled up and she opened her mouth to speak, but Edmund put his free hand gently over her mouth. He closed his eyes.

'If I don't get this out in one go, I'll never be able to say it, ever. So bear with me.' He opened his eyes and began the speech he had been mulling over all day, determined to get it right. 'These last months have been the happiest of my life, despite making such a balls-up of taking over this place. And now I have an opportunity to make a real go of things. Gray and I have been emailing a lot, and we realise that with his people skills and ability to organise, it makes so much more sense if he takes on the job of running Denhelm.'

Oh, crap, thought Liberty, *I have never got anything so wrong in my life! He is talking about running this bloody park and I thought he was going to kiss me!*

Edmund looked startled by her sudden change of expression; she now looked as though she had sucked a lemon, but he battled on. 'I have never been so happy and relaxed as when watching you prepare, build and nurture your future, and I want to be part of that future. No, don't worry,' he said as he read a flash of terror in Liberty's eyes, 'I am not going to ask to learn how to cook and start baking. I want to return to what I do best, which is continue to run my own company, advising on environmental and ecological issues, and to be there at the end of the day, to rub your feet and run your bath. To be with you.'

OK, thought Liberty, *this is getting better.*

'I love you, so very much. I love the way your beautiful mouth turns up at the sides when you are tired, the way your green eyes change to turquoise when you are anxious. I love the way your bottom wobbles when you whisk egg whites. I love your compassion. I love your huge, giving heart. I even love your silly dog. Be mine, will you? Be my wife.'

Edmund gulped. He was not used to being so open, let alone declaring undying love. It was terrifying, yet liberating at the same time. He looked at her and waited for a response.

Liberty surprised him. She didn't immediately say 'yes' and jump up and down, and she didn't immediately say 'no' and jump in the lake. She looked stunned, her mouth opened a little as if to say something, but then she just clamped it shut, snatched her hand from his, placed it over her forehead and turned away. She walked unsteadily a little way until she reached a stone bench, where she stopped and suddenly sat.

'Liberty? Have I offended you so much?' He saw her shake her head and then realised her shoulders were heaving. Racing to sit next to her, he grabbed her and turned her round to face him.

'It's not meant to be like this!' she sobbed, tears running down her face.

'What? You want me to get down on one knee? I can do that,' he said, starting to bend down.

'No, no,' she blubbed. 'I'm meant to look all lovely and serene and say yes, and gaze into your eyes before kissing you over and over. Oh, God, how I've dreamed of doing that.'

Edmund felt crazed with a mixture of confusion and lust. Couldn't they just do that, then?

Liberty made a noise rather like a walrus hiccupping. 'But I can't marry you.'

Edmund felt his heart stop. 'What? Do you mean that?' He was hoping she was joking, but it didn't sound that way.

'Of course I mean it, I can't do that to you. It would be unfair.'

Edmund didn't understand, but he recognised the utter horror of having to face life without this creature. He had no idea whether to hate her for letting him bare his soul as never before – but no, he could never hate her. He just shut down, his face a mask of hurt, made worse in the soft lighting as the sky was now pitch black.

He rose and said, 'Well, if that's how it is.' He was desperate to separate himself from the agonising wire around his heart. He needed to get away, and fast. He couldn't stand to see her any longer, to face his family now that he knew she wouldn't have him. As he turned to leave, hating to see her crying, and unable to stay and be crushed further, he couldn't resist one last turn of the dagger in his own chest.

'May I at least ask why?'

Liberty was howling with great heaves of her chest, she hurt so badly. She desperately wanted this man, whom she couldn't accept. 'Why did you have to ask me to marry you?' she wailed. 'If we had just been able to love each other for a little while, you may have simply gone off me when I had to let you down. At least I could have had you for myself for a while.'

She stopped, and blew her nose. 'You know why . . . why I can't marry you. I can't give you children.' She gasped as the words came pouring out, her body now shivering uncontrollably, so near to utter happiness, but so far from being able to hold on to it.

Edmund's heart blossomed as though midsummer had arrived with all its madness. He immediately sat beside her and took her in his arms again, this time holding her as if he would never let go, and that was indeed how he felt. 'If that, my darling, is the only reason that you will not have me, then stop being an idiot and accept my proposal. Do you not realise I have recognised that already? And I'm not such an idiot myself that I don't believe it is possible for us to succeed where you and Percy, thankfully, did not. Tell me you will be my wife, and I will love you with or without the blessing of babies. Let me enjoy you, love and care for you, let me worship you and tell you every day how much you mean to me, how my world turns on making sure you wake with a smile and a hope.'

Liberty stopped crying and stared at him through her puffy

eyes. He did mean it! She was loveable! Could she let him take her on? She knew she wanted to be with him so very much. She put her arms around him, and she sniffed and snuffled for a while into his chest, impressing his words on to her heart so she would remember them forever. Then she said, her words muffled, 'And here I am, crying uncontrollably and I look a mess. Why do I always look so muckymoo around you? I am making a big scene, which I know you hate. Have you completely gone off the idea now?' Hiccupping and sniffing, she kept her face pushed into his chest, covering his crisp white shirt with mascara and tinted moisturiser mixed with tears. It was the only way she could hide.

'My precious girl,' he said, as he wrapped his arms around her, relief pouring through his veins. 'I can honestly say you have never looked a mess to me, and I don't care if you do, so long as the answer is YES.'

Liberty withdrew her face from his shirt. It was streaked with black, and her eyelids were puffy. 'Oh, God, yes, of course yes!' she said, gazing up at him. 'A million times YES!'

Edmund took his chance before she began crying again, and grabbed her tear-soaked cheeks, drawing her mouth to his. As their lips touched she knew the electric spark needed no wind turbine to maintain its strength. The kiss deepened and quickly became passionate. Any other worries, responsibilities and hang-ups were engulfed in a delicious wave of love and desire.

Back inside, Paloma and Deirdre were huddled in the bay window under the pretence of talking over the day. They were, however, fooling no one.

Jonathan strolled over with his whisky and asked if they could see what the love birds were up to. 'Bother it, no!' replied Deirdre. 'They have been an age. I'm sorry, Jonathan, but if they come back and announce they just needed some fresh air, I may have to kill Edmund. I can't think why it's taken him this long to tell her how he feels!'

Paloma was, for once, more diplomatic. 'Perhaps he is unused to the feeling of being in love, so maybe he didn't recognise it at first. I believe that if sons grow up having lost their mothers at a young age, they constantly seek that strange reassurance of unrequited love. It must be very difficult to realise that adult love is so very different, and be able to give your heart when it could so easily be rejected.'

Jonathan and Deirdre looked at the worldly woman with respect, and then burst out laughing as she followed it up with, 'But good God, he does have a penis, doesn't he?'

Alain came over to join them, wondering what the happy noise was about and eager to take his own beloved back home. He had had enough of listening to how Percy had been such a let-down. Hadn't he always known? He was ashamed he had let his daughter marry such a feckless waste of space; Percy had hurt her so much, and now there was this ridiculous notion of getting him back under control by threatening him with the loss of a painting. The fact that if thirty years ago someone had offered him lifelong triple Michelin stardom, he would have given his right arm, didn't stop him thinking the idea was preposterous. Right now, he wanted his family as far away from Percy and his stuffy parents as possible.

Deirdre looked up at Alain's grumpy face and said, 'Don't even go there. I know what you are about to say, and you wouldn't have changed her mind. You couldn't have. She needed to feel secure and completely suffocated by Percy's love. Don't you realise that it was all our fault? Liberty needed a Percy. He told her what to do, how to dress, where to go on holiday, what to do for a job, because we hadn't. We told her how wretched and useless the other parent was, we told her what not to do in life, because we had so many regrets. She was looking for someone to give her positive direction, and she fell into it and loved and embraced it because of Isabelle and Cecil. Can you see how strong and united they are as a couple? That's what she was craving, and what we failed to give her!'

After Deirdre had concluded her alcohol- and exhaustion-fuelled diatribe, Alain calmed her, and Jonathan and Paloma discreetly left them to it. Alain sat next to Deirdre and said, 'A thousand apologies, but my darling, we are who we are. Liberty isn't doing so badly, is she?' And he gently wiped away the tears coursing down her face, the years of guilt finally finding an outlet.

Claude and Evangeline, having persuaded the CRs to come and stay in St Tropez if they were ever passing through, bade their goodnights, as they were pooped. Everyone understood, and waved and kissed them goodnight in a haze of cigar smoke and post-party tiredness. The long day, and emotionally exhausting evening, had got to everyone.

Savannah and Khalid were sitting cosily together, his hand on her tummy, while they encouraged Cecil and Isabelle to visit as many places as they could. 'Think of the travelling you will do now that you are well,' said Savannah to a charmed Cecil. 'And we won't hear of you being in France without staying with us, either in Paris or on the coast. It's lovely for the children to have as much family as possible, as Khalid's dear parents died so young.'

The CRs were feeling as though they had been welcomed out of an empty home into a gregarious, funny, if slightly crazy, family, and they were truly happy for the first time in months. They had always loved their daughter-in-law, and now saw why she was the person they knew. With so much love and friendship around, it was impossible to be selfish or unkind. They, too, were exhausted, though feeling better and less isolated than before, but the threat of Percy throwing them out of their home still hovered like a black cloud over a tiny sail boat in the middle of the ocean.

Bob and J-T were restless to get back to Duck End; they wanted to regale Liberty with ideas of looking for a suitable property to turn into a bed and breakfast business.

Neither couple wanted to retire until the elusive Liberty and Edmund returned. Therefore, the room fell silent as the door opened slowly. A hand appeared, a left hand. Suddenly, the flickering firelight drew flames from the diamond on the hand's ring finger.

'Darling!' screamed Deirdre and Savannah in unison, leaping out of their seats, Deirdre as quickly as she could in an alcoholic fug, and Savannah as quickly as she could release herself from Khalid. By the time the two had reached the doorway, Liberty's whole body had entered sheepishly, followed by Edmund, who was also feeling hopeful that Jonathan would approve of his removal of his mother's engagement ring from the safe. They had spoken of it and Jonathan had wished it to him, but Edmund hadn't wanted to wait, and took Liberty to his office to claim her for his own. The ring fitted perfectly, and suited her; elegant, understated, but of the finest quality.

As the women hugged, Jonathan strode over and shook Edmund by the hand before embracing him warmly. 'About time, and bloody well done!' he exclaimed. Alain was next in line, unable to get close to his daughter, who was being grilled by Paloma, Savannah, J-T and her mother, as to how the proposal took place, so he settled for giving the surprised Edmund a great kiss on both cheeks.

'I couldn't be more thrilled to welcome you to my family, dear boy,' he said, as he held Edmund's shoulders tightly. 'Thank you for making my daughter so happy.' And he started to weep.

Oh, Christ! thought Edmund, never able to stand visible displays of emotion, but he was surprised to find he didn't mind; in fact, he was feeling rather wonderful about it. Since Liberty had accepted his hand in marriage, he seemed to be floating, and didn't think he would mind if the sky fell in, which was lucky, as Cecil and Isabelle had now appeared in front of him, both crying and telling him that he and Liberty deserved every happiness. Jonathan was opening more champagne, and handing round glasses, J-T was asking if he could be bridesmaid this time and Savannah was laughing as she responded, 'As long as I get to be maid of honour when heavily pregnant, my dear friend will be depicting the perfect twenty-first-century wedding – although she should probably be a single mum as well!' Glancing at Liberty's suddenly blanched face, Savannah took her hand and whispered, 'You never know, with Ed it may all work out.'

After the mantel clock chimed two, the party decided that all good things had to come to an end. Liberty and Edmund, who was now becoming accustomed to being embraced, were hugged and kissed over and over, and even Claude and Evangeline had been back down to congratulate them. As the house went to bed and Bob made his way to the car, having offered Deirdre and Alain a lift, Edmund turned to Liberty and said, 'See you for breakfast, my love.'

Liberty's mouth opened and then shut again quickly. She could see the humour in his eyes. Having been nose to nose with each other all evening, stealing kisses only when sure no one was looking, which of course they were, they had mutually decided to meet tomorrow, rather than have their first night together with everyone aware of what they were up to.

'Oh, yes, see you tomorrow, unless of course . . .' A wicked gleam appeared in her eye and she quickly ran to the staircase. 'Bob!' she called 'Make sure to let Teal out and lock the back door. Sleep well!' And with a giggle she leapt up the stairs two at a time and raced into Edmund's bedroom, which, thankfully, she knew her way to. She had been dreaming of this moment for so many months, and she wasn't going to wait any longer!